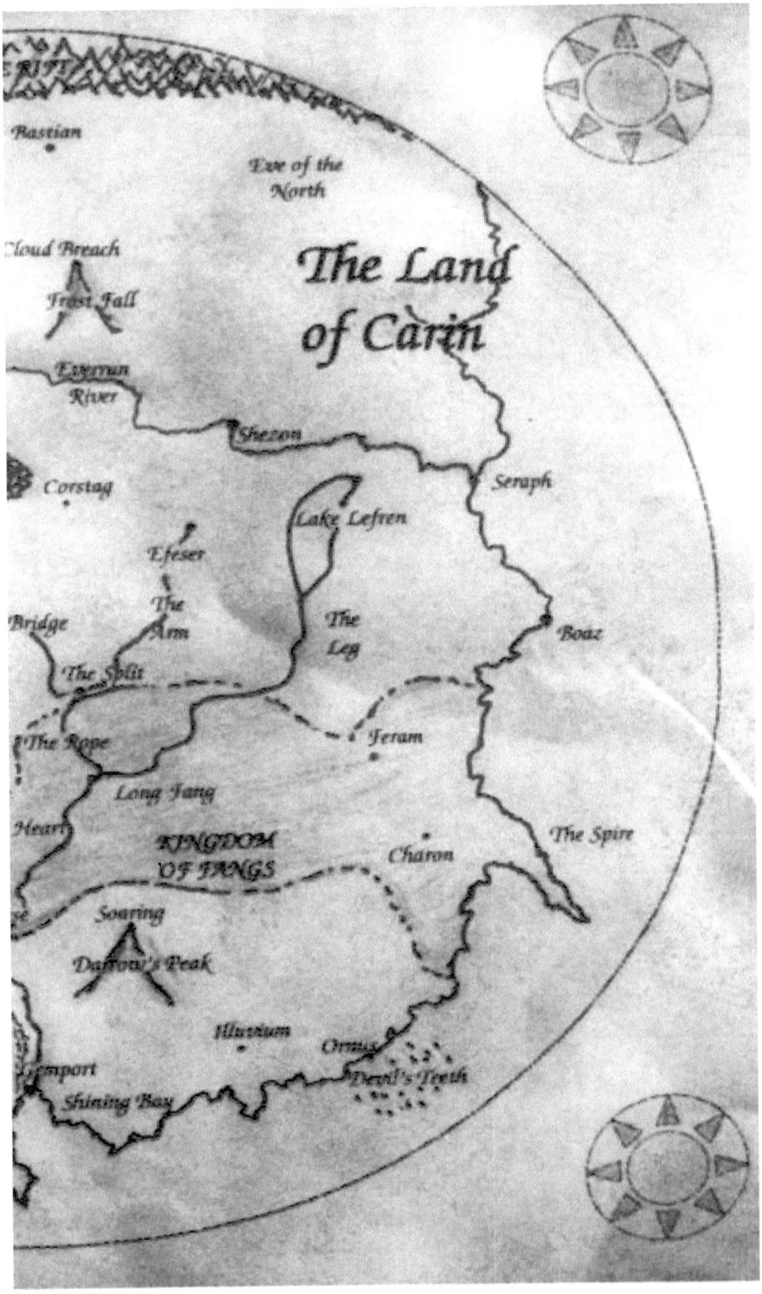

The Land of Carin

Bastian

Eve of the North

Cloud Breach

Frost Fall

Esserun River

Shezon

Corstag

Seraph

Efeser

The Arm

Lake Lefren

Bridge

The Leg

Boaz

The Split

The Rope

Jerum

Heart

Long Fang

KINGDOM OF FANGS

Charon

The Spire

Soaring

Darrow's Peak

Illustium

Ornus

Devil's Teeth

Shining Bay

port

Dawn of Darkness

J.D. Reding

Dawn of Darkness
Copyright © 2012 by Joshua Reding

ISBN (978-0-9834233-2-4)

Even Heroes Know When To Be Scared

Dedication

This book is dedicated to Brandon Michael Reding. You will never be forgotten, and you will always keep us from being alone.

Dramatis Personae

Aurum Guilden's Tale

Dane - Centaur Warrior
The Red Man - Unknown
Andusìl - Human Woman, Wife of Aurum

Rikard Karandash's Tale

Dorian - Human Wizard, Brother of Aurum
Qel of the Thousand Hammers - Unu Clansmaster
Terel of the Amber Stone - Unu Warrior
Breva of the Bleeding Moon - Unu, Wife of Dorian

Tendra Sumenel's Tale

Jeric Tybius - Human Light Monk, Betrothed of Tendra
Jonathon Sumenel - Human, Cousin of Tendra
Vizien Traenor - Human Grand Inquisitor
Rayn - Human Wizard, Brother of Aurum
Joven - Human Wizard, Brother of Aurum
Rowen - Human Wizard, Brother of Aurum

Galeerial Strongwind's Tale

Jariah Clearsky - Skyguard, wife of Ezekiel
Veriel Stormrise - Skyguard Lord Commander
Gabriel Highflight - Skyguard Lord Commander
The Wither - Unknown
Grey - Human Wizard, Brother of Aurum

Table of Contents

Preface

It has been four and a half years since I first began to imagine the world of Carin, and it is unrecognizable from what it was in the beginning. In the beginning, I had a broad outline of a world, it was all line work and no color, no inking, just the broadest of layouts. I knew the big story details of Galeerial's fall, of Aurum's driven nature, of the tragedy of Tendra, but I didn't know what was in the land of Thanatos or who The Wither actually was, or if Galeerial would ever fly again. Now, after working tirelessly on Dawn of Darkness, I have filled in the details of Carin. I will take you to the seas of the Thorne Coast and to the heights of Acheron. I will show you the majesty of Merhelden and introduce you to the Codex of the Seven. You will see the Seven as more than just warriors, but as a group of men that have their own problems, their own psychological hang-ups, and their own demons. You will see Tendra step into her place as the queen of humanity. You will see Galeerial struggle to find his place in the world. You will see sacrifice. You will see the layers of the world begin to peel back to reveal the players who have been manipulating events all along.

Welcome back to a darker, more personal, more emotional, and more dangerous Carin. Welcome to a land where even heroes know when to be scared. Welcome to *Dawn of Darkness*, book two of the Heart Quest Saga.

Four Months Ago
One

The spray of the sea stung Rikard Karandash's eyes. The large man felt his sinewy muscles twitch in anticipation. He watched as *The Nydian* tossed and turned beneath his steady feet towards the large gray monoliths that were the Devil's Teeth. Rikard had sailed from Seraph and was now rounding the edge of the world. The golden city of Ornus stood tall before him on the cliffs in the distance, and the Rift Mountains hung ominously in the haze behind him. Rikard narrowed his eyes as he carefully ran his thumbs along his two daggers: Bleed and Burn. The edges were sharp-real sharp: just how he liked them. They would need to be for what he was about to attempt. The cold arkaline metal of the blades was far sharper than any steel and could cut through solid stone. *The Nydian* rocked against the turbulent waters, and the sky was as dark above him as the tempestuous water below him. He carefully strapped the hilts to his hands and bound them tight. He couldn't afford to lose them.

Rikard licked his salty lips. This would be fun. The ship's captain knew him only as a friend of Damaen Longshore, the infamous pirate and reaver, captain of the *Finality*. Damaen had served as his brother Aurum's alias over the last few years. As such the captain was scared to death of Rikard, just the way Rikard liked it. It was better to be feared than questioned. Aurum had gathered quite the reputation as a pirate in the seven years' worth of ranging they had done prior to their emergence upon the world, and he had built up quite the system of favors; now one of them was being called in to Captain Ferion.

"Get us closer!" Rikard called down to him. Rikard stood at the bow of the ship and watched the massive stones grow closer as the crew wrestled against the sea for control of the boat. Beyond the Devil's Teeth lay Ornus, the capital-and only-city of the unu. The city was a fortress, unassailable by land and impossible to reach by water; nevertheless, it was his target. What he was about to attempt was suicide.

Rikard smiled. It would be a good death, dying at the hands of the gods who ruled the sea, the gods of chance, stone, and pain. Let them come. Let them break themselves upon his iron resolve and callous disregard for their seemingly infallible dominion over this expanse.

The boulders grew closer still.

"Captain!" Rikard called out. Ferion came scurrying towards him. Ferion was a mouse of a man: a trader and a businessman, not a sailor. He was no more a captain than Rikard was a king, but he called himself that nonetheless. "Your services are no longer required, and your debt to Captain Longshore has been paid in full."

"Thank you, thank you, sir." Ferion said quickly. His face betrayed his relief. "Is there anything…"

"Just die." Rikard didn't even wait for the confusion to register on the man's face; he simply took three steps back so as to arrive at the aft railing of the ship. The first stone was about three hundred yards away, and that was his starting point. He took a deep breath, "Boom!" He called before taking off running down the length of the ship. It took four steps before he took the six stair drop in stride, never letting up his pace.

Crewmen leapt out of his way as he ran, and explosions began to rock the ship behind him. The shock wave from the explosives he had placed on the ship would give him that much more of a starting edge. He would need every advantage he could get if he wanted to survive this. Rikard flew by the last sailor who was scrambling to jump off the ship as it exploded into shrapnel behind him. He hurtled onto the bowsprit. His ridged shoes cut into the wood, providing him adequate traction as he rushed forward. He hit the bow, braced his left foot, and leapt.

The shock wave of the final explosion hurled him forward. Rikard flew through the air and watched the first stone pillar grow closer. He knew that he was going to be nowhere close, but he had counted on that. He reached up and undid the clasp that let all of his clothes fall away from him. They would only weigh him down. He didn't want to make it too easy. That was his last thought before the cold water slammed into his arms and face. The shock of the water burst through his body, and his muscles threatened to immediately seize up. Rikard overcame nature by sheer strength of will.

He surfaced immediately and began swimming. It would be a long day, and he needed a hard start. He forced his arms to do his bidding, pushing stroke after stroke through the bitter, cold water. Rikard gasped for breath at every six count. He broke through wave after wave as he made a slow, beleaguered march toward the awaiting gauntlet. The waves were unpredictable and thrashed about like a creature in the throes of death. Rikard felt the ice-cold water flow across his entire body at every stroke threatening to seep in and drown him. It made him feel alive. The elongated shoes that he wore enabled him to swim faster and pierce through the water easier. As Rikard grew to within twenty meters of his objective monolith, he glanced back, searching for the wave he needed to ride. He couldn't just swim up to the stone; the waves would batter him to pieces before he would be able to make it high enough to get out of the barrage. Instead, he needed to ride a wave up to the stone pillar.

He gave one surge, pushing himself forward and to the left, toward his wave. He thrust his arms before him, and his legs were a flurry of motion as he finally arrived at his wave. It was a monster, at least thirty feet tall and was heading straight towards him. Rikard wheeled around and began to swim with the swell. He rode the wave up higher and higher until he was at the crest as it carried him towards the stone. The wave battered against the rock, and Rikard felt the blow rattle his jaw. He gasped for breath as he felt a rib crack from the impact of the unforgiving rock. He slammed his daggers forward into the stone while his feet scrambled for some kind of foothold on the slippery rock. The hard granite resisted the cold metal's sting, but the daggers were still able to slide into the stone.

Slowly and steadily, he made his way up the length of the pillar. His arms burned, and he could find no footholds on the treacherous stone, forcing him to make the entire labored climb one hand over the other. In a single motion, he kicked his shoes free; they would be useless now. The burn of his muscles working combined with the freezing water filled Rikard with adrenaline.

Rikard shivered from the biting cold but gritted his teeth and kept climbing. Failure was not an option: right, left, right, left. His arms worked furiously, allowing no time for rest. He grinned in grim satisfaction and pulled his eyes away from the stone to look upwards as his hand found nothing to gain purchase on but empty air. He carefully mounted the pinnacle of the pillar before looking out to behold the challenge that was laid out before him. There were about eight hundred meters worth of stone and sea spread out before him. The large stone pillars rose eighty feet out of the water, and the next closest one was spaced thirty feet to his right.

The top of the stone column in which he stood was about ten feet across; so he had some room to maneuver. Rikard moved back to the edge of the stone pillar and took off running once again. At the last instant, Rikard pushed off and went sailing through the air towards the second column. Rikard braced for the impact he knew would come but still felt it reverberate through his body, rattling his bones, as he forced his daggers once again into the stone. Rikard felt the unrelenting battering ram of the water cast him into the pillar again and again as he struggled to the top.

Rikard looked forward, charting his path to the shore. The outlying columns were farther away from each other, and he saw that as he moved closer to shore the stone pillars grew denser. Rikard smiled. He would do this. Not he could, but he would.

Rikard leapfrogged his way forward, repeating the cycle again and again. His arms began to grow leaden, and his entire body ached from the constant battering of the stone and the water, but he was making progress. He felt his rib go from cracked to thoroughly broken, and every intake of breath placed pressure on his ribcage, forcing a grimace to cross his face and a rasp to escape from his lips.

The shore was still a hundred meters away when he felt a sharp pain in his foot, followed by numbness. Rikard looked down and saw a small lizard glaring up at him curiously. He reached down and stabbed it through the back. It made a short cry as black blood oozed from the wound. He shook his head and prepared for his next jump. The pillar was close enough that Rikard knew that he could make it to the top. The trick was not sliding off. Rikard took a deep breath and felt a second nip at his foot. A second lizard had appeared right beside the first one, and his foot was now bleeding from the chunks of flesh that had been pulled from his foot.

Rikard reached down and picked the lizard up by its neck and looked at it. It was approximately a foot long, including the tail, and had a thin membrane between its arms and legs. It was gray with black stripes and blended in well with the stone. Its three-toed feet ended in long, curved claws that looked particularly vicious. It snapped at his face, and he was able to see the full set of teeth that the lizards possessed. Rikard held it over the side of the stone pillar and dropped it into the sea.

He watched it fall about thirty feet before its arms spread out, allowing it to glide over to a nearby pillar. Rikard then watched, fascinated, as the lizard climbed up to the top of its pillar before pushing off to return to its previous position below Rikard and begun to climb up once again. Rikard couldn't believe his eyes as he watched the lizard ascend. Rikard marveled at the lizard but thought no more of it as he prepared for his next jump. They were inconsequential and deserved to be treated as such. He gathered up and was about to start running when he caught something out of the corner of his eye.

He watched as the pillar to his left suddenly began to move. It began to ebb and flow, and Rikard watched in astonishment as well over a hundred of the lizards leapt off and glided over to his pillar.

"Oh Dread." He cursed. He took off running and leapt to the next pillar. He slid onto the top of it, and the combination of his wet body on the wet stone caused him to slide towards the edge, but he was able to get his knives dug in before slipping off. He looked back and watched as the lizards on his former pillar pushed off and glided over to where he was. Rikard cursed again and leapt to his feet. No more playing around. He crashed onto the next pillar and scrambled to move to the next one. The columns before him were very close now. He turned to look back and saw a lizard flying right at his face. He whipped his arm up, and the reptile's torso slid right onto it. The animal didn't stop snapping at him though, and Rikard threw it off and into the sea. He grimaced as one bit into his leg, and he kicked it off.

They were flying from pillar to pillar towards him by the hundreds now. "Dreadspawn," he muttered as he started to run. He leapt from one pillar to the next, letting his momentum carry him as he tried to stay ahead of the beasts chasing him. He had no idea how he was supposed to climb up to the top of the bluff and into Ornus with all of these things following him; he would be torn to shreds. The cliff face was just a short ways away, and anger clouded into his eyes. These Dread-forsaken beasts were screwing up his plan, and now he would get to kill them all. Rikard made his way to the last pillar before the cliff face. The cliff was about twelve feet away, and it stretched upward about two hundred meters before transforming into the golden hue of the city walls. Rikard turned to face the army of demon lizards following him.

"C'mon!" He screamed at them. "C'mon!" He screamed. "You want war? I'll give you war!" The creatures had stopped one pillar short of where he was standing. A single lizard propelled itself forward, and Rikard watched its trajectory. He prepared to slice it clean in half with one of his blades when a massive shadow swept in front of him. He watched as what looked like a bat with an eight-foot wingspan curved around his pillar snapping the lizard up in a single bite before flying back into one of the many holes in the cliff face.

A moment later, Rikard heard the sound of death screaming towards him. Instinct seized him, and he dropped flat to the ground as hundreds of the bat creatures exploded from the bluff. The lizards scuttled down the side of the pillar and leapt away as the demon bats plucked them from the air. Rikard shook his head as he watched nature's checks and balances. When it appeared like the last of the creatures had emerged from the cave behind of him, Rikard ran forward and leapt across the final chasm. He had planned on camping in one of these crevasses, but that no longer seemed like such a good idea.

The sky was awash with the creatures, and Rikard didn't want to attract any unnecessary attention away from their hunting towards him. He moved to the side of the cave to begin his climb up. He unlashed his daggers from his palms and tied them to his wrists. The rock here was not as weathered and smooth as it had been out in the bay. Here it was black and craggy and rife with hand-and footholds.

He was tired, his arms and legs ached, and his right leg ached worse than the other because of the stupid lizards. Yet upwards he climbed. He had work to do, and he would need every minute of every day to prepare. He couldn't afford weakness. That was one vice in which he did not partake. The stone was sharp, and he had to take care with every step to avoid being sliced to ribbons.

His right arm began to cramp about halfway up the side of the cliff, and he wedged himself into a small opening between rocks to rest and stretch. He looked out and saw the bat creatures finally begin their migration back towards the caves. Rikard slowly undid the bindings on Burn. He kept himself as still as possible. He didn't want to attract any attention, but, if one happened to come near him, he would be ready. It was

7

awe-inspiring to watch these hunters move back into their dens until the next time they would emerge to hunt. They were beautiful.

Rikard's eyes were a flurry of motion as he tracked the hundreds of creatures move through the air. Many of them dove into caves below where he was now situated, about a hundred feet up the cliff. He watched the cascade of flesh slowly begin to work its way up the cliff, and he made himself small in the nook. He wasn't afraid, but he didn't want to draw himself into a fight that he couldn't hope to win.

He felt the rush of air as the beasts began to zoom by him up to their lairs. So far none had noticed him, but he held his breath anyway. There were hundreds of them. Rikard hadn't realized just how many of them there were. Finally, the mass of flesh began to thin out, and eventually it disappeared entirely. Rikard re-bound his blade, pulled himself out of the crevasse, and continued his climb. It had been a couple of hours since he had begun, and Rikard could feel his body screaming out despite the small respite that he had provided it.

He kept climbing. The smooth stone of the city walls grew closer and closer. Rikard finally arrived at the top of the bluff and felt smooth grass instead of stone. In one final monumental effort, he heaved himself upward and rolled onto the ground. His arms were bloody from the cuts on his hands, and his feet were far worse. But Rikard felt none of that; all he felt was satisfaction. He wanted to scream in triumph, but he held his passion in check. He still had a job to do, and this was only the end of the first round.

The walls on this end of the fortress were purely for show. The front walls were towering two hundred foot affairs, but back here they were maybe fifty feet high. The ground the city was built upon was heavily sloped, so the height of the walls was even all the way around. He stared up at them. He would wait until nightfall before climbing them. It wouldn't do for a nearly naked human to be seen running through the streets of Ornus.

Rikard felt the adrenaline slowly seep from his body, and he once again collapsed to the ground. His muscles tensed up from the cold and the exertion. He began shivering, and his teeth clacked together. He had trained for this, but it was too much. He curled up into a ball to try to keep warm. It was still summer and the air was warm despite the gray sky, but he felt none of the heat.

He slowly began to massage his muscles: first his right arm and then his left. He dug his hands hard into them working through the biting pain. The effort pulled some of the pain out and warmed his muscles at the same time. He moved on to his chest taking extra time to rub it. He wished that he would have kept one of those lizards to eat, for he was ravenous, but he quickly pushed the thought out of his mind. He couldn't afford to dwell on the past.

He moved down to his legs and finished by launching into a stretching routine. He kept one eye watching the top of the wall. He knew that the unu didn't patrol the side and rear walls. In their arrogance, they believed themselves invincible due to the combination of the torrential waters, the stone monoliths, and, as Rikard was now well aware, the biological protections. He watched the cloudy ball of the sun descend into the horizon and began to prepare for the final part of his climb. He lashed his daggers to his wrists with numb fingers and began to climb the wall. The apparently smooth walls were, in actuality, just the opposite, and the climb was much easier than his first one. The dark of night descended slowly upon him as he made his way up the wall. The massive blocks of stone that made up the wall had decayed from centuries of being eroded by the elements.

Slowly, Rikard glanced over the top of wall and saw the great city of Ornus sprawled out before him. To his left, he saw one of the castles nestled against the back left corner of city; the second castle was directly opposite of it in the front right corner of the city. The unu and their balance. The rest of the town was laid out around a central bazaar and the Anvil. The Anvil was the massive central arena where unu fought as gladiators in epic confrontations for glory, or for the right to be made clanmaster. Every building in the city was short and made from the same golden, sandy stone that the walls were hewn from. He looked to his left and right for any sign

9

of the guards, but the way was clear. In a single motion, Rikard pulled himself up and vaulted over the wall.

He crept quickly across the ten feet and leapt across the chasm to the house that was directly in front of him and about six feet below him. He hit the roof with a wince and dropped into a roll to cushion the impact. There were rope lines with clothes hanging between houses throughout the city, and he made his way over to one of them. A roughly woven brown cloth shirt and trousers made for an unu child immediately caught his eye. He dropped down into the alleyway between two houses and pulled on the loose-fitting clothing. First order of business was done. He was not exactly looking forward to the second.

He began scouting through the back alleys of the city. Ornus had a strict curfew of sundown, and so he knew that he would be the only one on the streets besides the guards. Rikard stealthily made his way forward. He had been here many times before, and he knew his way around. More importantly, he knew where she lived. He navigated through the meticulously balanced streets until he finally came to a doorway that looked like so many others, instinctively knowing this was the correct one. He ran his fingers over the grain of the wood, and he took a deep breath. This would be…interesting. He quietly rapped twice in the top left corner of the door and twice more on the bottom right corner and once in the center. Then he waited and hoped that she hadn't been reassigned.

Rikard held his breath as he saw two hands slowly open the door. Before him stood a beautiful unu woman. Unu women were different than the men, though they retained the deep blue skin and slightly unnerving golden eyes and hair. They were thinner than the barbarian stature of their mates and had four arms instead of two. They also had longer bodies and faces and more pronounced curves in the hips and chests, like human women. The unu woman before him was of exceptional beauty, though at just over two meters tall she was considered exceptionally short for her kind. Two of her arms were opening the door, one was rested at her side and the fourth cupped her gaping mouth. Her blue skin shone in the candlelight, and her simple white dress perfectly accentuated her every feature. Her eyes were wide in a look of a surprise, and her unbraided hair cascaded down to the small of her back. He offered her his most Rowen-like smile.

"Hello, Breva." He said simply. She exhaled as if she had been holding her breath for all the years that it had been since he had seen her. Her voice was barely more than a whisper in the night wind.

"Dorian?"

Lightning in a Bottle
Two

Tendra Sumenel, the High Queen of humanity, gazed upon the shiftstone statue in the cathedral of Gemport. It had been many long weeks since the autumnal equinox. The sunlight through the lone clear window on that day had changed the brown stone of statue had changed from being that of a father to a flame. The flame echoed the unrest she felt in her heart, yet stood in stark contrast to the chill outside. The world was deep in winter now, and the solstice just two weeks away.

Every seat in the church held a soldier as all prepared for the coming day. It was dawn, and the soldiers of the first day's watch were knelt in prayer. It was a visage that would be repeated every dawn, every midday, every twilight, and every midnight with the changing of the guard. Tendra stood at the doors of the cathedral watching them. She knew that hundreds more waited outside to enter the cathedral after these ones left: two blessings for every watch. None of them knew if today would be the day that the unu and centaurs, known collectively as the Hammer, finally broke their hold and made their assault upon the city. Tendra knew they prayed in equal measure for the battle to come and pass and the continued reprieve. The siege was taking its toll.

The armies of the Hammer waited at their doorstep, though Clansmaster Qel of the Thousand Hammers had not yet arrived, and Tendra feared it was all that stayed their assault. Qel had returned to Ornus, the capital city of the unu, after destroying the feral city of Long Fang. Falcons sent from Light Monk scouts reported that the city had been razed, and all its inhabitants slaughtered. The city Ferum had been all that was left of the former Kingdom of Fangs, but even that had fallen a mere two weeks after Long Fang. The feral race was no more than a scattered few who had escaped the genocide.

"May Supremor's blessing be with you all; may he cloak you in strength, arm you with courage, and shield you with valor. Go in peace," Cleric Solom said with finality as he made a line on his forehead, one on his lips, and a third on his breast. The men began to move past her, each one greeting her and offering a salute. Upon her coronation, she had banned all bowing outside of the Royal Court. She spent most of her days wandering the city inspecting fortifications. She did not want soldiers stopping in their duties to offer meaningless courtesies in a time when courtesy was a luxury that no longer mattered.

The Hammer had halted their catapults the day that she had found her father murdered, and they had not resumed since. They were biding their time for the final assault. The Feast of Bejor, the celebration to mark the discovery of the Universal Balance, was occurring the day after tomorrow. The Universal Balance was the religious and cultural foundation of the unu. As such, all of the clan leaders would now be arriving at Ornus for the feast. Not only that, but if rumors were true, it would give Qel the chance to show off his latest prize. Whispers had it that only a single wizard remained alive and had been captured after the Battle of Long Fang, which

13

was being called the Wizard's Folly in hushed tones. Though there was still the issue of the mysterious seventh member of the wizard's group who had disappeared shortly after the Battle of Sterin's Throne, which had ignited this entire war. Tendra wondered how long he would remain hidden once news of his brothers' demise was revealed to him.

Tendra watched the last of the soldiers trickle out of the cathedral before rubbing her eyes. She'd been reluctant to sleep, for her dreams brought as little comfort in the night as the sight of Herdmaster Jeronious' banners did in the day. Therefore, most of her nights were spent restlessly wandering the barricades or speaking with members of the army, navy, or the Light Monks who were her constant companions. It was beginning to take its toll. At least she hadn't started speaking to the gallowglass that ever hung in the background, trailing her stealthily like her own shadow. Despite it all, her senses were not so dulled that she didn't recognize the presence of the man who abruptly materialized beside her.

"My queen," Grand Inquisitor Vizien said. His voice was rich and deep. It served as an ironic contrast to his silver tongue. Tendra did not turn to face the handsome man.

"You didn't used to be so formal, Vizien," Tendra replied.

"Dramatic circumstances call for dramatic actions," Vizien said. "I need to speak with you. Alone." Tendra stood watching the rank and file soldiers mill into the cathedral and down the rows of pews to the front.

"Do you have somewhere in mind?"

"Where it all began," Vizien said. He turned on his heel and began to walk. The click-clack of his boots echoed in her ears even above those of the soldiers. She waited until the last of the troops entered into the cathedral and the doors closed behind them before moving. As her minister of information, Vizien was a shadow of a man, always hidden yet ever present. His motives were as suspicious as his actions, especially of late. On top of that, Tendra had her suspicions that it was not an unu that had caused her father's death weeks ago.

14

She moved quickly and confidently through the throngs of soldiers arriving at the south gate of the chapel. She slipped out the west doors of the cathedral and made her way through the hallways of the castle.

Ever since her father and brother had been murdered, the walls had seemed much colder to her, like she was just now noticing that they were made of stone. She remembered running through these same hallways with Jakob and her cousin, Jonathon, who, despite being twelve years older than her, had never hesitated to indulge them when he had been allowed to come to the castle from Illuvium, home of the Order of the Light Monks. Their laughter had filled these cold stone hallways with life and, even until just a few weeks ago, they still had held the fires of hope. *But now? Now, everything was cold and grim.*

She shook her head to clear the ghosts from within. The past was gone; all that mattered was the present, and how she could prevent humanity's extinction, if it were even still possible. She arrived at the back door to the throne room, and the guards pulled open the doors and saluted her as she entered. She returned their salute: a simple forearm across the chest. Vizien was nowhere to be seen, and the throne room was empty but for the gallowglass, her silent guardian.

She looked into the upper corner of the ceiling and saw the flickering shadow of the gallowglass. The creature was an enigma to her. She had researched as much as she could on them and had come up with very little. No one who wasn't a gallowglass was permitted entry into their fortress of Daggerfall. The gallowglass always met with clients outside the gates. They seemed to be as much liquid shadow as solid flesh. They seemed to ebb and flow in the shadows like the tides. However, despite any misgivings she had regarding the gallowglass, she knew their prowess as warriors was unmatched in the entire world. There was not a single reliable account of their defeat in single combat. Every important political and military figure in the world, but for the Skyguard, had a gallowglass for protection. But she wasn't here for the gallowglass.

Tendra made her way towards the pillar that led down into the crypts. Passing the Unyielding Throne reminded her just how

15

uncomfortable she was claiming it as her own. It made even the light weight of her simple golden crown press down heavily upon her neck. The twin vipers of her house sigil were etched into the yellow gold of the crown and a single ruby was embedded in the front. This was one of several crowns in the royal inventory. Tendra had chosen the least ostentatious of them to wear for everyday usage.

A faded streak of crimson on the marble floor remained as a testament to where her father had been murdered. The palace staff had been unable to remove it. Tendra almost didn't want them to; it would remind every king from now until the end of time what had been lost.

She pressed her father's ring into the indentation of the eagle's eye in the pillar and twisted it, causing the door to open. A bitter wind whisked out and cut into her simple tunic and robes. Winter was fully upon them, and Tendra didn't like it at all. Vizien would already be down there she knew. She bit her tongue and closed her eyes a second before descending. She hated this place; it had caused the death of her family. The masons had wanted to begin work on her father's statue immediately, but she had refused their request. There was too much work to be done.

The masons were needed to reinforce every part of the wall. She had them working around the clock examining the walls around the city looking for any place that the unu could break through. She had placed rotations of sentry ships watching the cliffs around the palace day and night for any sign of an impending attack. She had placed carpenters at work creating ammunition for the catapults and trebuchets and arrows for the archers and ballistae. She hoped it would be enough.

She completed her descent, and Vizien stood there in the flickering light of the blue stone: the fake Heart of Fires. It was unfair that something so useless had caused so much pain. The ambient glow of the rock sent shadows spiraling around the room at strange angles, making the ghosts of the past dance atop the crypts of the men who bore them. The Grand Inquisitor wore black; of course, she had never seen him wear any other color in her entire life. His black hair cascaded smoothly around his shoulders almost as an extension of his cape. His handsome features were

16

accentuated by the glow and seemed to perpetually show him in a different light. She knew that he was quite dashing when he put his mind to it, but she knew some beauty was barely skin deep.

"What is it?" She broke the silence. She had neither the patience nor the will to play foolish games.

"You asked me to find out information on the stone. For some time, I have come up blank; I now know why. I have been looking in the wrong places for the wrong item. I had been looking for the Heart of Fires, when I should have been looking for something else." Vizien began. He ran his hand over the rock. Tendra could feel the same magnetic attraction to it that she had felt the first time she had seen the stone. She didn't know what it was, but in spite of whatever magic it held, she knew that this was not the real Heart of Fires.

"Four and a half years ago, a star fell from the sky. It passed over the Rift Mountains, beyond the ocean to the east. That is why the majority of us never saw it. The star landed in Thanatos, which was why nobody ever searched it out. I was able to get that much from some sailors who were in Terakeen at the time. Well, it turns out someone did go looking for it. I corresponded with one of my men at Evenfall, and he told me of a Skyguard who went searching in Thanatos for the star. Thirty days after the Skyguard entered into Thanatos, he emerged battered, and burnt to a crisp. Even more intriguing was that he said the Skyguard was bleeding." Tendra started at this.

"Skyguard don't bleed." She said, the confusion evident in her face.

"Obviously, but who knows what occurred in that forsaken place. My source said that the Skyguard came out of that cursed land with his wings on fire, and he crashed right near the border of Kana. And who, do you imagine, were the ones to find him?" Tendra considered this for a moment, before coming up with the only logical answer.

"The Seven."

"Precisely, though at the time no one knew who they were. However, knowing what we do now, five men with broadswords and staffs, I think that the evidence is conclusive."

"So what does that have to do with the fake Heart of Fires?" Tendra asked.

"I also have reports that say that Jakob-" Tendra glared at him at the mention of her brother's name "-did indeed enter into Thanatos, though he did so alone, and he exited twelve days later carrying something large on his horse."

"So my father did tell us something that was truthful." Tendra interjected, and Vizien nodded.

"There is more. Upon exiting Thanatos, Jakob was intercepted by three members of the Order of the Light Monks, who escorted him first to Illuvium before allowing him to return to Gemport."

"If this isn't the Heart of Fires, and it is indeed that same star that fell from the sky, then why would the Light Monks be so interested in it? And what about the White?" Tendra mused. The disease that had claimed her brother's life and that of so many more had appeared some time after Jakob had returned from what she now knew was Thanatos. Maybe there was no connection between them.

"I don't know. Perhaps that would be something you should speak to your cousin about."

Tendra nodded. Jonathon was a twelfth level Light Monk, a Brilliance, second only to the Council of Luminary's and the Radiance herself in the order. It was possible that he knew what had happened.

"As for the Seven, your father's involvement with them was most likely limited at best. You can't keep something like the Seven under wraps. It is mere probability. The amount of people who would have to be kept quiet to train them and take care of them seems to negate that as being a possibility. That isn't even taking into account the apparent disparity in the ages of the Seven."

Tendra took a breath. *So much deception*, it almost defied her ability to reason through. "So then who are they?" This was the question that really mattered.

"And that is where things grow even more uncertain," Vizien said.

"Because nothing is ever simple." Tendra interjected.

Vizien continued. "Information about them is unreliable at best, though it seems like the first accurate reports are from about five years ago. There is no absolutely concrete data, and they were more of a myth than anything else for seven or so years. I have heard rumors everywhere from Boah to Bicoln. The most notable evidence of their existence before the Battle of Sterin's Throne, was killing one of the remaining Horrors at Lake Lefron. Though any reliable informants most likely died with the fire that consumed the town of Thelon shortly after the Horror was killed. However, right after the Battle of Sterin's Throne, one of my agents was at a tavern called *Lingering Ocean*, which is near Lightwatch, and he observed one of the Seven enter into the tavern right before a centaur. He didn't know it at the time, but discovered his identity afterwards. The important thing, though, is that the man identified himself as one Damaen Longshore."

Tendra cocked an eyebrow up in disbelief. "Damaen Longshore: the Black Flag, captain of the pirate ship *Finality*? That Damaen Longshore?" Tendra asked, aghast.

"Indeed," Vizien replied simply. "And rumors are that another one acted as Qel's foster son for a number of years, and that a third worked at the Book Castle of Mesnir. The rest have been all over the map, with no concrete identities that I have been able to uncover."

"Are any of them still alive?" Tendra asked. She had to force herself not to hold her breath in worry over his answer. *By Supremor, Tendra, you might as well just ask if Rowen is alive*, she chastised herself silently.

"All that I know is that Qel is carting one to Ornus to be sacrificed."

"No knowledge of which one it is?" she asked. Vizien shook his head.

19

"Most people know their names but not their faces. In the seven months since the Battle of Sterin's Throne, most of their time was spent with unu and centaurs. Men heard the names of the wizards in stories, but few have actually met them. They are legends as much as men." Vizien replied.

Legends. Are these the days spoken of in the final book of the Stone, the book known as the Maw? Are these the days when legends die and heaven burns? Tendra did not voice her concerns to Vizien.

"If any of them are still alive, what is the likelihood that they will come here? And if that happens, can we trust them?" Tendra asked, fingering the handle of her dagger. It was the dagger, Heart, that Rowen had given her right before he had left.

"Do you even trust me?" Vizien asked her.

"Do I have a choice?" she replied.

"That's not what I asked."

"No. I don't." she said. Tendra stared into his blue eyes. They were like needles, always piercing, but she did not wither from his gaze. This was a man who needed to be stood against.

"You may neither like nor trust me, Tendra, but we both have something the other wants." Vizien said, his voice dropping low.

"Which is?" She was almost afraid to hear the answer.

"You want my loyalty, and, in return, I want stewardship."

Tendra had to force her jaw to remain closed: the sheer audacity. "I would die before I would see you on the throne." she spat.

"And die you will. Without my aid, you will not live out the week." Tendra forced herself to keep her jaw clenched. "You have no one to stand by your side. No one who will stay with you to the end. Jeric will take weeks to get here with the banners in the north, and in the meantime, your enemies will not wait for you to solidify your power." Tendra ran a hand through her hair. "You are far more vulnerable than you know, because you are a child living in a world of monsters in the skins of men. You do not even begin to understand what it is that you face. No one

20

believes that you can win this war. Not the Council of Elders, not the magistrates who have fled here for protection, not the people."

"So what is stopping them?" she asked.

"Me. They are waiting to see which way I will go. If I side with you, they won't dare move, because I know their identities. If I side with them, well, that makes their job simple."

"Have you no loyalty?" she asked. "Isn't your duty as a human to the crown?"

"Of course, My Lady, but who holds the crown at any given point in history divides patriots from traitors."

"Why are you telling me this?" she said slowly.

"Because having you on the throne better suits my purpose. If these others ascend, they will not be so easily controlled."

"Controlled?" Tendra's anger flared up. "Who do you think you are?" She had to use every ounce of her willpower not to rip her dagger from her sheath and hold it to his throat.

"Tendra, please. I am no more a puppet master than you are a puppet. Nevertheless, the fact remains, you are fundamentally altruistic, and I can trust you to always be selfless. So, in effect, I control you by you simply being yourself." Tendra considered this for a moment. She felt a shiver run down her spine as the freezing grip of the crypts enveloped her.

"What else do you want?" she said quietly.

"Nothing, there is nothing that you have to offer me. At least nothing less than what I already have." *By Supremor, he is bold.* Tendra hesitated.

"If I give you what you ask, what will you do with it?" she saw Vizien smile.

"You want proof of my intentions." it wasn't a question. A second unspoken question hung in the air.

"A queen will always trump a steward, but yes, I do."

"Your current course of action is wise considering what we are facing, but it not enough. We need to attack now, while their leadership is

21

absent, and before the centaurs move against Bicoln." It took Tendra a moment to realize what he meant.

"Are you insane?"

Vizien gave her a dubious look. "With the Heart of Fires no longer our secret weapon and the wizards scattered or dead, we have three options, and I intend to exploit all three." Tendra stood there for a moment thinking. She was no fool; she knew that there were people who thought her incapable of dealing with the current situation. She was young, inexperienced, and a woman. That combination made people uneasy. Vizien came from a good family. He was smart, charismatic, handsome, and ruthless. He would do well against the forces arrayed against them. If only she would hand him the keys to the kingdom. Tendra approached him slowly until she was only a step away.

"You presume far too much, Grand Inquisitor." Tendra hissed very slowly and darkly. "You dare to ask that of me? My father tolerated your ambitions for his own perverse pleasure in games of the mind, but I? I have far less patience. I will kill you myself if you dare to move against me," Tendra said, glaring at him evenly, and he met her gaze. A slow smile formed on his face as his deep eyes poured into her own.

"So the viper bares her fangs at last," he said. "If that is your decision and if you intend to survive the week, it's time for you to stop acting like a mother and start acting like a queen to these people. They don't need you watching over them. They need you leading them to some kind of victory. If we lose Gemport, they will blame you. They will all blame you."

"Let them come." Tendra stared into his eyes. "Know your place, Inquisitor, or prepare to grow comfortable in a new one at the bottom of the bay."

"It is not wise to cross me."

"The same can be said for me. It's past time you learned that," Tendra said. "Now, I am going to leave, and you would do well to wait for some time before coming out." Tendra turned on her heel and strode up the stairs.

"I can protect you, Tendra. I'm the only one who can." he called after her. "Or who will," he continued almost too softly for her to hear. Tendra seethed with anger. She didn't know how her father had managed to quell Vizien's ambitions for so long, but she wished she had some of his guile. She strode to the front of the grand hall, and the guards saluted her before opening the doors.

"Where is my cousin?" she snapped at one of the guards standing at attention far more venomously than she had desired. She silently cursed Vizien for putting her in this foul mood. She regained her composure with a breath.

"He, uh, he is in the aerie, My Lady. He requested some materials not ten minutes ago. One of the boys went to fetch them." The man stuttered through his words. He fidgeted under her gaze.

"Thank you," was all she could say as she struggled to maintain her hold over her anger. Tendra turned and began to make her way up to the tallest tower in the castle. The aerie was the common name for the north tower where the Light Monks had their quarters, and it was where Jonathon mixed and matched various materials in alchemical pursuits.

Every stair that she took seemed to add weight to her mind. Vizien had forgotten about Jonathon. He was with her, even if no one else was, but what if Vizien was right? Her grip on the throne was tenuous at best. The Council of Elders had been pressuring her to name a steward-only lightly, though-in respect and deference to the deaths of her father and brother. *Did her people need a king?* Tendra refused to believe that she could do a worse job than a man. If need be, she could name Jonathon her steward, and the man would gladly let her do whatever she wanted. Jonathon had no interest in ruling anything, which was why he had chosen the road that he was currently on. In fact, Light Monks were forbidden to marry; Jeric was a special exception given that it was the king who had bartered the deal, though compromises had to be made by both parties.

She wished he were here. Jeric had a quiet calm about him that allowed her to think clearly. Everything seemed to be happening both too fast and unbearably slow. It might have something to do with her lack of sleep. She just wanted to fall into his arms and breathe. But she couldn't. He wasn't here, and she was not just a woman. She was a queen, and not just a queen, *the* Queen.

Tendra wound her way up the tower passing the open doors of the rooms of the Light Monks. They always left their doors open. They had no personal possessions that they did not keep with them, save clothing, and therefore, nothing worth stealing. She did see the Y-shaped branch upon every open doorway marking the room as a Light Monk's quarters. The Y symbolized the divergence of the path of life that monks took: who they might have been, and who they now were.

She finally reached the upper turret after far too many steps. She twisted the brass ring latch on the ceiling and let the door swing down. The old wood thudded against the stone with a crack. The smell hit her first. It was the smell of ages of dust and rotting wood. She reached up and grasped the ladder, unhitching it so it rolled down to the stairwell. The well-worn wood felt soft against her skin as she climbed up into the chamber. She had never been inside; her cousin had always told her she could see it when she was older. Well, she was certainly older now, and she was curious to see just what it was that Jonathon did up here all day (and oftentimes through the night).

"Jonathon," she called as she stepped off the ladder. She was almost disappointed as she looked around and saw her cousin pouring over a text. Harsh light streamed in through the shutters of the west window, and numerous fires burned beneath glass bowls around the room. It was surprisingly warm despite the draft of a winter wind that blew in through the window.

Cabinets covered all of the walls from top to bottom around the circular room. Each had a half-dozen shelves cluttered with glass vials, ingredients, fluids, pieces of animals, alembics, tools and more. In the center of the room was a long table where Jonathon sat pouring over a recipe of some kind.

"Jonathon," she repeated. Her cousin blinked heavily as he looked up and saw her standing there.

"Tendra! What a delight. Come in, come in." Tendra moved gingerly through the chamber towards her cousin.

"What is all of this?" Tendra gestured around the room. A slow look of confusion formed on Jonathon's face, which quickly turned into a sly grin.

"You've never been here, have you?" he asked. Tendra shook her head.

"This is where the real work gets done. Domini and the other physicians may be doing the medicinal work, but it is here that the medicines are made. By combining plants and animal parts, as well as fire and water and even stone, we have been able to come up with amazing, amazing things. But you aren't here to learn chemistry. What's wrong?" a look of concern colored Jonathon's face.

"Did the Light Monks know Jakob went to Thanatos?" she blurted out. She didn't need to be coy with her cousin. He would be honest with her regardless of the answer. Jonathon's tongue played across his lips several times. He hummed softly as he tilted his head back and forth.

"Yes, but not until after he went. We found him with the blue stone after he had already emerged. Maybe you should sit down." Jonathon closed the book and gestured towards a simple four legged wooden stool next to his, across the table. Tendra took the chair. "Were you followed?" his voice dropped low.

"Of course not." Jonathon moved over to the door and pulled it closed. "There is nothing more powerful than information. He who controls it can control not only what people think, but what people *can* think. The idea that no one goes to Thanatos is not entirely accurate."

"What do you mean, not entirely accurate?" Tendra looked at her cousin. "Have you been there?"

Jonathon nodded slowly. "As you know, the Light Monk Order is set up into a series of levels with the fourteenth level being the Radiance, and the first level being that of Flicker. Now, there are also four divisions. There are the apprentices, who are the first through fourth levels. The vanguard, which are the fourth through the seventh levels. The knights,

25

which are from the seventh through the tenth levels, and the paragons above them. Now when a Light Monk has reached the tenth level, that of Lustrous, he is sent on a mission to travel what is called the Shaded Path. It is the path through Thanatos."

"Wh-?" Tendra managed. She appreciated that she was sitting. "Why? Why the deception?"

"There is a reason why that is a saying in the world. We made it so. Thanatos is worse than death. What I saw within was almost enough to cause me to take my own life." his words were thick with the dread of old memories.

"What did you see?" she asked slowly.

"That place, it is all of your nightmares. Everything you love taken and twisted into horrors beyond reckoning. Thinking of that land is enough to make my blood run cold even now, six years later. When someone enters into Thanatos, the Radiance knows. We don't know how it happens, but she does. When Jakob entered, she sent me and two others to wait for him. We waited for twelve days. We didn't think he was going to make it. Just for context, I was in for three days of absolute hell. I can't imagine what he endured in that Supremor-forsaken land. When he came out carrying that blue stone, I had never been so relieved in my entire life. The stone itself was marvelous. Rarely have I seen something as beautiful as that rock. He was ill though, and thin. We took him back to Illuvium for twenty-one days where I personally took care of him while the Radiance spoke with him at length regarding what he had seen within Thanatos, and no, I was not privy to those conversations." Jonathon said before she could interrupt him to ask. "After that time, he was fully healthy. We kept him for two more days, but he was anxious to return to you and your father. For two years he was fine...and then the White...and the Seven, and that brings us to our current predicament." Tendra looked closely at her cousin. There was something he wasn't entirely telling her. They both knew it. Tendra considered pressing the issue.

"Two years?"

"Yes." Jonathon looked at her.

"Two years," she repeated. "Then the White had nothing to do with Thanatos." he shook his head.

"Why did you never tell me about this?"

"That was your father. He had no idea what that blue rock was, but he knew the value of secrets. Made him a fine king, but a terrible father; though somehow you and your brother turned out just fine." Jonathon smiled as Tendra winced softly.

"You're all the family I have left now." she said to him. He nodded solemnly.

"I don't plan on dying on you anytime soon. I'll be here for as long as you need me. The Radiance has assigned me to Gemport and is sending reinforcements to fight off the Hammer. We have six legions of forty warriors each. They are the best fighters this side of the Seven. I can promise you that. These are all Brightness knights and above; any lower-ranking Light Monk that requested to join the fight was denied. We aren't sending children to their deaths." Tendra nodded gratefully.

"What about the Seven? Do the Light Monks know anything about them?" Jonathon shook his head.

"We were as unaware of their existence as the rest of the world until a few months ago. We think that one of them might have been the pirate Damaen Longshore, but beyond that, we have nothing, at least as far as I know. We have been searching for information, but the war has sent the world into a tailspin. The feral kingdom may be no more, but packs are still roaming the countryside marauding, and the Hammer isn't much better. The Watchers Black are holding Beth's Bridge, but they are assailed constantly. Centaurs are not staying here. They are slaughtering humans across Carin. The reason you have heard so little from the eastern cities is because the centaurs have set fire to most human cities in the lands between here and there. Not only that, but rumors are that the telos negotiated sea interdiction to the east as a condition for their surrender after Long Fang. We have Light Monks spread thin throughout the world searching for information and trying to keep some semblance of order, but we are not an army. We are a stopgap measure at best. Jeric needs to hurry. We need to break the

27

Hammer here. Fear is running rampant through the world. Men who answered your call for banners are now refugees, whose families have been slaughtered. We need to break this siege."

"That's what I am afraid of, Jonathon...I don't know if I can." she bowed her head as her words trailed off. She felt his well-worn hand on her chin.

"Tendra, I have been with you all your life. I have watched you transform from a mischievous child, to a struggling girl, to a woman who veritably glows with strength. You are more fit to rule this kingdom than any man or woman. You have the blood of the viper in you, same as your father. You are beautiful to look at, but you are dangerous when pressed, and don't let that schemer Vizien tell you any different. You have only to believe in yourself to succeed." Tendra stiffened at Vizien's name. She had voiced her suspicions about his role in her father's death. Jonathon had been investigating it subtly ever since, but they had been able to find nothing that indicated that it was Vizien's hand that raised the blade.

"Thank you," she said.

"You're not alone." he looked into her eyes. "You are never alone." the silence that filled the room served to make the sound that came filtering through the window all the more noticeable. Jonathon tilted his head as he rose from the stool and walked over towards the window. Tendra's gaze followed him and her legs soon after.

At first Tendra thought that maybe there was an attack, for the sound of raised voices caught in her ears; yet her eyes told her that the unu lines were the same as they had been for the last few weeks. She closed her eyes and focused harder. The wind seemed to die down, and she was finally able to make out the sounds. They were sounds she had not heard in what seemed like ages...the sound of cheers.

Spreading up through the town like a virus, cries of joy were erupting everywhere. It was like a clarion call to her ears.

"What is going on?" Jonathon shrugged in bewilderment. Tendra turned away from the window as she heard tattered breathing near the trap door. A pounding on the wood followed soon after.

"My lady, my lady!" Tendra crossed the distance in six strides dropping the door to see a young boy carrying a bucket full of various spices and leaves.

"Ah my supplies, finally." Jonathon proclaimed. "Give them here, boy." Jonathon reached down and snatched the bucket away from the young man.

"But…but…but." the boy stammered through strangled breath.

"Easy now. Speak." Tendra commanded.

"The birds just arrived, my lady. There are two of them, and they're coming." the boy's excitement was palpable.

"Who? Who is coming?" She asked.

"The wizards! The wizards are coming." his eyes were alight with delight. "They'll be here by nightfall. The wizards are coming." Tendra's breathing stopped for a moment: *the wizards…Rowen.* Praise Supremor, she had known that they couldn't be dead. She had known it. Tendra turned to Jonathon.

"Maybe there is hope for us after all." She smiled. "The wizards are coming."

Flight of the Fallen

Three

"I need to kill a demon." Galeerial Starheart, Supreme Cleric of the Skyguard, told the wizard Grey, who raised an eyebrow questioningly but shrugged indiscriminately. Their conversation was interrupted by a sound that sent a chill through Galeerial's hardened heart. It echoed through his bones and resounded in his mind. It was a clarion call. The horn rang clear through the air, as if it had been blown right next to him; yet Galeerial knew that it was being blown hundreds of miles north, in Cloud Breach.

"Are you okay? You look a little...not okay," Grey said, snapping his fingers at Galeerial. Galeerial shook his head as the sound of the Horn of Seventeen Sorrows faded from his ears. "What was that sound?"

"He's coming."

"Who?" the centaur Dane asked from his place in the aerie within the Skyguard city of Winter Crest, atop the mountain of Lightwatch. Next to him lay the wizard Aurum, on his deathbed. After being stabbed at Long Fang, they had led him to the Split to let him stabilize for nine days before heading here for him to fully recover. Gabriel, the former Supreme Cleric of the Skyguard, had told Galeerial that the wizard could help train him, that Aurum could show him how to kill Veriel. Now, Aurum needed to go somewhere else. He had been contemplating it for the last three weeks since they had begun the flight out of Long Fang. The wizard Grey would have to train him. Galeerial was reminded of what Gabriel had said to him. Galeerial turned from the centaur to the doorway. "Aurum, I know you can hear me; wherever you are, listen to my words.

Go where angels fear to tread,
And souls are alighted yet bound.
Where eyes from above watched,
And the beginning was found.

Truth spawns from lies,
The doubting heart dies

The Key to All Souls will be given,
The door to the Book will unlock.
The willing heart will bleed water
And Ruin will emerge from the rock.

Nobody moved for a moment as everyone's eyes flickered between Galeerial and Aurum. "Come on, Aurum." Galeerial whispered. "What does it mean?" Galeerial watched as Aurum's eyes opened to reveal a violet light.

"Ohm." his eyes flashed shut again, and the light vanished with his consciousness.

"I don't understand. What does it mean? And who is coming?" Dane's confused tone echoed his face.

"As soon as he is well, take him to Thanatos." Galeerial said. Dane's face grew slack in astonishment, and his expression was echoed on Grey's face. Galeerial stepped back and up from the bed where Aurum lay.

31

"As for who is coming," one word emerged from Galeerial's lips. It was a word of hatred."Veriel." *That horn meant Veriel was coming, and I will be ready for him.* Galeerial felt his blood run hot. Finally, that monster would get his bloody due for the torture that he had inflicted upon Galeerial. Veriel had cut his wings off and sent him to be tortured at the hands of The Wither. Everything that had happened in the last few months had been because of that creature. Galeerial would have his vengeance upon Veriel, and soon.

"Why Thanatos?" Dane asked.

"He has been marked by divinity. Thanatos will prove him worthy." Galeerial replied. "Grey, we have to go." they needed to get out of this aerie, and quick. He couldn't let Veriel find Aurum. Galeerial felt the cold wind on his face as he exited the room to the balcony. He gestured at their steward to come to retrieve them, but the boy was gone. Something was wrong. Galeerial could feel it in his bones. Silence filled the air as the first Skyguard rose into the sky clothed in the full battle garb of the Burning Host. The crimson and silver blend of steel and cloth chilled his blood.

Soon that Skyguard was joined by another, and another, and another. One by one the sky grew dark with ten thousand Skyguard rising into the clouds. Galeerial's heart stopped beating for a moment. Veriel wasn't coming here. He was calling the Skyguard to him, and they were answering.

"No." he whispered. This was the first day they had been in the city. He hadn't even met with the High Clerics yet, and now the city was being deserted as the Burning Host of the city of Winter Crest answered the clarion call of the Horn. "NO!" he screamed at them, but still they continued their ascent. "Grey! We need to get to the cathedral, now!"

"Dane, if he dies, I wouldn't tell Joven. I've heard Bastian is nice this time of year," Grey told the centaur.

"He'll live. He must, but Thanatos?" Dane replied, still bewildered.

"Grey!" Galeerial urged as he grabbed Eon, the Cardinal Sword of Time, given to him by Gabriel to mark his ascension to the rank of Supreme Cleric, and slung it across his back.

"Alright, I just hope you're ready for the fall." Grey sprinted towards him and tackled him out of the doorway. They plummeted earthward, and Galeerial had a strange feeling of déjà vu, but rather than sailing away on pearlescent wings he found himself gradually slowing. They touched down lightly.

"How did you...?" Galeerial began. Grey shrugged.

"Magic. Isn't that why you kidnapped me?"Grey said. Galeerial didn't answer the question for he was already sprinting up towards the Cathedral of Fate, which stood at the apex of the mountain. The skies had grown empty as the storm of the host moved away from the city. The Clerics must have a way to call them back. Sweat began to pour down his face as the thin mountain air caused him to gasp for breath. The winter's chill clawed at him, desperately seeking to pull him into the darkness, but his grinding muscles staved off its advances. The Cathedral of Fate dominated the landscape, and slowly it grew more and more imposing. He saw the doors rising up to meet them and reached up with both hands and pushed. The ancient doors stayed firm. Galeerial slammed a gauntleted hand against them. The metal plating on the wood doors rang out with a reverberating din, but nothing else happened.

"Let me try," Grey said. Galeerial stepped out of the way. "Open Sesame!" he cried and thrust his arms forward. Galeerial felt a ripple in the air around him, and the doors flew inward with a crash. "Guess I don't know my own strength," Grey said with a smile. Galeerial entered with trepidation. Before him was a gently sloping, crimson carpeted floor that led to the primary altar. The altar was a large, rectangular piece of black stone etched with divine runes in gold and silver. Surrounding it stood five High Clerics. In all three of the Skyguard cities, five High Clerics ruled, and all fell under the purview of the Supreme Cleric. They were garbed in simple high-collared robes with eagle helms, the symbol of the son of Supremor. None of them spoke until Galeerial arrived at the foot of the dais.

"The human cannot enter," they said as one.

"The human will do as he wishes." Galeerial said firmly. The Clerics said nothing in response. "You must call the Host back." No one

33

moved. Galeerial's eyes franticly searched each of theirs and found nothing. "NOW!"

"One of Seruvia's instruments has been awoken. The Skyguard are bound to answer its call. And you, Supreme Cleric, have overstepped your bounds. You may rule the Skyguard, but you may not so callously disregard tradition." all five Clerics once again spoke in unison.

"And you can stop the creepy simultaneity any time now," Grey said. The Clerics sent him a withering glance, to which he responded with a toothy smile.

"I don't have time for this. Veriel called them. He is leading them to war against humanity in the south."

"Lord Veriel is a trusted member of the Skyguard, and humans wielding unbound magic are a dangerous proposition at best and heretics at worst. The Burning Host will join Lord Commander Veriel in their destruction. We will reclaim the Heart of Fires and keep it safe within the bounds of our cities. This disease must not be allowed to spread. Magic was bound for a reason. It was Supremor's will, glory be his name. The heretics must be eliminated." the Clerics looked pointedly at Grey. "All of them." there was a rustle of wings, and a Skyguard cascaded down from the heights of the Cathedral. It was a Lord Commander. Galeerial glared at him coldly.

"If you raise a finger against the wizard, you will also draw arms against the Supreme Cleric." Galeerial's gaze drifted back to the Clerics. Galeerial slowly reached behind him and pulled Eon from its sheath.

"You cannot protect this blasphemer forever, Galeerial."

"But I will protect him from you." Galeerial's icy stare bore into the eyes of the Clerics. None blinked. They were as stone.

"Your position grants you power that is not to be abused in this fashion. Nor should you have revealed yourself to those gathered here. It is not befitting of your station."

"I didn't ask for this, but, as long as I have it, I will use it to make our people safe."

"You are no longer a Skyguard, Galeerial. We are no longer your people. You are merely…" they paused for a moment. "…human." Despite

34

the cold, Galeerial ripped his tunic off. The scars that he bore from his months of imprisonment at the hands of The Wither stood revealed, as did the protrusions from his shoulder blades that marked where his wings had once been attached.

"Veriel cut my wings off and delivered me into the hands of The Wither. He made me human, and it was humans who saved me: a human who rescued me from torture and certain death, a human who brought me back to health, a human who agreed to help when my own people sided with a monster. If that is wrong in the eyes of Supremor,, then I have sinned most grievously. Veriel will drag our people screaming into the abyss. Your ignorance will not save you. You see the fates intertwine; so how can you be so blind?" For the first time the Clerics looked uncertain.

"We see…fluidity in the future. The Seven block our visions. Their blasphemy muddles the very rivers of fate itself. They are an aberration; an abomination that must be eradicated."

"So you say, but what does Supremor say? He says *Trust in me with your faith. The abilities you possess are nothing compared to the weakness of me. Your wisdom is more foolish than the foolishness of me. When you trust in yourself or the world you will fall, but when you trust in me I will lead you to salvation.*" it had been a long time since the words of 1their holy book, *The Stone,* had flowed from his lips. Not since he had repeated them to himself over and over again in the months of his capture and torture by The Wither.

"You dare fight us with the very blood that runs through our veins?" they thundered. "We are Clerics chosen by the Son of Supremo-"

"And still you have been blinded by the world!" Galeerial felt his frustration mounting. His rage burned in his eyes and was reflected as a deep menacing crimson within the heart of the Five Eye gemstone which hung as a pendant around his neck. "Call. Them. Back." he felt a hand on his shoulder, and he whipped his face around viciously to behold Grey.

"Take it easy, Galeerial. They won't help us. We just need to leave before sharp pointy pieces of metal start sticking into soft rounded pieces of flesh."

"Shut up, Grey." The wizard took a step back. "Where is the rallying point?" He hissed at them. The Clerics looked back and forth without answering.

"Where, Clerics," Galeerial emphasized the word, "is the rallying point? One of you will die if I must ask again."

"Visir, in the Stonewood Pass between the end of the Sparkling Mountains and the west city of giants." Galeerial turned from the Clerics to the Skyguard Lord Commander who knelt to the ground, bowing his head.

"You will not leave Winter Crest until I call for you. You will under no circumstances join Veriel's host. You will prevent the High Clerics from leaving this cathedral as well. Is that understood?" The Lord Commander rose, offering a salute.

"Yes, My Lord." he replied. The Lord Commander who stood before them was a slight warrior, not thin, but lean. His wings were large and powerful behind him. He looked like a raptor.

"What is your name, Lord Commander?"

"Sevitel Starglass, My Lord."

"You are in charge here. My orders are to be followed to the letter. If Lord Commander Veriel arrives and demands you join his Host, tell him that you are under orders from the Supreme Cleric to refuse. Do not give him my name. Also, the wizard Aurum and the centaur Dane are to be protected at all costs. They will soon depart, but until then, Veriel must not know of their existence."

"I understand and obey, My Lord." Sevitel replied.

Galeerial turned back to the High Clerics. "As for the five of you, may Supremor have mercy on your souls, because I would not be so kind. Grey?"

"Still here."

"Let's go." Galeerial slowly began to walk backwards. His eyes were fixed upon the Clerics.

"Don't do this. If you help him, you will find only exile." the Clerics called after him.

"Too late." Galeerial replied. With that he turned and pushed past Grey and out of the cathedral doors. A chill fell over his body as he exited the walls. He felt every step as if a chasm was growing between him and the rest of his people. He had openly defied the High Clerics. He had blatantly violated ancient traditions. He breathed out heavily. He looked up to the sky and found no solace there.

"So what's the plan, boss?" Grey asked, matching his step. Grey handed him the tunic that he had pulled off in the cathedral, and he gratefully pulled it over his head.

"We're going to Visir. You are going to teach me how to use this sword, and I am going to use it to cut Veriel's head from his shoulders."

"What do I get out of the deal?" Galeerial recoiled momentarily. *What do you get? How about I don't kill you where you stand?* He tempered his flaring rage.

"The Skyguard will not burn your brothers and the rest of humanity to the ground. If you help me, your race will not be extinct by year's end." Grey considered this for a moment.

"Aurum would make a much better teacher." he said.

"That may be so, but you are all I have."

"Your faith in me is truly inspiring." he remarked sarcastically. He looked Galeerial up and down. "It won't be easy."

"If it were, then I wouldn't need you." Galeerial fired back.

"Fair enough, but if you want to learn to fight then you need to learn how not to be an idiot." Grey sighed as Galeerial's eyes narrowed. "Lesson one: fight first with your mind." the wizard pointed to his own temple but didn't offer further elaboration. "I'll explain as we ride. Let's go." Grey took off running downhill, and Galeerial followed. Galeerial's boots created jarring impacts on his shins and knees from the frost-ridden ground. As they ran, Galeerial was overwhelmed by just how similar Winter Crest was to his home of Cloud Breach: the same architecture, the same patterns of roads winding their way through the city from aerie to aerie.

"Not all pathways lead away from home." Ezekiel's voice echoed in his ears. Galeerial whipped his head around sharply searching for his best friend, but there was no one there. Galeerial began to slow his descent as he neared the stables by the gates. He looked up into the sky.

"Wherever you are, my friend, may the winds guide you," Galeerial said. He turned his head from the ocean of air. This wasn't the time or the place. Grey was already inside.

"You are going to have to be faster than that if you want to be one of us."

"Wait," Galeerial said through gasps for breath as he entered the stables. Grey pulled the horses they had acquired from The Split out of their pens. "What do you mean be one of you?"

"Let me talk slowly, 'cause I know you are kind of messed up. I could straight out teach you to fight, but then this Veriel guy would just kill you, and it would be a waste of both our time. So instead, I will make you a proposition. In order to last longer than four seconds in a fight, I will teach you how to be one of us. In other words, how would you like to become the eighth member of the Seven?" Grey offered Galeerial the reigns of a horse, followed by his hand. Galeerial stared at him for a long moment.

What extraordinary humans these were. He was offering to bring him into his host: to make him family. Galeerial thought about his own parents. His father Horishon, and mother Carinima. He thought of Ezekiel, his wingman, and Ezekiel's wife, Jariah. Both his mother and father had been rangers who had been killed young in Galeerial's life. Ezekiel and Jariah had been his only family. Now, he didn't even know if they were still alive. He stared into Grey's eyes.

"Why are you offering me this?" Grey shrugged.

"Because you seem to be pretty alright in my book, and I owe you for saving Aurum's life. He hates being in anyone's debt, so I figure I will use this opportunity to try to take down some of what I owe him."

"What do you owe him for?" Galeerial asked.

"More things than I could explain to you in a lifetime. Well?" Once again, Galeerial regarded the wizard's hand. Gabriel had told him that he could trust the Seven, and he *had* just violated the direct orders of a council of High Clerics. He had nothing to lose. Galeerial reached out and grasped the other man's hand firmly.

"I'll do it." the wizard's hand was thick, and his handshake hard. The calloused fingers squeezed tight around his own.

"Then welcome. We have a lot of work to do." Galeerial nodded in compliance as the wizard released his hand. Grey handed him one of the packs they had carried with them since leaving the Split. They were growing short on food and water; they would have to restock soon. The Skyguard required neither, so they would need to reach a human city or town in the next three days or so. Galeerial threw the saddle bags over the back of the horse along with a riding blanket and saddle. Galeerial swung up onto the horse with a grunt. His legs were still stiff from the days of riding it had taken them to get here.

"As a more obtainable and immediate objective, I want you to do something that may prove difficult. I want you to think." Grey guided his horse ahead of Galeerial's as they maneuvered out of the stables. "You fly off half-cocked wherever you go with little to no regard for the long term plan. You go where you are told, which may be admirable in some walks of life, but as one of us that equates to stupidity. Think first with your head. Why would Veriel marshal at Visir? It makes less than no sense. Cloud Breach, on the other hand...Cloud Breach is almost directly north of Gemport, which is where the Clerics seem to believe that the Heart of Fires is located. Visir is completely out of the way. If they were to marshal anywhere, it would be at Amul Kon."

"They lied." Galeerial breathed. "Skyguard High Clerics lied within the shadow of the shiftstone statue. How dare they? How dare they!" he thundered.

"Not necessarily." they guided their horses slowly down the mountain. The path was old, almost as old as the world itself. The sound of the hooves through the chilled air was sharp and poignant. "You asked them where the marshaling point was, and they told you Visir. You never asked where the marshaling point of the Burning Host was. Despite their desire to commit wholesale slaughter upon my brothers and me, I believe they don't

39

want to see the Skyguard destroyed. So why would they send us to Visir? Think." They rode in silence down the mountain path. Galeerial racked his brain. *Why would the Clerics from the Cathedral of Fate send us somewhere that we didn't want to go?* "Think what you told me about Veriel. The first time you descended into the stone cells." Grey urged. A feeling of dread began to grow in his stomach as he thought about the conversation he had overheard between the being named Terel, The Wither, and Veriel.

"Veriel's army."

"The army." Grey repeated. "They can see into the annals of fate, so perhaps they see the growing darkness there and are sending us there to hold the line. Someone has to. I know that you want to take your shot at Veriel. But some things have to come first."

"No." Galeerial said. Grey reared his horse to block Galeerial's path.

"Excuse me?"

"Veriel comes first. You know what he did to me. Everything else will fall apart when he falls."

"If you go fight him now the only thing that will be falling will be your head from your shoulders. You need to be trained, that was the entire point of you rescuing Aurum and I. You need to be taught not just how to fight, but how to win. You are an infant in a world of adults. If you can't handle this, then I will kill you right now and go to Visir myself. Got it?"

"You think so little of me, Mage? You were fleeing from a dozen unu when Dane and I rescued you. You are the least among a group of your betters." Galeerial said.

Grey laughed mockingly. "Fine then. You want to waste time with a pointless fight? Let's go. I will beat the living daylights out of you, tie you to the horse and go along my merry way. Or you can stop being a petulant child." Grey sighed. "I'm repeating myself. That is how annoyed I am at you right now. Look beyond your own pain. This world is about to ignite. We are the only chance Carin has of delaying the fuse. I asked you not ten minutes ago if you wanted to be one of us, and you accepted. Now act like

40

it. Starting today, you don't doubt me. You trust me; you accept my judgment and leadership. I am not your enemy or your antagonist. I'm your friend who is trying to help you. It's your call." Grey said. Galeerial glared at this infuriating wizard. He took a deep breath.

"Very well."

"Very well what? Grey asked.

"We'll do it your way. I'm all yours."

Grey smiled."That's what I like to hear. Though usually from attractive females, but I will make an exception for you." The wizard winked before whipping his horse around and taking off at a slow but progressive trot down the twisting road of the mountain. Galeerial gazed skyward at the harsh sunlight one last time before turning his head downward and following the mage wherever he might lead.

It's All Part of the Plan
Four

Rikard remembered that day well, the day that he had arrived at Ornus. Breva only hit him five times before he could explain, three less than he had expected considering they had abandoned the unu woman a year ago. Dorian had loved her, and it had rent his heart in two when they had left. There had been matters that they had to attend to, and there had been no way for Dorian to return. Unless that return was in secret or in chains. Now, it had happened both ways. Just as Joven had said it would all those months ago. Rikard marveled at just how well Joven had planned all of this. He truly was masterful. He could see pathways layered on pathways and wheels within wheels.

Clansmaster Qel of the Thousand Hammers was arriving today along with his royal guard, the unum, and with Dorian. The unum were a particular sect of the unu, the best of the best warriors were selected to be a part of them. Rikard wasn't impressed. Rikard lay atop one of the rooftops, covered in sand and hay, overlooking the entrance to the city. It wasn't easy being a human in a city of unu, but he had made do while making his preparations. Everything was prepared for the game, and now the pieces had been delivered to him.

Qel rolled into the city with a crown of trumpets and gold. All commerce in the town had stopped for the day to welcome home the clansmaster of the unu. The clansmaster looked suitably noble but for his missing arm. Rikard smiled. That was new. He wondered briefly which of his brothers it had been who had delivered the blow.

"Nice work, brothers," he murmured. The unum were also decently ravaged. Usually it was one hundred strong; now there were only twenty-eight. Rikard briefly wondered if there had been an odd number, and Qel had ordered one killed to preserve the balance.

Rikard grimaced as the cart rolled in with Dorian atop it. Dorian was laid out with only the slightest bit of clothing left upon his body. His arms and legs were stretched out and bound by heavy iron chains. His skin was a deep red from sun scarring, and his hair was grown long. Dorian looked delirious; if not unconscious. Rikard wondered what had happened at Long Fang. He had managed to get out only single message to Joven, but beyond that, he knew only what Breva could find out. He knew that the feral race was destroyed at Long Fang and teetered on the edge of extinction with the destruction of Ferum. Now, the Hammer turned to Gemport and, after the Feast of Bejor, Qel planned to sack the capitol of humanity.

"Not if I have anything to say about it," he whispered aloud. The Feast was tomorrow, and that would be when the fire fountains would begin. He watched Qel through his spyglass. He could kill the bloated scaler right now, but he wouldn't. That would be too quick. He had to make him scared first. Make him terrified. Make him fear the name of the Seven.

The one-armed unu had his hand out, clasping the hands of the common folk. There were smiles everywhere. Qel was a hero to his people: the annihilator of the ferals. This was the greatest singular deed since those of Kam of the Swift Arrow during the Jaws War. Rikard had watched a dozen leaders of the various clans filter in over the last few days, and they

43

were a talkative bunch: most notably about a coup. With Qel down to a single arm there was quite a bit of talk about who would replace him. Terel of the Amber Stone was a name that had been tossed about quite a bit.

Terel had been the leader of the Amber Stone Clan and had been a contender for the title of Clansmaster after the death of Shane of the Bleeding Moon. The battle between him and Qel for the souls of the unu had been fierce, but, in the end, Qel had won, and the official tale had been that Terel had left in disgust. But everyone knew the truth. Qel had sent him ranging northward, and then sent the unum to kill him, but they had failed. Now rumors were that he was coming back to claim the throne.

The other two options were Qel's son Nod and Gorn of the White Pike. Nod was exactly like his father, and Gorn was a one of the heroes of the current war. He had led the unu at the Face Off where he had supposedly taken the fortress without losing a single soldier. Rikard didn't put too much stock in Gorn. He was a follower, not a leader. And Nod...Rikard bristled at the very thought. Nod was a conniving, scheming spawn of the Dread who deserved a knife in the throat and three in the back.

Rikard had gotten to know him well while serving off and on as Qel's foster child. He had taken Dorian's place twice during the three years they had spent with the clan, and, in that time, he had survived three assassination attempts by Nod. Rikard grinned. He had paid him back with a scar underneath Nod's right eye. He licked his lips. That had been a good fight.

Rikard brought his attention back to the present. He needed to kill someone. He hadn't killed anyone since he had arrived while the brothers had been fighting a war. It just wasn't fair. He should be doing some killing. He watched Dorian's slave cart roll past on its way to the Gold Castle. The sightseeing was almost finished, and he had a meeting to keep.

The unu keep their prisoners in the Gold Castle, which stood in direct opposition to the Blue Castle. In Ornus, the town was divided diagonally down the middle, and each side was a mirror image of the other to preserve The Balance. The Blue Castle was the home of the clanmasters, and the Gold Castle held the prisoners and the servants. Kings and pawns treated as equals: such foolishness. During the night they were kept in the dungeons, but during the day the prisoners were kept in the courtyard in front of the castle.

Rikard slid his spyglass back into his sheath, crawled to the edge of the building, and rolled off. The Gold Castle was behind him, and, with everyone watching the parade, he was free to make his way there. He dropped down to the ground. He took off running dodging through the alleys of the houses. It was surprisingly temperate for this time of year, but Rikard knew it wouldn't last. The winter was a harsh mistress, cold and unforgiving.

Rikard arrived at the stone walls of the castle. The castle stretched about two hundred feet into the air, though the walls surrounding it were only about fourteen feet in height. He moved around to the back corner, where the castle walls met the outer walls of the city. He ran up the outer stone, kicked off with his left foot, and leapt onto the one surrounding the castle digging Burn into the wall and using it to pull himself up. He swung his leg up and ripped his dagger from the wall as he rolled into the inner courtyard.

He sprinted across the courtyard, keeping an eye out for any unu, even though he knew that none would be there. These fools. They thought themselves invincible here in their inner sanctum. Rikard smiled. He would show them just how safe they were.

The inner courtyard used to be comprised of trees, water, and stone, but with winter descending, the branches added just another shade of brown to the land and the fountains had been blocked so there was no more blue: just dreary brown.

Rikard ran up the castle wall and gripped the gaps between the stones. He had spent three nights mapping out the ideal way to climb each of the towers: observing every outcropping, every misplaced stone and wooden ledge. He knew the two castles like he knew the face of his father. Rikard didn't really think about his father much. Rerem had been a hard man, a strong man, a noble man. He had been a curiosity within the world of Cambria: a land of cowards hardly worthy enough to lick his father's

45

boots. He had died gloriously, though. *That was what mattered: how you died.*

Rikard reached the final stone before the window. The wooden shutters were flung open, and Rikard kicked his leg up and into the room. It was a simple guard's quarters with a bed in the middle and two nightstands on either side of it. The wash basin was immediately in front of the bed. Everything was perfectly symmetrical, balanced.

Rikard grabbed one of the nightstands, lifted it up, and moved it to the far corner of the room. He wished he could see the look of abject horror on the guard's face when he walked in. An unbalanced room was grounds for dismissal and shame. He could almost taste the panic that was to come and had to refrain from laughing; these pathetic unu living their pathetic lives. Well, not for much longer. Rikard had done his job well, just as soon as he spoke with Dorian. He had to know what happened. He had to know how bad it was.

Rikard glanced out into the hallway and stealthily crept out. He moved quickly and silently up three stairwells and into the dungeons. There had been a few prisoners in the unu dungeons in the time that he had been there, but they were all empty now. One didn't survive long in an unu prison. The stone hallways were wide and tall to accommodate the large unu figures, and Rikard met no resistance on his way up. He was lucky. He knew getting out wouldn't be quite as simple, and that was just fine by him. He didn't mind getting his hands bloody.

The tower where prisoners were held was the mirror image of the clanmaster's quarters. This meant Rikard had plenty of practice finding every nook and cranny to hide in, every beam to hold on to, and every window to climb out of, all without ever having to break into the palace. Interestingly enough, the unu dungeons looked just like all the other rooms, except that there was nothing in them but chains. Rikard found the irony of this hilarious.

"Which one...which one?" he said as he twirled up into the interior stairwell of the turret. Every eight steps there was another door. Dorian was a high profile prisoner, which meant that he would be in the highest cell.

46

Rikard ascended the steps two at a time to the top. He stopped for a moment at the second to last door. He stopped because of the screams. Normally, screams wouldn't bother him; it wasn't like he hadn't heard them before. But these were different.

He slid Bleed from his belt and Rikard turned the handle. The door slid open easily, and he rolled his eyes. Inside, against the back wall, a girl was chained. She looked to be about twelve years old. A tall slender unu stood in front of Rikard, his back facing him. A whip was unfurled in his right hand, and the girl's tattered clothes and long scars indicated that it had been well used. The unu turned around, and his eyes had just enough time to register surprise before Bleed embedded itself in between them.

"Now look what you made me do," he sighed. "Who are you?" Rikard circled around the young girl, staring at her. She had short black hair and was wearing a black shift. Her wrists and ankles were raw and bloodied from the chains, and she had a series of needles pressed into her skin along her arms and legs. Her eyes were wide and full of fear as they warily followed him around the room.

"I'm not going to hurt you. Well, I might kill you, but I'm not going to hurt you. Now, what's your name?" Rikard walked up to the girl and touched his hand to her chin. He jerked it back as her teeth tried to take a chunk of his flesh. "You're trying my patience. So, either I leave you, or you cooperate. Those are the only options." The girl sniffled as her tear stained face stared at him. "Fine." Rikard knelt by the dead unu and ripped his dagger free. "Have fun."

He pulled open the unu's shirt and carved a D into the flesh. That was going to be his call sign. Every time someone died, there would be a D on their body: D for Dorian, D for death, D for desolation. Whatever Qel came up with as an explanation would suffice. Rikard pulled open the door and prepared to walk out when she spoke.

"Hope."

Rikard didn't turn around. "Excuse me?" he called over his shoulder.

"My name's Hope."

"Well, I hope you have thought up a way to get out of here not involving me. You had your chance." he closed the door and continued up the stairwell. Did he feel bad? *A little*, but he had a job to do, and killing an unu, well, that was part of the job. He was in the business of death, not salvation, and he was exceedingly good at his job. Having a little girl follow him around? Not so much. He reached the top of the stairwell and slipped out the small window. He would wait on the roof. He swung out into the air, reached up, and grabbed the ledge of the roof. He felt the stone scrape against his fingers as he pulled himself up with his left arm.

It was late afternoon, and the sun was beginning to fade into the horizon. The wide roof was circular in shape and twenty-four feet in diameter. Rikard stayed low as he peered over the ledge. There should be twelve guards stationed on the walls, and his observations agreed with his prior knowledge.

The lack of sound from musical instruments caused him to peer down at the main road. Below he saw the crowd dispersing as Qel and the rest of the war heroes moved into the Blue Castle. He laid back and began to doze as he waited for nightfall. He heard them drag Dorian up. He smiled in satisfaction as he heard them kick the door down that he was seated right above. He was moderately surprised by the lack of torture that occurred after Dorian's arrival. He thought for sure that the unu guards would have a little fun.

He watched the sky burn with red and purple fire before vanishing beneath the black curtain of the jagged mountains that shielded the Rift. He watched the stars rise up into the sky. He had never cared for the patterns in the sky that others claimed to see. To him, they were simply the last bastions of light in a world of darkness: much like his brothers. As shadows fell, Rikard watched the pairs of torches begin to light up. It was time to move.

Once again, he swung down to the ledge and slipped into the window. He pressed his ear to the door, slowing his breathing and listening carefully, but he heard nothing. He tried the door and was surprised to find it actually locked. Interesting.

He pulled his dagger from his belt and began to saw away at the lock. He made it through the bolt, and he pushed open the door. Two unu stood guard over the chained body of Dorian. They stared at him in astonishment. Rikard smiled. Apparently, in this world, no identical twins had ever been born before, and it was something they planned to use to their great advantage.

"Hello, gentlemen," Rikard's first blade pinned the left unu's hand to the wall and his second pinned the other. He dodged the thrust from the staff of the other unu, leapt up against the wall, and pushed off around behind the unu soldier. He latched onto his neck, pulling him backwards, before twisting his neck, and snapping it. The unu collapsed to the ground in a ragged heap, and Rikard turned to look at the other one.

"What-what are you?" he breathed. Terror was evident on the unu's face. Rikard relished it. It was a great reward for all of his hard work.

"I am the spirit of Dorian Waterborne of the Thousand Hammers. Here to wreak vengeance upon your race for your betrayal." Rikard almost laughed, both at the absurdity of what he was saying and at the belief in the unu's eyes. "Now run like a whipped dog to your master. Tell him that this city is mine." the unu was shaking, and as Rikard ripped the daggers from his hands, the unu fell to the ground. "Go." the unu spat at Rikard and launched a savage kick at Rikard's right leg. He leapt over him and snapped off a kick of his own that hit with a satisfying crack upon the unu's chin. His head flicked back, and Rikard buried Bleed into his neck.

Blood began to fountain from the wound, spraying him in the face, and Rikard tossed the body to the ground in disgust. He turned back to his brother. To the untrained eye, his brother didn't look to be in too bad of shape, but he knew better. Rikard could tell Dorian had lost weight, and his lips were dried out beneath a scraggly beard. Both shoulders were covered in bandages, though it looked like only one of his arms was actually injured.

"You look terrible," Dorian said. Rikard leaned down and brought his canteen up to Dorian's lips allowing a small bit of water into his mouth. He drank it gratefully.

"Funny, I was about to say the same thing to you. Where do we stand?" he said as he gave his brother a little more to drink.

"I think we all made it out."

"Think?" Rikard asked.

"Qel and his cronies have said differently, of course, but we planned for this eventuality." Dorian replied. That meant that ideally Joven, Rayn and Rowen were back in Gemport; Aurum was at Soaring trying to convince Gabriel to join the war, and Grey was in King's Port.

"So, there were no complications?" Rikard asked.

"You mean besides this?" Dorian said, nodding to his bandaged shoulder.

"What happened?"

"I was hit with a ballista on the first day of the Battle for Long Fang. My breastplate collapsed into my chest. It took them two hours to pry it off. I was given a temporary suit of centaur armor: cheap garbage. I took an arrow an inch above my heart. I passed out from the blood loss and woke up three days later on the bloody caravan on its way here."

"Anything else?" Rikard asked. His brother would heal fast; they all did. Inexplicably fast, now that he actually thought about it for a moment. Rikard shrugged off the puzzling thought.

"Jakob is dead."

"Vizien."

It wasn't a question, but Dorian replied anyway. "Of course."

"I told you he would screw up our plans."

"It was nothing irreparable. Besides, it was inevitable that Jakob die. Now that death will not be on our conscious." Dorian said concisely. Rikard looked his twin in the face. Something else was bothering him.

"What's wrong?"

Dorian paused for a moment before responding. "You know back when we were at the Star Chamber, and Uraban came and spoke to us?" Rikard nodded. "Remember when he said that if everything seems to be going perfectly, it usually isn't? Well, things have been going too perfectly. Tendra's brother just happens to be sick at the same time that we emerge

50

from an illness that Rowen can treat? For that matter, the mere discovery of the Heart of Fires at the advent of campaign; the centaurs being the first to find us, and Jeronious and Qel both joining our quest that easily: even our conquest of the ferals. I mean, six months and we obliterated the Kingdom of Fangs. Too many things have been falling into place too neatly."

"What are you suggesting?" Rikard asked. He knew that whatever the answer would be, it would be a challenge.

"What if-just bear with me-what if all of this has been planned? Everything from the gallowglass prophecy to all of our current activities. We spent seven years here, and none of us died. This is a dangerous world, far more so than the one we left. We infiltrated the unu. Aurum and all his work as Longshore worked perfectly. Too many disparate things have gone right for us. I don't like it."

"Sounds like the musings of someone with too much delirious time on their hands. Dorian, no one could have planned every event. It would take an astronomically complicated mind to even think of it. That's not even considering the resources necessary to pull it off. We could barely do it, and that's with all seven of us. Let's be honest, we are much, much smarter than the people here. We have abilities they don't, and it still took us three years of planning in Cambria before even arriving."

"Yes, but what if part of it was ourselves? The gallowglass have given maybe three 'prophecies' throughout history, but all of them have come true with their interference. There is a theory that if you are told your future, you will make it come true. What if the words of the gallowglass entered into our lower minds, and we influenced ourselves to do their bidding? The rest of the coincidences could have been more subtly influenced by this presence. What if all of this is just a game of Crowns with us on one side, and some hidden player on the other? What if we are playing a game against an opponent we know nothing about?"

Rikard looked at his brother. If it was any of the others, Rikard would have questioned his sanity. But this was Dorian. Dorian thought and prayed about everything for days on end before voicing his beliefs or opinions on anything. He was patient with an idea. The fact that he had voiced his suspicions meant that he had thought long and hard upon it.

"So who is this player on the other side of the table? Hostile?"

"Most likely. I think we need to look back to the Heroic Age." Dorian said quietly. Rikard didn't comprehend his words for a second. When he did, a smile grew upon his face. He licked his lips.

"You really think he's back?"

"Seven years ago was the thousandth anniversary of when he emerged the last time. The same year we arrived. That's not all. When Aurum went to Amul Kon," Rikard shot him a questioning glance. Dorian sighed. "Aurum has been having visions of a red man talking to him." Rikard stared at him dubiously. "He knew Aurum's Thul." at this Rikard started. Nobody knew that. Not even his brothers. At the age of twenty years, each man chose his Thul, his surname, and it was something that was told to none but the spouse of the person. The fact that this person in Aurum's dreams knew it was disturbing.

"Dreams. They are one of the more annoying and inane aspects of this world."

"Indeed, but that's not all. He told him to go to Amul Kon, to rescue a man who was being tortured there. So he did, and everything played out exactly like the red man had told him." Rikard didn't like this at all. "Anyway, at Amul Kon, Aurum fought a being so fast that Aurum couldn't even see him move. This is Aurum." The stress in Dorian's voice told Rikard all he needed to know. "He shot him point blank with a bolt of galvanic energy. It vaporized a hole in his chest, and threw him across the room. Yet the creature stood back up, as if nothing had happened."

"Was it him?"

"I don't think so, but what if we awoke something? It is no coincidence that we arrived when we did. Supremor is in play, and so is his opposite." Rikard didn't put as much stock in deities as Dorian. It was foolishness to put faith in anything that could not be felt, heard, smelled, tasted, or seen.

"I seem to recall you saying that Midox wasn't allowed to take an active role in the affairs of this world." Rikard said.

"According to ancient Skyguard texts I was able to see when meeting with Gabriel, he can only work through intermediaries, like the Dread. There is hardly any mention of Midox in this world. However, I studied the dead faith of Cambria, and their supreme deity was the All whose antithesis was known as Midox as well. Don't you find that odd?" Rikard didn't know much about Midox, but of the Dread he knew much. He had heard the stories, of course, of this evil that had spread across the world, almost annihilating all life in Carin with his passing. Rikard smiled.

"Sure."

"Something bigger than us is guiding us. We need to find out what or who."

"Can't wait." Rikard said. Dorian shook his head with a knowing smile. Rikard was always looking for a challenge, always the next war. Now he would get a death worth dying "I've seen Breva."

Dorian's eyes lit up. "Is she...?" his voice trailed off.

"Your wife's fine, though none too happy that you abandoned her for a year," Rikard said.

"I can scarcely imagine. Did you sleep with her?" he asked.

"Of course not," Rickard said with disgust. Dorian chortled lightly and winced for his efforts. "We don't look that much alike."

"Just keep her safe," Dorian said, and Rikard nodded in return.

"Other than that, I'll start my efforts today. The Feast of Bejor is tomorrow, and that's when the opening gambits will be played. After midnight tonight, no one will leave this city unless it is by ghost."

"Nice work." Dorian said.

Rikard grinned. "Thanks, you too. I saw Qel's arm, or lack thereof. Your work?"

"Hardly. That was a feral berserker," Dorian answered. Rikard nodded appreciatively. "It's dead, before you ask. But anyway, keep an extra eye out. My life's on the line."

"I always was looking out for you," Rikard said. He hoisted one of the dead unu onto his shoulder after carving a 'D' into it while Dorian watched impassively. "Let me take out the trash for you. I'll see you in a few days, but you'll be hearing about me much sooner than that. I guarantee it." Rikard kicked open the door and made his way over to the window. He grabbed the torso of the unu with both hands and pushed the corpse down onto the newly stationed guards in the courtyard below.

"Was that really necessary?" Dorian called out. Rikard pulled the door closed with one final grin.

"Absolutely."

Wheels Within Wheels
Five

Like everyone else in the city that night, Tendra stood atop the battlements watching and waiting. The line of torches that marked the unu barricades was clearly visible just over three hundred and fifty meters away from Gemport: fifty meters outside of trebuchet range. The entirety of the battlements was prepared for the arrival of the wizards. There was not a single man in his bunk that night. No one knew how they would arrive, but no one wanted to miss it. The moon was halfway to full height when the fog began to roll in. It was thick and deep.

"I can't believe this." Wesley, her captain of the guard, came up next to her. "Not a man is at rest right now, despite my explicit order. I swear if anyone falls asleep on watch tomorrow, he will find my foot in his hide," the stocky man grumbled through his black grizzly beard.

"Of that, I have no doubt," Tendra said with a smile. Wesley's gruff and dry demeanor was eternally entertaining. Her introduction to him had been one of the few bright spots in the past few weeks.

"It's them," Jonathon whispered. Her cousin stood on her left with Wesley next to him, and Vizien stood to the right. Tendra didn't like him being so close, but she tolerated it. He wasn't going to try anything in the open. He wouldn't dare. The unu lines became tiny glimpses of light in the fog, but slowly they began to build in strength and intensity. Seconds stretched outward into minutes.

"Bonfires," Vizien said. His voice was as cold as the air.

"It won't work; the wizards are already through. Those six minutes were all they needed." Jonathon said. Jonathon did not quite believe in the tales of the wizards in their entirety. He had met Rowen, albeit briefly, before he had left for Long Fang.

Suddenly, one of the fires vanished. Tendra's eyes were immediately drawn to where the absence of light now existed, desperately searching for something. Then the second one went out, and people began to notice. Their hushed whispers began to grow into a crescendo as the fourth and fifth fires were doused. Then they heard the first scream.

Tendra's eyes glazed over as a flash of light blinded her, and she felt tears run down her face as her eyes tried to cope with the sudden infusion of light. Everywhere people were screaming. Tendra wiped her tears away and blinked heavily, squinting to see what was going on. She saw two black silhouettes hurtling towards the gates.

"OPEN!" Came a shout from below, and Tendra heard the creak as the gates slowly groaned open. She turned from the wall, leapt down onto the ramp below her, and walked quickly down to the main level where the two men came streaking in on horses of fire. The wizards leapt off of their mounts, cutting their robes with daggers where they had ignited. The wizard on the left whipped his dagger across the black horse, and a dark burning cloth fell to the ground. He repeated the motion with the second animal as they bucked wildly, terrified.

56

"The gates!" she called, and the operators quickly turned from the spectacle to bear the cranks, causing the massive doors to inch closed. "Stay back," she warned the people.

"Sentries, to your posts," Wesley called out. No one moved. "Now!" he commanded, "or it'll be your hide on the wall if I catch you. All eyes on the unu lines." his voice left no room for discussion. Reluctantly, they turned away from the wizards on the ground. Tendra stood waiting for them to slowly mill back to their positions on the wall and their various armaments. The wizards slowly pulled back their hoods. Tendra gasped as their faces were revealed. They were entirely covered in black paint such that they looked like creatures from a nightmare long forgotten by human imagination. But it was not the faces, but their lack of eyes, that caused her to recoil. There were simply two black ovals. The two wizards stood and bowed before her.

"My Lady," they said together. Such sorcery, such power-it would serve her well to have them here. The shorter of the two stepped forward.

"My name is Joven. It is a pleasure to see you again. I apologize for our appearance, and our... grandiose entrance, but we couldn't risk getting captured by the thirty thousand unu that currently reside on your doorstep. Nor could we stay away when our people were in such dire straits."

She turned to the other and felt jubilation fill her heart as she saw the other one clearly for the first time. He had Rowen's eyes and Rowen's face.

"This is Rayn," Joven said. She paused for a moment, disbelieving. The man before her looked so much like Rowen, but she slowly felt her heart fall back down. He was her height, whereas Rowen had been half a hand above her. His hair, while being similar in look to Rowen's, wasn't quite right. His eyes were less playful, and more...inquisitive.

"Greetings." She fumbled for a moment. "I speak for all of my people as High Queen, and as a human, when I say that we are most grateful that you have arrived." It seemed as if everyone were holding their breaths for something.

57

"Why don't we go to the castle, and we can talk about how we are going to burn every last one of those unu away?" Joven's voice rose with every word until he was veritably shouting. He raised his staff, and a lightning bolt cracked out from it.

A tidal wave of cheers erupted from the epicenter of the gates. People began to cry and shout and scream. It was a mountain of jubilation. It was the sound of hope. The wizards were here. Everything was going to be fine. In spite of her worry, Tendra found herself smiling. They began to walk up towards the castle, and everywhere applause erupted around them. Four men came forward, lifted the wizards up on their shoulders, and carried them forward in a surge towards the castle. Despite the darkness, the light of hope that enraptured the city refused to be quelled.

As they walked up through the tiers of the city towards the castle, Tendra saw an old woman approach from directly before them. The crowd pushed forward right towards her and began to bury her in its riot.

"Stop!" Joven called out, and the entire procession came to a grinding halt. "Set me down." The men lowered them to the ground. They moved forward and pushed into the crowd to where the woman huddled over, shivering on the ground. "Grandmother, are you well?" As she rose to her feet, Tendra saw a bundle in her arms. At first, Tendra wasn't sure what it was, but soon she saw very clearly.

"Please," the woman begged, "Bless my granddaughter. The White took her parents, and now she has nothing and no one but me. If you would but bless the child, she will grow and prosper," she pleaded. Her eyes were a mass of tears and belief. Joven looked down upon her. He whispered something into the ear of the old woman, and then placed his lips upon the head of the girl. She was no more than five months old, a tiny thing, pale of skin and clean of the filth of the world.

"I am a wizard, not a priest, but I swear upon what I spoke to you." the old woman nodded. A smile ignited upon her face. "Now go." Joven reached down and lifted her to her feet. "You there." he pointed to one of the young men in the crowd.

"Me, My Lord?" he pointed to himself.

"Yes." Joven replied. "Your name."

"Hallen, My Lord."

"See that this woman is returned to her home with all due care."

"Yes, My Lord." Hallen rushed forward, took the old woman by the hand, and led her to the west. The crowd parted before them.

"Soldiers of Gemport...of humanity. Your lives, each and every one of your lives, are precious: even that of an old woman and a fragile child. The old are the past. They speak with the wisdom of footsteps that have endured years. Children are the future. They are those who come after us to replace us, to fulfill our dreams. Cherish them as you would your own. Now go-go guard your city. Protect her and love her and know, deep in your hearts, that you are safe." Celebration broke out as Joven finished, and he and Rayn turned and joined Tendra in the plaza. The hollers followed them into the throne room and ceased only when the doors were closed behind them.

Vizien stood next to the throne; his arms folded waiting for them to arrive. Tendra, rather than leading them towards the throne, instead turned back to the two wizards as soon as the click of the doors occurred.

"What can we get you? We heard that you have been riding for two days straight. We can wait until tomorrow for business if you need to rest."

Joven offered her a smile. "As tempting as a bed sounds, I'd like to talk first. If we could get some hot water to wash our faces and some wine..."

"Of course," Tendra gestured with her eyes, and one of the guards bowed and turned to hurry to the kitchens. "Please, sit." She gestured towards the auxiliary table off to the east, and they gratefully sank into their chairs. Tendra heard the heavy click of Vizien's boots as he walked towards them. She took great satisfaction in thwarting him, pompous creature that he was.

"We had heard scattered reports of your demise at Long Fang. What happened?" she asked. Joven grimaced.

"Qel made his play, and he failed. The Hammer betrayed us and tried to wipe us out, but we survived: all of us." he made a point of his final words. Tendra felt relief flood through her body. Like a glass of cool water on a hot summer day, she felt her entire being refreshed. "We regrouped, and now our plans continue as conceived," Joven continued.

"What plans? Where are the others?" she paused as a servant arrived. "Thank you, Balfor," she said as the servant set down a large basin of hot water with two rags and two towels before retreating to retrieve the wine.

"They each have their own assignments, the details of which I would prefer not to speak about while prying ears are nearby." Joven nodded to Vizien, who had taken up position standing behind where Tendra sat.

"I am the Grand Inquisitor. It is my job to know everything," Vizien replied tersely.

"Ask me again if that matters to me." This caused Vizien to pause a moment. "I know all about you, Vizien Traenor, and I will be happy to speak with you as soon as the High Queen and I are finished. Speaking of which, when did it happen?" He and Rayn dipped their rags into the hot water and ran them along their faces. "We heard word of your father's death and your coronation in Midway, but no one knew details." The black began to bleed off of their skin, and soon the water was murky with the inky shadow.

"A few days after the Battle of Long Fang. I returned from Bicoln and found him dead. Killed by an unu who had somehow infiltrated the most protected place in the city. My father who, while old, was still an accomplished swordsman in the middle of this very room apparently without him even attempting to fight back." Tendra said purposefully. "We have yet to be able to determine his method of entry. The unu arrived the day of your battle, and we have endured their siege since then."

"I am sorry for your loss. I know what it's like to lose a father," Joven replied. He had finished wiping his face down, "Ah perfect timing." he took the goblet of wine from Balfor's hands, and Rayn gratefully accepted the second. Tendra declined her own cup. "So what are your plans? It makes no sense for the unu to be here all winter. We ran from storm clouds all the way from just south of Whisperwood. They can't hope to break your power at sea; so what is their play?"

"We hoped you might be able to shed some light on that subject. We are hardly pleased with an army of the unu on our doorstep. The nature of Qel's movements has us greatly disturbed. I believe we should attack during the feast tomorrow," Tendra said.

"No."

"No?" she replied.

"No. Two of us are working as we speak in Ornus. They were able to infiltrate the city and will be holding all of the clan leaders' hostage until Qel gives the order to lift the siege. Right now, the city is well stocked and supplied, I presume, and as long as they remain out of range, then we should do precisely nothing."

"The soldiers are getting restless." Vizien cut in.

"Better restless than dead," Joven interjected. "What about the cliffs?"

"We have frogmen patrolling on their boats, and the sentries keep the walls to the south well lit." Vizien answered.

"And they are all men that can be trusted?"

"These men are fighting for the survival of their race," she said angrily.

"And might that fight be easier with a bit of silver in the pocket and a cottage in the north? We may be patriots, my lady, but others…" Joven looked directly at Vizien, "let us just say that not all loyalty is certain."

"I understand," Tendra replied slowly.

"So what is there that is left to be done?" Joven asked.

"Nothing, we can do nothing but wait. This place is a fortress; they won't unseat us easily from here, and their losses will be catastrophic once the battle begins," Tendra said.

61

"What of humanity's army?" This was the first time Rayn had spoken during their entire exchange, and a shiver went down Tendra's spine. He sounded just like him. It made sense that they were brothers, but unlike Joven or Aurum, he was the very image of Rowen: his voice, his posture, his face, like the Rowen of six years ago.

"My betrothed, Jeric, is at King's Port raising the last of the banners; they sail south in three days time. In the east, my cousin Jonathon tells me that the Order of the Light Monks is preparing their own war march. The lays have, by all reports, been burned to the ground after being pillaged by centaur or feral marauders. The eastern kingdoms are bunkering down. We've lost communication by falcon, and no ships have come from either Seraph or Boaz for almost two weeks. We don't believe them to be destroyed-" Tendra paused-"yet."

Joven nodded pensively. "Vizien, if you will excuse us for a moment, I wish to speak with Her Majesty alone," Joven said firmly. It was not so much a request as an order, and Vizien bristled.

"Of course, I will await you in the gardens when you finish." Vizien said through pursed lips.

"I am sure that you will," Joven replied. Vizien turned on his heel and retreated. Tendra was surprised at how easily dismissed the man had been. He had not protested at all; it was quite unlike him.

"Can you trust him?" Joven asked as soon as the guard acknowledged that he was truly gone.

"I asked him the same question about you before you arrived. I don't know who you are. I thought I did, but in light of events after my father's death, it appears that my knowledge was faulty. So in answer to your question, it is better the devil I know."

"So does that make us the devil you don't?" Joven pressed. Tendra thought for a moment.

"Yes. You have to earn my trust. Rowen proved himself to me and my people, but that doesn't mean that you don't have to do the same."

"Well, you're not stupid, that much Rowen was correct about." Tendra didn't know if she should be offended or feel complimented. "To be perfectly frank, we have given you no reason to trust us outside of our actions. You trusted us enough to allow Jeric to travel to Amul Kon with Aurum. You trusted us enough to allow us to run the war without interference. You trusted us enough to allow one of our own into your home. We have never pretended to be anything other than what we are. Wizards from the land of Cambria here to start a war."

"To what end?"

"Our reasons are our own."

Tendra snorted in reply. "And that is why I don't fully trust you. You have fought well so far. You have eradicated a species for Garen's sake. But now you have brought that war to my city, to my people, and I will do whatever I must to protect them. If that means throwing you from the city walls, so be it." Rayn smiled, and Tendra fixed him with a hard stare. "You find something amusing?"

"Rowen described you perfectly," he mused.

"Oh?" Tendra asked.

"He said that you were a hawk in the guise of a butterfly."

"Not for nothing is the crest of my house the viper."

"My Lady," Joven broke the long silence, "I won't tell you that you should trust us, but I will tell you that you must. We are here to protect not only you, but humanity, that is our principle objective in this world: to ensure humanity's survival."

"Then in that, at least, we are in agreement," Tendra said with a sigh. Joven nodded. Tendra wasn't sure whether she believed him or not. Yet she realized, just like he had said, she didn't have a better option... in fact, she didn't have *any* other options.

"You didn't come here to just tell us to keep in a standing pattern. Why are you here? What do you want to know?"

"We are here to win a war. We can do more good leading than on our own. As for what we want to know...who are your current advisors?" Joven inquired.

"Vizien acts as my information gatherer. He knows what I need to know, but he is too ambitious for his own good. My cousin Jonathon is a member of the same order as my betrothed. He might as well be a Skyguard for the amount of history that he knows. He is a Brilliance in the order as well as an alchemist. Merinam is my tactical strategist. He is a fourteen-year-old prodigy and a master of the game of Crowns. He has never lost, and he attained the rank of Grandmaster three years ago. Braken is my ear to the city council. She lives politics and is able to tell me the will of the Council of Elders. They were not happy during my father's reign. They have little real power, but it is useful to keep them content. Retren is the bookkeeper. He is manages the food and water rationing and payment of the troops. Finally, Wesley is the leader of the city guard. He organizes the troops. He is invaluable in helping morale and making preparations." Tendra wished she had accepted the offer for wine. It was late in the evening, and she felt the hours upon her eyes.

"I think that will be all for tonight. I will want to meet with all of them tomorrow, of course, but I am sure that you need more rest than we," Joven said, as if reading her mind. Tendra rose with them, and they bowed before her. "And of course we wouldn't want to keep Vizien waiting." he offered her a wry smile as he arose, which Tendra reciprocated.

"Are you going to speak with him tonight?" Tendra asked.

"Absolutely not. He is not my superior, and I am not his serf," Joven said.

"Still, it is not wise to make an enemy of him."

Once again, Joven smiled. "That won't be a problem. Trust me." she didn't, but she did believe that he could handle the Grand Inquisitor.

"Rooms have been prepared for you. Balfor, please take them to their rooms. Thank you." she offered the boy a smile as he bowed before her. She watched the wizards move off towards the east turret behind Balfor. She sighed and turned towards her own rooms.

She rubbed her eyes wearily as she walked. It was near midnight, and she knew she would be forced to awaken far too soon for her liking. Every step was an effort. The adrenaline of having the wizards here had now fully worn off. She pushed open the heavy wooden door to her rooms, nodding to the guards who stood sentry there. She closed the door behind her and walked over to her washbasin.

She ran a brush through her long brown hair with one hand as she slipped out of her shoes. Her father had loved her hair. When she had been a girl, he would brush it for her. It had been their special time. They would sit for an hour, with him brushing and telling her stories, and she loving every second of it. She held the same brush in her hands as he had used all those years ago. It was one thing she would never get rid of. She carefully laid it back in its faded wooden box before moving over to her wardrobe.

She absent-mindedly pulled out a lavender evening gown and slipped into it. Her bed had already been prepared for her, and the hot coals in the bottom kept it warm in the cold of winter. She slid into the heavy blankets and felt them envelop her in their comfort. A bed had never felt as wonderful as it had that night. She fell into the darkness of sleep with a single feeling: that some hope still existed.

*   *   *

"Was that entirely necessary?" Vizien's voice rang out from the shadows near the window. Joven sat down on the bed and pulled his boots off. It had been three days since he had done so, and his feet ached from it. The fire in the mantle flickered upon Vizien's face, but the rest of his body was masked by his long black cloak.

"Yes. She had to see me completely in control. Your impudence, while entirely within your character, was not appreciated under the circumstances. It made you look weak. You shouldn't allow yourself to be placed in those situations." Vizien bristled. "Good work by the way, killing Jethro and framing it on the unu. Though a deaf man could see she suspects you."

"Nothing is ever perfect."

"Obviously, I didn't teach you well enough because you killed Jakob." Joven pulled his sword and staff off his back and laid them against the wall. He poured himself a glass of water. He tossed the first glass into

65

the fire, which hissed as the water turned to vapor with no apparent change in coloration. It was clean. He proceeded to sip it slowly as he sat down in the simple wooden chair directly opposite Vizien rather than on the bed.

"That, surprisingly enough, wasn't me. There is a growing faction within the city that wants to see the Sumenel line fail. They tried to kill Tendra, too. I know how important she is to your plans; I wouldn't do anything so deliberate." Joven swirled the water in his mouth.

"Who is involved?"

"A couple of members of the Elder Council, Torin and Berili, lead the group, which is made up primarily of a few minor lords. All told there are fourteen who would rebel should the call go out. In total, there are somewhere around six hundred swords within the city itself. They are far bolder than I would have given them credit for. Also the physician, Domini, don't take anything that he gives you. Rowen was well on his way to fully endearing himself to our beloved king when Domini sabotaged his efforts."

Joven nodded. "Give me your analysis of the current situation with the Hammer."

"There are between twenty and twenty five thousand unu on our doorstep, with an additional twenty thousand centaurs, sixty-one siege towers, a hundred catapults, and sixty trebuchets. The current commander is Het of the Amber Stone. All of the clanmasters are in Ornus for the Feast of Bejor. Our troop strengths are twenty five thousand soldiers in the city, with another fifty to sixty thousand marshaling near King's Port as we speak. They should be under way any day now under the command of Jeric Tybius, Tendra's betrothed. There is an additional force moving to attack Bicoln in conjunction with this one. Kana must be all but empty, and all the clans have been called in on this. They are veritably drunk with the victories Qel has given them."

Joven considered this for a moment. "Tactical assessment?"

"We send a group of small expeditionary forces into their camp at night, twenty groups of no more than ten to sow confusion and dissension in the ranks. Do it one night, and they will grow nervous enough to post guards at night. Then use night archers to take them out from a distance.

Slowly whittle down their ranks while they wait for their leaders to make a decision."

Joven nodded approvingly. "I couldn't agree more. I want names of all the conspirators against Tendra. Don't eliminate them unless you have to; they may prove useful to us in the future. Also, I need you to compile as much information as you can on the Light Monks for Rayn to devour. See if you can get him a meeting with Tendra's cousin."

Vizien said nothing in response, and the silence lingered. "Is there anyone remaining in the Council of Elders who might recognize me?" Joven asked. Vizien thought for a moment. Joven had once been known as Lord Daramont, and he had graced the Council of Elders off and on for almost three years in the past. Vizien nodded.

"Four. There are only fifteen still in the city. The rest have fled to King's Port or Seraph. Pequo Beers, Kore Thoft, Teis Cringe, and Jhons Geoffs."

Joven considered each of those names. Out of them, he had only had extensive dealings with Teis and Jhons. "See to it that Teis and Jhons do not make the meeting tomorrow. It is best that my presence is not recognized at this juncture."

Vizien nodded but made no motion to leave.

"Yes?" Joven inquired.

"It's good to have you back," Vizien admitted.

Joven offered a wry smile. "It is good to be back." his eyes burned in the soft glow of the fire, and he licked his lips. *This can still work, even if it is just Rayn and me. This will still work.*

All Hope Abandon, Ye Who Enter Here
Six

"You have failed, Aurum. You have forgotten the name of your father, and so you have lost your own." I awoke slowly to a barren landscape: a world of black rock that every so often a rippling wave would carry energy through but was otherwise completely still. "You are Aurum Guilden no more. Now, you are Aurum Nameless. You have forgotten your Thul, and the oath that you swore upon it."

The man of red skin stood before me. His black eyes were condescending, and his face was a mask of disappointment. The intricate tattoos told stories on his body: stories of predators and prey, of life and rebirth, of good and evil. I glared at him: this man with no name. I had seen this man before. It was he who had told me to go to Amul Kon and find Galeerial, and it had been he who enchanted my daggers, Havoc and Dream. I had not seen him in all the long months that we had waged our campaign with the unu and centaurs against the ferals, and now, now he chose to manifest himself before me, with accusations such as these.

"How dare you?" I said quietly. "I have made three oaths in my life, and I have kept every one of them. How dare you? How dare you!" I screamed at him. "You sit here in your world of dreams manipulating me-and who knows who else-into playing your games. No more. You think you can take my name? Who do you think you are?" my eyes were steel, and his reply was with thunder.

"I am the son of the god, and you are a fool! You have been chosen like all others of this and all worlds. You have been chosen."

I shook my head. "I do not think you understand. I want you gone. I am done with you. Leave me. Now." there was a note of finality to my voice.

"Why?" he replied simply, the anger gone from his voice. "So that you can go back to your meaningless, lonely life that you have been leading since your family died? You are not living, Aurum; you are surviving. You have been for years, but you have been too blind and angry to notice. Face it, Aurum; you want to die, do you not? You are pathetic." my hand was a fist, and my fist was flying towards his face before I even thought about it. It stopped by some unknown power just before it struck the man.

"Plan your next move carefully, Aurum. You are full of rage, but you are smarter than that. We both know that you do not let emotions rule you. You are your own master, and look where you are because of it. You are on the edge of death. All your plans, all your strength and genius; they will all fail you in the end. For in the end, there is only a long, slow spiral of despair that awaits you until death takes you. You know it because you searched and came so close to finding it after your wife died. Where did Joven finally find you, Aurum? Not in some library or great hall of science but in a cathedral. The last testament in your entire world not dedicated to the vain gloriousness of man. When reason failed, you turned to faith, and for the briefest moment in your heart you came close to achieving something that you have not in all your years in Carin. I know what you seek, and I know that you will never find it without me."

"How can you possibly know that?" I stared at him.

"Because I know you, Aurum. I know the coldness in your heart that has frozen over your rage, your pain, your loneliness, your despair, and, most of all your pride. You have made yourself a blank slate walking through the world in a self-assured daze. Your pride binds you and powers you. It is your will and your downfall. I have seen you, Aurum." His voice softened. "I have seen you over and over and over again; I have watched you in a thousand lifetimes. You are special. You know this in your heart, but you deny it. You relegate yourself to a commoner when you should be a king. You pull yourself away from others when there is power in unity. You have lost yourself, but, if you will follow me, I will show you all that you could be."

"What do you want from me?" I asked. I felt weary. I wanted this being to be gone from me. The sky around us grew darker.

"You have lost so much. My path is one of redemption. You have already started upon it. You call yourself a man of reason; yet you have already placed your faith in me," he replied.

"What are you talking about?" I asked.

"You saved Galeerial. You questioned, and you doubted, but you leapt. That is something not many men do. They take the road well traveled. But not you-never you. You're searching for something more. I can give that to you. Come and follow me, and I will give you what you truly desire."

"And what do I truly desire?" I asked. He smiled.

"That you must discover for yourself, and you will discover it." he strode forward and placed a finger on each of my eyes. "Ohm," he said, and I recoiled.

"What did you just do?"

"I sent you on your path. If you want to break from this cycle, you will follow the path I have set before you. If you survive, then we will begin."

"If I survive what?" I inquired.

"Your nightmares."

I shook my head. "Why are you doing all this? Why will you not

70

just leave me to my pain?"

"Because I believe in you, Aurum. I always have." his smile dazzled my eyes. "Now go. You must wage this war. Go." he raised his hand to dismiss me.

"Wait." I stopped him. *What had just happened?* "I have not agreed to anything." he looked at me.

"Come now, Aurum. We both know your relentless drive is such that you could not turn from the path even if you wished to do so." I considered this for a second: something was not adding up. For all his predictive power, for all his influence, he had limitations. A revelation came to me.

"You need me." I said simply. The man said nothing in return. "You say that you took my name, then give me yours." he looked at me with an odd tilt of his head.

"My name has not been spoken by a human in centuries upon your plane, much to the regret of the clerics who allowed my name to die." his name seemed to echo from everywhere in the world, like an echo from a bygone year. I didn't even see his lips move so smooth of the tongue was it. It was a name of majesty.

"Now awake, prove your worth, and embrace the ruin that lies within you." I stood watching him fade way. *Embrace the ruin that lies within me.* I thought to what the Orrery of Words had told me in Cambria all those long years ago on my Naming Day. *You will be the ruin of the world:* words that had haunted me for years. They were words that had made me almost abandon my wife. I suddenly felt very afraid. I closed my eyes, and, moments later, I awoke to cold stone walls and a colder wind. There was a soft beam of light that was shrouded by snowflakes. I was wearing only a pair of rough tan breeches with a coarse heavy blanket thrown over me.

My hand reached down to where Jeronious' sword had pierced my flesh in the middle of my stomach. My chain mail armor was lain out on the floor next to me, with my leather over clothes beside it. I stood gingerly and gritted my teeth in disgust at the pain that accompanied it. The wound had been expertly treated, but only time could heal the rest of the damages. I had no idea how long I had been unconscious or even where I was, but the oppressive aura of judgment hung over me. It was familiar, distantly familiar. It took me several minutes to pull my armor on. I didn't want to leave this room without it, but the pain was extensive. I couldn't lift my arms higher than shoulder-level without pain spiking through my abdomen.

The wooden door gave easily. It wasn't locked: a good sign. The citadel in which I found myself was a series of rings. There was the stone wall, then a ring of a courtyard, and finally a tower in the center of the bull's-eye that stretched into the sky. A man regarded me coolly from his wooden chair where he sat skinning a rat with a rusty knife. He spat out a wad of blackweed on the ground in front of me. The man's face was covered in a brown mangy beard that obscured most of his lower face, leaving only dull gray eyes left to stare at me.

"Where am I?" I asked. The man said nothing, but just gestured with his eyes towards the central tower. I immediately began to walk around the outer perimeter until I reached a staircase. There were forty-eight stairs before I reached the ground level.

I was regarded with a mixture of hostility and indifference as I picked my way through the people living there. Most were gathered around the sporadic fires as the snow began to pile on. Some people were sweeping the snow off of the higher levels, and it showered down upon those below. I arrived at the tower and slammed my fist against the wooden door, which opened of its own volition. I looked back and saw all eyes upon me. I turned around and stepped uncertainly into the tower.

Inside was a series of benches and tables sprawled out with a bar covered in bottles of wine and rum. A man stood there running a cloth through a cup as a woman covered in soot and dirt scrubbed the floor. Immediately to my left, a spiral staircase began and twirled upwards into the next floor. Neither said a word to me, but the man pointed to the stairwell. I began to climb. The next floor was empty of life. I kept climbing and finally came upon a single man at the thirteenth level, staring out from the top of the tower. I followed his gaze and saw my suspicions confirmed.

This was either Sentinel or Evenfall. I was in one of the two watchtowers of Thanatos, and before me stood the cursed land itself.

The land of Thanatos was a sprawling wasteland that had claimed the foolish and wise alike. 'We don't go to Thanatos.' That was a saying of this world, and it was easy to understand why. In all the history of the world, only disaster had accompanied any who entered that forbidden land. It was gray and dark, an impenetrable shell of gloom that ravaged any who dared to test it. The Horrors had been born from that land and, many believed, the Dread, and farther, back, dragons as well all originated within that dead land. At its center stood the City of the Damned: Acheron. The smack of wood on stone caused me to turn back to see the stairwell now covered by a door.

"My name is Praetor Praxus. I am the guardian and ruler of Evenfall. Your centaur brought you here two days ago. Since then you have done little but sleep and murmur nonsense, Mage. So speak and do so quickly. We do not tolerate idiocy here at the shadow's edge."

I eyed the praetor. He was a hard man. His face was one that had known darkness. The lines of age had been grilled onto his face, and he may as well have been made of the same stone as his surroundings, so emotionless was he. His hair was white from many winters, both on his scalp and his face, and it was wispy where once perhaps it had grown thick. Around us stood only a spyglass and a torch, along with the stone throne upon which Praxus sat. I knew the throne to be named Vigilance, and its twin, Guardian, lay at Sentinel.

I looked out at Thanatos before me. It was vast, a land whose name was only whispered in terror. Six times in recorded history had men entered into that land, and each time the world had been plagued by disaster. Yet still fools sought entrance, whether it be for knowledge, fame, or glory. The two watchtowers existed to kill such fools. As I looked out at Thanatos, I had no doubt that I was going to be one such fool. The red man had sent me here. I didn't know why; I didn't know how. All I knew was that I needed to walk this path. To do so, I needed to stare down a man whose life was centered on stopping men like me.

73

"I mean to enter." I poured confidence into my voice where none had any right to exist.

"Entry is forbidden," Praxus replied coldly. He refused to meet my gaze, instead staring out towards Thanatos.

"Praetor," I began. I worked to put on the same sureness that I had always had. It was difficult. It felt like something had changed: something irrevocable. I didn't like it, but I pushed it to the side. I could afford no weakness now. I had to be Aurum-. My hands began to shake. My Thul…it was gone. I shook my head to clear it, but my hands wouldn't stop shaking. "I…" I breathed to still the quake in my voice. "I will enter regardless of your permission. Your permission is a courtesy, not a necessity." I paused, taking a long breath to steady my voice. "I want information, not your blessing." It was then that he turned his eyes to me. They were glassed over. I quelled a breath of relief. He hadn't seen my weakness. He had heard what I wanted him to, a calculating precision in my voice. I strained to maintain it. I would maintain it.

"You think you can scare me, Mage? Blind though I am, I can still see in my dreams, and in those dreams I have nightmares that are beyond anything your magic can hope to create."

"Even so, I am like no other human who has ever entered into this land," I continued.

"Yes, even as far as this Supremor-forsaken land, we have heard of you and your Seven Sorcerers. To the rest of the world, magic may be something that has not been seen in generations, but here, on the edge of damnation; we know magic. We are assailed by it. We reek of it." The Praetor held his sword across his lap. It was a hand-and-a-half sword, with a golden handle. I saw a pyramid upon its crest: the sigil of the House Loring. This man was a member of the ruling house of Mesnir-perhaps Mahrvel's brother or uncle. A harsh winter wind whipped by us, and our cloaks rustled and flew about.

"I can make it to the dead city," I said. Praxus harrumphed.

"I believe you can. Don't think I don't. Your companion though, he is not made of the same mettle as you. If he goes with you, he will not return."

"How can you know that?" I asked.

"Because Thanatos demands a sacrifice. Make no mistake, if you go there: death will plague you for the rest of your days."

I had faced death since I had arrived here. "Death…death would be a release, not a shackle." I spoke resolutely.

"And to those to whom it is a shackle? Will you accept all of the deaths that will result from your actions by entering Thanatos? The moment after you enter, it will be my men who die. I won't allow that."

"You can't stop me, Praetor," I said quietly.

"Have you no conscience, Sorcerer?" Praxus glared coldly into my eyes.

"My mission supersedes everything. Your lives, while precious, may have to be sacrificed to complete my task. I must see what lies at the end of this road."

Praxus smiled a cruel facsimile of a grin. "Then perhaps Thanatos is indeed where you belong. You would fit right in with the prisoners who man our walls." the comment caused me to recoil for a moment. I was nothing like these men. These were thugs and rapists and murderers. What my brothers and I were doing…it was something that had never before been achieved.

"Why are you here, Praxus? You are the brother of Magistrate Mahrvel of Mesnir." I guessed. "Yet here you are. You are here because you are bound by your duty, as am I. My duty draws me down this road. You cannot stop me."

Praxus shook his head. "You are right about all you say save one thing. I am not Mahrvel's brother. I am his son." the blood drained from my face. Mahrvel had only seen maybe fifty winters at the most. This man looked to be older even than that. Praxus chuckled without joy.

"Thanatos demands a heavy toll. I have been here six years, and I look and feel older than my father. You don't know the cost of your actions.

75

Do you even know what you seek? Is your need so desperate that you would threaten destruction upon us all in order to quench your lust?"

"Yes," I said simply. I had to know. I had to follow this road. These men were expendable. I had to know why that man was in my dreams. "I'm sorry, but I must walk this path, and if that means bathing in the blood of your men before I enter, then so be it." I couldn't let him see any weakness, any cracks in my resolve.

"Very well then." Praxus sighed. His face grew forty years older, as if he had been pouring every ounce of energy into convincing me not to enter Thanatos. "We will hold the line, as we have for the last twelve hundred years. We will hold the line," Praxus replied heavily. He stood from his throne and stomped on the floor. Next to us the trap door was flung open, and he gestured for me to descend before him. "Your centaur awaits you outside the walls. This fortress was not built with their kind in mind." he said as we descended the ladder down to the balcony. A man in a deep crimson cloak and whose hood was drawn stood watching us. I peered beneath it to see the tattoo of a fist upon his forehead. I eyed him as we passed down the stairs. "Give me a moment, Lord Malachi." Praxus said to the man who didn't answer but kept his narrow gaze upon us.

"Then why the charade?" I asked.

"It wasn't a charade. They were prepared to kill him if I gave the signal." nothing more needed to be said on the matter.

"What can I expect within?" I inquired.

"I don't know, but we on the fringe all experience different effects from the land. Nightmares becoming real. Your perceptions will change: hallucinations. You must anchor yourself to whatever it is that drives you. Thanatos will use that against you, but if you believe, then you can make it. The lord of that land is pervasive. He will worm his way into your mind, and his claws will tear your will to shreds. When you emerge, you will be changed."

"In what way?" Praxus shrugged his heavy shoulders. "I don't fear death."

"It isn't death you need to fear, but rather the draw of the azure deep: the madness of the mind." I glanced uncertainly his way, but he offered me nothing more. I pushed open the wooden door and walked out into the cold winter air. It was November now, and the world was growing colder. Soon it would be naught but ice. I had to be back before then. Black glares watched me as I strode towards Dane, who stood fidgeting nervously and staring at the men around him. I nodded to him.

"Let's get going," I said simply. Dane looked at me with some concern, but my glare silenced any response that he might have made.

"No argument from me." Dane said quietly.

"Your weapons await you outside the walls," Praxus said. "And Aurum, don't come back this way, if you come back at all." I shot one last glare back at Praxus before throwing my right leg over Dane's back. I winced as my stomach tightened over my wound. It still hurt-all the time-it hurt, but I knew when we rode was when it would really burn.

We found a man holding our weapons for us. I gratefully grasped Andusíl, my staff named for my too-long-dead wife, and Widower's Wrath, my sword. I sheathed my dagger, Havoc.

Dane was quiet as we began our journey, which I appreciated. It gave me time to think. I had not been conscious consistently since Long Fang. I had scant memories of waking in the Split and again on the road.

I thought back to the feeling of cold steel filling my breast. It was like water had been stuffed into my veins and then frozen. My veins had burned from the cold, and I had seen *them*.

Andusíl and Hope had stood there waiting for me. I had reached out to touch their hands. Hope had been so small, a babe in the arms of her mother, as I had imagined her being before...before she had been taken from me. I would kill Qel for them. I would make him burn. My thoughts remained distant as I thought about my brush with death. I had stood on the precipice that separated this world from beyond, and I had stepped back.

I thought about Joven. Ten years ago, we had found Desmond adrift in the sea. Ten years ago, our entire world had changed. Before then, Joven, like all but Dorian, had believed in no god. We existed not at the

77

whim of some superior being, but because of the choices our forefathers had made. But after Desmond had made his way into our lives something had changed in Joven. He had been a vagabond before then since the death of Rerem, but he had seen in this man words that had been all but stricken from our world's vocabulary: freedom of destiny. Joven found a purpose in that man. He had dedicated himself to their mission, just as I had when my family had died. I had nothing left to live for in Cambria after they had passed, and so I had joined him, and all my brothers as the final cog in the wheel. Dane shook me from my reverie.

"Are you going to be alright?" Dane asked with concern in his voice. He knew how close I had been to death.

"How long since Long Fang?" I asked him, ignoring his question momentarily.

"A month or so." he told me. *A month-one days. Had it really been that long?*

"I'll be fine. That is what we do; we endure." a jet of pain stabbed through me, but I gritted my teeth and did my best to ignore it. I had faced pain before.

"You have endured much already, Aurum."

"And I will endure much more before my quest is finished."

"What is your quest?" he probed. As much as he had been through, as much as he had seen, he was still so naïve. The centaur had traveled with me since the very earliest days of our campaign. We had met just after the Battle of Sterin's Throne, and after a rough start he had become one of our strongest supporters within the centaur ranks.

"I'll tell you when I figure it out for myself," I replied as he began to gallop for the entrance into Thanatos. The gray lands were about fifteen minutes' ride from the fortress, and I knew soon enough that oppressive land would bind us.

"What are we doing here, Dane?"

"Galeerial told me to bring you here. He helped to save you at Long Fang. We went to Winter Crest for a short time before departing to come here. You have been unconscious, babbling nonsense, at least to my

78

ears. Galeerial recited some poem to you, and then you said 'Ohm.' I don't know what it means, but Galeerial seemed to recognize it and told me to bring you here."

"Do you remember what he said to me?" I asked.

"Some of it," Dane replied.

"Tell me."

"Go where angels fear to tread, and souls are alighted yet bound. Where eyes from above…see and something is found. Truth spawns from lies, the doubting heart dies…I don't remember the rest. Something about the key of souls, and a book unlocking…the willing heart will bleed water. I can't remember the last line." it was gibberish to me.

"Too much doesn't make sense." I murmured to myself. Dane snorted. "Yes?"

"Things don't make sense to you; how do you think I feel? Grey told me less than you have about what exactly you all are doing here." Dane chided. "I have followed you this far; I fought with you and for you; I saved your life; yet still you remain silent." I sighed. I knew what would come next. "You owe me at least some answers."

"I owe you nothing, Dane. I never asked you to save my life, and I never asked you to follow me. Those were choices you made."

"I made them because you are my friend. I am not asking for much. Just give me something, anything. Reward my faith," he pleaded, turning back to stare at me, while still continuing his gait towards the border. We would arrive soon: very soon. I thought back to the conversation in my dreams.

"Alright. Three questions, whatever you want answered, I will do so." I saw Dane tense up slightly. He hadn't counted on that. He had expected me to keep being evasive, but I knew how much I could push him. We needed him if we were to control the centaurs. I didn't like having him here, though. Whatever lay at the end of this road was for me. But before he could ask, we arrived at the edge of the end of the world.

"Hold." I told him, but he was already slowing to a stop. Before us stood Thanatos, the Land of Eternity's End, The Gray Wastes, The

Forbidden Land, The Source of All Shadows: it had a hundred different names, none of them good. It was like looking into a glass globe. A line could be drawn in the prairie grass before us as to where Thanatos began and the living world ended.

It was a globe of black and white that stood before me: transparent yet viscous. Of all the places in Carin, this was the only one we had willingly and deliberately avoided in our rangings. I swung myself down from Dane's back knowing that it would hurt to return to his back but not caring; I had to feel this place first.

I placed one foot before the next, slowly but steadily making my way towards the line of absence. I reached out my left hand as I stepped forward. I had expected some kind of feeling, like pushing through water, upon entering into the land, but there was no resistance at all. It was as if there was just more air in front of me, same as everywhere in the world. I almost laughed as I breathed a sigh of relief, but then I felt it.

It was like maggots crawling on the skin. My very veins and blood felt old and dry within the land, and I ripped my hand out. My hand had gone stark white, and no matter how much I shook it, I could not get any color to return. I wiped it with my cloak, and it came away as brown as ever, but my hand was a perfect white. I looked back at Dane one final time. Fear colored his face.

"You don't have to come with me," I said. "You have done more than enough."

"Where would I go, Aurum? I am a traitor to my kind and a deserter," his voice betrayed no remorse. "Besides, before I met you I was already dead as far as everyone in this entire world was concerned. I have nowhere to go but with you." I was struck by just how sad Dane truly was, but I nodded and turned back to Thanatos. I set my jaw and entered the void.

The black tower stood against me as I entered. The sensation that had been lacking with my hand slammed into my face, and suddenly the entire world became black and white to my eyes. I looked back outside to where I had just stood and saw no color there. I reached my hand back to try and recapture the light, but instead found the barrier that I had looked for when entering. It was barely perceptible, but I when I pushed my hand against it I saw it ripple, like the stomach of an animal. I pushed harder, and as I strove against it, the invisible wall rose to the challenge. I pulled my sword from my back and pressed it firmly against the unseen force, but the blade could no more cut it, than my hand could penetrate it.

I was trapped.

I strove to maintain calm as I replaced my sword upon my back and looked out at Dane. A look of concern on his face betrayed his alarm as he watched my spectacle of trying to free myself.

He was not stupid; he had to know what had happened. He uneasily began to walk forward. His tail swished back and forth behind him anxiously, and he pawed the ground in between steps as he unsteadily strode toward me. His hoof entered into the land and then his leg. I watched him fully enter before speaking. I turned to stare at the black tower in the distance. Even against this landscape devoid of light Acheron stood tall against us.

"To Acheron?" he asked.

"To Acheron."

I had never seen so desolate a place. Even the Burning Waters far to the north were not as devastatingly bleak as Thanatos. The air was stifling in its stillness. There was no motion, no wind, no sound-nothing but the shuffle of our footsteps as we walked.

There was nothing in this land. No markings to indicate the passage of time or space. The only landmark of any kind was the massive tower of Acheron. The tower was black and stretched high into the sky, ending in a terrible crown of obscure iron. As we walked closer and closer, the tower seemed to grow no nearer, though it continued to grow more terrible to behold. Around us there was only a flat sameness to everything. The world seemed to be coated in a perpetual shell of white ash, which we could never scrap away. Our long strides became shuffles after hours of slow plodding. My mind slowly began to wander away from my trek.

I thought about all that had happened in the last three weeks: about Galeerial and Long Fang, being stabbed and the red man. I had seen him two nights ago, or was it three? *How long have we been here?* I looked up to see the sun, but was greeted with a gray glob of sky. There was ambient light everywhere, so there was no way to tell when it was light and when it was dark. Still, we plodded on.

I licked my lips. They were rough, and I tasted something upon them. It tasted slightly metallic, but still good. I licked some more. I rather liked the taste of this fluid, I decided as I walked. Slowly, ever so slowly I walked, always one foot before the other, and I began to wonder why.

Why was I walking? Why couldn't I just stop and lie down? Why not now? After all, now seemed to be a perfectly acceptable time for a nap. I looked to my right and saw nothing but the blades of gray grass, and then, I turned my head to the left and was greeted once again by the gray grass. I concentrated hard. There was a reason I was here. *Truth, I am here for truth.*

I grabbed on to the abstract construct. I had come for truth. *Go where angels fear to tread.* That was the poem that Galeerial had left for me.

"Go where angels fear to tread, and souls are alighted yet bound." I whispered. My head began to clear, and I realized that I was lying face down on the ground. "Where eyes from above watch, and the beginning was found." *How do I know these words?* I reached my hands out and pushed. Slowly, I rose to my feet. My limbs felt like they were made of stone. I could barely move as I staggered forward, stumbling more than walking. I saw Dane trip a few steps ahead of me before falling. I fumbled towards him. I fell to the ground again and was forced to crawl. My eyelids weighed a thousand pounds each and pressed deep into my eyeballs. My wound throbbed. I knew if I could only sleep, then everything would be alright.

"Truth spawns...spawns from lies," I muttered. I reached a hand forward and felt the scars on Dane's back. I gripped the hair that grew there and pulled myself towards him. I then grabbed Dane's shoulder and his other shoulder. His eyes were in a grayish state of catatonia. I drew my left hand back and smacked him in the face.

"DANE!" I yelled in what I hoped was a bellow. I slapped him again. "Focus," I said wearily. "You must focus on something. A phrase or a...something." even my thoughts felt like they were swimming in a stew of filth. "The doubting heart dies," I said, completing the bridge stanza of the prophecy. The centaur blinked twice as if dazed, and I struck him a third time. Finally, the centaur shook his torso, causing what looked like ash to tumble off him in a great flurry. "Turn back, I can do this alone. You won't make it."

"I...I can," he stuttered. There was desperation in his eyes.

"Then focus. One leg in front of the other." slowly, we pushed onward. The heaviness in my limbs began to break after several steps. It was like a ship stuck in ice and just now was beginning to find cracks. We pushed onward. The wasteland stretched farther and farther, and at the end, omnipresent, stood Acheron. The dark tower beckoned like a woman every time we dared raise our eyes to gaze upon its fearful beauty. And yet she mocked us with our inability to reach her. After an eternity in silence, Dane's voice rang out.

"You once told me that I may ask three questions."

I took my time before answering. "Yes? Yes. Yes, I did. Ask." *give me something to focus on...anything.*

"Why me?" Dane asked. "Of every centaur you chose me to befriend... why?"

"You were damaged. We saw that, knew we could use that. We saw it from the beginning all the way at Midway, we chose you. You had no friends, no family. You were perfect." I said. Dane looked at me, startled, before replying.

"You mean you don't know?"

I looked back at him. "Know what?"

"I told you that I killed my family, my father, mother, brother and two sisters, but that wasn't all my family. I had another brother who didn't perish in the blaze. Herdmaster Jeronious. He is my younger brother."

"I had no idea," I lied. I had promised honesty only in answering the question. Of course we knew. Nothing we did was by chance; the only question had been who among us would 'befriend' the centaur. Albeit nothing since Long Fang had been planned, but my interactions with Dane were all carefully plotted before they had ever occurred. Despite it all, I had grown somewhat fond of the centaur.

I looked back towards Evenfall, and the world we had left behind. There was nothing to see except long gray plains. There seemed no beginning and no end to this place. I looked forwards toward Acheron. It, too, seemed to be even farther away now than when we had begun our journey. "You still have two more questions," I told Dane.

"What is your plan for the future of Carin?"

"That is a rather broad question. Are you sure you don't want to narrow it down a bit?"

"Very well then, why are you here?" I rolled my eyes in annoyance. That narrowed it down for sure. It was like talking to a giant stupid insect. I was amazed he even had the capacity to speak sometimes. Nevertheless, I had told him I would answer his questions. I marveled only slightly at my wildly swinging emotions

"The Seven of us are all here for different reasons. Rayn is here because he thirsts for knowledge. Rowen is here because he liked the idea of women as maidens to be rescued from foul creatures. Joven and Dorian are here because they are running from what the world held for them. Rikard was because of the death of one of his best friends. Grey just thought it would be funny. I came because I needed a purpose, and coming here gave that to me... in a way my old home never could again."

"So you truly are from Cambria," I simply nodded in response.

"What about the Heart of Fires?"

"We don't have it. As far as we know, it still lies buried wherever the secondborn laid it to rest seventeen hundred years ago."

Dane shook his head. "Incredible."

"No. What's incredible is how hard you tried to forget us," a voice whispered into my ear. It was the same voice that had guided me to sleep and had woken me for years. The voice that I had spent my every waking moment longing to hear. The voice that I loved. I turned slowly, and my hands began to shake as I saw her. My eyes could scarcely comprehend what they were seeing. They could barely comprehend that my wife, who had been dead for ten years, now stood before me, holding the hand of my ten-year old daughter.

Actions and Reactions
Seven

The last day had been busy. He had killed twenty-seven unu, all left with the mark of the D on their body. The last two hours had been spent preparing for the feast of Bejor: some long dead unu. The grand mead hall of the unu was laid out beneath him. He lay hidden in the thatching of the roof with his package. It was to be a very special delivery: a bloody special delivery. Below him stretched three banquet tables. The sweet aroma of burning meat and cold ale filled his nostrils. His stomach growled, but he quelled it.

He watched the hundreds of unu file in; they were magnificent. First, came the unum. Their gaits were strong, and their adornments brilliant. They were covered in golden chains and golden cloaks. They held massive ceremonial staves of solid gold. They were the only ones allowed to hold weapons during the feast. There were seventy-two of them, Rikard took care to count. They arranged themselves along the second banquet table. The table that stood between the rabble and the clanmasters.

Then the clanmasters came. From all across Carin, they had answered the call of history. Bleeding Moon and Amber Stone, Shimmering Glass and Endless Blaze, among others, and above them all stood the Thousand Hammers.

Qel.

He had been Dorian's surrogate father in this world. He had taken Dorian into his home and into his clan, and now Rikard was going to tear it down piece by piece. More than that, he was going to enjoy every second of it. Qel's swagger would have given him away immediately if his single arm was not so apt at defining him. Rikard would enjoy stealing that boastfulness.

The clansmaster strode through the room in silence until he reached his own immense throne. Qel clapped his hands twice and every head was bowed for the prayer. He raised his cup, which had already been filled with wine.

"To he who brought us Balance." Qel shouted.

"Bejor!" the unu chanted.

"To he who shined the light."

"Bejor!"

"To he who brandished the scales."

"Bejor!"

"To he who brought us here."

"Bejor!"

"We salute you."

"Bejor!"

"And your current sentinel."

"Qel!" the final call was greeted with silence as everyone drank deep of the draughts. Qel slammed his golden chalice down upon the table, and the rest of the unu echoed the action. In unison, they took their seats, and the food began to arrive in the hands of the spouses of those assembled. The female unum were served by their husbands. They were especially dangerous as their four arms made them unpredictable.

Even though Rikard had eaten before ascending, his mouth watered as his eyes feasted upon the sight before him. Roasted boar adorned with honey apples and crackpoppies; blackened gazelle, the skin of which had been charred to a shell that held within it the sweet, tender meat. The plates kept coming: pork, rice, stew, full loaves of bread. The food cascaded down upon the gathered feasters. The unu lacked what might be considered traditional gender roles. Men cooked and women fought. All that mattered was if you were good at it. The reason Ornus had never been sacked was as much due to the power of the women in the unu clans as it was to its geography.

Rikard turned his gaze to Qel, and he saw confusion appear upon his face as his daughter brought out the first course and whispered into his ear. Rikard knew that Qel was demanding to know where his precious Aurora was, and why she would dare to shame him in this way. If only he knew. Rikard waited until the fourth and fifth courses had been delivered, and the majority of the unu had become filled with wine and water and meat, before raising the small whistle to his lips.

The sound of a thousand screams filled the air in a cacophonous burst, that shook the unu from their stupor of merriment and several of them fell back in their chairs. Rikard smiled in satisfaction as he watched the clanmasters frantically search in confusion for the source of the sound. He lowered the screaming whistle from his lips, carefully tucking it into one of his pockets. Rikard cut the latching on the package, and the body parts began to rain. First fell the hands and feet, followed quickly by the arms and legs, then the six pieces of the torso, and finally the head of Aurora dropped to the table, landing directly in front of her husband.

Cries of outrage assailed Qel's lips, and the look of horror on his face at the sight of his wife told Rikard that now was the time. He dropped from the rafters of the roof and took care to slow his descent enough that it looked like he was falling but not so fast that he ended up injured. His boots slammed onto the table upturning cups and sending pieces of bone and skin flying from the table. Rikard went down to a knee and bowed his head. All motion in the banquet hall ceased. Rikard felt the entire world come to a halt, and he had caused it. It was enough to make one drunk with the power of it. Rikard slowly rose; his eyes focused on Qel.

"Hello, Father." Rikard took care to make a grand show of his twin knives in his hands.

"You dare…" Qel breathed.

"A message needed to be sent." Rikard kept his voice even. Qel's face was a deep shade of blue. Rikard could see the fury bubbling up inside of Qel. Rikard smiled. This part would be tricky. Rikard glanced around the room at the assembled clanmasters. "Today marks the beginning of the end for the unu. The betrayal by the clansmaster illustrated very clear that the unu cannot be trusted with their own survival. So they will be eradicated from this land."

"You wouldn't dare, Dorian." Qel said. *Even Qel can't tell the difference between us.* His voice was eerily calm. Rikard was almost impressed how well Qel was able to maintain his composure. He had expected an outburst of some kind, but Qel's voice was flat.

"These are your people. More than the blood you call family. She was your mother." Qel said. At the last sentence, his voice caught with emotion. Rikard smiled.

"You betrayed my brothers. You assaulted my clan. Did you not think there would be consequences?" Rikard thundered. "I am your reckoning."

"You come into my house," Qel rose to his feet, "kill my wife, tell me that my people are going to die, and you expect me to do what? Besides drink wine from your caved-in skull." Qel asked.

Rikard wasn't sure how to answer this so he just shrugged. *Why isn't anyone attacking me already? Bleed is hungry.*

"I expect you to die with the rest of them. Though being the clansmaster, I expect you to die last, as the burning remnants of your empire come crashing down around you."

Qel smiled, a sad, grim, empty smile. "You're arrogance is beyond what I ever thought you capable of. You always did think you were smarter than me. She didn't deserve this." he finally looked down at his wife's remains. "Especially since I am no longer the clansmaster." confusion and astonished gasps rang out around the room.

"I am." a voice rang out. Rikard turned just as a gauntleted fist slammed against his chest, sending him flying backwards. Rikard skidded across the table, brushing plates and cups off the table as he hurtled backwards. Two hands grabbed for him, and instead found themselves removed from their appropriate wrists.

Rikard threw himself to his feet and beheld the unu in front of him. The unu that stood before him was the epitome of distinguished, which only made it all the funnier to see him standing atop the table. Rikard cursed silently.

"Terel of the Amber Stone," Rikard said darkly. "An unu worth killing." Rikard licked his lips in anticipation. The unu warrior priest regarded him dispassionately.

"Sit, Dorian Shamesword, once called Waterborne, and your transgressions will be forgiven. You presume much in your words here, but we both know them to be hollow. If I will it, you will never leave this room alive. We both know it. You have proven your point. So sit, and be humbled at my generosity, and tomorrow we will march to war together and put the human queen in her place. Remain standing, and you will die like a dog."

Rikard laughed a bone-chilling laugh that reverberated through the banquet hall. "You think you have power, Terel? Your power is nothing. Your flesh bleeds and burns just as easily as any other unu."

"Maybe so, but even you Dorian Shamesword, whose blade is as renowned as that of Geraldean himself, will admit that a Skyguard Lord Commander would be more than a match for you."

Rikard snorted. "Skyguard are weak. They have not left their cities in generations." Rikard heard the flap of wings and immediately regretted his words as a massive Skyguard glided over his head and came to rest on the ground next to Terel. He had only the slightest moment of astonishment. He stared at the Skyguard, studying him. Something was wrong with this man. His every motion, the way his muscles curved, and his hair flowed, none of it looked real. He looked like a painting of a man made flesh, like he had been sculpted, rather than born. For the first time that night, Rikard felt genuine unease rise up in his belly.

"You were saying?" the Skyguard asked. His smile was devilish in its confidence.

"My first action as Sentinel of the Scales," Terel's voice rose with every word, "is to form an alliance between the unu and the Skyguard. This is Lord Commander Veriel. With his forces supporting our own, we will destroy the humans down to the very last child." Terel glared at Rikard with a look of easy superiority. Rikard returned it coolly. "We will take the Heart of Fires as our own to be distributed evenly amongst the races. Jethro will pay for his treachery, and his people with him."

Cheers broke out amongst the assembled unu, but Rikard barely heard Terel's speech. He was focused on the Skyguard. It was a fascinating specimen. Every contour, every facet of the Skyguard's body was perfect, like a painting come to life. Rikard knew this Skyguard. He would be a worthy feast for Rikard's blades, but not now. The Skyguard changed things irrevocably. He searched again for a weakness, and once again found nothing. In a one-on-one fight, Rikard had no doubt that he could take him down, but it would be a war of attrition. With all the unu as well as the Lord Commander, a fight would be stupid. Rikard wasn't stupid. Terel returned his gaze to Rikard.

"You have been warned, Dorian. Sit," Terel commanded.

Rikard smiled. "Thanks, but butchering Qel's wife took a little bit of the appetite out of me. Instead, I will leave you with a bit of advice. The gates to this city will never open again. Throw yourself from the battlements, because the only way any unu is escaping this city is as a corpse." Rikard stepped down from the table and walked by the Skyguard and the new clansmaster, both of whom watched him intently.

"Your fate is sealed, then. As you walk out that door, you walk out on your people."

Rikard stopped at the doorway that led out into the city. "You have no idea what you have unleashed. But you will learn. Oh yes, you will learn."

"You killed her." there was no question, just a cold hardness to his voice. Devoid of subtlety, devoid of passion, devoid of life.

"Yes." Rikard replied.

"She loved you, Dorian. She loved you as much as life itself."

"What are you doing, Qel?" Rikard asked. The unu sat upon his prayer mat staring at where his wife's place would be. The flicker of the lantern was the only illumination in the room, and Rikard made sure to keep to the shadows. More than that though, the unu could see heat signatures, and so Rikard was wrapped head to toe in clothing that contained the heat from his body.

"I'm winning," Qel looked directly at Rikard, even as he stayed mired in the darkness. "You and your brothers are so brilliant. Such shining stars in the darkness of this world. Where does that leave me?" Qel drunk deep from the chalice in his hand before hurling it and only narrowly missing Rikard's head. It bounced away with a clatter across the room. "But I won. You had this all planned, but I saw through it. When Jeronious stabbed Aurum through the chest at Long Fang. It felt so good. So good to watch the tide turn against you all. All except for you. I told them not to harm you. Aurora wouldn't have wanted that. Why?"

"Why what?" Rikard answered.

"Why did you kill her? You didn't have to. She, she was an innocent."

"There was a price to be paid." Rikard said, "and you care about so little in this world beyond your power. I had to take something from you. Something you cared for before I took everything."

"You're wrong. It's you who have nothing. Come, try and kill me. Even if you succeed, you will never walk a day on this earth without the unu hunting you. I took your brothers; I took your plan." the unu laughed twice. "I've taken the Citadel in this game of Crowns."

"Poor, deluded Qel. You think this levels the playing field? You think you have achieved something with your gambit today? You are so far out of your depth that you cannot even imagine what the surface looks like. You think you foiled me today? But I don't even exist. You have been speaking to no one. No one but your imagination: your deepest, darkest fears. Check my cell and you will see that I have not left the entire day. You speak to shadows." Rikard slid down the wall. Qel's golden eyes attempted to track him through the darkness. Rikard watched him grab the lantern and hurl it against the wall where he had just been.

"Where are you?" a fountain of anger erupted onto his face, and Rikard slipped out the open window onto the balcony outside. "WHERE ARE YOU?"

Rikard leapt up and grabbed the wooden slats and pulled himself up to the roof. He stealthily crept atop the roof, away from Qel's frustrated screams. It was the first moment of satisfaction that Rikard had felt since Terel had become clansmaster. *How had Qel done this?* Qel had always been smart, but not this smart. He knew something. Rikard's thoughts went back to what he and Dorian had discussed. Maybe they hadn't been too far off the mark. Was that Skyguard the player on the other side? Or Terel? He didn't know. But now he needed to figure out what in Garen's name he was supposed to do.

This was not how things were supposed to happen. How had Veriel arrived in the city without anyone noticing? He was hardly an unrecognizable figure. Neither was Terel, and now he was the most powerful unu in the world. Rikard scanned the skies but saw nothing. He knew he would be paranoid about that for the rest of his time here.

Rikard descended into the city. He carefully scaled the rocky walls of the stone castle. His muscles rippled against the evening's chill and his thoughts. *Why would he place his most hated rival in charge of his race? Why would Qel willingly give up power?* All other questions stemmed from this. Qel was a lot of things, but neither humble nor acquiescent.

Why, why, why? Dorian would know.

Terel had been gone long before Dorian and he had arrived on the scene. Terel's clan, the Amber Stone, had bred Terel from birth to be a leader. He was strong and dedicated to the Balance. He was composed, smart, and, worst of all, noble. He had everything a leader needed, except for one thing: ruthlessness. Terel was a flute, and Qel was a knife, and the people had chosen the knife. The Amber Stone clan had been devastated at Terel's subsequent exile. The clan had lost not just a great leader but, in essence, their father and priest.

In the first few years of their rangings before they had joined up with the unu, they had heard rumors of Terel all over the place. A single unu roaming the country away from the unu's traditional nomadic routes was big news for many of the small towns and even bigger in the cities. Grey had made it his mission to find Terel but had come up blank. He had tracked him from one end of Carin to the other, but it had been to no avail. Grey had lost his trail up north near the Burning Waters.

From what he had heard from Grey, Terel had not been happy with his situation, especially after Qel's kill crew had come after him. What Rikard had never understood was why Terel hadn't just come and killed Qel. The whole screwy religion of the Balance had never made sense to him. Rikard finished his climb at the prison cell. He heard the guards' voices before he saw them.

"…really as good as they say?"

"I saw Dorian fight near Illuvium. A group of ferals had gone outside the bounds of what the clanmaster had deemed proper. He was amazing. The only better fighter I have ever seen was a gallowglass. We used to joke about him being magic with a blade, but a real wizard. I never would have guessed."

"If he was a real wizard, why is he still locked up in there?" the first one replied. This one had a burn on his right bicep just below where his breastplate ended on his arm. The second one was missing a finger on his left hand, which held his pole arm.

"Order!" the soldiers snapped to attention, and Rikard ducked down under the window sill.

"Balance!" the two called back in reply. Rikard peered over the bottom of the window. It was Qel and two unum. *Hmmmm.* It had taken him longer to get here than he thought if Qel was this close behind him...or he had just spooked Qel that much. Rikard smiled at the thought. Now that he actually thought about it, he enjoyed so little about living with the unu with the exception of being able to kill relatively indiscriminately...and the Anvil. He loved the Anvil. It reminded him of Cambria.

The unum entered the chamber along with Qel. The two guards peered in after them, and Rikard leapt over the window sill and crept up behind the closer of the two, the one who had the burn on his arm.

The unu was about eight inches taller than him, and Rikard contemplated the best way to contain the situation. Kill one, and scare the other one off, or kill them both. Which one, which one? Kill them both. Life was more fun that way. However, then there wouldn't be anyone to run scared. Fine then, kill one. The door slammed in the faces of the two unu, and they started to turn back around.

Rikard crept quickly behind his victim. He saw the flash in the eyes of the other unu right before he jabbed Bleed into the back of his target's knee. The unu cried out in pain and fell to his knees. Rikard wrapped his arm around the unu's left side, grabbed the pole arm, and pulled the edge of the blade down onto the unu's throat.

"Speak and he dies." Rikard said quietly. He had no intention of letting the unu live, but it was better if the other one didn't know that. Four Finger held his right hand up in a gesture of peace. "You are going to leave now and tell everyone that Dorian isn't happy about being locked up and that until both Qel and Terel are dead, not a single unu will leave this city alive."

"What are you?" the unu gasped.

"I am the Spirit of Vengeance. Now run." Rikard said. The unu backed away slowly. Rikard could taste the man's fear. It was delicious, like bloody meat. As soon as the unu rounded the corner, Rikard slit his captive's throat and left him to drown in a pool of his own rapidly spewing blood.

95

Rikard pressed his ear to the door. He couldn't hear anything through the thick wood. It was by design, he was sure. These were torture rooms as much as prison cells. Rikard pulled a small vial from his armor. He smiled. Breva had thought he was performing some brand of alchemy when he had cooked this up as per Rayn's specifications. The week after he had arrived, he retrieved the plans that he and Dorian had placed years ago for when this time would come. So far, the potions had worked perfectly. He hadn't been able to bring any of his tools for magic due to his arrival method; so brewing potions was the next best thing.

This particular potion was a nasty piece of work. Rikard's kind of nasty. It was an flesh-eating something or other that would, if sprinkled the right way, leave nothing but a skeleton lying dead on the ground. This would be its field test on a living being. Rikard hoped it worked.

The bolt on the door still hadn't been fixed, so the door was opened freely from its moors, and Rikard pushed it open slowly.

"…break you, Dorian. You're like a son to me. So fight me. Prove your worth to your father!" Qel proclaimed angrily. Dorian's face was swollen and bloodied as Qel viciously thrashed him for what Rikard could only imagine as being the twenty or thirtieth time, judging by the damage. Dorian didn't answer but rather looked right at Rikard.

"*Breva*." he mouthed. "*Go!*" Rikard nodded in disappointment. It made sense to get Dorian's wife someplace safe, but he had been itching for a real fight. "*GO!*" Dorian mouthed urgently. Rikard slipped back out the door. He pulled the plug on the potion and sprinkled it on the body of the unu. The acid ate through the armor to the flesh, and Rikard watched, enraptured. *Brilliant Rayn, bloody brilliant, or perhaps not so bloody.* Rikard smiled; delighted at his own humor, before slipping back out the window for the long climb down to the city streets.

Eighth of Seven

Eight

Galeerial grunted from the exertion. His twin scimitars were held above his head, grinding against Grey's broadsword. He dived right, sliding his blades along Grey's, and came up from his roll in a low guard. Grey made no move to continue to engage him. Galeerial felt the sweat pour off his body. He felt sticky and disgusting. The moisture clung his clothes and hair to his body, and he felt dirty. He raised the sleeve of his robe and wiped the sweat from his forehead. His eyes stung, and his muscles were heavy.

He had never felt the exhaustion of fighting before today. The burning of his limbs frustrated him. He waited for Grey to put his sword away before he followed suit.

"Well, the good news is that you aren't terrible; the bad news is that you're pretty close."

Galeerial bristled.

"If you want to learn to be one of us, we are going to have to start at the beginning. Think of it like climbing a mountain. At the peak is where I am, and you are at the base. Before you can begin your journey you need the tools, and you need to understand that you are at the bottom. Here you have the rules, or the Codex as Dorian calls it. If you follow the Codex, then you will begin your climb. Eventually, if you are strong enough, you will reach the crest," Grey said. "On the bright side, I'm just going to tell you the Codex. Dorian made us outsmart him before he would tell us anything." Grey added with a smile. "Aren't I generous?" Galeerial was just now getting his breath back but managed to glare at Grey, who responded with an even wider smile.

"So what is this Codex?" Galeerial gasped.

"Less talk, more ride." the mage did not even appear to be winded after their battle as he swung up onto his horse. The wizard seemed to have boundless amounts of energy and endurance. Galeerial realized just how badly outmatched he would have been against Veriel. He had not made a single scratch against Grey in their six-minute battle, yet his every muscle ached from strikes that the wizard had made with the flat of his blade. But he would learn. *Oh yes*, he would learn. He squeezed some water from the skin on his steed. They had resupplied in a small town called Lavin this morning.

They had followed the western edge of Whisperwood and passed the city of Sharn two days ago. They would arrive at Visir by midday tomorrow. There they would find whatever it was the High Clerics had desired for them to find. Whenever Galeerial thought about the coming days, grim foreboding descended upon his mind, as if they were riding into days without sunlight. It caused a pit to form at the bottom of his stomach that threatened to absorb his resolve. Galeerial joined Grey in his riding and listened closely to the human. The last six days had been what Grey called his proving. The wizard had tested him with a half a dozen different weapons and challenges. Now it seemed they were ready to begin in earnest.

"Before we get to the Codex, I need to talk to you. I know you aren't used to being human, but you have to sleep." Galeerial cocked his eyebrow as Grey continued, "Yes, I know. I don't care how tough you think you are, you're driving your body into the ground. Last night was the third night in a row that you haven't slept. Right now your limbs have to be jelly."

"I don't need to sleep."

"Yes you do." Grey's voice took on a hard edge. "Why aren't you?"

"Because every time I close my eyes I see him."

"Who?" Grey asked. Galeerial looked back at Grey who had lagged a step behind. "The Wither?"

"Supremor." silence lengthened like an evening shadow between them. "Now give me your rules." Galeerial said, shouldering through Grey's confused gaze.

"Rule number one is that you do what I tell you at all times until I repeal this rule."

"I am not a lackey," Galeerial growled.

"And I won't treat you like one, unless you want to be, in which case that can be arranged." Galeerial felt the Five Eye burn red on his chest. *This mage is so infuriating.* He didn't take anything seriously. "But you will do as I tell you. Look at me. Do I look like someone who is going to take advantage of this rule?" Grey flashed him a goofy smile, which Galeerial replied to with a dubious look of his own. "Well, maybe if it was for a laugh. In all seriousness, though, this isn't a game, Galeerial. I am not just teaching you how to kill. Anyone can kill. I am teaching you how to become a killer. By the time we are done you will be changed. Some people can't take it: some people forget who they were before and become consumed with the killing. You have the potential to be consumed, Galeerial. Ideally, that won't happen. By the end of this, hopefully you will be one of us in spirit as well as in mind and body. Each and every one of us can take on an army. Aurum did at the Face Off, and he killed every single feral without losing a single man. We know what we're doing absolutely at all times, and if I can't trust that you are going to do that, then I can't be your teacher."

Galeerial took a moment to consider what Grey was saying. Like it or not, he needed Grey. He wouldn't stand a chance without him and the power of the Seven behind him.

"Alright. What would you have me do?"

Grey smiled.

"Free ussssss" the sounds of the spirits of Whisperwood called out to them. Galeerial glared into the depths of the forest. It was oppressive in its atmosphere. The canopy of ithacan ash stretched high above them, and it grew tight very quickly as they gazed into the swirling depths. It was daylight outside, but the trees created a solid barrier of darkness broken only by the screams of the spirits trapped within. There were no paths through Whisperwood, as the trees vied for survival.

"Tell me when they shut up, for starters," Grey said. The sounds of voices had followed them since they had begun their journey. Always pleading, begging them for something. Some wanted freedom, others gold, others ascendance, others power. Their voices disturbed him greatly. They were all that was left of the Cult of Ephemus, curse his eyes. The voices gave shape to the shadows, and Galeerial felt his eyes constantly roving at the slight flickers of movement.

"The second rule of the Codex is that you must know your fears." Grey said. Galeerial turned away from the disturbing dance of the spirits to focus on Grey.

"What good is knowing fear?" Galeerial asked.

"A few reasons. Firstly, there is no greater fear than fear of the unknown. This fear is the most pervasive and binding of all fears. Fear of danger, death, darkness-all of these stem from the fear of the unknown. We call this the base fear. So if you know the base fear and are able to recognize its power, that gives you power over it. Secondly, fear is a matter of escalation. Everyone feels fear, even us. However, the difference between us and everyone else is that we understand fear, and we use it. If you don't know what you're afraid of, it is easy to be blinded by it. This leads to hesitation, which leads immediately to death. If you hesitate, you're gone. No question about it. At Long Fang, I watched you. You were raw and untamed, yet you cut your way through seasoned warriors, because you weren't afraid of them. The greatest warriors in the world fear not each other, but rather the novice for whom the point of a blade is as foreign to them as being a woman is to you. These are the dangerous ones. People who are more likely to hack off their own arm as their opponents. That's not to say that they can't kill you, for they quite surely can and will. The important thing to take from your experience at Long Fang is that you never hesitated, not once. That is why you, Aurum, and I are still alive. Thanks by the way, I rather like my body in its present cohesive form."

"I'm not afraid," stated Galeerial as a bark of laughter escaped from Grey's mouth.

"Good joke."

"I have passed through hell, mage…"

Grey stared at him.

"Grey." Galeerial corrected himself. "My fear was burned away with my compassion." Galeerial saw Grey move his horse right next to his and then felt a fist slam into his face. Galeerial staggered backwards as his reigns flew from his fingers. His horse reared, and Galeerial went tumbling to the ground. An instant later, Grey stood poised on top of him, his sword in hand.

"Rule three, absolute trust in your brothers. That is the last time that you will lie to me. Is that understood?"

Galeerial felt the cold metal press against his throat. "Is this…necessary?" Galeerial asked. The blade pressed slightly harder. "Yes, I understand." Galeerial felt the pressure lift from his chest and took the hand that was offered to him.

"I understand you, Galeerial. I understand your pride, by Supremor; you are just like Aurum in so many ways. The difference is that you still feel something besides grim detachment, which is why we are going to be such great friends." Grey remounted his horse, and Galeerial ran ahead to latch onto his own.

101

"You *are* afraid, of so many things. It is nothing to be ashamed of; it isn't weakness to feel fear. On the contrary, that means you're alive. It is just like love, happiness, desire, and anger. There's nothing inherently wrong with any of these emotions, what can be wrong is the actions that come from them. For example, when you feel fear you have two responses: flee or fight. Fleeing does not indicate cowardice any more than fighting indicates bravery. Which brings us to rule number four. Technically this is rule number two, but this is the fourth one I am teaching you so you don't know any better." Grey tossed back a wink. "Think with your mind."

"What?" Galeerial asked, confused. Grey simply smiled.

"You'll figure it out. Now, tell me what you know."

Galeerial hesitated a moment. "There is a Codex that must be followed at all times. The first rule is to do what you say. The second rule is to know your fears. The third rule is to trust your brothers absolutely, and the fourth is to think with your mind."

"Good. Tell me what you have learned."

This time, Galeerial hesitated for more than a moment. He thought about how Grey's mind worked. "That I don't like having a knife to my throat."

"Well, looks like you have learned something after all. So, what do you fear?" Grey asked. Galeerial fell silent. He looked to the right at the souls of those who had been betrayed. Ephemus had been a Skyguard hundreds of years ago who had fallen from the Radiant Path. Despite all efforts to reclaim him, he refused and continued to spread lies about ascendance to godhood. He had amassed thousands of followers among all races. His words were powerful, wrought with confidence and majesty. He had ensnared those discontented, those hungry for power, and those disillusioned with what they perceived to be an unjust deity. He had led them to Glimmerwood to seek the Glade of the First: the stone where Garen had been created at the beginning. When they had arrived, Ephemus attempted to shatter the stone with the Third Cardinal Sword known once as Justice. The sword cracked the Shrine at the center of the Glade and every one of his fifteen thousand followers perished, but they were denied

102

entrance into the Halls of Supremor for their blasphemy-for their quest to recreate themselves as gods. Thereafter the sword took the name Ripper. It was the blade that had stolen his wings. There had been no other faith to challenge Supremor since that time.

Galeerial thought of Veriel and of The Wither. He hated them with every iota of his being, but he didn't fear them. He thought of snakes, and fire and spiders, of the darkness within the bowels of the earth that was the bane of Skyguard existence but each of these thoughts was accompanied with a chilled indifference.

"I don't know," Galeerial said.

Grey sighed, "Until you know what you fear, until you can acknowledge its existence, you can never be one of us. You can never be truly free." they rode in silence for a few moments. "Alright, we will work on fear later. Get off." Grey slowed his horse to a trot.

"We need to keep moving." there was an edge to Galeerial's voice. "Veriel will not wait for me to be ready."

"Neither will death, and the faster we ride, the faster death will take you. You need to learn, and while I don't need to teach, I would greatly enjoy the opportunity to channel my inner Dorian." The wizard dismounted, and Galeerial begrudgingly followed his lead.

"To fight, you need to use all of your body." Grey took one step forward and then hurtled into a back flip. "Don't worry, I don't expect you to be able to do that yet. But you need to be stronger, faster and more flexible than anyone else. The only way that works is through lots of work. Do you know what a push-up is?" Galeerial shook his head. "Watch." Galeerial watched as Grey demonstrated lowering his face to the ground, then pushing back up until his arms were straight. "Now, do forty." Galeerial didn't move. "Now." Grey said. Galeerial dropped to his knees and began the exercise.

Galeerial reached twenty, and his arms began to burn. It was one of the many side effects of being human. Galeerial was discovering more and more of them, and he liked it less and less with each revelation. Being a Skyguard meant being freed from hunger, age, sweat, blood, weariness, and

103

thirst, but being human was about being limited by one's own body. It was like being imprisoned. Galeerial gritted his teeth as he hit thirty. His body felt far heavier than it should have. His arms were liquid. Galeerial slowly rose to his feet.

"You are weak now. I have no idea how the whole transition from Skyguard to human works, but you appear to be roughly a twenty-eight year old human. You are still in decent shape, but your muscles have atrophied from disuse. It probably ties in as much with the fact that you were a Skyguard to the fact that you were tortured and malnourished. We are going to remedy that. We will reach Visir in about a day of hard riding. We are going to make that two days, because we are going to be training the entire time. Before you protest, just remember that you are no good to me dead, and only marginally good to me alive."

They spent the next half hour running through stretches, and Galeerial slowly felt his muscles lose their soreness and grow warm. He marveled at Grey's knowledge of the human body. It seemed that he knew how to work any individual muscle as well as groups of them at the same time.

"Are you a physician?" Galeerial asked when they had mounted up once again.

Grey chuckled. "Hardly. Rowen is actually the physician, and he did a bang up job of fixing you."

"You are obviously a healer of some sort. You know too much to be a common human."

"Is that discounting the fact that I am a wizard?" Grey replied with a grin. Galeerial nodded. Grey shrugged. "We each have our own talents. I enjoy magic that has lots of pretty colors. Dorian and Rikard don't use too much magic in general. Aurum will use whatever he can come up with. Joven enjoys the subtle magic, and Rayn wields the boom-boom magic. Rayn is always burning stuff. So we are all special, just like everyone else. But in answer to your question, we all have a certain baseline of knowledge and separate from there."

The rest of the day grew blurry in Galeerial's eyes. He no longer spoke to Grey since he used the time between their workouts to recover from the beatings. The sun began to grow low on the horizon when they finally slowed to a halt. Grey dismounted heavily.

"I will tell you straight up, Galeerial. You are one stubborn son of a pig." Galeerial numbly climbed down from his own horse without responding. His entire body was black and blue, and it hurt to move anything.

"Help usss," the spirits of the wood called out to them.

"Help yourselvesssss!" Grey called out back to them. The spirits grew quiet for a moment. "Thank you."

"Pleaseeee." the call rose out again.

"Oh, for the love of a motherless goat."

"They cannot hear or understand you, Grey," Galeerial murmured as he laid his blanket upon the ground. "They are cursed to dwell beneath the shadow of the wood, into which they followed the heretic, unto the Ravishing of the World."

Grey appeared to be mulling this over for a few moments. "Ravishing of the World huh? Sounds like a party." Galeerial took a long drink as he watched Grey break off pieces of the ithacan ash from Whisperwood. The forest was growing out beyond its borders. They had seen the giants marching while they had ridden from the Split to Winter Crest. The temperate winter had only served to allow for the forest's growth, despite the giants trimming.

Every year on the equinoxes, the giants would depart from their cities, making a circuit around the forest, and cutting back the frenzied growth to acceptable borders. The rivers and coastal lines would run brown with timber that would flow to the entirety of Carin. The rest of the year, the massive doors of the Four Cities remained closed. Having flown over the cities, Galeerial knew that they were more like provinces in their own right. Galeerial also knew that the lands around The Eye of the North were entirely made up largely of farmlands for the massive animals of the giants. Galeerial didn't know how the animals grew that large, but they did, and on

105

those two days, the giants in the north would pilgrimage south with food enough to last for the next six months for the four cities in the south.

"What is it with your people and prophecies? Where we come from, we don't even have a word for fate or destiny. Things just are. We have the path set out for us by the Orrery, but no such delusions of foreboding and grandeur. Yet here, it seems that your world is bound to follow a pathway based on ancient prophecies. Like the one you told Aurum. What was that?"

Galeerial paused before answering. The Book of Arestephan was one of the greatest secrets of the Skyguard, yet somehow, Aurum had been murmuring phrases from *Twilight of Ages* and *Day of Destiny*. However, Aurum had not spoken a single one the lines from the middle prophecy, that of the *Dawn of Darkness*. The piece that Galeerial had told Aurum was the first of two pieces to the *Dawn of Darkness*.

"It is from the Book of Arestephan." Grey's blank look told Galeerial that the wizard knew nothing of the prophecies within. "While Aurum was dying, he muttered phrases from the book. It is a book that only Skyguard are allowed to see. There is no possible reason or way for Aurum to have read it. It is a book of prophecies in which the final three take guidance from The Maw, the final book of *The Stone*. As far as I know, every prophecy in that book has come true except for the final three. That book foretold the coming of the Dread, the massacre, and the subsequent construction of Sterin's Throne. It told of the emergence of the Horrors."

"I am more interested in history than prophecy. I know of it only because my friend Ezekiel would speak often of his belief that we are living in a time where the *Twilight of Ages* is coming to pass." Galeerial was aware of the pain in his voice as he spoke, and he hated himself for it. He knew Ezekiel was dead or being tortured. He knew too much about Veriel to be allowed to run free. He prayed that someone had saved Ezekiel as Aurum and Jeric had him.

"I know of it. I mean, I haven't read *The Stone*, but I have heard Aurum and Joven talking at length regarding it."

"Yes, well, that was the first of two parts of the prophecy of the *Dawn of Darkness*, which follows *Twilight of Ages*...wait, you've never read *The Stone*?" Grey shook his head. "How curious. The first part was written for an unknown person, most believe it to be for a Skyguard; I believe that person to be Aurum." A spark ignited the combination of wood and kindling that Grey had acquired and soon a fire was roaring.

"You said the first part. What is the second part?" Grey asked. Galeerial ran the oiled cloth across the pommel of Eon.

"The second verse goes like this:

> *A black sun rises over a broken plane,*
> *a new day dawns in night.*
> *Darkness will be speared by time;*
> *a ruin will befall the light.*
> *Gods speak from on high,*
> *a human burns with might;*
> *magic stands revealed,*
> *as the world succumbs to blight."*

With every word Galeerial was reminded of Ezekiel. He wondered where his friend was.

"I don't really understand any of that."

Galeerial shrugged. "That is why it is a prophecy, because we don't understand what it means until after it happens."

"Going back to Aurum, the question again is why? I mean, just muttering phrases from a book doesn't mean that it is a guideline for him."

Galeerial replied, "his eyes were also flecked with gold, the mark of one who has beheld the Son of Supremor." with this comment, a pensive look crossed Grey's face.

"This Son of Supremor doesn't happen to come to you in your dreams with red skin and black eyes, does he?" Grey asked slowly. Galeerial started.

"He has told you about his sighting?" Galeerial asked. Grey nodded.

"Then I was correct," Galeerial said. "It is him."

107

"I don't understand."

Galeerial basked in the turning of the tables. He was now the expert and Grey the novice. "The game of Crowns revolves around three principle pieces." Galeerial grasped three sticks and laid them out into a triangle on the ground between himself and Grey. "At the top is the Imperial. Here is the Son of Supremor. At his left hand is the Will, and at his right is the Champion. Each needs the other to function or else the whole falls apart. The Will pushes the Champion forward to protect The Imperial, who provides the Will with the power it needs to propel the Champion. It is an endless cycle of might."

"You think Aurum is this...Imperial?" Grey asked.

"No, the Imperial is the Son of Supremor. Aurum is the Champion."

"And the Will?" Grey asked. Galeerial shrugged.

"No idea, there have only been two Champions before, and next to nothing has been written about the Will." Galeerial stared into the crackling flames. If he was right, then the world would see something that hadn't been seen since Geraldean. But if he was wrong, he had just sent Aurum into the most dangerous realm in the world armed with nothing but a prophecy and a centaur. He had sent him to his death.

Ghosts in the Shell
Nine

"Andusíl?" I whispered. My hand stretched out to feel the skin of my wife. She was flawless. Her skin held a radiant luminescence that threatened to pull my heart away from me once again. Her hair cascaded down to the small of her back. A spattering of freckles highlighted her perfectly formed cheekbones. She was the most beautiful thing I had ever seen. At her side was my daughter, Hope, and she looked just like I had always imagined. Wetness stained my cheek as I beheld her. I knew it was her the instant I saw her. She had her mother's eyes, that same smile, so eager to uncover everything that life had to offer. She waved at me as I curled my hand around my wife's chin.

"Aurum?" I heard a voice behind me, but I dared not look. My fingers grazed her cheek, and the light of her body recoiled from my grasp. My wife's face turned to horror as she turned and began to run.

"No. NO!" I hurtled after her with reckless abandon. "Andusíl!" I screamed. I tripped on the mountains of ash that barred my way. Ash coated the inside of my mouth, and I lost my vision for a moment as my face became stark grey. I shook my head as I stumbled to my feet and stumbled after her. I couldn't see, and rubbing my eyes served only to produce more ash within them. I ran blind as the ash shook itself loose. I looked frantically and saw my family rising into the air. "ANDUSÍL!" I screamed.

"Aurum?" I heard a voice behind me, but my eyes remained locked on my wife. She merely shook her head at me. My daughter frowned, and her tongue emerged from her mouth towards me. I dropped to my knees. I watched helplessly as they ran into the sky to join a symphony of dancing lights; there were thousands of them.

"Please," I whispered, "don't leave me again."

"I'm here, Aurum. What-what did you see?" an unfamiliar voice rang out, but I wasn't listening. My eyes desperately searched for the last whispers of my family.

"Please. Please." I stared skyward, but I couldn't find them. I couldn't find them anywhere. *Where were they!* They had been afraid of me. They had seen what I was, who I was, and they had run. I heard a footstep behind me. A monster approached. I turned and saw a towering black horse in the shape of a man stalking toward me. Its eyes were white, and they bore into me. It hadn't been me they were afraid of.

"You," rage funneled into my eyes. "It was you!" I fumed. My fingernails dug into the skin of my palms, and my knuckles burned as the bones strained to be unleashed from the skin. My fist flew upwards and caught the centaur on the chin. The creature staggered backwards, and I leapt atop its back. The crux of my elbow wedged itself on the creature's throat, and I pounded my fist into its face. Once, twice, three times. My fists pummeled him mercilessly. "She ran because of YOU!" the centaur tried to defend himself, but my blows showed no remorse.

"She didn't believe I could protect her." I screamed. The beast's hands grasped for me. I pushed a foot into its spine and kicked off to the side. The tear in my stomach groaned, but I paid it no mind. I would do whatever it took to kill this creature.

"Aurum, it's me!" it pleaded. Suddenly its face changed to that of a friend. This creature sought to deceive me, but I would not break. My knuckles flowed with the lifeblood from his face. I ducked under a swing and launched three punches and a savage kick to his solar plexus, but a stray blow clipped my chin, and I was hurled backwards. My ears rang from the force of the kick. The hoof might as well have been stone. I curled into a ball as I hit the ground. I sprang back up to my feet and looked for my killing blow. I saw it perfectly in my mind's eye. I knew how I would fell this creature. I sprinted forwards, planted one foot on his chest, and a second landed solidly upon his chin as I continued the flip backwards. The centaur stumbled drunkenly about for a moment before crashing to the ground. I circled my prey, launching a vicious kick at the stomach and a second to the face. I circled this Garen-spawned piece of trash. This mistake of Suprem- my mind hesitated for just the briefest moment, but it was enough to send spikes through my mind. My every nerve yearned for me to push forward, forward, to destroy this thing. My body shook as I fought back against the mind-bending rage. Hot knives of pure hatred plunged into my brain, sending it aflame.

I screamed.

I fell to my knees, clutching my head as the pain intensified, pushing my hand towards my knife and my knife towards the horse's throat. Every second I resisted sent more and more jolts of pain coursing through my body. I couldn't resist. I...

"Get out of my mind." I shouted at the sky. My body jerked against itself as two minds struggled for control of a single body. I fought against the heat to raise myself from the ground. "I am Aurum the Nameless. I am the Sword of the Seven. I am the storm within. I am fire. You want war? I will give you war! I am Aurum Nameless. GET OUT!" This wasn't me. I was stronger than this. This land was a parasite. It had wormed its way inside me with my wife and child. I was no creature's puppet. I fell to the ground convulsing. I heard laughter and glanced into the sky. There were hundreds of them: thousands even. I recognized some, but most were unfamiliar to me. It wasn't until I saw a feral that was missing an arm that I knew who they were. They were everyone I had ever killed, and they were all laughing at me.

"I will not bow to the likes of you." I pulled one foot up to rise, and I was driven down again by the pain. I gritted my teeth together and tasted blood as I bit my tongue. "You want a war? I will give you war." Every muscle in my body tensed as I pushed upwards. The exertion threatened to shatter my spine. It was like lifting the world. The mocking laughter of those over me drove me higher. They were dead. I had beaten them. I won. That was what I did: always and forever. There was nothing I couldn't beat. I am Aurum. I pushed with all my might. I ascended. Inch by inch, I conquered the best Thanatos had to throw at me. I pushed higher the last few inches until finally I stood wholly erect. I breathed in, and the air tasted dry and foul in my mouth. I swallowed heavily and licked my parched lips.

"Is that everything?" I shouted at Acheron. The black tower said nothing in return. I grinned in satisfaction. "You cannot stop me, not even death could...stop...me." I circled looking up at the mocking spirits. My halting laughter grew choked as my gaze fell upon the growing pile of ash in the form of a centaur. My hands grew chilled at the sight, and I looked down. They were wet and dripping. I did not need color to tell me that the liquid would be red. Pain shattered its way through the adrenaline, and my hands began to spike with pain. I couldn't move my fingers. I couldn't move at all. I could only stare at the mass of flesh that had been a centaur named Dane. I began to lose awareness of anything but the laughter of those above me. A hissing, halting laughter approached me. It grew louder in my mind and more pervasive in my ears as it approached.

"All you know is death. All you can give is death." the sound of his voice allowed me to break my gaze from the corpse and saw the feral captain floating above me. "You are an animal, Aurum. A truly feral animal. A rabid animal. You have come to our world to kill us all. You are a demon in the guise of a savior. You are a warmonger."

"Silence," I managed, but my voice was weak, even to me. I took my first begrudging step forward. The ash was thick around my feet, and I had to slog through it like snow. Each step was a burden. Each step seemed an eternity. My foot took an eon to rise and a millennium to fall. Yet still, I arrived at the body too quickly. I pushed his shoulders back and gazed at the broken jaw, the puffed face and the ravaged skull. My hands screamed in protest at the weight that I put on them, and I was forced to drop the centaur's torso.

"You killed him. You broke his face against your knuckles, and you enjoyed it. You delight in destruction and devastation. You are a messenger of death. You are the crow that bears the storms to the innocent children who want naught but to play in the fields of mirth for all eternity. Breaker of Innocence, I name you, the Ravager of Peace."

"No." I once again reached for Dane's shoulder, but the inferno of agony in my hands wouldn't even allow me to touch it.

I dropped backwards into a seated position. I stared at the body of my friend. Still the spirits laughed. I looked up, and I saw Dane staring at me. His face was a horror. The bones of his nose had been caved in, and his eyes were puffy with bruised flesh and blood. His jaw hung limply at a canted angle. I searched for words, for thoughts, anything. All I saw were his eyes staring condescendingly down upon me.

"How could you do this to me, Aurum?" his mouth pantomimed words in unnatural ways. "I followed you; I saved you. I gave up everything for you, and yet you lied to me. You broke my body with your bare hands, and you enjoyed it. I was blameless; yet you could see nothing besides your own rage. Your own failure; you are no savior. You are nothing but death in human form. You will ruin this world, Aurum. I was merely another casualty."

I didn't answer as I rose to my feet, staring at the black tower that taunted me in the distance. I placed a single step forward, and then a second. I looked back at Dane's body.

"You don't even care! You don't care about anything or anyone! You may have broken my body, but your heart was shattered long ago!"

Dane screamed after me. "Your wife would be ashamed, and your daughter would be afraid." I swallowed and kept going. His words meant nothing. His words meant nothing. His words meant nothing. I repeated these words over and over in my mind as I stumbled forward through the ever-gray waste. Thousands of spirits hovered over me. Their gaze propelled me forward, pushing me like a wind on my back and weighing me down at the same time. Dane was not the first person I had killed--the ghosts were evidence enough of that-but I had never killed a man with my bare hands.

I looked down at my hands. I couldn't feel them. They were just...numb. Everything was numb. I looked back at Dane's body. It was now nothing more than a pile of ash. I couldn't even see him. All I could see was the bleakness of the world around me and the dark tower ahead. I walked onward. I kept walking. The ground seemed to slope down as I continued, as if I was descending into the pit at the end of the world.

"Curse you for sending me here, Galeerial. Curse you." I walked onward. I looked at the ghosts swirling around me.

People's beliefs about killing were... misinformed. People believe that when you kill a man it is like seeing beauty for the first time. That it is burned into your mind as a scar that you will never forget. That was true for the first maybe ten men I killed, but now I don't even see living beings. I see pieces to a puzzle. If they are useful, then they belong in our puzzle as part of the plan, and they are to be spared. If not, they die or are discarded, whichever is most expeditious. That was what I had forced myself to think of people as: puzzle pieces. *But Dane?* Dane was an ally. He was a...friend, and I had killed him.

I didn't know how long I had been shuffling along, but I couldn't remember the taste of water on my lips, or the smell of grass. My face was masked by a ripped piece of cloth to keep me from suffocating in the blinding wind of ash that swept around me like a hurricane. I didn't even remember when I had put the scarf on. Still the dark tower stayed in view. The ash piled around my ankles, and I was slogging through it like snow made of paper shavings. Slowly I walked, onward towards the black tower. It stretched high in my view, yet never seemed to grow any closer. Every

114

footfall was harder than the last. I was so weary. I looked up and still the ghastly visages of the dead followed me, with Dane leading the cursed procession.

Everything began to die. I knew there was blood on my hands, but it was the same sickly pallor. I tried to think of what the color red looked like, but I could conjure no images beyond the endless gray. I could no longer even remember why I was here; all I knew was to just continue walking. I began to wonder if there even was a world besides this, or if all that had ever been was the endless gray expanse. There was nothing beyond these hills of ash but more hills of ash. There was nothing else... there was nothing else.

I could no longer raise my head. My eyelids were weighed down by lead, and I shuffled along in haggard strides. My mind began to slide as it tried to grasp memories-anything to propel me forward, anything to escape the horrible reality of what I had done. I had lost control, completely and utterly. This place was infecting me like a virus, and so I began to build walls around those things most precious to me. It had already poisoned me using my wife and daughter, that wouldn't happen again... never again. I reinforced the walls of my heart. I locked it within a block of ice inside a steel box. I allowed my eyes to close for a brief moment, and when I reopened them I blocked myself from all emotion. Whoever ruled this place would be unable to seep into my heart again. He would try, but he would be found wanting. *I am Aurum, and I win*. There were a thousand reasons to win... *make that a thousand and one*, as I gave one fleeting thought to Dane, my resolve hardened to stone.

"You win?" a voice whispered. I couldn't recognize it; though it seemed like it came from a long-forgotten memory. "Like you won at Long Fang?" The memories grew clearer and clearer, as if a fog was lifted. I felt the pain in my stomach as Jeronious' blade slid through my flesh, and shock... as I fell to my knees. Fleeting images... the grin on Qel's face, and then shallow breathing.

115

"Oh yes, you win," the voice continued. I staggered in my walking. "And now you don't even have a name. Aurum Nameless. Aurum the Fool. Aurum who walks for no reason other than that he is too afraid to stop."

"I…" I whimpered through cracked lips. "I'm not afraid." my throat was raw, and every word was an effort.

"You are afraid," the voice slid to my left ear from my right.

"You were afraid the moment that sword pierced your flesh. You are afraid of death. You are afraid of waking up on the other side and realizing that your family sees you as the monster you are. You have killed and maimed and destroyed thousands of lives."

"Nnnn…no." I fought back. I was so weary. I was so…afraid. A cold pit welled up in my stomach and each breath became a labor.

"You are afraid of losing control again. You are afraid of failing your brothers again. That's what you did, Aurum, you failed them. You failed us. Because of you, I am dead." I turned finally with blank eyes as I slowed my plodding steps. Rerem stood there. His neck snapped, and his head lolled to the side as hateful eyes gazed at me.

"Not you." I felt tears on my face. "Not you." my eyes sagged.

"I'm ashamed of you. You failed to step up after I left. I believed that you would lead this family, that you would guide them, and that you would be able to save them." my father shook his head. "You have forgotten my name. You are an embarrassment." my body began to shake, and I turned away. I couldn't bear to see him. I looked up at the monolith so far away. It was so far away.

"You fear what lies there, because it will send you back into battle. You fear failing again. You might as well give up now, because nothing but failure will accompany you. You have failed since the day I died." I fell to my knees. Sorrow filled my eyes.

"I'm sorry." I looked back at Rerem, who hadn't moved. "I am so sorry. I am sorry I couldn't save you, but I can't stop."

"You can't stop, because you don't care. You never cared about any of us. You can't love another human, because you aren't human. You are just an animal. You left Cambria, because you were afraid you couldn't

116

control it. The Orrery told you what you would become. You have feared your fate since that day. It has haunted you through all your life. You were afraid then, and you are afraid now."

"You always were. That was why you never spoke to me." A second voice cut into the conversation. It was Dane. He shook his head in disgust.

"Come, my friend," Rerem put his hand on Dane's shoulder. "Let us leave him with the only person he could ever love…himself." They turned and walked away.

I could only stare back at them with forsaken eyes. They slowly faded into a storm of ash. My head spun. I couldn't tell the difference between my eyes being closed and opened. I sat there…not moving. *Why move? Why even bother? Nothing but failure lay ahead of me, just as it lay behind me. I failed to save Dane; I failed to save my brothers at Long Fang; I failed to save my wife; I failed to save my father, and I failed to save my mother. I failed them all. There was no one left to fail. I was alone. So alone. There was no one left to fail.*

There was no one left to fail.

There was no one left to fail.

There was no one left to fail.

I pulled myself up to my feet. There was no one left to fail. I took a first step forward. There was only me. There was only me now. Everyone else was gone. Everyone else was dead. I was alive. I couldn't hurt anyone else. I couldn't fail anyone else. I couldn't lose anyone else. There was nothing left to do but walk.

To walk.

To walk.

I would walk to the edge of the world and cast myself from its shores. My final failure would be for myself. There was nothing left for me. Nothing left. There was just ash and dust. Just the smoky ink of memories of pain long faded from a knife to a club bashing…breaking all resolve, all desire. I was nothing. A shell of a man…a boy. A shell. An animal.

…

117

...

Not an animal. I could still feel. I fumbled to pull the knife from its sheath, cutting my hand. The pain was dull, but it was there. There was still something left of me. Something left of a man inside. I begged for the Black Tower.

My head slammed into a wall of darkness, and I thought that I had fallen. I pulled my eyes from the ground and found myself facing a black wall of fireglass. I reached out to it, not quite understanding what it was. The stone was so hot it scalded the skin from my hand, but it felt good. It was a physical pain, a pain I was much more accustomed to dealing with. I felt a slit against my hand as I came to the corner and blood began to flow from my finger. I pressed it to my lips. It was cold and metallic and gray. There was no way that I had made it here, without even noticing. I began to back up, sensing treachery yet again. I took two steps back; the world swirled like water and the tower once again appeared to be far in the distance. I began to sidestep in a circle around the circumference of the barrier, stepping back towards the tower every few steps and arriving a couple hundred meters away from my last point, eventually arriving at the massive structure. I searched for some kind of doorway to enter. Ten, twenty, thirty, seventy times I worked my way around the tower before I finally found what I was looking for.

A white portal stood in stark contrast to the black of the tower, and I knew that I had finally arrived. I turned back to gaze back at everything that I had been. Whatever lay beyond this door would change me. I didn't know how I knew, but this trial by fire had burned me so much that there was no going back. I looked at the tower and saw the massive doors.

"Good bye," I called out, but the spirits had vanished. I swallowed heavily. I was completely alone: as alone as I had been since they had died. There was nothing left for me but to go forward. I would walk this path to the finish. There was no turning back, no compromise, only victory or death. And with any victory there was sacrifice. I merely prayed that the price was not too high. I placed my hands upon the gate. The tower shuddered beneath my fingers, and the gateway began to swirl. I pushed my hand forward, and it slid through. I took one final breath before thrusting myself into the unknown that was Acheron.

Eye of the Beholder

Ten

"You feel it." Tendra glanced up from her novel that she had been reading. *A Spring of Glass* was its title. She was sequestered in the back of the library and had been for the last three or so hours. After this morning's meeting with her council of advisors, she had been ordered to take the day off to go somewhere where no one could, or would, bother her with anything. She had been told that she was 'meddling.' The council had been none too pleased with Joven. He had stormed in with a flurry of ideas and basically staged a coup of the meeting. She had found the reactions of her fellow council members to be quite humorous as they gaped at Joven's audacity.

120

Her father had stolen time for her and Jakob, but now, with Jeric gone, she had nobody. So she would have to steal time for herself. However, it appeared as if the wizard Rayn might be attempting to play his own game at being a thief.

The wizard, though similar in appearance and voice to Rowen, was in actuality quite different. He was the youngest of the wizards that she had met, seemed to be in his mid-twenties. He was buried behind a stack of books that almost totally obscured him from view. He was peeking at her from around the corner of his stack and from above his own book.

"How long have you been there?" she asked without taking her eyes off her own reading. Every time he spoke, she felt her heart twinge; the similarities between him and Rowen were far too striking to be ignored.

Rayn was apparently quite the scholar. Since he had arrived, while Joven had gone about making war preparations, he had all but disappeared. She had discovered later that he had been wandering around the city speaking with the elders, and his evenings had been spent here in the library. Not only that, but last night Jonathon had come to her to tell her that the young wizard had spent hours in the aerie speaking with him about all manner of subjects. Most especially, they had spoken about the stars in the sky and the nature of the heavens above. Jonathon had been quite impressed with the young man. Since that time, she had kind of hoped that she would run into him while she was here. She was curious about him, and why he looked so much more like his brother than the others.

"About an hour," he replied somewhat sheepishly. She grinned. He was shy and polite, that was what the people had told her, and apparently it was true. She found this to be quite at odds to her experience with the others. They were all so focused and... intense. Even Rowen, in his unabashed playfulness, was still carefully directed in all of his actions toward achieving whatever goal the wizards had laid out for themselves. But not Rayn. He seemed to be just asking for stories.

"And have you been reading, or just watching me?" he smiled: that Rowen smile.

"Reading... mostly, just taking occasional peeks." Tendra gestured to the chair next to her. The wizard was wearing the same brown robes that they always wore. He didn't have any weapons, though. At least none that she could see, but that didn't count for much with magicians she supposed. He sat down slowly next to her.

"You said that I could feel it. Feel what?"

"That gaping hole in your stomach, like someone poured liquid darkness down your throat, where it lies eating away at your body and soul." her confusion must have been evident on her face because he continued his explanation. "Loneliness. You are lonely." Tendra chuckled.

"You certainly have an odd way about you, don't you? My father and brother were killed, and the man I love is far away, what did you think that I would be exuding? Happiness?"

Rayn chuckled softly before quickly sobering up.

"I meant that you have no friends. You are always alone."

"Maybe I just like being alone." Tendra said with a smile. Rayn set his book down.

"I don't think so. You run yourself ragged trusting not even the minutest things to others. You don't trust anyone, but I think you want to." Tendra considered this man more closely. He had big eyes.

"How do you know so much about me?" she asked as a smile crossed his face.

"It's my job, as well as a hobby."

"You speak to me about loneliness, but you are quite the vagabond yourself," she quipped. "You go to and fro about the city gathering information, lost in thought."

"Well, maybe we can uh, be alone together," said Rayn. He reminded her of a young Jakob, awkward yet cute. Tendra folded her book and laid it down on the table. He was eager to please, and this might be the first and only chance she would get to learn real information about the Seven.

"Would you care to walk with me?" she asked. His face lit up.

"Of course; just let me put these away." he leapt to his feet and quickly began gathering his books. She waited patiently for him to finish gathering his materials. He was like Rowen if one substituted the silky smooth layer of Rowen's skin, and left a bookish exuberant exterior. She watched him carefully replace each book in its proper place. He didn't even have to look at the titles. He simply knew where they belonged.

"So, Rayn, tell me about yourself." The wizard replaced the last of the books and followed her as she made for the exit. The library of Gemport was second only to the one at Mesnir. Cases of books stretched high into the air, such that one needed one of the rolling ladders in order to reach them all. The library smelled of old paper and even older leather. It was one of the largest single rooms in the castle, smaller than only the cathedral and the throne room. She loved the old wood and earthy tones that permeated the room. They made it feel homely and warm even in the dead of winter. The ceiling was a tapestry of colors and images that had been painted in the Far Away Times, before painter's names were remembered. Two thousand years was a long time. Tendra considered the age of her world. Much of that time could be found here, yet there was time that no book had ever, or would ever record. She was saddened by that thought; yet the books here were enough to fill a dozen lifetimes.

The books were mostly of the older variety, most specifically from the Age of Exploration. During those few hundred years, thousands of books were written about the plant and animal life of Carin, and copies of many of them were kept here, while the originals were in Mesnir. They took the horticultural details that had been written in *The Stone* and expanded them out in exasperating detail. She personally cared less for those than for the books of stories: books that told tales of faraway places, beyond her realm of experience and beyond the entirety of Carin. Books of heroes that had never lived and told stories that had never happened. Those were the books that she loved: the fables.

Magic was on the move in Carin and war not far away. Five of the seven pillars were embroiled in it, and she feared that soon the other two would join. She struggled to think of what could possibly possess the

123

Skyguard or, Supremor-forbid, the giants to enter a war among the small races. Yet she had a sinking feeling in the bottom of her stomach that the furnaces of war that had been stoked in many of their hearts would spread into a wildfire that would consume even the giants and their disregard for the small races' affairs. Tendra's mind struggled to refocus as Rayn said something. She shook her head absent-mindedly.

"I'm sorry?" she asked. All she had heard of his response was faded murmurs. Rayn offered an apologetic grin, as if he had been at fault.

"I said that I am what is called, in Cambria, a weaver." he repeated. Tendra nodded respectfully to the guards as they left the library. She liked the idea that the only three rooms in the castle that had permanent guards were the Throne Room, the cathedral, and the library. Power, knowledge, and spirituality were what were most worth protecting. She loved that. She didn't know who had made it so, but she imagined that whoever it was had been similar to her.

"And what, pray tell, is a weaver?" Tendra asked. They moved slowly through the stone hallways of the castle. She had no real destination in mind; she merely wanted to move freely through her castle, through her city. She loved the feel of the city. It always felt welcoming to her. Even with the gray pallor of death and winter hanging atop it, she still felt at home here. Not just in the castle, but everywhere: on the walls, on the towers, in the small bakeshop that sold the sweet rolls with honey, in Jaycen's Forge with its rolling fires and proud axes hanging in the windows. She loved everything about the city. They entered a throng of people who all saluted at her approach, but she waved them on with a slightly chastising glance.

"A weaver is a storyteller. Someone who gathers disparate threads and finds commonality. I am gifted with branded sight. If I see anything, I remember it. It makes me...useful," Rayn explained.

"You remember everything?" he nodded in response. "Interesting," she murmured. He was right, that was a useful talent. She tried to imagine what that was like. Often times she couldn't remember various information, from tiny things like which color was to be worn with which festival to major things like the names of magistrates of the various provinces.

"Yes to all of the things you are thinking about right now," Rayn said with a light-hearted chuckle. She realized that he had been studying her face as her expression had changed with her thoughts. She smiled in return. "Would you like a demonstration?" he asked.

"No," she said after a moment's consideration.

"No?" the surprise was evident in his voice. She felt the tug of a smile. She felt oddly connected with this man through his brother. Perhaps not in the same romantic attraction she felt with Rowen, but more like the protective spirit she had felt with Jakob. Rayn was so innocent to the horrors of the world. She wondered how he managed that when it seemed that death was the name of the Seven's shadow.

"Everyone probably asks for a demonstration, but your word is enough for me."

"Well, so much for my idea that you don't trust anyone," Rayn replied.

"Indeed." the smells of the kitchen aroused her stomach and reminded her that she hadn't eaten since a light breakfast of bread and cheese at sunrise. She looked expectedly at Rayn who nodded vigorously. The mage eagerly followed her through the doorway into the kitchens. Piotr's eyes lit up when he saw her.

"MY LADY!" his broad shoulders and deep stomach bellowed at her approach. His black bristled beard kneaded itself around the corners of his chin as words boomed from his mouth. "And her honored guest! Welcome, welcome to my kitchen!" He muscled his way through the throng of people working. He placed his hands on her shoulders and guided her through the maze of chopping, slicing, searing, and smoking. "Is it a meal or something a little lighter that you be wanting?" Piotr thundered.

"Just something light, my good man," Tendra replied. Piotr was as much a fixture of the castle as the stone walls themselves. He had been here long before she was born and suspected that he would be here many years after she was dead and gone. He was of a hearty stock. As he would always

125

say, being bred for the north keeps one young when the folk of the south grow old and tired.

Tendra remembered back to when she had been a child eager to learn everything about everything. Piotr had welcomed her into the kitchen and had taught her for three days everything she had wanted to know until she had grown bored and had moved on to horseback riding. She had still come back, though. Her father had made sure that his children knew everything about how to live self-sufficiently in case, Supremor-forbid, something happened to them.

"And for you, young master?" Rayn seemed slightly abashed by the cook's overbearing manner, but maintained his intense sense of politeness.

"Whatever the Queen is having is more than good enough for me," he replied. "Thank you."

"Bread and meat and cheese for the Queen!" Piotr hollered, and moments later two sandwiches appeared before them. Tendra feasted first with her eyes. The roasted venison steamed from the melting cheese, and the lettuce and carrots provided color to the brown concoction. Tendra took a seat in one of the large stools that Piotr pulled up to the counter. "EAT!" he commanded. Tendra was more than happy to oblige as she stifled a rumbling in her stomach, and Rayn was just as cheerful. The bread was crusty on the outside, but it gave way with a small amount of pressure to the delicious blend of food within. Tendra found herself enjoying each of these little things more and more as the days of the siege went by. Every hour that held the oppressive force of the Hammer on her doorstep coupled with the unrelenting pressure of the gloomy weather seemed to send her farther and farther away from the freedoms of past days.

She had never felt such pressure upon her as she did now, nor had she ever felt so thoroughly beat down. Three weeks. For three weeks, she had been moving so fast that she had given herself not a moment to breathe and think: to think about her father's murder. Tendra set her sandwich down and dug into her palm with her fingernails. She refused to muse upon it

126

now. The sharp pain threatened to expose blood, but she never pushed that hard. Pain was the only thing that kept his ghost away.

"Your father would be proud of you." Rayn said quietly. Tendra's eyes flashed open, and she didn't realize that they had been slowly closing.

"I...I don't know what you're talking about." she replied stiffly. Tendra turned her gaze to Rayn, who sat next to her. His large, almond-shaped eyes watched her carefully, and then he blushed and bashfully returned his focus to his food. She remembered her father telling her about how Jakob had been a feeler: someone who could sense others' emotions and thoughts as if they were their own. She wondered if her father would have characterized Rayn as such. She had scarcely interacted with the man, and yet he seemed tuned to her thoughts. It unnerved her. Tendra slowly took another bite of her quickly dwindling sandwich.

"I'm sorry," Rayn said quietly. He took a sip of water. "I am usually better mannered than this. I was just excited to meet you, and you are everything I was told to expect and more." Tendra cocked her head inquisitively.

"Explain," she said simply, eating the last bites of the bread. She noticed then that Rayn had long ago finished his meal. She held up a finger and gazed up at Piotr who was still shouting orders, though his voice and the noise of the kitchen itself had seemed to fade into the background din of the world as she had eaten. Now that she was again focused on it, however, she found that she could barely hear. The cook took notice that they were finished and hurried towards them.

"It was delicious, Piotr. You never cease to outdo yourself," Tendra said gracefully, meaning every word.

"You are much too kind, my queen. Though you should not skip the dinners I prepare for you so often," Piotr teased with a smile. Tendra waved her hand.

"Work." She gave a tired smile, and Piotr nodded in understanding. "Speaking of..." Piotr nodded once again.

"It is always a pleasure, my lady." Tendra rose. The chef bowed, and Tendra nodded her head in agreement. She motioned for Rayn to follow

127

her, and they maneuvered their way through the ruckus of the kitchens. Cooks hollered to servant boys for water, and one could see knives flashing as vegetables and fish were cut and sliced with a skill and speed that would have given an accomplished swordsman pause.

Tendra narrowly avoided stepping on a chicken as she slipped out the back door and into a long hallway that led to the emissary chambers on one end and the gardens on the other. Tendra chuckled as she turned back to see the larger man attempt to follow the narrow pathway through the maze of activity and fail. He offered her a smile that contained both bemusement and mock panic. The wizard narrowly avoided being hit with a cudgel and ducked under some low-hanging pots, only to trip over that selfsame chicken. Rayn caught himself moments before falling by grabbing a table. He shrugged at his own clumsiness as he righted himself. She cocked her head as she watched him. If she hadn't already known it, she never would have guessed that this was one of the men that had so radically changed her world: one of seven honest-to-Supremor wizards that had taken the world by storm. Right here and right now, he was just a man, with slightly overlarge feet, who seemed more comfortable with books than with people. He reached the doorway and bowed for his performance.

"Well, if you can survive the kitchens, then ten thousand unu ought to be no challenge at all," Tendra told him.

"What can I say, My Lady? I take on all challenges, great and small," Rayn said.

"You said I was everything you expected. What did you expect?" she prodded. She gestured with her head, and he eagerly began to walk with her. They wandered through the castle halls with no destination in mind.

"Well, Rowen wouldn't stop talking about you when he arrived at Long Fang. He was quite smitten. It was quite funny actually to see him so. He well, he has always had a fondness for ladies," Tendra cocked her eyebrow, and Rayn grinned sheepishly. "But," he held a finger up, "I have never seen him talk about a woman like he talked about you. He was excited about you."

"Really?" she asked.

"Absolutely. I hadn't seen Rowen that excited since before Father died." as he said that Tendra saw a brief flicker of panic on his face. *Interesting. I don't think I was supposed to hear that.*

"You are an orphan as well?" she asked. He looked at his feet as they walked.

"Yes," he said hesitantly after a moment. "Rerem was my father's name. He died just before I came of age. It was…difficult for all of us. I know what it is like to lose your father…or rather, to have him taken from you." *So not just an orphan, but he had a father who was murdered.* The conflict regarding the matter was evident on Rayn's face. She didn't want to push him.

"You know, Rowen told me some things about you as well," she said. At this, he lit up, regaining his previous jubilance.

"What did he say about me?" he asked eagerly. Tendra thought back to the long road from Midway to Gemport and the months spent in Gemport while the war had been going on, when Rowen had acted as liaison between the Seven and her father. It had been when he had trained with the city guard and took care of healing Jakob and the Skyguard. It seemed like a lifetime ago.

"He said you were the conscious of the Seven. That it was you who kept the rest of them honest and true." a massive grin lit up the young man's face.

"No, he didn't really say that, did he?" he asked. She nodded with a smile. "What a rascal," he said. Tendra chuckled at this. She hadn't been paying attention to where they were going, and she was startled to realize where they were. Before them was the southern entrance to The Haloed Gardens. She gestured to them.

"The gardens are my favorite part of the castle besides the library," she explained. "They are called The Haloed Gardens. They are divided into eleven concentric circles. The doorway for each one is right next to the entrance, but you must walk the entire length of the gardens in order to get to the center. Being so far south means that we have little of the beauty of

129

the northern cities, but here, in these gardens, we can pretend that we live in a world that is less stone and more life." Tendra continued.

"What lies at the center?" Rayn asked.

"Would you like to find out?" Tendra inquired. She looked at him quizzically. Then she wondered at herself. The gardens had always been a place for her family: for her and Jakob and her father. Now, it was only hers. She had brought Jeric there several times, but now the first person she had even thought of bringing was Rayn. She hadn't even brought Rowen to the gardens. She suddenly felt timid. She knew that the feeling was silly, but she was afraid of what he would think of the ornate display that her father had crafted with his own hands. A small dose of fear crept into her stomach, and she almost hoped he would say no.

"I would be honored," Rayn said. His voice held only sincerity, where she knew that Rowen's would have contained some slight amount of teasing. She felt an urge to take Rayn's hand and lead him, but she suppressed it. She motioned for him to go first so that she could see the reaction on his face.

Rayn pulled the doors open, and the sunlight through glass ceiling dazzled her eyes. As her eyes adjusted to the harsh light and she gazed at the gardens themselves, her mind was soothed. The hedge before her was made from intertwining firebloom, and the light shimmered off of the flowers in dazzling reds, yellows, oranges and blues. She looked at Rayn's eyes and saw the wonder as he reached out to finger the plant.

"No," Tendra said softly, and Rayn's hand jerked back as he looked at her inquisitively. For all his reading, he obviously did not know anything about horticulture. "It's firebloom. If you touch it, your hand will burn for weeks."

"Beautiful, but dangerous," he whispered, and she nodded in agreement. The firebloom twisted around in a circular pattern, and Rayn began to trail along the pathway. His eyes roved upwards to see the high walls surrounding the gardens covered in vines and moss. The entire room was heavy with moisture and heat. Tendra breathed deep of the heavy air, the smells twirled in her nostrils and mind. Remembrances swam up from the murkiness of her memory as she thought to when her father had been designing the gardens.

He had stayed up late into the night drawing on his big parchment board. She remembered the first time she had entered. Her father had refused to allow her and Jakob in while it was being constructed, but after it had been finished, they had all gone in as a family. She had wanted to touch everything, but her father had guided her hands just like she was guiding Rayn now.

She saw that Rayn had meandered out of sight, and she moved to catch up. Every time she came here she would always speak in hushed tones, even though no one was ever here but the single omnipresent gallowglass who hovered in the southeast corner of the ceiling. There was an air of reverence that pervaded the gardens and not just because of who was at the center. She saw Rayn waiting for her at the entrance to the second tier.

They entered together. The second layer was a swirling mass of rainbow colors that wove in and out of one another in a lavish tapestry. She saw Rayn's eyes rove through the entirety of the hedge. He was memorizing it all, she realized.

They wandered through the second ring and came to the next which told the story of Gemport as woven by horus and porus. One was a black vine with white blossoms and the other was white with black blossoms. It told the story of Garen before weaving into his sons building the city and the trials and fires of tribulation that lead all the way to her family. The Line Sumenel began four hundred years ago and came to an end with her brother and her. Rayn's eyes were completely absorbed by the story being told upon the walls of the garden. His gaze was pensive, almost awed, and she delighted in this fact. Her stomach uncoiled in relief.

They moved to the next layer, one made entirely of a sheer wall of flowers. The one after that was simply hedging with only a single sunblossom in the center. The layers grew gradually smaller and smaller as they progressed inwards. The sixth was stranglethorn, which brought a somber brown to the gardens that highlighted the brilliance of the snow lilies in the next row. Then came the red asp that created a feather-like pattern and texture, followed by a wall of hollywhite that transformed into magen and back again as the year progressed. As the year wove to its end, that wall was almost entirely magen. The first day of spring would bring the first blossoms of hollywhite, and they would again fight their battle for control.

Tendra fought the urge to take off her boots as she strode through the grass into the ninth ring. It was the one place in the castle outside her room where she felt comfortable with walking barefoot. Even this late in the season when most grass had faded to brown, the grass here was lush and green. She didn't know why or how, but the sunstones laid within the ceiling captured the sunlight during the summer and kept the gardens alive for as long as she could remember. The glowblooms bathed the next layer in an olive light whose rays played back and forth across their bodies. Tendra didn't know how long they had been walking through the gardens. Time always seemed to stretch out while she was here. Minutes seemed to last for hours, but it was never enough. She always wanted to spend more time here.

The penultimate ring was so small that it only took a few moments to walk all the way around the teardrop-shaped bell lilies. The final layer was phoenix bells. They died everyday and remained dead through the night. Then, with the first light of the new sun, they arose. The retained light of the sunstones did nothing to stave off the cycle. They responded only to natural sunlight.

They moved to view the final circle. There a stone hand grew out of the ground with an inscription dedicated to Tendra's mother, beneath which her body was kept. Tendra stood next to the wizard as he regarded the remembrance stone.

"It's beautiful," he whispered. Tendra reeled. He had said nothing through the entirety of the gardens, but here, at the grave of her mother…

"Yes," Tendra murmured. It was all that she could manage.

"What was she like?" Rayn asked.

"I…I don't know. She died just after I was born. My father always told me that I had her smile, and her hair." Tendra fought back tears for a moment. Now, they were both gone. She felt Rayn's hand envelope her own, and she looked into his eyes through her own increasingly cloudy ones. He pulled her close into an embrace, and she could hold her tears no longer.

"It's alright," Rayn murmured. "Even a stone may weep when enough of a burden is placed upon it. And you are burdened." Tendra barely heard his words, as her face was buried within his shoulder. "You're not alone, my lady. Not at all. Rowen loves you, and that makes you family." Hot tears streamed through her eyes and down her cheek or into Rayn's cloak. It took her several moments before her mind understood what Rayn was saying.

"W-w-what?" Tendra asked. She swallowed hard, cutting off the flow of tears. She wiped her eyes with the sleeve of her tunic. Rayn smiled softly at her.

"When Rowen met us at the Face Off, you were all he would talk about, and not just in that Rowen way. Rowen knew how to handle women, but you…you were different. You challenged him. It was so hard for him to leave you when your brother died. He argued heavily with Joven to let him return, but Joven insisted that he come for the battle. We knew the unu would betray us sooner rather than later, and Joven wanted all of us there to try to deflect their attention from any one of us. But his mind wasn't on the battle." Rayn smiled at her. "It was where his heart was, with you."

"No, no no, you said 'loves.'" Tendra said pushing forward. Despite his words, this was what was most important. "Rayn, is Rowen alive?"

"Of course he is," Rayn said confusedly, "he is one of us. We don't die easy, and arrows can't penetrate our armor. I watched Rowen get peppered with arrows and fall into The Heart, but that was to escape the unu. He's alive, and he's coming." Tendra searched his eyes for any sign of deception but found nothing. She had not found anything but honesty in the

133

young wizard's eyes. "I promise." his eyes shone as he looked into hers. Her tears dried as quickly as they came.

"Thank you," Tendra said. "Thank you so much."

*   *   *

A shadow moved silently through the night's pathways of Gemport. A black cloak hugged the broad male figure as his boots stepped with little regard to the freezing puddles and grimy streets. There were no beggars left in Gemport to disturb this man's progress towards the docks. He moved with purpose, and yet his heavy boots made almost no sound as they impacted the city streets. He turned and twisted through the winding ways ever lower towards his final destination: a boat that, every night for as long as anyone could remember, was transformed from its legitimate daylight business into a nighttime congregate for those who knew about things that others did not. By day it was known as *The Light's Maiden* and by dark, to those smart enough or desperate enough, *The Night's Maiden.*

The City Guard wove in well-known patterns through the city enforcing the strict curfew that Queen Tendra had imposed in the wake of the unu interdiction. No man was permitted to leave his home after dark unless an alarm had been raised. The wall was the only place men were awake. Joven had made sure that shift changes occurred randomly throughout the evening, changing each day so as to avoid the enemy attacking in the middle of one. Each day the change time was posted on the cathedral doors. Three shifts, each roughly eight hours in length, manning the outer walls or surveying the sea pathways.

This man evaded the guards with the practiced ease of a thief. Shadows embraced him like lovers, and the silence seemed to deepen at will as the man wound his way through the guard's pattern, always aiming straight and true for the lower docks.

The man's boots made not a sound until the first step set upon, not weathered stone, but rather on plated wood. The hood that obscured the man's face turned, slowly surveying the assortment of vessels: everything from the small schooners to the massive warships that served as pirate chasers along The Thorne Coast. The man cautiously turned westward and made his way along a pier at seeming random, but nothing about this man was random. His every step was confident along the wood. His breath formed a mist around his head before dissipating quietly into the night. At the fourth vessel on the pier, the man stopped.

The man's hands held a circular piece of iron. Despite the gnawing cold, his fingers worked deftly to unclasp the small latch that held the two pieces together. His hand enveloped the front piece and pressed the bitterly cold metal to his face. The black eyes enabled no man to gaze into the wearer's, but allowed him to gaze outwards. The nose was sharp and angled, and the mouth was drawn tight in a glare of malice. As the metal pressed against his flesh, the man winced. The back piece slotted firmly into place with the latch snapping just below his right ear. The already midnight black of the world took on an even darker hue as the fading moon was obscured by the filter of the lenses in the mask. He felt the mask bond to his flesh with a grimace.

The man turned around and walked back down the dock, he continued three piers down before stepping onto the first boat there. Instantly, steel glittered with the starlight as daggers and cutlasses were bared at his approach of their domain. The forms of men seemingly melted away from the shadows of the boat, but the man showed no sign of worry. He reached his gauntleted hands up and cast back his hood. His mask reflected no light and sucked the starlight into its abyss. Instantly, the hostility that had been emanating from the men changed to fear.

"Co...Co...Corrigan?" one of the men asked.

"Naw, he's dead, disappeared with ole Longshore and the rest after *The Finality* was ghosted," another said, but the bravado in his voice was laced with terror. "This ain't him."

"Let me in," the man called Corrigan said. There was no permission requested. There was only an order. The voice was heavy and dark. It was as thick as oil and almost as black.

"Right away," said the first man, and he shuffled to the floor a mere footstep away from where the man called Corrigan stood. Still the man called Corrigan didn't move. The man's fingers slid into a small ring on the floor that revealed a trap door leading to the lower decks where the dim light of lanterns wafted up into the night. The man called Corrigan took a step forward, and the man scrambled to get out of his way. The man called Corrigan raised his hands in preparation to descend and made his way down the ladder, leaving behind him the sound of the gurgling blood of the man who had dared doubt him.

The man called Corrigan's feet hit the deck simultaneously, and all eyes turned towards him. The stink of sweat, liquor, candle wax, and fear assailed his nostrils. This was the part Rayn hated most: the mask, the fear, the bribery, the backstabbing, the murder, and the treachery. But he needed information, and this mask and this name gave him what he wanted. Evil men trembled at his approach. Rayn knew power, and it terrified him.

RUN!
Eleven

Rikard sprinted across the rooftops. If Breva was gone, Dorian would not be pleased. He felt the wind breeze through his hair. He sighed. *This is why I make no attachments. They just slow you down, and what's life if not lived at breakneck speed?*

The stars shined brightly upon him as he leapt to the next roof. He did a front flip in midair as he ran. He enjoyed the exertion. He had been slinking in the shadows for too long; all that mattered now was speed, even though he knew it wouldn't matter. This wasn't going to be a running mission; this would be a rescue mission. He would get a fight. He grinned.

He plunged down to the streets, snapping into a roll as he hit the ground and came up running. He charged around the corner. Two more houses and he would be there. He pulled his daggers out as he rounded the last corner. An unu stood with his back facing him, and Rikard leapt forward and stabbed his twin blades into the unu's temples, ripping them out as he pushed off the unu's shoulders, keeping his momentum intact.

Her door had been broken. Rikard quickly began to calculate. Her home was big enough for six unu to fit comfortably with enough room to maneuver their weapons. Six against one. He almost pitied them.

"DORIAN!" he heard a scream from down the road and his head snapped right to see Breva being hauled away by two massive unu carrying battle axes. They would be fun to kill. "It's a trap!" *No way! A trap?* Rikard couldn't believe such a thing. He rolled his eyes and then saw the archers.

They were lined up along the rooftops, all with arrows pointed at him. *Oh yes, this is what I've been waiting for.* The sound of arrows being released was as close to pure beauty as Rikard was likely to experience, though at the moment he was less concerned with being awed as he was with staying alive. Rikard eyes became a blur of movement as he tracked the arrows coming towards him. He had been born for this. He watched each and every bowstring draw back and let loose. His blades were a flurry of movement. The unu archers were good, but he was the best ever. He leapt upwards, folding himself into a ball, and his blades flashed, blocking the arrows as they came. One, two, three, four, five…nineteen in total; he got them all.

Breva loomed large before him. Rikard could almost see Dorian's smile when he told him that he rescued her. He tossed his blades up into his hands and hurled them into the two unu's foreheads. It was a shame that he hadn't been able to actually fight them. A shadow crossed his view, which Rikard thought was odd considering it was night: such was the size of the unu. It was Nod, Qel's son.

Rikard slid to a stop as the unu thundered to the ground. He gazed at the rooftops. The unu archers stood at the ready, but held their fire. Nod had wanted to take a shot at Dorian for years, and this was as close as he was likely to get. Rikard wondered briefly if Dorian would mind him killing his step-brother, but that thought was instantly dispelled.

"You always tried to take what was mine!" Nod snarled. His axe whistled as Rikard leapt backwards, avoiding half a dozen slashes. Rikard gritted his teeth. Breva was just watching them fight. *Run, you idiot!*

"Run!" he yelled at Breva. He got clipped in the shoulder with the flat of the blade and went spinning backwards. He launched into a cartwheel, nabbing the polearm of the unu he had killed. It wouldn't do much good blocking, but if he could get a shot to the neck it would make all the difference.

"You tried so hard to be his son, but you never were; you were a fake." sparks thundered as the axe slammed into the ground. The unu didn't even flinch at the jolt. Rikard launched a flurry of jabs and sweeps, but the unu's defenses were as sharp as his blade.

"What can I say? You always were second best, Nod. Your own father was ashamed of you," Rikard taunted. Rikard glanced under the unu's arm as he prepared another heavy sweep and saw Breva running. *Good. Time for me to run too.*

"You know nothing! You are naught but a thief and a charlatan," Nod roared. The unu feigned a swipe and bull rushed Rikard, who lost the ability to breathe as the powerful unu's shoulder slammed into his stomach. Rikard was slammed back into the wall of a house so hard that his teeth rattled. He saw stars get cut in half as Nod's axe whistled through the air towards his head. His eyes flashed wide open and ducked as the axe broke through the wall. Rikard leapt to the right and nabbed his fallen polearm. He hurtled it at Nod, who was turning slowly around. Rikard turned his back, confident in the hit, when he heard the crash of metal.

"Unless you have a steel head…" Rikard said, slowly turning around. The polearm lay shattered on the ground, and Nod's axe gleamed. Rikard sighed. "Well, that wasn't supposed to happen."

He ran.

Arrows pinged after him as Nod charged. Rikard couldn't afford to waste any more time with this buffoon. He would have to end it quickly. Rikard leapt through the air to avoid arrows and slid to where his daggers had embedded themselves into two unu's faces. He swiped them both simultaneously and threw himself to his feet. He needed to get to Breva, but she could wait. He had his babies back. Now, he could kill Nod.

The unu was like a rhinoceros charging at a tree, so still Rikard stood. Rikard saw the unu's every footfall in exquisite detail: two more. As the second one hit, Rikard dove forward underneath the unu's axe. His arms were a blur of vertical motion as his knives worked their way up and down the unu's right arm, his stomach and right leg. Slices of flesh flew into the air along with a geyser of blood and screams of pain and the clang as the axe hurtled into the wall. Nod crashed to the ground in a hazy state of pain and disbelief. The right side of his body looked like the leftovers after a bear had mauled a wild animal.

"I'm Dorian. Did you really think you stood a chance?" Rikard asked. "I always liked your right eye. Can I have it?" An arrow whistled by Rikard's neck. The archers had caught up with them. "I guess that's a no." Rikard slit Nod's throat with one blade and cut his eye out with the second as the golden rain began to grow in number. "Then again, I never was good at following orders." Rikard took off running after Breva.

The archers were only able to follow him a few blocks before he lost them, but by this time the whole city was awake. Rikard cursed. It would make everything more difficult. Hopefully, Breva had made it to the safe house. He took off in that direction.

It was the middle of the night, but torchlight was everywhere. Nod had made way too much noise, and Rikard wished he would have killed him faster. Not only was he forced to traverse from shadow to shadow, but he was bound by the roads. The rooftops were swarming with archers and hunters trying to find him. He needed to get her out, and fast.

The sound of clashing metal caused Rikard to hurl himself into an alleyway. He counted footsteps as they passed by out of sight: twelve of them. As soon as the last one passed, Rikard took off running in the opposite direction. Near the south side of The Gold Castle there was a storeroom. He had told Breva to go there at the first sign of trouble. *That had worked well.* Rikard kicked a stray dog that refused to move out of his path as he threaded his way through the city streets.

The door to the storeroom was open when he arrived. He crept slowly inside. It was pitch black inside. His eyes were accustomed to darkness, but this was deeper than that. This was a void.

"Breva?" he whispered.

"Not exactly." the Skyguard seemed to materialize out of the darkness. Rikard drew his knives. "You are endangering an alliance that has been generations in the making, and that is something that cannot be allowed. I have been greatly looking forward to meeting one of you. You have quite the reputation."

"I can't say the same about you. I don't know who you are, nor do I particularly care. But I will be happy to kill you." The Skyguard smiled as if scolding a foolish child.

"We may yet cross blades, but not tonight. That honor goes to my associate. This is Frosh, and he will be your executioner this evening."

This was wrong. Rikard could feel it in his bones. Everything about this place was wrong. He launched into a back handspring out of the door. A shadow followed him, and Rikard heard the whistle of steel cut through his hair. He landed on his feet and was immediately met with a foot to the stomach. He flew backwards and crashed against the wall.

Rikard licked his lips as his assailant regarded him coldly. The man's armor was the same deep black, matching the void within the storeroom. The only sign that it was in fact a living creature were the eyes. The eyes were a striking blue, like skin on a body that had been frozen to death.

"Frosh, huh?" the man carried a marvelous broadsword. "Nice sword. It'll look good on my back." the sword swung up in a diagonal strike, which Rikard easily blocked. He countered by thrusting Bleed towards the eye slit. The man moved impossibly fast, grabbing his wrist. Rikard prepared to vault with the inevitable attempt to snap his arm, but instead the man lashed out in a savage kick to his knee. Rikard ripped his leg up, but pain still reverberated through his body as the steel boot landed solidly on his shin. The man held tight onto his wrist and brought his sword up before sending it whipping around in a circular motion. Rikard twisted out of the way, and the man ripped backwards on his arm. Rikard threw himself back onto the ground to avoid having his tendons shredded.

The man's boot landed on Rikard's elbow and shattered it. Rikard swung his left arm around, jamming the dagger into the knee joint of the armor. As his right arm flopped to the ground, useless, his left was dealt a reverberating shock as his dagger impacted against a metal that was stronger than the steel of his blade. He had only a moment to register his displeasure at the outcome when a realization dawned on Rikard.

He was losing.

He swung his feet up around the man's neck and latched on, twisting his torso. The torque flipped the man over and hurled him down the alleyway. Rikard pushed himself to his feet with his one good arm. He needed to get out of there. He took off in the other direction. His shin screeched, and his arm screamed as it dangled at his side. Rikard looked back and saw the man slowly rise to his feet with no apparent discomfort and walk towards him. Rikard stopped to regard this man.

The man striding towards Rikard filled him with an inexplicable sense of unease. This man had thrashed him thoroughly without any effort at all. Rikard knew he was a great fighter, but he hadn't believed that anyone could be this much better than him in Carin. Frosh and his impressive suit of armor was enough to convince him otherwise. Rikard played his eyes up and down over the armor, searching for some kind of avenue of attack.

Any attack on the plates would be foolish considering the joints themselves had resisted the dagger. That left the eye slit as the only viable target. It would take a one in a million shot. Rikard grinned. Those were his kind of odds. The alleyway turned ninety-degrees, and so Rikard did an about face and waited for his relentless pursuer. He looked down at Bleed and hoped it would live up to its name today. The man was ten meters away. Rikard prepared for the throw... five meters.

He flicked his wrist, hurling the blade sideways. It spun twice in the air. The hilt rotated before Frosh's face, bringing the blade to bear at the eye slit. The blade went true and stuck right into the opening. For a moment, the man stopped, and a grin of triumph formed on Rikard's face. The grin quickly vanished as the man pulled the still gleaming blade out and cast it to the ground.

"That should have worked," he murmured. A gloved hand shot out to his face in the blink of an eye. The heavy gauntlet easily fit Rikard's face within it, and he shot an arm up to break the grip, but his fist simply clanged clear in the sharp chill of the moonlight against the impenetrable armor. Rikard felt his entire world rock as his head was slammed backwards against the wall. The first blow dazed him. The second had him seeing only half the world. The man let go of his face, and Rikard slumped to the ground with the world spinning everywhere. But Frosh wasn't done. The man grabbed the back of Rikard's head and pulled on the hair, bringing Rikard to a stunned standing position. His face was ground into the stone wall. The coarse surface ripped the flesh from the bone. Blood clouded his eyes, and his nose flattened to mush. He heard steel and knew that he was about to die. He tried to smile. This was a warrior. This was a man who could kill him.

"Wait." A voice rang out. Rikard couldn't see anything anymore. "Let the unu kill the traitorous brothers together. It will cement Terel's hold on the unu."

Rikard couldn't see it, but he imagined a sadistic grin lighting up the Skyguard's face.

Smug son of a b... he didn't even finish the thought as blackness encompassed him.

Know Fear

Twelve

Galeerial was weary. He was not simply tired, but weary. The last few days had been an unending onslaught of mental and physical challenges. Every moment of their ride, Grey had been filling his mind with knowledge. Everything from fighting tactics, to historical events, to scavenging techniques all fought for space in his mind. When they were not riding, they were stretching, fighting, lifting, pushing, pulling, and breaking. By the end of the first hour of the first day, Galeerial had gained an enormous respect for humans in general and the Seven in particular. The burning ache of his muscles and the weariness of his thoughts were things foreign to him as a Skyguard, but now they were constant companions. The rawness of his legs upon the horse's saddle caused Galeerial to stand in the stirrups, and Grey's eye once again fell upon him.

"Tell me the best strategy for fighting an unu," Grey said.

"Quickness or distance." Galeerial recited immediately. "Unu have remarkable stamina, which makes outlasting them a difficult proposition. Bows are ideal, but only a shot to the head will cause the unu to fall. If you must fight hand to hand, do so up close, using the unu's size and anger against him. They are fast, so using daggers and hand axes is the best course of action."

"And what is the most important rule of combat?"

"If you can't win, you aren't thinking fast enough," Galeerial said. The wizard had drilled that phrase into him over and over again. There was no such thing as an unwinnable battle. Grey told him how Aurum had managed to destroy an entire battalion of ferals at the Face Off because he had outsmarted them. Galeerial found it interesting that the benchmark for success was how Aurum did things. Whenever Galeerial needed an example of how a certain piece of knowledge was applicable, Grey had a story of something Aurum had done. Galeerial wasn't sure if it was idolatry or if Aurum had quite simply done everything.

"Can you catch an arrow?" Grey asked him. The wizard had slowed his brown charger to a trot, and Galeerial's own followed suit automatically.

"Of course not," Galeerial responded automatically.

"Why not?" Grey asked with a shrug. Galeerial's mouth started to work before his mind, but he silenced himself. Rule 4: Think with your mind. Galeerial's instinctive response to the question was an immediate dismissal of the seemingly impossible task, but he had never honestly considered the proposition of catching an arrow. It was all a matter of speed, and Galeerial knew about matters of speed.

"Because I am not thinking fast enough," Galeerial said. Grey smiled in approval.

"Precisely." Grey reached into his saddlebag and withdrew a bow and a small quiver of arrows. Grey tossed the two of them to Galeerial, who instinctively dropped the reigns of his horse and caught the bow. The quiver bounced off of his gnarled left fingers and fell to the ground. Grey eyed him disapprovingly. "You were supposed to catch that."

145

"I never would have guessed," Galeerial replied darkly.

"Now, now don't be fresh."

Galeerial dismounted, and Grey rode a short distance away. Galeerial reached down and flexed his left hand in and out, restoring circulation to the cramped fingers. They had been grasping the reigns all morning and had become locked in that position. Galeerial worked the bones lose. When the pain finally broke, Galeerial barely noticed it. Pain was like air; he always expected it to be there. He slowly retrieved an arrow from the ground where they had spilled out. There were seven of them. Each one was carved differently. Galeerial ran his fingers over the grooves on the shaft and back into the fletching. It was a hawk's feathers. Most Skyguard arrows used trimmed white feathers from their own wings for their arrows. It was a sign of losing oneself when a life was taken. The golden feathers on these arrows were remarkably pure in hue. Galeerial marveled at them. He watched as Grey dismounted from his horse about sixty meters away. The wizard pulled an apple out from his saddlebag.

"You want me to shoot you?" Galeerial asked.

Grey did a double take. "Are you crazy? Why would you shoot me?"

Galeerial shifted his eyes back and forth. "I thought you were going to catch the arrow." Galeerial replied.

"Did I ever say I could catch an arrow? No, I didn't think so. I want you to shoot this apple off of Ole Rover here." Grey took a bite of the apple and placed it on the horse's saddle. Ole Rover stood remarkably still as Galeerial nocked the arrow. He squinted. The red apple was slightly blurry in his vision; yet another facet of being human that he hated. Galeerial had spent most of yesterday being rebuked about his awful technique firing a bow, and so was prepared today. "You have seven arrows, and one minute to fire all of them, unless of course you hit the apple, which you won't."

Galeerial gritted his teeth. The constant rebuking had not bothered him at first, but like the wind whipping sand along the skin that would eventually grind you to dust, so were Grey's insults grinding him down. He

146

focused on the wizard's head. It would be so easy to end it now. Kill this wizard, ride for Cloud Breach, and strike Veriel down in the same manner. Instead he lowered his aim back to the apple. Galeerial's fingers strained to bring the arrow back to his chin. The twang of the string followed the arrow as it leapt from Galeerial's hands.

His human eyes struggled to track the dart, while his hands reached for the second missile. He stopped in mid-reach as he watched the arrow go low. It was going to hit the horse. A cold feeling of dread shot through Galeerial in the space of an instant. Then it was gone-not the feeling, but the arrow. Galeerial blinked and saw it in Grey's left hand. The wizard shrugged.

"You owe me six more arrows, Galeerial," Grey called out with a smirk. Galeerial obliged him, and each time the brown streak was deftly picked out of the air with the precision of an eagle grasping a fish. When the last of the projectiles was spent Galeerial mounted up and rode forward to meet the wizard.

"Teach me," was all Galeerial said.

"I have been," Grey said. The wizard took the quiver and arrow from him and replaced it in the saddlebag. "Everything has been leading to this. I'm really sorry about this, Galeerial, but now comes the hard part. I figure we are about twenty miles outside of Visir." Galeerial said nothing. "Now is the part where you have to die." Galeerial was able to see the dagger clear its sheath, and even managed to throw his arm upwards to protect his face while scrambling for his own weapons when something hard struck his temple, and the world went black.

*   *   *

Galeerial awoke naked and freezing. His every inch of skin was cold to the point of numbing, but was just short of that line, and the pain mocked him. A blue fire flickered a few feet away from him as Galeerial felt the familiar bite of steel against his wrists and ankles. He was chained and bound. A hooded figure sat only a few feet away. A cold seeped into

Galeerial's blood that had nothing to do with the bitter chill. He knew this creature. A knife appeared in its hand and a fork in his other. The creature sparked them together. The grinding of the metal assailed his ears.

"Did you honestly think you could escape from me?" every "t" was pronounced. Galeerial couldn't move. He couldn't speak. His mind achieved the numbness that his body desperately searched for, but he could only think a single thought. It was a lie. It was all a lie. This couldn't be happening. A cruel haunting laughter filled the room.

"Of course it is, and it can. I thought you liked games, Galeerial." the figure's hood fell off of its bald elongated head. Grapefruit-sized sockets lacking eyes gazed at the former Skyguard. Its lack of nose and leering smile was the visage of disgust. Its skin seemed to almost be flaking off. The Wither's breath smelled of death. The creature stood and walked forward to him. An ashy, decaying hand reached out to his chin. Galeerial fought his stomach back from his throat. He jerked back from The Wither's touch. This response only prompted the manic grin to widen on the creature's face. "This is the best game yet." Galeerial's breathing grew shallow and afraid.

The heavy air stank, and despite the former cold, Galeerial broke out into a sweat as The Wither began to run the tips of the fork along his skin. Bumps ignited across his body, and he shivered.

"I hope our fun will never be done, run, sung. It deserves to last forever." The fork traced a circle around Galeerial's chest as the knife ran straight down his torso. Galeerial shivered as he felt a sliver of blood follow the knife's pathway down his chest. The momentary warmth only served to make the following chill that much more pronounced.

"No, this...this is a dream," Galeerial stammered. The howling laughter in Galeerial's ears was exactly the same as it had been those countless nights: those long, dark nights, when he would howl out for his god to save him and hear nothing. He had cried over and over and over again until his throat bled from his pleas for help, for deliverance.

"Oh please, Galeerial. Do you think you are the first Skyguard we have made to disappear? Veriel has been delivering nosy Skyguard to me for centuries. Not one of them broke, but you…you are the weakest of your brood. You are a disgrace to your people. You are so afraid."

"That's not true…it's not," Galeerial murmured softly to himself.

"Of course it is. You are a Skyguard that has no faith in anything. You have nothing. You are just a human now: just a pathetic, worthless human. One of tens of thousands of vagabond sewer rats with no purpose for which to live."

"No…" Galeerial's mind trembled, "no…" a shiver echoed through Galeerial's body.

"Yes, yes." a second shiver ran through his body as The Wither's blade trailed down his stomach. This had nothing to do with the fear or the cold that permeated his bones. It was one of rage.

"I… am… not… worthless. I will kill you," Galeerial said through gritted teeth. He glanced about the edges of The Wither's body, and it looked like it was cracking.

"You deny, reply, supply me? You are nothing. You have nothing. You are just a-"

"I am Galeerial Starheart!" Galeerial roared with every ounce of strength in his bones. He didn't know how this beast had managed to reclaim him, but he would accept no more from this monster. He was no longer a prisoner. He was one of the Seven. He was a warrior. "I am not yours." Galeerial's fingers balled into fists so tight that his skin cracked and broke. Blood flowed down his wrists as he strained against his chains.

"You can't break them. You are still too afraid, and you should be," The Wither hissed in his face. "You really should be, Galeerial. Your way of dying is not to be silently in the twilight of the world, but wrought with pestilence."

"No. No more lies. I will break you. I will break you in half," Galeerial thundered. He felt the chains rip his skin open, and his muscles shook. He had escaped this creature. Aurum had saved him. This was all a trick, some nightmare demon of The Dreaming. "You are not real."

"I'm more real than whatever kinship you think you have with an imaginary wizard," The Wither hissed. "Did you really think someone

149

could, should, would save you? There is nothing in you worth saving. I made sure of it. You're broken and dire, like me. You are nothing but what I have made you."

For a moment, doubt crept into Galeerial's mind, but he refused its advance. It had to be true. Grey and Gabriel and Long Fang and the Codex. It had to be true. He couldn't believe it could possibly be fake. He looked into the hollowed eyes of his captor, and all of his hatred came to life. He couldn't let fear win, so instead he hated. He seethed with anger, and he poured all of it into strength. All of it poured out in an eruption of titanic proportions. His chains shattered, sending metal splintering outwards. Galeerial collapsed to the ground and leapt towards The Wither. Both of his hands wrapped onto the creature's skull. Galeerial dug his fingernails into its soft decayed scalp. "You have breathed your last." His fingers pushed downwards into the rotting skull. He felt the flesh giving in to his claw-like fingers. The Wither's hands grabbed his own, desperately hacking to try and break his hold, but Galeerial refused to let go. A putrid stink arose from the tear that began to form in The Wither's scalp.

"I will always be there," The Wither hissed. "The extra shadow in your steps. The hidden dagger at your throat in your sleep. The voice just out of reach. You can't destroy me." For a moment, The Wither resisted before its skull split in half in Galeerial's hands. And he was bathed in light. "...because I am in you." The words echoed in his mind.

Galeerial's eyes flashed open to behold a small underground chamber that was well lit by torches. In the far corner sat Grey. Galeerial's exhausted eyes passed over the wizard's body.

"Grey?" Galeerial asked. His mind was muddled to the point of incomprehension, and he stumbled over the words.. "What?" Slowly, realization began to dawn upon him. "What...What in Supremor's name did you do to me?" Galeerial's voice rose in volume until the last word was a nigh incomprehensible scream. He tried to lunge at the wizard, but he was tied to the wall with heavy ropes that wound around his wrists and body. "What did you do?" Galeerial roared.

"Sorry." the wizard said almost timidly. "Rage huh?" the former Skyguard pushed against the ropes. His whole body strained to be free. "Easy there, bucko." The wizard slowly rose to his feet. "What you just did was remarkable, but it's freaking me out. For all of us Seven, we overcame the drugs by willpower. But you broke your chains of fear with rage." Grey was lost in thought as Galeerial seethed. "And quite quickly too-slightly less than eleven hours."

"How dare you? I trusted you!" Galeerial bellowed. Galeerial jerked against the ropes again.

"If you had honestly trusted me, then this would not have been necessary. But your soul is guarded. Not that I blame you, but it is locked down tight. As much as I can teach you how to fight others, you have to learn how to stop fighting yourself. You aren't free, Galeerial, you have just traded one set of fashionably gray chains for some burning red ones. While I admit they go with your eyes, they do have the side effect of, y'know, burning." Galeerial felt his anger slowly began to simmer down. His fists slowly pulled back.

"You have no idea what you put me through!" Galeerial growled.

"I showed you that you were still afraid, and you are just too proud to admit it. You have known such pain I can't even imagine, but you are using that pain as a crutch. You are enslaved to your past. You are enslaved now just as you were when Aurum found you. You need to release those chains."

"You want me to forgive him?"his words were incredulous.

"I want you to forgive yourself. Accept what happened to you. Accept that you are a human. Accept that what happened to you was not your fault. You blame yourself for being imprisoned. You blame yourself for being human. Let it go now, Galeerial, or you will never be able to move on. You will be stuck hunting him until it destroys you. Even if you find and kill him, your lust for finding someone else to blame will not be satiated. There is nothing down that road but a lonely death."

"Are...are you going to untie me?" Galeerial struggled to keep his tone under control. Grey had crossed a line. *How dare he?*

151

"Will you try to eat me if I do?" Grey replied. Galeerial shook his head slowly.

"No." The wizard considered for a moment before crossing the ten paces to where Galeerial was bound, and Grey reached out and cut the cord. Instantly, the entire rope grew slack, and Galeerial's hand shot out onto Grey's throat. His other hand grabbed the wizard's hand and locked it into a grip that caused him to drop the blade. Galeerial's feet swept out and knocked the wizard's out from under him. Galeerial followed Grey's descent down to the floor, and the wizard's head hit with a thump. Galeerial's hand was still locked onto his throat. He made no attempt to resist.

"Do you think this is a game?" Galeerial thundered. "How dare you?" Galeerial's fingers tightened about the magician's throat.

"I...did...what...you...needed...not...what...you...wanted. I-" Galeerial pressed harder. He wanted nothing more than to snap this wizard's treacherous neck. Galeerial's eyes bored deep into the magician's. Grey's eyes were steady.

"We are done," Galeerial said. He forced his fingers to withdraw from the magician's neck. Galeerial rose to his feet. The wizard began to hack as air filled his lungs after its explosive denial. Galeerial searched for a door or window of some kind.

"You..." Grey coughed, "do. You do think this is a game. You still think that you can remain who you are and still be one of us, but you can't. You have to let go of your past failures and look to the future, Galeerial. You can't do this without me."

"How do I get out of here?" Galeerial ignored the wizard's words. Grey gestured unsteadily towards a point on the floor of the room. Galeerial stood on it for a moment. A white light shone, and he felt himself ascend on the very air itself.

He emerged into the plains of Carin. He looked around uncertainly in an attempt to gather his bearings. The evening sun was setting, and he could see a massive inferno inside a city in the distance to the right of the sun. That was Visir, and that was north. Galeerial searched for the horses within the shallows of Whisperwood but saw nothing. He grunted in dissatisfaction and began to walk.

No one followed him.

This almost surprised Galeerial. He thought for sure the wizard would try to justify himself in some way, but there was nothing but the howling of the winter wind and the voices of the wood to protest his northern progress.

Galeerial hugged close to the forest to serve as a break against the torturous wind. It whisked southwards, and the trees provided some protection, but the omnipresent floating rivers of argent that were the specters of the wood kept Galeerial from descending deeper into the cover of the trees.

"Where will you go?" a voice whispered. Galeerial jumped, and his scimitars leapt into his hands.

"Grey?"

"Where will you go?" the voice again asked. It didn't sound precisely like Grey's, but it was close enough that Galeerial knew it was his.

"To Cloud Breach. I'm going to kill Veriel. I've had enough."

"No. Not enough, not yet. If you fight Veriel, you will die."

"That's why I am not going to fight him; I am going to kill him." Galeerial replied. He was sure that Grey had been stalking him in the forest. His eyes searched the shaded boughs in the last lingering remnants of sunlight. The rising moon was bloody and full: a hunter's moon, a killer's moon. "Now leave, or I will kill you, Grey."

"You have neither the means, nor the will. All you have is your anger. You are a fire that, if left on its own, will rage out of control and consume the entire forest." Galeerial reached down and found a smooth stone amongst a small bank of pebbles. His eyes darted back and forth and found a likely candidate. His hand flicked outwards at the shadow. "Did you really think I would be that careless?" a voice whispered in his ear. Galeerial whipped his arm around and found it intercepted by the wizard's hands. Galeerial spun away as the first stars crept into the sky. The Eternal Host shone down upon Galeerial as he regarded the magician.

Grey was smaller than he was, both in height and build. The wizard looked different, though. He held himself in a manner that Galeerial had not seen before. Grey had his staff in hand with the tip pointed towards the ground and the remainder running up the back of his arm. His robes twirled around him in the wind. His hood had been thrown back, and his square face was lit by the light of the moon.

"Get out of my way." the two faced off against one another. Galeerial fingered the hilts of his blades. He considered taking out Eon but rejected the proposition. Grey knew how he fought with Eon, but he hadn't seen him fight with the scimitars since their first round of sparring. Grey made no motion to pull his own sword from his back.

"Are you really going to fight me, Galeerial?"

"I will if you don't turn around and go back the way you came. And I will kill you," Galeerial said. His voice was unwavering. It had the cold cut of anger on the edge of every word.

"If I beat you, then will you stop being so melodramatic and imbecilic and let me finish teaching you how to survive?"

"No," Galeerial replied.

"Well then, I am just going to have to tie you back up in my secret lair until you finally wise up." Grey sighed. "I won't lie. This will hurt." Grey took three steps forward, cutting the distance between them in half, but he didn't engage. Galeerial stepped forward, swinging his left scimitar overhead and wind-milled through with the second one close after. The wizard blocked both with his staff and lashed out with a kick at Galeerial's stomach. Galeerial took the blow with a flex of his muscles, and then launched into a five part series of hacks and slashes. Grey parried each of them with ease and countered on the final stroke into his own flourishes. Galeerial had never fought Grey while using his staff, so he had to adapt quickly to the new style.

Galeerial leapt into a retreat, hastily moving backwards with the wind to escape from Grey's carefully placed blows. Grey swept his left leg out, and Galeerial leapt upwards. The wizard stopped mid-swipe and lunged forward catching Galeerial's stomach in his shoulder. They both tumbled

154

backwards to the ground. Grey hit Galeerial in the stomach with his staff. Grey grabbed Galeerial's wrists as he attempted to stab the magician's heart and thigh simultaneously. The magician threw his forehead forward into Galeerial's face. Galeerial felt the bones of his nose crunch backwards. He slumped back, dazed for a moment, but cast the pain back. Galeerial hurled his hips upward, throwing Grey off and onto the ground behind him. Galeerial whipped one of his scimitars through the air, and released it. The blade cut the night air in half. Grey's hand moved impossibly fast.

"You cut me!" Grey cried. He moved his fingers up to his mouth as he dropped the scimitar to the ground. Galeerial watched impassively.

"Go home, Grey."

"Like heck. Lift." the wizard stretched his hand out, and Galeerial felt his whole body suddenly seize and rise into the air.

"Cheat!" Galeerial said furiously. He struggled against whatever magic the wizard was using, but to no avail.

"You think that matters to anyone, much less Veriel? You use everything at your disposal to win. You never hold back. You..." Grey stopped. His hand whipped to the ground, summoning his staff, and Galeerial fell fifteen feet to the ground. He hit hard and fell into a roll as his feet touched the ground. "Show yourself!" Grey called out into the darkness. Galeerial's eyes followed Grey's gaze. His nose alerted him first. The smell of wet hair, rum, and rust filled his nostrils. Green fire erupted in the being's hands. With every movement, the limbs of the being seemed to grind against one another. Galeerial shot a confused and wary look at Grey.

"Who are you?" Grey called out. The creature ran towards them. Every footstep was accompanied by a hard thud as what had to be heavily plated boots sent reverberations through the soft ground. It was shorter than Grey and much shorter than Galeerial. Its body reflected none of the starlight and moonlight, rather seeming to absorb all of it. Galeerial was having a hard time pinning down what exactly this being looked like, but as he got closer and the light from the fire in his hand shone brighter, Galeerial was able to see that it was a man: a man made of iron.

"I am The Fifteenth Finger of the Left Hand of the Iron Giant. The Dread has been reborn, and his army assaults our capital city beneath the mountains. Will you aid The Iron Giant?"

Galeerial looked at Grey. The wizard's green eyes looked back. Grey spoke first.

"Sure, sounds like fun."

Shadows of Acheron
Thirteen

The hot stone exterior gave way to a chilled interior. I felt the goosebumps grow on my arms, and I could see my breath. Torches of blue flame lent the entire palace an ethereal glow. The hallway was long and made entirely of the same black glass as the outside. Torches were placed at every ten or so feet. The walls warped upwards, ultimately combining into a tip nearly thirty meters above me. The walls were entirely smooth, inducing a sense of vertigo in my mind, and I closed my eyes to stave off the dizziness that engulfed me. Slowly, I counted to five, opened my eyes again, and centered them on the first in the long series of torches. The blue was deep, almost azure, and the flame danced a hypnotic dance in front of my eyes. They were held in cruel circles of barbed iron wound tightly, binding the torches to the wall.

I took my first tentative steps forward. I wasn't afraid; I was wary...no, I was afraid. The cold pit in my stomach was fear. Something was wrong. At first I couldn't place it, and I attributed it to the unnatural stillness of the air, but as I approached the first torch I realized what was wrong. There was no sound. I snapped my fingers and heard nothing. I stamped my foot on the ground...again, nothing. I tried to speak, and though my mouth formed the words, nothing was emitted.

I crept slowly down the hallway. I pulled Havoc from its sheath and Widower's Wrath from my back. My bruised and bloodied fingers ached as they wrapped themselves around the handles of my weapons. I kept walking. The hallway seemed to stretch on and on. I began to count my steps. 493, 494, 495. At my four hundred and ninety seventh step I came to the first door. I almost walked past it, but my eyes caught the slivers of light that formed the left edge of the door, and by stepping forward twice more I found the right edge. It looked exactly the same as the rest of the black metal that the corridor was forged from, but for the cuts along the sides. I briefly wondered how many of these doorways I had passed without even noticing. The hallway continued to stretch down, but I stopped and looked at the door. I raised my hands. pressed them against the barrier, and pushed. Nothing happened, and so I stepped back to survey my options. However, any ideas I might have had were superseded by the words that slowly began to form upon the door.

You are not one of His.

"Who are you?" I was surprised to hear my own voice. It was raw and broken. My throat felt like it was full of shattered glass. I tasted blood.

You are not one of Mine.

Enter Other. The light at the edges of the door began to spiral inwards, creating the same elliptical swirl as had been on the doorway at the outer wall. I stepped forward. The door allowed me to pass into and through it. The strange mix of heat and coolness again embraced my skin for a moment before I emerged once again into a long hallway. The walls were covered in mirrors-hundreds of them-that appeared to span the length of the hallway. The walls of the room itself bent upwards into one another and

158

became the ceiling. Once again I felt the vertigo begin its onset, but I fought it back.

I took my first tentative steps forward. To my right the glass mirror showed my reflection and to the left it did the same, but they were different from how I appeared now. To the right was simply my reflection, but the other was shaved, and his body was burned red by sun scarring. I continued walking forward. At the next junction I was dressed in a coat of nine colors, and the fourth I had a hook for a hand and was dressed similarly to how I had been when I had lived as Damaen Longshore.

"Who are these men?" I recoiled from the sound of my own voice. It sounded…warped, old…broken.

These are who you could have, should have, or would have been. I kept walking, seeing dozens of alternate versions of myself. I only stopped when I saw one. It was the interior of an intricate terranite faux-wooden house, like something from the city of Veridian back in Cambria. The walls were decorated with paintings that I knew had been made by my wife. I sat in a rocking chair, facing the hearth, with a book in one hand and a pipe in the other. A fire blazed with color, and I could almost feel the warmth from where I stood. My face was far removed from the dozens of lines that now pervaded it in the real world.

This could be yours. All you have to do is step into the glass. The words appeared in the stone around the doorway. A woman entered in from out of the frame.

"Father." *father.* This was my Hope. This was my daughter. She was so beautiful. She looked just like her mother, but taller. Her skin were of a more golden hue, more like my wife's than mine had been. Her face was kind and soft. She wore a beautiful gown of white and violet, and a single feather held her hair together in an ornate display of craftsmanship. My other self smiled at the young woman. "I am going out tonight to the observatory. The comet Seronos will be the closest it has ever been tonight. Will you come?" she asked.

"Yes, say yes," I murmured, urging myself on. My other self simply smiled.

159

"No, I think I will spend the night with your mother. Her soufflé didn't come out right, and you know how she is after that."

"I heard that, Aurum." a voice from another room rang out. It was her. It was my Andusíl. I loved her voice. I loved everything about her. I saw my daughter, all grown up, walk out of the frame. I forced myself to tear my eyes away when I wanted nothing but to watch. I knew that if I watched any longer, I would walk through.

"Enough," I said through gritted teeth. "Whoever you are, that's twice you have tried to use my wife and daughter against me. Don't you dare try to do it again."

Twice you have been tempted, but only once have you resisted. Your fate is yet to be determined. I continued walking down the hall. It was a puzzle. The hallway just kept on going. I turned back towards the way I came and found that the entrance had vanished. Everything up to now had been a test. Everything. From the moment we had entered Thanatos until now. Now, they were testing my mind. I continued to walk, looking at each one of those windows, searching for the one that was unlike all the others. I saw myself as a farmer, a ranger, a jail keeper, a librarian, a king, a knight, a sailor, and a writer. But none of them fit. *What was to be gained from this test?* I stopped walking. I knew what the being wanted.

"I hate you," I said. "and I am going to kill you. Slowly, so when death finally comes you will reach for her embrace, but even then, I will deny you her comforts. I am going to break you and bleed you until you are naught but a hollow shell. I hate you." I said. My eyes blackened with fury. I turned on my heel and stalked back to the portal that showed my reflection, though it was slightly changed now. Now, there was a black skull laughing behind me as I stared at myself. My knuckles were red and bloody, my face haggard and drawn. My body was rendered thin and gaunt with hunger and exhaustion. I could see the bones in my face through my ashen skin. I could have anything I wanted here: wealth, power, freedom, family, wisdom. But in the end, the only thing I had earned was the pale deathly visage that stood before me. The only thing I had earned… was nothing.

160

I plunged into the looking-glass and materialized in a large, cylindrical black room. I look up and see a platform and an archway far above me. Ringing all around the spiraling tower are bars and platforms.

"What game am I to play now, you sick son of a..." I halt as words once again form on the wall.

The game of survival. I jerk my head back as an arrow whizzes by my face and flies straight through the metal, evaporating into nothing as it hits the wall. From all across the room arrows begin to rain down. My doorway is gone. There is nowhere to go but up. I don't move though. I observe. I shunt my anger and misery to the side. I need to think now, not feel. *Curse your eyes. If I need to go through this to get to you, then that is what I will do.* I watch as some of the platforms recede into the wall and then push back out. I watch as the bars begin to rise and lower or swing in the air. It is a game of inertia, momentum, and timing. I will need physical perfection. This time I do take a deep breath. I watch the pattern unfold before me. In times like these, the physical world ceases to exist as everyone knows it.

The world becomes a black and white diagram. I see angles plotted out, trajectories mapped with mathematical precision. The world becomes alight with circles and lines. It is like they are drawings in one of my architecture classes. Every line tells me one thing, I need to move fast, and I can't stop. Shadow darts fly towards me, but I dodge them with only the slightest movements as my mind solves the puzzle before me. I feel a strength in my limbs beyond what the haggard reflection had shown me.

This mechanism is like a clock, every gear becomes perfectly aligned in one sequence. I blink heavily and open my eyes with purpose. I take off running. Sixteen steps to the edge of the platform. I push off with my right foot, grabbing the first pole. I swing up and carry my momentum forward into a front flip. I land on a thin beam, balancing precariously as it closes towards the wall. I wait until the last second and leap upward to a globe that is spinning with a pole stretching out from its side. The globe spins around as I swing back and forth to gather my kinetic energy. I leap

161

backwards, grabbing the bar above me with the crux of my legs, and swing my torso forward to grab another bar above it.

I grit my teeth as I feel sweat start to bead on my forehead. I pull myself up so that I am standing on the bar. The pole begins to swing inwards toward the wall. I look up and see a ledge above me. It is too high to jump. I watch the wall approach. I leap forward, cushioning my knees onto the wall, and then ricochet back to the ledge. The hard black stone bites into my fingers. I pull upwards with all my might. I feel the wound in my stomach tear open, and the ache in my hands becomes a flood of agony.

"Oh no, you don't," I whisper. I pull myself up with all my strength. Blood courses down my forearms as my fingers are cut to the bone. My hands are slick as I scramble for some kind of purchase on the platform. I feel sick. My whole body is overcome with weakness. I grimace as I throw one leg over. I feel the inside of my mail grow wet with my own blood. I mount the platform and lay there as blood begins to pool around me. I stagger to my feet. The doorway is right before me. I press one hand to my stomach. The wound is like a hole in the very fiber of my being. I stagger and fall to my knees. A jolt of pain shoots through my body. I scream in agony as the ache sends fires of electricity through my veins. *You do not have to continue.* The words appear on the wall, but I ignore them. The blood seeps through into my hands. It is sticky and hot. I can smell it, and my mouth immediately withdraws a metallic taste from the scent. I begin to crawl. This is a test of my body. I failed my body once at Long Fang: never again. Never again would I be beaten. Not by Jeronious or Qel, or whatever twisted game the creature that ruled this tower was playing.

I am Aurum. I win.

I throw my right leg forward and push myself to my feet. I take two more steps forward. The gateway is just a step away. My vision is going black as stars of darkness eat away the light. I stumble for half a step.

"You want a fight," I whisper, "I will give you a war." I cross the threshold and collapse. The gate closes behind me as I draw in a ragged breath. I stare almost drunkenly at the ceiling. A white light glares down at me from the roof. I close my eyes heavily.

I feel myself transition. It is like awaking from a dream so real that it might as well have been reality. The light forced that shift upon me, and I held my hands up to my eyes. I was standing again with no memory of rising. I stumbled forward exhausted, but still I pressed onwards. I had to be close. *Please...let me be close.*

I took stock of my surroundings. I was in a long corridor, much like the first, except the ceiling seemed to stretch infinitely higher, and the walls were not black but a stark white that almost hurt my eyes to look upon. Some distance ahead there was an austere black cylinder upon which a staircase spiraled around. I walked forward warily. I pressed my aching hands to my stomach as I approached. I could feel blood welling up inside me. It made me vomit. The bile scratched my throat as it erupted from my mouth. The smell brought forth a second heave. I couldn't remember ever eating. I stumbled forward, wiping the last bit of vomit from my mouth. The vile taste lingered in my mouth. I spat blood on the ground. Slowly, I arrived at the staircase and I saw that the hall was in fact shaped like a cross. There were others in the room, approaching from each of the different sides. As I walked closer, the others did as well, with equal pace to their movements.

To my right I saw a Skyguard. I didn't recognize him, but his face was ragged. He looked like he had been through worse than I. He said nothing to me as he looked up the winding staircase.

"Did you come seeking the keystone?" he asked. I shook my head.

"I'm here because I had to come," I said, struggling through the words. The Skyguard nodded. It was then that I saw a gaping wound in his side. There was silvery blood seeping out. His face was burned, and boils covered his skin. His wings had black streaks within them. To my left was a human bald of head and long of tooth. He wore the garb of a Light Monk.

"My name is Samuel. Remember me, if you should ever escape, and I do not," the Skyguard said.

"Who are you?" the Light Monk asked me. "You aren't one of us?"

"I'm just a man," I replied heavily.

163

"You don't belong here. You have not been prepared. Tread carefully, for you will be hunted when you arrive on the outside. Watch yourself, friend." he said. He peered into the stairwell. "I never knew it would be like this. She didn't tell me it would be like this."

"Who?" I asked. The Skyguard entered the stairwell and descended. He walked down the staircase...*down*? It was only now that I noticed that the staircase also descended. I couldn't believe that I hadn't noticed it at first.

"Any of them," the Light Monk said. It was then that I saw blood seeping from a wound on his head. He was delirious. "It's not my time...it's not my time...it's my time." he moved to follow the Skyguard. I watched him take two steps before collapsing. I reached to help him, but my hand was stayed by some invisible power. He tumbled down the stairs, and I heard a crack not long after. I didn't flinch. I moved to follow close behind him, but found that I could not. I could not see the being on the other side. His face was obscured by a heavy cloak, but he appeared human. There was something about his walk that was familiar. I couldn't place it, though. He made the sign of Supremor: a line on the forehead, a line on the lips, and a line on the chest towards me. His every step was deliberate, as if he had been wounded grievously, but I could see no visible sign as I had with the others. He took the ascending stair.

This is the balance point. Your final chance to return to the life that you know. Take the Falling Stair and rejoin the world as Aurum Nameless. Take the Falling Stair and return to your life. You can even have your pet centaur back. Take the Rising Stair, and you will emerge as something terrible. Take the Rising Stair, and only death will follow you. Choose.

"Death comes to all things. I have come this far. I will not stop now. I cannot stop now." I took the Rising Stair without any hesitation. I climbed for hours. My mind grew distant and delirious. My every bone ached with exertion, and every step was an effort. Higher and higher into the tower. The walls grew close in upon me until I was climbing in a tunnel of stone. Still, I climbed. The black glass showed my reflection as I walked.

164

It distorted my eyes and my arms, my neck and my feet. I paid it no heed. I just kept climbing. My legs burned, and my mind wandered. But the stone blocked even the freedom of my mind. I could think of nothing but the stairs. I could see nothing but the steps. I could hear nothing but my feet rising and falling on the stone.

My eyes began to falter. *NO!* I couldn't stop now. This staircase should have ended long ago. There was no way it could have kept climbing. Therefore the only logical solution was that I was no longer climbing. I turned to the inner wall and reached out. My hand slid easily through the stone. I wanted to allow myself a moment of triumph, but I was so weary that I couldn't even manage that. I stepped fully into the center column. I felt the pressure of air and a blinding light. I instinctively closed my eyes as I collapsed on the floor with sheer exhaustion. I don't know how long I lay there without even moving. Slowly, ever so slowly, my eyes cracked open to behold the world.

Around me were what looked like windows that showed thousands of different areas all around Carin. I saw Grey with Galeerial riding on horses. I saw the *Lingering Ocean* with Rose still there serving drinks. I saw the Face Off, and Midway, Bastion and Ornus. I saw every city and the thousands of people in Carin. In the center of the room there was a pedestal. On that pedestal a book lay open. To either side stood a staircase with three stairs leading to an oval of light. The oval on the left was white, and the one on the left was black. I staggered to my feet to slowly approach the book that lay at the center of the room. The whole room was surrounded in a dome of those images. I placed my hands on the edges of the book and looked as words formed on the pages.

Aurum places his hands on the edges of me for support and looks as words form within. He reads them carefully as they form before his very eyes. A look of slight puzzlement encroaches upon his face, but this quickly becomes full surprise.

"What are you?" I breathed.

I am Ohm, and I am the Book of Ohm. I am the Chronicler of all of Carin. Within my pages are the stories of every person, place, and thing that has ever manifested itself within this Plate.

"Why am I here? Did you bring me here?"

No, you have been brought here to face judgment. Judgment. Is that what all this was? A test to determine my guilt or innocence. I thought back to the legions of ghosts following me through Thanatos. My guilt was not in question. That wasn't why I was here. I wanted answers. I wanted to know how this book knew my wife and daughter. I wanted to know why my friend was dead. I needed to know.

"I am guilty," I said.

Of course you are. Yet you have also caught the attention of one who would forgive your heinous crimes.

"Who?"

You know.

The Red Man.

"Where is he?"

He is coming. He does not rule here, but somewhere close.

"Do you rule this place?" I asked.

This is my domain. My eyes squeezed into a narrow glint.

"Then you are the one that I am going to kill." My voice was cold.

I implore you to do so.

I glared at the book. It was becoming more and more difficult to contain my emotions. *Why?* I had always been able to separate logical mind from my emotional side, but here I was losing that ability. I dug my nails into my palms. The pain gave me focus.

"You said that you contain the stories of everything. How is this possible?" beyond the stairwells, there was a door that led to a staircase that spiraled down. I heard the noise of what looked like a crank, and suddenly the floor grew transparent. Below was a sight that, despite all I had seen in the last few days, threatened to stagger me. Spiraling down hundreds of feet, shelves and shelves of books lined the walls. Every book was fitted with a number on its spine in silver. They were stacked thousands high. I couldn't see the bottom; all I saw was the never-ending wall of books. There must be millions of them.

Three hundred and forty-four million six hundred and fourteen thousand and six. The knowledge of all the world. It is yours if you are willing to pay the price, the book replied.

I blinked several times attempting to fathom that number of books. It was all but impossible.

"What price?" I asked.

Ultimate knowledge for utter imprisonment. Whomsoever enters my library, is doomed to never leave it save by being replaced willingly by someone of equal potential.

"How are you doing all this?" I breathed.

My curse has been in place since this world began. I have watched and recorded the poison that the Garenspawn have inflicted upon the body of this Plate. This Throne of Farsight that I am anchored to shows me every action and thought of every being in Carin, and I am bound to record it.

"Why?"

Because Supremor is a cruel being who gives love to some of his children while abandoning others.

I considered this for a moment. I concentrated on why I had come.

"Tell me about the Dawn of Darkness."

Written by Arestephan the Farsight in 790 as the second of the three-part prophecy known as The Final Mourning. The first part is The Twilight of Ages, and the third part is The Day of Destiny. The prophecy is meant for a being who can survive the Trials of Thanatos. A being such as you, Aurum. It is the last series of prophecy known to the people of Carin. There is nothing beyond them.

"Why am I here?"

Because you want answers.

I contemplated this for a moment.

"Why should I trust you?"

You shouldn't. But you are not the spawn of Garen, so I bear you no enmity. You passed the Trials of Thanatos. I cannot lie to you, only ignore you. Time for some real answers: answers that we had been searching for a long time, starting with the gallowglass prophecy.

"You know everything?"

Much.

"What is the Key to All Souls?" I fell to the ground beside the book.

"Are you prepared for the answer? Are you prepared to become my student and to learn the truth behind the war that you have thrust yourself into? Are you prepared for the coming breaking? Are you prepared to embrace the Champion within you?"

I turned, but I didn't have to in order to know who it was standing behind me at the top of the stairwell that led to the swirling black door. I could scarcely believe my eyes and ears, though. I had heard that voice many times in the last few months but never truly heard it. Yet there was no mistaking the being before me as anyone but the being from my dreams: the being named Alizar. He wore royal robes and a crown of light upon his head. His red skin glowed in the dim light of Acheron. His black eyes were inscrutable.

"Yes," I said breathlessly. He held out his hand to me.

"Then take my hand. Come with me to The Dreaming. Come, and bleed water for me." I took his hand. His skin was smooth. He turned and walked through the black door, and I followed him. As I passed through the door, my senses were assailed with color and light. It was like seeing for the first time. There was a vibrancy to everything in the grand throne room in which I stood. I saw Skyguard standing in glorious ceremonial armor and pillars of glass. The floor was the purest marble, and the air was like water. It was clear and fresh.

Alizar turned back to me. "Welcome, Aurum Guilden. Welcome to The Dreaming. Welcome…to Merhelden."

The Second Horseman

Fourteen

This war would be over before it even began. Tendra's eyes told a tale of horror at the sights that she was witnessing before her. The Skyguard had come to war against humanity. There were thousands of them, and more still were descending from the skies like a swarm of locusts. They were marshaled directly behind the unu. Even from so far away, she could see the sheen from the battle garb they wore. The sheer amount of steel was astonishing. They had come in the midday sun when the entire world could see them, and now a single Skyguard, centaur and unu marched toward the gates of her city. They came under the guise of a white flag. They were here to demand her surrender of the city, and she could not think of a single reason not to give them what they wanted.

Her city walls might as well have been two feet tall for all it mattered to the Skyguard. This wouldn't be a battle, it would be a slaughter.

Tendra looked to her right and saw Joven, and to her left she saw Jonathon, Merinam, and Wesley. Merinam looked scared. He was just a child. He had refused to leave with his mother two weeks ago. Instead, he had spent the last six days with Joven, Wesley, and Vizien drawing out battle plan after battle plan.

"Why are they here?" Tendra asked. *How could they possibly be here?* There was no answer from any of them. How could there be any answer? The Skyguard had not flown in force since the Fisherman's War six hundred years hence.

"We could not have predicted this," Merinam broke the silence with a whisper. "My Lady, there is no victory here. No matter what happens we will experience eighty percent casualties. The sea gives us no protection now," Merinam said.

"Hush, boy. When I want your doom saying I'll ask for it. Till then, hold your tongue," Wesley said. The men were all three standing strong: calm in the face of the coming onslaught. Beyond them stood thousands of her warriors: they would die for her without a second's hesitation, and die they would-by the thousands-as arrows rained down from foes beyond reach. Joven turned away from the visage and came in close to her.

"You need to recall everyone from the wall. Abandon it entirely." Joven broke the silence with a whisper.

"What?" she responded sharply.

"Any soldier that remains on the wall once the battle starts will be dead. That is a promise. Fighting Skyguard with open skies is suicide. Worse, it is stupidity, which is something we can ill afford. Give them a Jamon's Victory."

Jamon had been a human warlord who invaded Tyrin, an old unu city that was now only ruins. They had taken the city after a brutal three hour battle. The soldiers had been so eager to reach the city palace that they had not bothered to search the city on the way there. Unu troops had

170

withdrawn from the wall and had hidden in all of the houses of the city just waiting for the human army to pass them by, and had then slaughtered all of them that night while they had celebrated their victory.

"This is no longer a battle that can be won through conventional means. We need to put into motion every emergency plan that we have devised. We put everyone on ships and burn the rest. Place as many soldiers as can fit into the palace and various homes and businesses around the city, but we evacuate everyone else. As fast as possible." Joven said.

"What will prevent the Skyguard from simply killing us in the boats as we sail away?" Wesley asked.

"Us," Rayn broke in. Tendra hadn't noticed him approach. "But you need to be on the first boat out of here after you meet with the emissaries." Tendra turned on her heel as the five men and one boy fell in step behind her. She thought furiously. She needed a plan, and her next words would change everything. She crossed the battlements and poured confidence into her steps down to the ground level.

"Merinam, I want you to make for the boats. You will be on the first ship out. Make for Bicoln, send falcons to Jeric, and tell him to meet you there." Tendra said.

"My Lady, Terakeen would be better. The Star Tower will provide some defense against the Skyguard. Bicoln would just be a second Gemport." Rayn said. Tendra looked to Jonathon, who nodded his approval.

"The boy makes sense," he replied.

"Make it so." she said.

"I want to stay," Merinam said stubbornly. She almost smiled at his stubbornness.

"The time for planning here is over. You have done everything you can, but now Jeric will need you to defend the next city. You will be no use in this battle. Go. Your queen orders it." Merinam bowed and ran. She watched the boy slip between the ranks of soldiers as he ran.

"Queen Sumenel, I need to finish booby-trapping the aerie," Jonathon said. "I have enough volatile chemicals in the aerie that I will send Light Monks through the city doing the same to every food shop in the

171

city as well. Wesley, can you spread the word telling the soldiers not to enter there?"

"Aye, I'll get the word around."

Both men looked expectedly at Tendra.

"Go," she bid them. It was just her and the wizards now.

"Are you ready?" Tendra looked around for Vizien. She couldn't believe the man wasn't lingering around her waiting to meet with the Skyguard and with Qel. Nevertheless, she refused to wait for him. "Open the gates." She said. The gates let out a steady *clink clink clink* as the massive doors strained against the chains. *The Skyguard*. Fear gripped her. This was worse than she could have imagined.

"Give the order to abandon the walls," Joven urged.

"Not yet. You aren't the only one with plans," she said with a smirk. Rayn chuckled softly. Three horses were brought out to them, and Tendra swung up on her chestnut stallion. She tapped her heels into the horse, and rode out to meet her opposition.

"You don't seriously think they will give you time through negotiation?" Rayn asked.

"No, but we might be able to learn why the Skyguard are here." Tendra said. As they rode, Tendra marveled at how things had changed. There were no Light Monks, no Vizien; just her and two men that fancied themselves wizards going to meet an army made up of unu, centaurs, and Skyguard. It felt almost surreal.

"The Heart of Fires isn't real," Joven said in hushed tones. Tendra stiffened. She had never told him about the Heart of Fires. How could he possible know of it? She filed it away in the back of her mind. She would confront him later if she were still alive to do so.

"They don't know that," Tendra replied.

"True, but when you don't field it against them during this battle they will know it isn't here. They will be cautious, fearful even, but that won't last long. That must be why the Skyguard are here. The centaurs and unu are here to satisfy Qel's insatiable ambition. He doesn't care about the Heart save as a means to increase his own power. If you tell them you don't have it, they will think you are lying to them." Joven's words were the last between them as they approached the ground where a lone unu, a centaur, and Skyguard stood waiting.

The Skyguard was exactly what she had imagined a Skyguard to look when she had been a child, and her father had told her stories of Darrow and Myriel and other famous Skyguard. His muscles bulged in his armor, and his face was made of chiseled marble. His skin was the perfect hue. His black hair cascaded down around his shoulders and pooled onto his chest. She stared into his eyes, though, and found them to be disturbingly cold.

"Queen Sumenel. It is a pleasure to see you again. Wizards, I am surprised to see you alive." Qel of the Thousand Hammers greeted her. The last few months since the Council of the Five Pillars had not been kind to the unu, as evidenced by his lack of a right arm. The unu's taut muscles were covered in the pelts of ferals, and his gold hair remained long. "This is Lord Commander Veriel Stormrise of Cloud Breach. He leads the Skyguard. And you already know Herdmaster Jeronious." he Herdmaster inclined his head slightly to the ground before glowering at the wizards.

"You are a long way from home, Lord Commander," Tendra said.

"We have come for the blasphemers and for the Heart of Fires." the Lord Commander's voice dripped power. It sent a shiver down her spine.

"Seems we get to kill you again," Jeronious taunted. Qel ignored his companions' comments. "We are here to negotiate the surrender of your people and the Heart of Fires."

"And the formal execution of the wizards," Jeronious added. Tendra felt her stomach turn to knots at his words. Surrender. As if that was even an option. Qel would hunt humanity down from Bastion to Ornus, and then he would turn to the telos, then the giants, until there was nothing left that wasn't ground beneath the heel of his boot.

She could feel the silent calm radiating off of the two members of The Seven and the anticipation from the unu. From the Skyguard she could feel only a hunger. The Skyguard didn't want her to surrender any more than Qel did.

Tendra felt the entire world around her. It was stretched taut. The air was still, as if being held between the stares of all the eyes that were upon them. This was a balance point. From this moment on there was only the slow inevitable plunge downwards until one side fell into the abyss of extinction. She did not know how far away Jeric was with her army, and she feared that the star of her reign was about to enter its twilight.

"Then I am afraid we have nothing to talk about," Tendra said. Her voice was resolute and betrayed none of the fear she felt. There was not a single shaken note, not a single twain to her pronunciation of the words that she would be remembered by, for good or for ill. Qel's smile broadened. Jeronious stamped the ground impatiently.

"This is the only chance your people will be given. After this there will be no quarter. We will push and push until the spine of every human being lies broken and bloody by our axes and hammers."

"Be that as it may, there is but a single road for us to walk-" Veriel seemed to drink in her fear, and she felt it growing the more that she looked at him, "-that of war. She arrives on her black horse to take all us fools alike," she said simply. "We await your blood, Qel of the Thousand Hammers and Jeronious, and your wings, Veriel Stormrise." Veriel smiled. His eyes furled into something cruel. She suppressed a shiver as it wound its way up her lower back.

"I will enjoy watching you die." Jeronious said after her. She turned her back to them and began the ride back towards her people. She was numb the entire ride back. This was not the way things were supposed to happen. This was not the world that she had been raised to believe in. This was something far more dangerous. This was not what her father had prepared her for. The earth was hard beneath her mount's hooves, and every step seemed to be the tick of a clock counting down to their doom. Winter's chill had sapped the life away from these once-green fields and had left only the hard rock to survive.

"So it begins," Joven murmured.

"Would you have had me do anything else?" she said quietly.

"Given the circumstances, no, this was the only way it could have happened," Joven commented. A shout was hurled forth from the forward turrets as they approached. Tendra swung her eyes around, but they were drawn not to the ground but instead rose with the shadow of light that took shape. The Skyguard host slowly began to take to the air in a massive phalanx that spelled desolation for her city.

"My lady," Rayn began, "with the Skyguard here, we will not be able to hold the army here for more than two days."

"I will not abandon the Unyielding Throne. No non-human has sat in it since its construction. I will not allow my Citadel to fall." Tendra's words were desperate and sounded hollow even to her.

"You don't have a choice," Joven said, "and they will not wait for you to come to that realization." A second cry went out, and Tendra once again averted her eyes and saw a shift in the mass of swirling wings. They were wasting no time. The Skyguard forces began to break in waves, gliding down from the heights towards her city. The unu were not far behind as the dormant siege towers awakened from their slumber with bellows of protest. The iron gears turned iron wheels. There were thousands of them: tens of thousands of them. For the first time, she felt despair. *Where is the hope here?*

"My Lady!" Joven called. She snapped back to reality and put heel to horse forcing a full gallop for the gates. The large cast iron doors creaked slowly open as they hurtled forward. Tendra was through the doors first just before Joven, who followed a moment later, but Rayn was nowhere to be seen.

"Rayn?" Tendra looked back through the doors to see the wizard leap off his horse and offer her the same smile that Rowen had given her over and over again.

"Watch," Joven urged into her ears. The sky grew dark with the forms of the Burning Host coming to obliterate her city. The flapping of their wings created furious gusts of winds that blew her hair back from her face. Rayn began to stamp his staff against the ground. Seventeen times he did so as the wings grew louder and louder in her ears. Arrows began to scatter around Rayn's stoic form, but he didn't move, and no arrow could touch his form.

"Rayn!" she yelled at him. This time he didn't acknowledge her. On the eighteenth tap, she saw his body change. He went from relaxed to coiled. He was like a wolf prepared to pounce on his prey. Even through the loose brown robes that Rayn wore, she could see his shoulders and neck tense and his stance brace.

"FURY!" Rayn thundered. Hearing the monstrous tone come from so reserved a man shocked her. The wizard cocked his staff back so that the tip was on the ground as if gathering power.

"FURY!" again he bellowed and cast the staff forward. The air deformed and rippled around the wizard's staff and exploded from the tip. For a brief moment, Tendra couldn't hear anything. Then she heard cries. The wave collided and passed through the ranks of the Skyguard as it coursed upwards into the air. The Skyguard screamed and plummeted from the skies. The angelic beings desperately flapped their out-of-control wings as they spiraled downwards in a torrent of pain and confusion. The walls of Gemport erupted into a cacophony of cheers.

"Arrows, you fools!" Joven cried as Skyguard began to recover from their downward plunge. At his command, hundreds of arrows began to fly through the sky at the recovering Skyguard that shot towards them in a tight phalanx close to the ground. Tendra winced as dozens upon dozens of Skyguard didn't manage to recover from the spell that Rayn had cast and slammed into the ground, becoming naught but a mass of broken flesh on the fields. Rayn turned and sprinted into the safety of the city, and the doors creaked closed. Tendra embraced him. His staff smoked and the blackened wood at the top had peeled back like the petals of a flower.

"That was incredible," she breathed.

"Thank you." Rayn said panting. "We need to go." he pointed towards the walls. Tendra nodded and turned to lead the way, but a hand on her shoulder gave her pause.

"You need to get to the boats. You need to lead the retreat to Terakeen. Make sure Jeric gets there quickly." Joven said.

"Not a chance!" Tendra shot back.

"Go. Or by Supremor I will carry you there myself." Joven replied. Tendra gritted her teeth as a thought slowly formed in her mind. She turned from them and shouted.

"STEEL CEILING!" the command was echoed up and down the battlements as soldiers combined into echelons of six, with four holding shields to protect the two who held bows ready to fire. Joven nodded approvingly, but she didn't stay. She took off running towards The Eye. There was no chance that she would leave her people.

The Eye was a bakery, whose name was not actually The Eye, which had been converted into a forward command center so that the leaders could rendezvous somewhere closer to the walls than the castle. It also happened to be in the same direction as the docks.

Tendra's boots pounded the streets as she dodged soldiers rushing from the gates towards the castle and to various places within the city. *Tick, tick, tick*, the slight sounds grew in her mind. Tendra at first didn't realize what they were until she slid into the bakery and looked back out upon her path. Two dozen arrows lay strewn about in the space where she had just come from. A whistling and a blur of motion caused Tendra to jerk her head back inside the doorway and a long, perfectly fletched arrow embedded itself in the frame. She was being targeted.

The wild-eyed look of Wesley sent her rushing to him. Her chain mail and sword were fully displayed out on the table. Her head of the city guard knew she would be coming. She pulled the mail shirt over her head.

"Am I that predictable?" she asked.

"As the tides, My Lady."

"Everyone has been informed as to my cousin's plans?" she asked as she pulled on her breeches over her clothes.

Wesley nodded. "Yes, My Lady."

"Excellent. Then I want you to go to the aerie and get him out personally. I want you on one of those ships, Wesley. You will not die here."

"Never planned on it." Wesley said. "I didn't live through the Candlestick Wars to be put down by these animals."

"What do you know of the seas?" she asked.

"No Skyguard have been sighted offshore, nor have any ships been seen. Tendra mulled this over. *What did the unu hope to achieve by leaving the sea route undefended?* The unu had neither the equipment, nor a strategy, to deal with human naval superiority. It bothered her that so big a point was simply being ignored by the unu. As long as humanity had ships, then they contained a massive advantage in mobility. The problem was in offensive, and indeed in killing unu, centaurs, and Skyguard, which was markedly more difficult onboard a ship. Tendra fastened her sheath to her belt as she pulled her simple helmet on her head. "This is a very poor idea, Your Majesty."

Tendra looked into his eyes. "That it may be, but that is for history to decide." Wesley looked gravely at her for a moment before moving to the cages that stood in the back corner. Several falcons glared at her with their large, impassive eyes. Wesley handed her the rolled paper and a small well of ink.

"What are these?" Tendra pressed her ring into the ink and then onto the paper.

"Retreat orders to Terakeen and the announcement of the Skyguard entry into the war. They will be sent across the provinces." She finished pressing the last one and made ready to run. She pulled her gloves on. The leather on the inside rubbed hard against her fingers.

Her armor made her look just like any other commoner. She had done nothing to distinguish her station; all that would accomplish would be to attract attention, which was the last thing she wanted. Tendra looked into the skies, and her blood chilled. The Skyguard had recovered from Rayn's onslaught and now were raining down arrows upon the soldiers. The sky

178

was a mass of white streaks across the pale grey sky. Tendra took a breath and felt Wesley's arm upon her shoulder. She nodded.

She took off running into the corridors of the city. Her eyes flicked back and forth through the skies as they searched for Skyguard and Skyguard arrows. Instead she found something different: bodies. Soldiers on the roofs of houses and on the wall itself fell by the hundreds, with arrows sticking from every part of their bodies. She couldn't remember the last time she had been so scared. Everything was falling apart. The Skyguard were coming for them… and they were coming for her. She looked in the corner of her eye and saw her gallowglass bodyguard standing in the shadows. She approached it.

"Will you defend me?" She asked. The gallowglass wasted in and out of view, and its scaled skin covered its clawed hands. It tasted the air with its long forked tongue.

"Yesss," it hissed.

"Then listen to me now. I want you to follow Wesley and make sure he and my cousin get out alive."

"I am paid to protect you."

"You are paid to do what I tell you. Now go." she said. *I can't lose Jonathon too.* The gallowglass faded into the shadows, and she took that as acknowledgement and acquiescence.

She took a deep breath and went once more into the breach. She burst out into the main courtyard and saw the gates shuddering under the weight of the battering ram. It was noisy. The sound was so deafening she wondered how she could have been so oblivious to it before: The sound of shields smashing against spears, drums beating, fires crackling, orders being shouted.

She was drowning in the noise.

Her eyes flashed to the top of the wall where her soldiers were firing desperate shots at the Skyguard who were weaving through the air. The Skyguard were firing arrows to pave the way for the first onslaught of unu siege towers and ladders. Buckets of oil and torches were being hauled towards the gates. She traced a group of three Skyguard threaded through a group of arrows and slice through the six humans on the terrace. They barely had time to scream before they hit the ground. For an instant she was paralyzed by all of it. She tried to see it all, hear it all, feel it all. A soldier's body slammed to the ground in front of her with a ballistae bolt that had shredded his armor and penetrated through the man's entire body. She watched as the heavy rope it was chained too grew taut and pulled it back towards the wall.

Thrum! The sound of catapults cutting loose with burning pitch sailing through the air shook her from her stupor. Soldiers flooded away from the gates towards the buildings around her to prepare for the unu and centaurs. She pushed through the other way. She needed to get to the wall. She took the stairs leading up to the battlements two at a time. Tendra pulled Valiant out of its sheath as she reached the top. She looked out upon the fields before Gemport with despair.

Dozens of siege towers made their slow, steady approach only scant tens of meters from the walls. Hundreds of centaurs were rolling forward a forty-foot long steel ram that was being used to break the gates. The true force of the unu had been hidden from her until now. Twelve battalions of soldiers coursed forward in echelon with spears and war hammers raised high.

The wall shuddered as a tower let loose its warriors upon the top of the tower. Soldiers flowed by her towards the breach. She pushed through them. She had to find some kind of order to this chaos. She broke free of a group and found herself momentarily alone on the wall. She looked out up to the sky, searching for Veriel. He was the key; if they could take him out she was sure that she could reason with the Skyguard free of Qel's influence. A blur of air brought Tendra's sword hurling to the right. It was met by twin scimitars.

The Skyguard stood tall in comparison to her. His armor was all gold steel and white cloth. It flowed around his body. His purple eyes shone through his eagle's helm. He was awe-inspiring. An angel of death had come to claim her.

The jolt carried up her arm, and she recovered quickly into a downward slash that tried to bisect the Skyguard from shoulder to hip. The Skyguard moved fast, side-stepping and bringing his smaller swords to bear. The scimitars worked a hundred cuts at her, and she desperately parried as the Skyguard forced her backwards. She leapt backwards and lashed out in a flourish that carried her blade in a right feint before following with a blow to his neck. She carried her sword around and down the edge of his blade. Sparks flew as the metals screamed furiously at her.

The Skyguard blade trapped her sword with one of his own blades before following through with a strike towards her head with the second. She leapt out of the way, coming out of her roll just in front of the edge of the wall with the Skyguard in pursuit. A spear exploded through the Skyguard's neck, and he instantly went limp as his body was rent to the ground by a burly man in armor. He put his boot on the Skyguard's head and ripped the spear out. He reached his hand out to help her to her feet…as his head was lopped from his shoulders by the twin scimitars of another Skyguard.

She looked at the Skyguard's face with fear. A smirk rose to his lips. She looked at his eyes. He wasn't looking at her. She whipped her head around as she felt a steel gauntlet wrap around her wrist, and she jerked towards the edge of the wall and fell.

Valiant slipped from her grip, and she struggled to grasp it as it fell towards the earth. The steel somehow remained sharp in her view as she whirled towards the sky. Her captor soared upwards, carrying her with him. Tendra felt her skin tingle and her hair rise an instant before the lightning bolt caused the Skyguard's head to explode in front of her. The wings convulsed twice, and Tendra's entire body shuddered from the strike. The Skyguard's wings burst into flame around her, and she ripped her hand free.

She was falling.

Tendra used to think about dying every day. Right after her mom died, the nightmares were born. She would have nightmares of poison, and fire, and spikes, and swords, and assassins. She would wake over and over again, screaming into the night. Her father would come in and light a fire in

181

her room and would sit with her until she would fall asleep, and he would still be there when she awoke again and again during the night. In all those nightmares she had never had one of falling to her death. Now she knew why.

The wind streamed through her face as she fell. Her heart, which had been pounding in her ears, was now deathly silent. The wind drowned out everything. She could no longer see the ground for so many tears whipping through her eyes.

The reason why she never dreamed of this death…was because for the first time since her father had died, she felt at peace. The surrounding battle lost all importance, color, and description. There was only her, and her steadily approaching demise. She was the eye of the storm.

"I will see you soon, Jakob," she whispered, and with the wind, she was sure that only the two of them could hear it.

The Iron Men, The Stuffed Men

Fifteen

"Where is my horse?" Galeerial asked. The burning hand of the Iron Man sent shadows flickering throughout the bitter night. It cast no warmth however.

"Good idea. He looks heavy; we will put him on yours," Grey replied.

"No. I'm going to Cloud Breach." Galeerial saw Grey audibly sigh and mutter something under his breath.

"How about I just kill you here, and then we will take the horses to Dynast and not waste any more of anyone's time?" Grey replied. "You have been saying the same nonsense over and over again. It hasn't even been two weeks. Less than two week's worth of training. That's not enough. This detour, however, provides a unique opportunity. You can get the training you need, and I can watch you get some blood on your hands." Galeerial stared at the wizard. Galeerial's entire body was shaking. Galeerial reached down and picked up the scimitar that Grey had dropped to the ground. He was inches away from the wizard's face.

"You want to see blood on my hands?" Galeerial hissed. "Veriel is marshaling my people to burn this world to the ground. You would have me waste time fighting in the north while my people die in the south. Curse you, wizard. Curse you."

"Wizard?" the Iron Man's voice broke the silence between them. "The Fifteenth Finger thought his eyes were deceiving him when he saw the other human being held aloft by your hand."

Grey nodded sheepishly. "Yeah, I'm good like that," he said. "But if you could hold off on your accolades for one minute, I need to beat some sense into my...narrow-minded friend." Galeerial seethed. His hands were fists, and his fingers dug into his palm. "Listen to me, Galeerial. Rule Three; do you honestly think that anything I've done is because I wanted to? Do you think I want to be up here teaching you how to not be such a self-absorbed, self-destructive psychopath? Aurum is on his deathbed, and the rest of my brothers are down south fighting and dying while I am here with you. I may not be the best swordsman, but I am here because you saved Aurum's life. Every day I look to the south and wish I was there. I asked you to be one of us, and you agreed. So I really don't care if you don't like what I have been doing. You need to stop whining and start living in the real world. Now if you give me another outburst like what you just did, I'll slit your throat...period. We're going to Dynast. You're not going to sulk, and you *are* going to train all the way there. When we get there, you are going to help me kill troops until I am satisfied you have learned enough to be of use *and* stand some semblance of a chance of not getting yourself killed. Then we will go to Cloud Breach. I understand you're worried about your people, but right now you won't make a single bit of difference to whether a single Skyguard lives or dies. You said you weren't afraid, but you are. You are so very afraid. I showed you a taste, and you ran like child. If you want to become a man, you have to push past all this. You are so

184

angry. We'll use that anger to burn Veriel to the ground starting with his army at Dynast. Now go get on your horse, and let's go."

Galeerial stood in the bitter cold of the darkness. Smoke burned from his mouth as he watched the wizard walk over to confer with the Iron Man. He fingered his scimitar. Galeerial breathed in and out. He watched the smoke from his breath rise into the cool sky. He slowly unfurled his hands. He had made a deal. He was better, stronger. He could kill Veriel now. He knew that he could, but he had set himself on this path. Now it was time to walk it.

Galeerial sheathed his blades and followed Grey towards where the wizard stood with the Iron Man. The Fifteenth Finger stared at him as he walked towards them.

"We had better get going," Galeerial said. "You can explain everything on the way." Grey nodded.

"We'll ride Grey's horse; the iron man will take the other. We need to get there as fast as possible."

Grey whistled, and the two horses came trotting forwards. Grey swung up onto his brown charger.

"The Fifteenth Finger can't go with you," the Iron Man interjected.

"Excuse me?" Galeerial replied.

"The Fifteenth Finger must travel to Harin's Dale. He must reawaken the old fires. The rusted bonds must be polished." Galeerial looked up at Grey.

"Ummm. Fifteenth Finger...the centaurs are in no position to help you right now. The south is at war. The centaurs can spare no soldiers to help here," Grey said. "I'm sorry." The Fifteenth Finger stood emotionless for a moment. The fire in his hands flickered, and Galeerial thought he saw a face within the fire. He was communicating with the Head of the Iron Giant.

"The Fifteenth Finger will guide you to Dynast," the Iron Man's voice was flat, completely devoid of emotion, "but he does not need a horse. The fire makes the iron strong."

185

"Very well," Galeerial leapt astride his own horse. "We should waste no time." The Finger moved fast, easily keeping pace with them on their horses, and the green fire on his hands illuminated the night before them as they rode. Galeerial waited for Grey to ask the Iron Man questions, but none were forthcoming. Galeerial followed his lead and kept silent. They cut away from the forest towards the lower rolling hills that led up into the Sparkling Mountains.

They rode through the bitter night, and by the time the world was greeted with the first light of day, Galeerial was practically numb. He rubbed his chest over and over again to try to keep warm. His clothes seemed to do little to keep him warm, but neither Grey nor the Iron Man seemed to feel it.

The Snake River greeted them as they rounded the southern crest of the Sparkling Mountains. The only mountain range in all of Carin, the Sparkling Mountains, held nearly all the ore that made up all of the weapons and tools of the people in Carin. There were extensive silver mines to the east of Lake Lefron and some farther north, but nothing compared to what the Iron Men delivered. The Iron Men had lived there for as long as anyone could remember. They had dealt exclusively with the centaurs after the Dread War, but before that, it was not uncommon to see Iron Men enjoying hospitality everywhere from Winter Crest to Ornus. Everyone depended upon the Iron Men, and so they were kept out of most conflicts, and everyone provided them aid should they ask it. Steel made the world go round, and steel flowed from Dynast like water.

The Sparkling Mountains were visible from afar, but it was not until they reached the base of the massive range that Galeerial realized just how high the peaks stretched into the sky. When he had been able to fly, he and Ezekiel and Ezekiel's wife Jariah had flown through these mountains many times, but he had never once landed on the ground and looked up. The world seemed much taller viewed from the earth than it did from the sky.

The heights of the mountains strove through the clouds to reach the sun, and their snow-covered tips brought an inadvertent shiver to

Galeerial's spine. Their physical training ground to a halt as they drove relentlessly towards Dynast, but the mental training remained vicious in its pace. Grey interrogated him endlessly about Veriel. Every scrap of information that Galeerial could dredge from his memory, Grey soaked up with an edgy calm. However, everything they spoke about was in hushed tones, away from The Fifteenth Finger. Neither of them trusted him, and Galeerial doubted their hushed tones garnered much confidence from The Finger either. Galeerial thought about Jariah and Ezekiel. He hoped they were alive, but knowing Veriel, they were both probably enduring the same kind of torture he had been subjected to. But there was no wizard to come and save them.

The sun brought with it tentative warmth that was nowhere near as strong as Galeerial hoped it would be. They cut north near midday and were soon rewarded with a winter freeze. The ground was covered with frost, and storm clouds gathered menacingly in the north. They kept up their northern march, but it slowed from the evening's pace to a steady trot. They would still arrive at Dynast by nightfall, provided they didn't get caught in the storm, which Galeerial didn't believe they would be lucky enough to escape. As the day wore on, finally Grey asked the Iron Man about the force that was attacking them.

"The Left Hand of the Iron Giant is not a warrior, but that is not to say that the rest of the body is unversed in the art of fighting. The Iron Giant sequestered itself within the mountains to escape the wars of the surface, and for the most part it has worked. With the exception of the Dread, no one has dared to threaten The Iron Giant in The Iron Giant's underground home. The ways are dark and small in the farther reaches, perfect for Caminus, what the world calls Iron Men, but for the other races, not as much. The Iron Giant began to lose contact with the outer tributaries in the middle of the summer. A small expeditionary force was sent to investigate, and none returned. The Skull of The Iron Giant then determined that The Iron Giant was at war. All mining stopped, and the old vaults were opened. The Iron Giant withdrew all the Arms and Legs of the Iron Giant back to Dynast, the head city, Huginn and Muninn the shoulder cities, and Heidrun, the body

187

city. All was quiet for three days, and then drums were heard. Drums pounded day and night to a steady rhythm, never ceasing for three days. Still, The Iron Giant held fast. Caminus are, above all, patient. Caminus are like the stone itself in that regard."

"On the seventh day, they attacked. Humans and ferals combined into a single force. They had to have dug through the other side of the mountains. The Iron Giant doesn't know how long it might have taken them, but this was not some raiding force: this was an army sent to destroy The Iron Giant. In the intervening months, The Iron Giant has made them pay for every inch of ground that they have taken, but they have taken it by the meter. Now, only Dynast stands. The tunnels were sealed, but they are coming. That was when The Skull of The Iron Giant sent The Fifteenth Finger to rally the centaurs to The Iron Giant's cause. A centaur trading party normally comes to meet with The Left Foot of the Iron Giant on the first day of each new month, but none came. For seven months, none have come. The Fifteenth Finger was sent to find them."

"The war," Grey rationalized, "Tell me about this force; how do they fight?"

"The Left Hand are not warriors; The Left Hand knows the trade, naught else," The Fifteenth Finger replied.

"Do you think this is Veriel's army?" Grey asked Galeerial.

Galeerial thought on this for a moment. "I don't know why Veriel would bother fighting against them. They pose no threat to him as they stand, and as long as he prevented any centaurs from reaching Dynast, then they would never know of the southern war. It makes no sense to me. Ferals and humans aligning themselves with Veriel doesn't either."

"Money is a powerful motivator. Greed may hold no power over your race, but in humans it is an all-too-common flaw. As for the ferals, I thought they were all wiped out in our war. How would they have gotten to the other side of the world? More importantly, why would they abandon their lands while the war was occurring? Unless they just had no idea about what is happening in the south, but why would Kaelish allow such an army

188

to go unused if his people were in such dire straits?" Grey pondered aloud. The Iron Man offered no insight.

"There are too many questions lacking rational answers," Galeerial replied. "I don't like this; I don't like this at all. But if we can fight through the front ranks, we may be able to find a leader who can tell us what we want to know. That is our first priority. Has a leader revealed himself to you? Have they attempted to talk with your people at all?" Galeerial addressed the Iron Man.

"The Left Hand is not one of the Skull of the Iron Giant. The Left Hand knows the trade, naught else." The Fifteenth Finger repeated.

"You said the Dread has been reborn. Why did you say that?" Galeerial inquired.

"The first day of the attack on Heidrun, a man entered the chamber before all others. The Iron Giant's arrows greeted him. He took six to the chest; but they fell out of him as he turned into a shadow dragon and proceeded to kill hundreds of Caminus," The Fifteenth Finger said.

"A shadow dragon…" Grey mused. Galeerial considered this for a moment. What if Veriel had found the Dread? The alternative was almost too horrifying to consider. The Dread War had all but destroyed the world and had laid the seeds for the rifts between nations that persisted to this day. No one had quite known what the Dread was; only that he had marshaled a vast army quickly and had laid waste to everything that had been thrown against him. The Radiance had assassinated him in some unknown manner. It hadn't been some epic noble confrontation between light and darkness, but rather what needed to be done to end the war. If it was true then, why had the Radiance lied about what happened to the Dread? What was he doing moving against the Iron Men? Why now? Tdo many questions and not enough answers. It was becoming a motif. Though the answer to the last question Galeerial had some suspicions about, namely, the Seven: Galeerial didn't know if it was possible. He looked at Grey. Could this man, his brother, be in league with the Dread? Or was he merely a catalyst? Galeerial kicked his horse to move up to where the Iron Man was jogging along with them.

"You have remarkable stamina. Don't you get tired?" Galeerial asked.

"The fire makes the iron strong. The Iron Giant keeps The Fifteenth Finger strong," The Fifteenth Finger replied.

"I guess there is a more than one reason they call you Iron Men." The Iron Man turned his head to glare at him. "What?" Galeerial replied, slightly taken aback.

"Iron Men is a name of mocking that the humans gave when they thought The Iron Giant was but men with steel grafted to the skin, but Caminus are much more than that. Caminus are the fire born. Yet the world knows only Iron Men."

"I am not human either," Galeerial replied. "Well...I wasn't. I was a Skyguard once."

The Iron Man's eyes betrayed no emotion. "You were cut from the Angel's Body and crafted onto the Human's?" Fifteenth Finger asked. Galeerial considered this for a moment.

"Something like that," he replied.

"Every piece of the body is valuable. When something is cut off the entire body weakens. Fire must be used to burn away where the cut was made, this hurts the body. The Angel's Body is less for not having you, and the Human Body is more," Fifteenth Finger said. Galeerial regarded the squat being that strode next to him. For someone who proclaimed to know naught but trading, he seemed of incredibly sound mind.

They rode along in silence as the clouds beckoned them closer and closer. They were growing near. Galeerial had never seen Dynast, since the city was underground, but the gates on the north side of the mountains were visible from the air. The terrain was different when viewed at ground level, but on the whole Galeerial knew that they were getting close. A flicker of movement in the mountains to their right almost caused Galeerial to start, but he held himself in check. He nonchalantly focused his eyes on the stone, and slowly shapes began to take form. Half a dozen Iron Men glared down at them, motionlessly propped against the sheer cliffs that trailed along with them. Their black metallic skin blended perfectly with the stone behind them, and Galeerial struggled to make out each of the individual forms. Galeerial noticed that he had fallen slightly behind Grey and kicked his mount to speed up slightly.

"How many did you count?" Grey asked quietly as Galeerial brought up his horse next to the wizards.

"Six on the bluff," his eyes wandered back up, and he spotted two more creeping along with them. "Two others are keeping pace."

"Very good, but you missed the one right in front of us." Grey grinned, though when he spoke his mouth appeared to not move at all. "Are you worried?"

"Can our swords cut through iron?"

"Mine can. I don't know about yours, but I figure a blade like that can cut through whatever it wants."

"Then not at all."

"Tell them nothing."

"Fifteenth Finger, would you like to explain to me why we are being shadowed?" Grey asked. Fifteenth Finger stopped and turned back to them. The Iron Men stared at them.

"The enemy has spies everywhere. You two happened to be right on The Fifteenth Finger's path to Harin's Dale. You prevented The Fifteenth Finger from going farther. The Skull of the Iron Giant wants you to tell exactly who you are, and what you were doing there." Galeerial and Grey exchanged glances as they brought their mounts to a halt. The rest of the Iron Men dropped to the ground, encircling them.

"It would be most unwise to raise arms against us," Galeerial replied darkly. His hand wrapped around the hilt of Eon on his back.

"Forgive The Fifteenth Finger if he does not take your word."

"I will not accept The Fifteenth Finger's apology. You asked us to come, and so we came. Now we have already diverted too far from our path to turn back. We are going through Dynast and the darkness beneath the mountain either with you or through you," Grey said. "I have magic, big magic. You really don't want to tempt me to bring it down upon you."

"Actually, a demonstration is what the Skull of the Iron Giant requires for your passage through the tunnels, and in fact entrance into the Sparkling Mountains. You will never find the gate without a Caminus to show you the way."

Grey licked his lips and exchanged a glance with Galeerial. Grey shrugged.

"What kind of demonstration does the Skull require?" Galeerial asked. The Fifteenth Finger gestured to one of the Iron Men, and he strode forth. "This is the Seventh Artery of the Body of the Iron Giant. You will kill him with magic."

"No," Grey said. No one moved for an instant. Galeerial felt the tension in the air, and he tightened his grip on Eon. Grey swung down from his horse and reached out with his hand. "Like heck, lift." This struck Galeerial as odd. Those were the same words he had said outside of Whisperwood right before he had used magic to lift him into the air. Galeerial watched as the Iron Man rose up into the air. *Some kind of magic words?* Grey held the Iron Man in the air effortlessly. He maneuvered the Iron Man around in the sky above them. "Satisfied?" Grey asked.

"The Skull is satisfied in your abilities as a magician. Have you woken the Drowned Flame?" The Fifteenth Finger replied. Grey lowered the Iron Man to the ground. The Iron Man kept the same stoic impression on his face as always. Galeerial studied his posture but could make nothing of it.

"I don't know what that means," Grey replied. "Our magic comes from our own land, the land of Cambria across the Rift." The green flames in Fifteenth Finger's hands flickered rapidly, but no questions were forthcoming for a moment.

"Why should The Iron Giant believe you?"

"Because we have no reason to lie," Grey responded.

"Why did you agree to come?" The Fifteenth Finger drilled.

"Because he needs to learn how to fight people that want to kill him," Grey answered, jerking his thumb in Galeerial's direction. "Now, you can either accept our help, or we can kill you all and go on our merry way.

What is it going to be?" Grey's voice went from light-hearted to deathly serious.

They hadn't talked much about fighting Iron Men; in fact, they hadn't spoken at all regarding it. There had been really no need. The Iron Men had had no dealings with the outside world in several generations, outside of trading with centaurs. Nevertheless, Galeerial was still a far better warrior now than he had been a week ago. Fifteenth Finger looked at the assembled members of his collective. The flame flickered in his hand and Galeerial thought he saw a face in the depths of the green fire. Galeerial's eyes shifted. He didn't know how this would go, but he would be ready if it went south.

Galeerial's eyes shifted back and forth. *Awareness is everything in a battle. You can't block a sword that you don't know is there.* Grey's words echoed in his mind, and at first Galeerial thought the wizard had spoken to him, but Grey's eyes were firmly locked on Fifteenth Finger.

"You will accompany the assembled to meet with the Skull of the Iron Giant. They will decide if your tale is truthful or not. If it is not, then you will be summarily executed; if it is, then The Iron Giant will welcome your assistance against the enemy."

"I can live with that," Grey replied. "What of our horses?"

"Leave them. They have no place beneath the mountain." Galeerial dismounted and began to unpack his saddlebags, stuffing the contents into the pack he wore on his shoulders. It wasn't much: a firestone, some dry bread, salted beef, the water skin, skinning knife, and a length of rope. They had traveled quick and lean from Winter Crest. "Shall we?" Grey asked.

"Yes." The Fifteenth Finger gestured instead towards the cliff face, and two of the Iron Men backed slowly away from them. They seemed to pull the stone apart to reveal a tunnel leading deep into the bowels of the mountain. The flat of an ax on Galeerial's back prompted him forward, but he dug his heels. "Move," The Fifteenth Finger said. Galeerial stared into abyss before him. "I said, move." he was shoved violently forward. Galeerial whipped around and kicked Fifteenth Finger in the chest. A half dozen crossbows were raised against him.

"WAIT!" Grey bellowed. "Galeerial, listen to me. We have to go in there."

"No." Galeerial shook his head. "I can't go in there. I can't go in there." His throat clenched with every word. Galeerial hated himself for his fear. He could smell the staleness of the air before him.

"What is his problem?" Fifteenth Finger asked.

"He's afraid of close spaces." Grey drew in close to Galeerial and dropped his voice low. "Listen to me: this is not your greatest fear. You saw it with the drugs and The Wither. You saw it, and you beat it. You beat it with your anger. Use that anger now. That road," Grey gestured behind him, "that road leads to Veriel. It is the only road now. There is no turning back. If you want your vengeance, then you will walk the dark road. You will march into the darkness, or you will be too late to make a difference."

Galeerial's eyes were transfixed by the darkness in the cave. He could scarcely see five feet into its depths. He swallowed hard.

"Don't ask this of me," Galeerial said.

"You already agreed to it," Grey snapped.

"I didn't know it would be like this."

"It doesn't matter. This is reality. This is our road. There is nothing that can change that. We go forward or we lose. Down that road," Grey pointed to the hole in the mountain, "is your revenge. Down that road is your destiny. I will walk with you, but I will not let you cast your life aside out of fear."

Grey turned away from Galeerial and strode boldly towards the entrance. He took one step into the mouth.

"Wait," Galeerial called out. Grey stopped and held out his hand. Galeerial took the first tentative steps forward. The cave grew into a mouth, a gaping maw waiting to swallow him. He was marching down the gullet of a beast. He grasped Grey's hand as he entered into the cavern, and immediately the light of one of the Iron Men's flames ignited around them.

Galeerial's breathing immediately grew shallow as they entered the close air of the cave. He felt the rising tightness in his chest, and he struggled to fight it down. The walls were close, and his fear made them feel even closer. The cold air threatened to freeze his muscles in place.

"Know your fear and overcome it," he heard Grey whisper. *Know fear. Know fear. I am afraid.* Galeerial slowed his rapid breathing as he was pushed along. He focused on each individual breath as if it were the most important thing in the world. They were simultaneously descending and moving farther east into the mountain. From what Galeerial could perceive through his focused haze, they were traveling in a relatively straight line, but he couldn't be sure.

"Now you are going to run," The Fifteenth Finger hissed. He pressed his axe into Galeerial's back, but he couldn't focus on that. Their pace quickened, and Galeerial had to focus less on his breathing as on the pace the Iron Men pushed them into keeping. The running distracted him from the brown stone walls that led down, down, down into the heart of the mountain. His feet stumbled as much as ran forward, and all the while he could hear the pounding footsteps besides Grey's; that and the omnipresent axe on his back told him they weren't alone.

As they ran, a faint blue light began to fade into view before them. At first Galeerial thought it was a fire, but it was too soft and too steady to be so. As they moved closer to it, he realized it was an end. He would have breathed a sigh of relief if all his breath wasn't being used simply to keep pace. They had been running for what seemed like hours with all-too-infrequent stops for rest and water, They were trying to wear Grey and Galeerial down, and they were succeeding. His legs burned as much as his lungs, though the air had grown substantially warmer as they moved farther and farther underground. They grew closer to the doorway, and Galeerial was forced to duck as the tunnel ceiling began to lower. A few meters beyond the doorway, was a wall with a ladder that stretched upwards. The blue light came from the stone of the walls and floor. They slowed to a walking pace as they emerged. The stone of the floor changed color from a soft blue to a harsh, fiery red everywhere they stepped. He looked closer and saw that it was not rock but a hard algae of some kind growing on the rock. Galeerial turned his eyes away from the burning crimson light. He

195

looked up and saw the ceiling about twenty five meters above them with a gap between the ceiling and the top of the wall. The Fifteenth Finger was already halfway up the ladder, with each rung glowing a brilliant red as he put pressure upon it, when Galeerial was pushed towards it.

"Climb." Galeerial reached out to the iron ladder and began his ascent. It took him only a few seconds to reach the top, and while scrambling up he tasted air that was lacking in the damp close texture of the air below. He looked up and gaped.

What he beheld could only be described as majestic. Even having lived his entire life in the awe-inspiring vistas of Cloud Breach, he was still rendered speechless by the sight he found before him. Dynast, the head city of the Iron Men, exploded outward from the side entrance into a massive citadel that easily dwarfed Cloud Breach, and even Gemport. Stone towers scraped the glowing blue stone of the sky. The algae provided constant illumination from above. The city itself was a sprawling mass of stone houses that stretched as far as he could see. Massive tunnels split away from the city, and Galeerial could only marvel at how high the ceiling itself was- at least a thousand feet. Twelve Iron Men stood with weapons drawn as Galeerial rose, while behind them were eleven others with violet fire in their hands. They watched him with wary eyes. The Fifteenth Finger held his hands out before him. Hundreds more Iron Men wove about the city going about their daily lives. Grey clambered up behind him with his eyes wandering just like Galeerial's.

"Well isn't that something?" he murmured.

"Indeed," Galeerial breathed. No other Iron Men followed them up, and Galeerial peered back to see all of them gone. Galeerial strove to memorize every facet of the city, for he knew he would never be afforded an opportunity such as this again.

"We are the Skull of the Iron Giant. We have heard your story. We want to know what you have to offer us." One of the Iron Men with violet fire spoke up. Grey looked at Galeerial.

"How do you feel about assassins?" Grey replied. Galeerial fought back a puzzled look to instead remained stoic.

196

"What?" a different Iron Man cut in.

"We will assassinate the leader of this army for you, and then we will be on our way through the same tunnels that they used to enter your home, and destroy them. This will prevent your enemy from escaping and the lack of leadership will allow you the perfect avenue to kill them all in one fell swoop."

"That is all?" still another Iron Man asked.

"That's the deal. Just consider us two concerned citizens trying to help out. We go, we kill;, we destroy, we leave; simple as that," Grey said. Again, silence for a moment, as the violet flame in their hands flickered briefly before going out.

"Are you mocking us?" *I hope you know what you are doing, Grey.* Trying to discern emotion on the Iron Men's face was all but impossible. Their lips didn't move at all when they spoke, and only their eyes offered any hint of expression.

"Not at all. I'm respecting the fact that you don't trust us, and don't exactly want us to be here. Also, the fact that you need serious help, which we can provide, means that you really have nothing to lose in this agreement." in each of their hands the same violet fire ignited. The flame made no sound this time, though, and the flickering tongues offered no strained images for him to try and guess what was happening.

"Very well. We accept your offer."

Grey smiled.

"However, you will be blindfolded while walking through the city. Should you be captured, you would not be able to reveal anything about our city through torture."

"Outstanding. Now is there any chance I could get my hands on one of those axes you are carrying?"

One of the Iron Men stepped forward and pulled his axe from its loop on his belt offering it to the wizard. Galeerial cocked an eyebrow at Grey.

"Souvenir," he said with a shrug. "Now, let's go, and you can show me what you got."

197

"With pleasure," Galeerial replied.

"But first, we need a nap," Grey proclaimed.

The Head of the Iron Giant exchanged glances. "The Fifteenth Finger will show you to quarters." Galeerial smiled. He was exhausted. Sleep would be a blessing.

The Fifteenth Finger approached them with a black velvet hood. Galeerial was pushed roughly to his knees, and the hood engulfed him. He squeezed his eyes closed as it did so. The world went dark around him, and they began their slow trek through the city.

Two Share a Single Face
Sixteen

"Rikard... Rikard...Rikard." At the sound of his name spoken a third time, Rikard slowly passed into the conscious world. His every motion brought fire to his limbs. He couldn't see out of his left eye and generally felt like he had been beaten on an anvil for days before being allowed to slide off in a liquid form. He began to run through an assessment of his injuries as he slowly tensed each of his muscles. He grunted in dissatisfaction as he found he could not move his right arm at all. The entire world was fuzzy, and he struggled to focus on the voice that was shattering his eardrums.

"Shut up, you stupid petulant voice. I dun wanna talk right now," Rikard mumbled. Even that soft effort brought a splintering pain to his temples. He blinked heavily and rapidly to see the blurred image of himself staring back at him from a wall rack.

"Stop your moping, Rikard. I need you to focus. Breva," the strain in Dorian's voice was evident, "is she alive?" Rikard looked towards his brother and saw the coolness of his demeanor contrast with the need evident in his eyes.

"I dun know," Rikard said regretfully. "Nod tried to take her; I killed him. She ran, I lost her, fought a human: blue eyes, black armor, got my teeth kicked in." Dorian didn't say anything for a long time. He just hung there in considered silence. Rikard felt something stir in his mind; it almost tickled. Not in the good, humorous, or affectionate way, but in the annoying and disgruntling way that perturbs you. It was disappointment. Yesterday had been a day full of failures. Rikard didn't have to see the calm of Dorian's eyes to know that he blamed him for the loss. Dorian would never admit it; Dorian didn't let anything disrupt his outer presence. At least, not since Father had died. Before that he had been a stew of emotions. Not anymore, though. It was unnerving to most people, but Rikard could see through it, just like he did now.

"Have you seen the Skyguard?" Dorian asked in his same measured voice. That was his brother, always thinking.

"Yeah, the knight was his. How long have I been here?" Rikard said through a pitched groan. A fractured humerus, with some shredded muscles no doubt, a concussion explained his inability to think clearly, and the lack of sight in his eye probably had something to do with the ached swelling on the left side of his head. He felt around his mouth with his aching tongue and found a missing molar. He was pleased that only one was gone. His left hand had some semblance of movement, for which he was grateful, though his right lower leg was completely numb. Rikard's entire face ached, as if it was one big scar.

"Here? Just over a day, but it has been four since the feast. Terel has been cementing his hold on the unu. He has been waiting to sacrifice us for the final day of the feasting celebrations." *Four days? I have been unconscious for four days.*

200

"Lucky us," Rikard muttered. That would give them time to mount an escape.

"Rikard, that's today., Dorian replied. *So much for that plan.* "Not only that, but I hear that Qel is gone along with the Skyguard to join the frontlines at Gemport. Terel and the rest of the clanmasters leave tomorrow-with our heads, most likely."

"Well, you know how much I love family reunions," Rikard grimaced.

"Do you know how I know when things are really dire?"

"I bet you are going to tell me," Rikard replied.

"When you start trying to make jokes." Silence lengthened between them. "What did you do to the gates? I heard pounding on them for the better part of a day before the splintered and came crashing down."

Rikard tried to smile, but it brought a splintering pain to his head, and so he abandoned the effort. "Rayn cooked it up. Some kind of corrosive acid; it reacts with the iron, causing it to fuse with other iron molecules around it. I coated the gap between the gates with it, so when they closed the doors they just stuck together."

"Brilliant," Dorian replied.

"It would have been more brilliant if it would have kept them caged for a while longer."

"Fair enough. Tell me about the knight. You said he was a human?" Rikard merely wanted to sleep. He strove for that oblivion, but the height of the sun coursed on his body, causing his wounds and eyes to burn.

"It was a big human." Rikard opened his eyes back up and looked at Dorian. "Twenty feet tall, giant fangs, acid dripping from his sword." Dorian looked at him disapprovingly. "Alright, he was half a hand taller than me. Like I said, black armor strong enough to block the knives, blue eyes. Really fast. I hit him right in the center of the eyes, through the face plate, and it didn't even stun him."

Dorian's eyes grew pointed. "Are you ready to die today, Rikard?"

"Always," he replied. "But I know Joven gave us a contingency plan for this."

201

"Not exactly. This is my plan." Rikard regarded Dorian dubiously. "Trust me." *I always did, and look what you did to my life because of it.* Rikard kept his mouth shut.

Rikard's view faced the almost-risen sun, and he squinted out at the rooftops. They were in a different cell from the one that Dorian had been placed in previously. He saw a figure in the distance. His mind worked to reconcile the difference and came to the realization that the person was human and quite small, a child even. As his eye adjusted, he saw that it was a young girl. He blinked heavily to try to clear his vision further, but she was gone. Rikard shook his head. *Just what I need...hallucinations.*

A rustling of the door caused Rikard to shift his gaze back to the room in time to see Terel enter. At nine feet tall and probably close to four hundred pounds, the massive unu's presence filled the room as easily as his girth did. His golden eyes regarded them dispassionately.

"Extraordinary," Terel whispered as he looked upon them. "You continue to amaze me, Dorian of the Thousand Hammers." Terel turned his attention to Rikard. "And you? What is your name, human?"

"Chuckles," Rikard said dryly. A backhanded blow to the head threatened to send him back to oblivion. Rikard held onto the fractured remnants of the lights around him and struggled for consciousness.

"His name is Rikard," Dorian answered. Rikard pulled his head back upwards to glare at Dorian, who simply shook his head. "I would know of my wife, Clansmaster."

"Spoilsport," Rikard spit.

"Quiet, Rikard. Clansmaster?" Dorian's gaze did not waver from the massive unu.

"Your wife will pay a traitor's death." Rikard watched Dorian's muscles flex against the chains that bound him.

"She's innocent," Dorian's words passed through gritted teeth.

"I take no pleasure in the fact; you know that Dorian of the Thousand Hammers. But by the actions of yo-"

"She's INNOCENT!" Dorian bellowed.

Terel glared down at him. "You and your brothers, you have condemned her to death."

"What actions have I committed that would be counted as treason, Clansmaster?" Dorian asked. Rikard smiled. Now the real Dorian was starting to come through: Dorian the warrior. His voice was sharp in the air.

"You attacked and killed members of your own clan."

"In self-defense," Dorian countered.

"So you say. Yet, other tales have reached my ears. This is not all. You and your brother mock the Balance by your existence. You threaten to destroy everything we have built. You are The Storm that has come to destroy us." Rikard started at this. Even with the little regard he held for the Balance, he knew enough about it to know of The Storm. The Storm was the antithesis of the Balance. The Storm existed solely to create chaos and to topple the scales that held all things. The idea that Terel believed them to be The Storm meant that he feared them. "But it won't happen. Even a storm needs time to build; time we will not give to you. We will quell your rise before you have built the strength to end us."

"You are mistaken," Dorian said. "We can save you." Terel paused his pacing. He had, at this point, seemed to completely forget Rikard existed. So Rikard relegated himself to simply glaring at the back of his head. Perhaps if he focused hard enough he could set it ablaze with his mind. Rikard smiled again as he thought of old Tanyo. Tanyo had been a crazy old man that had lived near them when they were kids. He had thought that if he focused hard enough on something, he could set it on fire. As far as Rikard knew, it had never worked. However, this didn't discourage Rikard from attempting the feat. Rikard had never successfully eaten fire either, but he knew that it could be done.

"Save us? From what?" Terel inquired.

"Something is happening in the world. Surely you can see it. Events are progressing whether you accept them or not. Look at us. Do you think this is chance? Never have twins been seen in Carin. Not till us. There is no chance; there is only the Balance." Dorian's voice forced the words into Terel's mind. Rikard could see the words weigh upon the unu.

"Things are changing. It matters not if I like them. Qel has set us upon a course that cannot be deviated from, but the damage can be mitigated. Contrary to many, I do not want to see humanity destroyed. The ferals were one thing; humanity is something else entirely. Your people were the Template. We will seize the Heart of Fires and drive humanity from the south. I will not commit genocide, though. That is the best that I can offer you, Dorian."

Dorian hesitated. "You can end this now, Clansmaster. I have heard stories of you. I know you are an honorable being."

"There is too much momentum, and Veriel requires certain…sacrifices. I cannot stop this now." Terel paused. "We met once, you know." Dorian tilted his head.

"It was four months after you passed your final trial in the Anvil to enter the Thousand Hammers clan. We were hunting, following the bison migration north near the border of the Kingdom of Fangs. We came across a herd of taurus, and you roped one." Rikard started. That had been him, not Dorian. "You took the wager from one of the Diving Spears. You were fearless. I respect that greatly. I know of your exploits, Dorian Waterborne of the Thousand Hammers."

"Then please…" Terel held up his hand against Dorian's pleading voice.

"If you want your wife to be saved from the taste of the flame, then I will need something from you," Terel said. *Here it comes.* "I want you to tell me about the Heart of Fires. Where it is, how Jethro found it, and who else has touched it." Dorian looked at Rikard, who shrugged.

"The answers to those questions are not trivial," Dorian replied. "Jethro doesn't, and to my knowledge never had, the Heart of Fires. Our magic is something else entirely. We truly are not of Carin. Our magic comes from our own land, to the west of Carin, across the Rift Gate. We strongly believe the Light Monks have the Heart of Fires hidden deep in Illuvium." Terel accepted all of this information stoically.

"You are willing to wager the life of your wife on the fact that Queen Sumenel does not have the Heart of Fires?"

"Queen?" Dorian asked.

"Answer the question," Terel pressed.

"Yes." Dorian said. "One of us spent the last three months assisting the King while the war was being fought in Gemport. He found no evidence that the Heart of Fires was ever there."

Terel looked back to Rikard who continued glaring at him. "This one?" Terel asked.

"No, a different, more subtle one." Rikard rolled his eyes. *More womanizing perhaps.*

"Very well then. Your execution is in one hour. The Balance will be served, and your blasphemous names will be stricken. You will die by burning, as is the old way. You have one hour to make your peace with whatever god to whom you pay homage." The unu turned and pushed the door open. Rikard saw half a dozen unum standing at the ready outside in the hallway.

"Clansmaster! My wife?" Dorian hollered.

"The Balance will determine her fate. I can offer you no more than that." Dorian sagged in his chains. Rikard felt the uncomfortable quiet hanging in the air.

"What does that mean?" Rikard asked. Dorian was quiet for a moment.

"Two stones will be placed in covered bowls. One stone heavier than the other. The Arbiter will choose an unu from the crowd to come forward and choose which bowl will be placed upon which side of the scales. If the right side is heavier, she lives."

Rikard gaped. "That's the stupidest thing I have ever heard." Rikard shook his head in disbelief. "The whole stupid Balance is…stupid." Dorian let out a light chuckle.

"What?" Rikard asked.

"Do not be so quick to caste the Balance into the flames. When they come for us, we will go quietly with them, and when the torchbearers come for us, it will be Terel's reign that burns instead." Rikard looked at Dorian expectedly, but his brother offered no more of an explanation.

205

Instead his eyes closed, and he bowed his head. Rikard knew Dorian was actually praying. *What are you planning?* Rikard tried to puzzle through it, but he didn't know enough about unu culture to know what was coming. Regardless, it was going to be a gamble. There was no way it couldn't be.

Gambling. That was what they were reduced to, all because of a Skyguard. Rikard shook his head in disbelief. Dorian would say it wasn't chance, but destiny. Even before they had fished Desmond out of the ocean, Dorian had believed in a greater destiny for himself than what Cambria had to offer in the wake of Rerem's murder. The Orrery had told Dorian as much. Rikard had not put much stock in what the Orrery had told him-at least, not until Rerem had died. Rikard had known that it would happen, but he hadn't wanted to believe it. Just like he hadn't wanted to believe Dorian would abandon him for Breva when he had needed him two years ago. Dorian had always believed in destiny, and that was what had pulled him away from Rikard, who was supposed to be Dorian's best friend…his confidant.

That was why Dorian, along with Joven, had been the ones who spearheaded the decision to leave Cambria. His twin had never been comfortable in Cambria. He had been a pariah before Rerem's murder for being weak, and after, for his strident belief in The All. Even though Dorian had embraced The Universal Balance as espoused by the unu, he still followed The All. Rikard didn't know what Dorian saw in that kind of crazy, but he didn't disparage him for it anymore. Everyone in this world believed in some kind of a god. To Rikard it was all just a bunch of posturing and an easy way out.

While Dorian went into prayer, even mumbling a bit, Rikard took the opportunity to attempt to sleep. Sleep eluded him, though. *Go quietly? Go quietly?* Why shouldn't they fight? Even beat up as he was, Rikard knew he was still more than a match for most of these unu. Well… maybe that wasn't entirely true, but they could go out better than like a goat strung up and burned for dinner. Rikard did not support this plan, and he couldn't believe Dorian was actually espousing it either. Yet his twin seemed content to keep his own council, so Rikard contented himself with the idea that Dorian had a plan. As long as that plan involved him not dying in such a weak way and killing a handful of these fools, Rikard was content with it. If not…well, then Dorian could go down like a lamb while Rikard went down like a lion. With that thought Rikard closed his eyes and let the aching pain into his mind. The pain served to make him drowsy, and he passed into sleep.

Rikard started as a fist impacted his stomach. He looked up noiselessly. There were four unu in the small cell. One held a long spear aimed straight at his heart. *That's encouraging.* The second was the one who had hit him. He memorized the unu's face. He needed to be sure that he killed this one before he went down. The unu's nose was broad, and he had a black line of ink stretched in a half circle across the left side of his face. Oh yes, he would be dead by day's end.

"I'm going to kill you before this day is over," Rikard looked right into his eyes.

"Let's go, meat." the unu grunted with a mocking laugh and hit him again. He watched as the unu unlocked first his feet then his hands. Over the unu's shoulder he could see Dorian getting a similar treatment. Rikard waited, looking patiently for some kind of a signal that meant that they could take action, but there was nothing. Dorian merely looked serene and made no motions whatsoever.

Rikard sighed as he rubbed some feeling back into his wrists. They were extremely drained of blood, despite what the bloody, raw skin would have one believe. Two heavy cords were lashed around his wrists, and a leather cloth was thrown over his head. A cord was wrapped around his neck and drawn tight. It smelled like fish. Rikard hated fish.

He was pushed roughly along and almost tripped twice as he stumbled down the stairwell. The cord that bound his hands jerked forwards, and Rikard gritted his teeth together. He thought about mapping out exactly where they were but decided it wasn't worth the bother. He knew they would be taken to The Anvil for execution. It was how the unu did things: by tradition.

They would be led in through the east side, so they could watch the end of the day as the end of their lives approached, or some other such ritualistic nonsense. They would be led to the execution platform and then burned at the stake. Cheery stuff.

The feeling of wind and the change of texture in the ground at his feet told Rikard that they were now outside. He felt kind of insulted, upon reflection, that only four unu were leading them to their demise. For all the grief they had caused the unu, Rikard figured half a battalion would be barely enough. The unu armor clanked in his ears, and he heard the crowd. Terel wanted this to be public.

"Traitor." the word snaked into Rikard's ears. He suspected Dorian would be dismayed by this, but he really didn't care. He owed these people no allegiance. They were just more corpses waiting to happen, for all he was concerned.

"Traitor." the word echoed again. And again. And again.

"Traitor." the word started out as a chant and turned into a roar. Rikard knew that they were now in the central plaza and that momentarily they would stand revealed to the unu people. Joy.

Rikard's foot hit the bottom step of the platform, and he dropped to his knees. He grunted with pain as his mind flashed to the beating Frosh had inflicted upon him. He was pulled gruffly to his feet. He made it up the rest of the stairs without incident. Still, the resounding cry of *traitor* hung in the air, booming down upon him. It was really quite annoying. So he started chanting it.

"Traitors," he said simply, as if tasting the word. "Traitors," he said again. His hands were unbound, and he was hauled backwards. His back was thrust against a hard wooden pole, and his hands were lashed once again. "Traitors," he said again, but his heart wasn't in it. He hoped Dorian had some kind of miracle in store, because from his perspective it wasn't looking too promising.

"The traitors have been brought before us to be sentenced for their crimes against the clans. Crimes of murder, treason, and disruption of the Balance. Crimes for which they now must pay." What had to be at least ten

208

thousand spears crashed against the ground. Once again, the outlook looked-or, more accurately, sounded-none too promising.

"The Balance will not be denied!" Terel boomed.

"The Balance!" The unu replied in joyful chorus.

Oh boy. Rikard thought. *This can't be good.*

"Let the traitors stand revealed!" Terel called. *And here we go.*

Light poured into his eyes, and water began to stream down his face as he blinked over and over again to compensate. His left eye managed to see a little bit, but his right eye showed him plenty.

They were in the center of The Anvil, the great gladiatorial combat ring in which warriors proved their mettle and made their bids for clanmaster. Before him stood Clansmaster Terel in a high box, amidst numerous other clanmasters and unum. A staircase led down from the center of the box. Behind them and around them the stands were swarming with unu. Rikard glared at Dorian in the corner of his eye as silence swept through the circle. Everyone was staring at him. Rikard had a nigh-incontrollable urge to stick his tongue out at them in a childish display of defiance. He restrained himself. Antagonizing these people was probably not the best idea for whatever plan Dorian hoped to implement. Instead, he glared in what he hoped was an incredibly menacingly way at Terel. Pitch was laid to rest around their feet by unu children in ceremonial robes. The children were barely smaller than Rikard was, but their faces were pudgy and eyes wide. They wore tall funny-looking hats that he had never seen before.

As Dorian's hood was ripped off it was as if a wave had broken across the stadium: a wave of silence. It spread like wildfire as the people got their first good look at the two of them. Even with his face as brutalized as it was, it was not difficult to see that their features were exactly the same. He hadn't expected this. There was not a sound throughout the entire plaza. Rikard saw something that looked an awful lot like fear pass onto Terel's face.

"You stand accused. You stand guilty. Your sentence is death," Terel announced. "On this, the final day of the Feast of Bejor, let the taint

209

that you have inflicted upon the unu be exorcized." Terel gestured, but the two unu carrying torches standing next to them didn't move. They were slack-jawed and frozen in fear. Rikard wasn't sure what was supposed to happen now. Everyone was just staring at him.

"Dorian," Rikard whispered out the corner of his mouth.

"Patience," Dorian replied under his breath.

"By the Balance, they are perfect." an unu spoke out.

Rikard looked to where Terel and the rest of the clanmasters stood. Rikard had no idea what the unu's name was, but he was the clanmaster of the Shimmering Glass. His robes held the white circle that was inside of a silver one upon his breast. He moved through the rest of the clanmasters and approached the stage where Rikard and Dorian stood. He walked up the steps slowly, his golden eyes flickering between them. "Extraordinary. This-this is a sign." *Huh?* Now, Rikard was really confused. "The Balance has delivered us perfection: perfect Balance in mortal flesh." The unu fell to his knees with his head bowed. Rikard had no idea what was going on now. "Forgive us," the unu continued. He rose to his feet and turned back to the clanmasters.

"Don't you all see? These humans are not traitors, but saviors sent to us by the Balance itself today, the celebration of our devotion. Clansmaster Terel, surely you must see it. You were returned to us to pave the way for them. You are the prophet, the herald, the instrument of their ascension." The unu gestured back towards them. "They will lead us to a glorious future of Balance!"

"NO!" Terel erupted. All eyes turned to the clansmaster. "I am the Clansmaster, and they will bleed, and they will burn. I command it," he proclaimed.

"Clansmaster, I recognize that you see within them the Storm, but perhaps you were so focused that you missed the perfection that has been revealed here." the Shimmering Glass clanmaster replied with equal vehemence. *This is getting interesting.* "You have been away from us for a long time. This human," he gestured to Dorian, "has been among us. We all can testify to his commitment to The Balance. He passed the trials and

210

gained acceptance into the Thousand Hammers clan in a way that no human ever had before. He has fought hard for order in this world. And this other shares his face. He is his mirror opposite. T'was he that has perpetrated acts against the unu, but is it not in the devil's nature to sow discord? What is your name?" he asked Rikard.

"Rikard," he said after a moment, not realizing the unu had been addressing him.

"Rikard is Dorian's counterweight. They balance each other, and they will bring balance to the world. It was through them that we have eradicated the ferals. Now, they shall lead us onward until there is not but balance in the world of Carin." A crash of a spear against the ground somewhere in the crowd was echoed by a second and a third. Over and over until the ground shook in thunderous approval. Rikard smiled as he saw panic erupt upon Terel's face. He watched the clanmasters exchange uncertain glances before two stood adding their own spears to the chorus: The Bleeding Moon and the Burning Ember clans. Two more rose to join in: the Black Rose and the Diving Spear. There were now five clanmasters speaking out against the other seven.

"Stop!" Terel commanded, rising from his seat and casting his voice forward in a thunderous bellow. Rikard saw the Shimmering Glass clanmaster look to Dorian with panic on his face.

"I'm sorry," the unu whispered. "I tried." Rikard started at this. Terel passed by the clanmasters who stood. Terel walked down into the arena. The dust swirled around his feet as the winter wind whipped into the arena, sending a chill through Rikard's spine. Terel approached the platform.

"You named me clansmaster, did you not?" Terel called out.

"AROO!" The stadium erupted. Terel climbed the steps one by one.

"Clanmaster Qoren has put forth these humans as my replacements." Terel said to the assembled unu. He turned to regard Dorian. "Do you, Dorian Waterborne of the Thousand Hammers, make claim on the title of clansmaster?" he asked.

211

"I do," Dorian replied.

"And you, Rikard of the Seven, do you make this same claim?"

Rikard froze for a moment. He had no idea what was happening. "I do." he said. It was the only thing he could have said. *What is going on, Dorian?* Rikard hoped his bewilderment didn't show on his face.

"You have the support of five clans. Clanmaster Qel of the Thousand Hammers is gone, and the Amber Stone rules the clans, so it appears that support is divided. Therefore," he paused, "let the Balance decide." Terel nodded to the sentries, and they strode forth to cut free the bonds that held Rikard and Dorian to their posts. Rikard rubbed his raw wrists together. Rikard moved over next to Dorian. He looked over and at the edge of the platform saw an unu woman with a black cloth over her head. It had to be Breva.

"Arbiter." a tall but thin unu strode forward. He wore the same silver robes as the boys who had placed pitch on the platform earlier. In his hands he carried two covered bowls and a balance. The cleric ascended the platform, and two attendants brought forth a table that seemed to be dipped in gold. They placed it before Terel, and Dorian moved next to Rikard and gestured that they step forward. The cleric took position on the other side of the table. He placed the balance on the table. The scales perfectly aligned, perfectly balanced. The cleric passed one bowl to his other hand. Each hand now held one.

"Clansmaster, as you are defending your title before the holy balance, the right to choose or defer is yours." Terel looked out into the crowd before looking back to study each bowl. Rikard could see not even the slightest bit of concern on his face. Dorian would say it was because Terel had 'faith.' Rikard had never heard of faith saving someone's position, but privately he hoped, just in case, that Dorian's faith was the stronger. Each bowl was bold and held intricate designs in some kind of emerald ink. Rikard studied the way that the Arbiter held them. He focused on the fingers, on how hard the muscles were tensed. It was the left hand. Rikard grinned.

212

"I will defer." the clansmaster said. *Idiot.* Rikard thought. *How could you possibly think that placing your fate in someone else's hands was a smart idea?*

"We choose the bowl in the right hand for our claim."

"NO!" Rikard's voice came out louder than he had desired. He reached out and grabbed Dorian's arm. "It is the left," he whispered into his brother's ear. "You can tell by how he is ten-"

"Rikard. Trust me. Have faith." Rikard stared into his brother's eyes. Twice these eyes had betrayed him, and yet still he did trust him. Rikard felt his nails digging into his brother's arm, but Dorian showed no sign of the pain he had to be enduring. He just met Rikard's eyes. Dorian's eyes pleaded with him to trust in him.

"I can't die like this, Dorian. Don't let me die like this." Rikard said. Dorian hesitated for a moment.

"I won't." he licked his chapped lips. Rikard exhaled and slowly released his grip. "We chose the bowl on the right," Dorian said again. This time Rikard remained silent. He watched Terel smile. The Arbiter reached up with both hands and placed the bowls upon the scales. As he withdrew his hands, Rikard held his breath just like everyone else in the arena. He searched with his periphery, planning his escape route. *Kick to the knee of the guard, thumbs to eyes, wrest control of polearm, use to kill Terel. Leap from platform, ignore pain in left leg, use adrenaline to run hundred and fifty meters to west exit. Use surprise to minimize number of unu coming down to the arena floor. Three blocks, take a left, two doors down enter through hole in the wall where window was broken, hide in the dry cellar. Three days recovery, hiding in barrels when unu com-*His thoughts were interrupted by shouts. Rikard's blurred vision refocused on the scales, and he saw the bowl that Dorian had chosen slowly sinking to the table.

"What does that mean?" Rikard whispered. Terel's face was an impassionate mask.

"The Balance has spoken. Rikard and Dorian of the Thousand Hammers will be the Clansmasters of the unu!" The Arbiter's deep voice echoed through the entirety of the arena. The arena exploded into a cascade

213

of noise. Cheers, bellows of defiance, anger, victory, and defeat mingled together into a grotesque amalgamation that assaulted Rikard's ears. He saw the Shimmering Glass clanmaster rush forward, and Dorian embraced him.

"Thank you, Qorem. You did well." the clanmaster bowed. "Your debt has been paid in full." Dorian turned to Rikard.

"I don't know how you pulled this off, but you are either insane or a genius," Rikard murmured.

"Oh ye of little faith," Dorian said with a smile.

"Me of no faith," Rikard muttered. Dorian reached his hands up to silence the crowd. It took several long minutes before the noise dimmed to an acceptable murmur. Rikard was still tensed, ready to move at a moment's notice. He didn't think that Terel would take this defeat easily. They could very well be looking at a civil war here. "Clansmaster Terel, the Balance has spoken. Will you relinquish your position so I and my brother may take command of the clans?"

"Your brother is not one of us like you are Dorian Waterborne of the Thousand Hammers," Terel replied evenly. His voice was strained, though. He had lost control. He had been undone by his own folly. Rikard watched Terel's muscles tense. He was coiled and ready to spring. Rikard prepared to grab the spear of office from the Shimmering Glass clanmaster should the need arise. All eyes were upon Terel. Rikard would have felt bad for the unu if it weren't for the fact that he was going to have them executed a moment before. Actually, no-no, he wouldn't.

"He will learn our ways, when we have brought our current conflict to an end. He is a warrior, that much has been made readily apparent to those assembled here. He will pass the challenges of the Loredai. The question stands, Clansmaster." Terel looked out at the unu people once again. The stiffness of his shoulders broke just a slight amount, but Rikard saw it.

"I-I will relinquish command of the clans." Terel said.

Rikard couldn't believe that it was this easy. Well, not easy, but without bloodshed. Rikard didn't like it. He didn't like it at all. There should be killing: lots of killing. Starting with the clansmaster, and then

214

Frosh and that Skyguard. Rikard didn't trust anything that wasn't born in blood; words were empty. Words are easy to forget, but you never forget the men who make you bleed. Frosh was the fourth such man on Rikard's list. The first had been his father. His father had taught him to be strong. Blood...blood was strong.

"Give me a knife," Terel told the unum standing with him. The honor guard pulled a small jeweled blade from his belt and handed it to the clanmaster. "In my blood is the blood of the Clansmaster. This blood has flown through all those who came before and flows now into you. Carry it well." *Creepy.* Rikard was slightly taken aback. The clanmaster drew the blade slowly across his right hand and then his left before passing the blade to Dorian. Dorian cut his right hand and handed the blade to Rikard. Rikard stared at the blade. It was unnerving how Terel had known what he was thinking, but Rikard would play along at least until he could punch Dorian in the face for this stupid plan. Rikard made his own incision on his left hand, and they both placed their hands onto Terel's.

Blood mixed with blood, and peasants became kings. Rikard felt like there should be fire fountains or drums or something. Instead, it was just him holding an unu man's hand.

"I accept this duty to preserve and defend the Balance," Dorian said solemnly.

"I...uh...accept this duty to preserve and defend the Balance," Rikard echoed uncertainly.

"May you preserve it evermore," Terel said. He pulled his hands back and stepped away from them. Dorian turned to Rikard.

"It's time, brother." Dorian addressed the clanmasters. "You do my clan, the clan Thousand Hammers, a great honor. We have destroyed the ferals, but we reach too far with humanity. We have restored the Balance as Supremor originally designed it. Six scales. Send birds to Gemport to inform Gorn to hold off on the attack. We will lose no more unu to this war." The clanmasters exchanged glances.

"We will move northward into the Kingdom of Fangs. We will make it our own. The Kingdom of Fangs is no more. The Kingdom of the

215

Golden Scales shall rise in its place. This is the day of the unu." Spears crashed onto the ground. Rikard was basked in the cheers of the crowd and the clanmasters, as one by one they descended the steps and knelt before them. The entirety of the stadium knelt to the ground in the seats. Ten clanmasters knelt before them. Terel looked at his brethren, and Dorian looked at him. The unu man slowly descended from the platform to join the remaining clanmasters and sunk to a knee. Dorian waited for a moment. Rikard basked in the glory of the moment.

"Rise. Today is the last day of the feast, so let us FEAST!" The roar was deafening. Spears echoed his words. "Tonight, we feast! Tomorrow, we march!" Dorian turned to Rikard and gestured for him to follow. He walked to where Breva stood on the edge of the platform. *She is probably as confused as I am.* Dorian reached up and slowly pulled her blindfold away. Breva's golden eyes blinked three times as she looked at her husband. Rikard offered her a small wave, but she didn't even look at him. She looked right at Dorian.

"Clansmaster Dorian of the Thousand Hammers clan?" she said. Dorian nodded with a smile. *Or not.*

"Breva of the Bleeding Moon clan," he replied.

"No," she corrected, "Breva of the Thousand Hammers clan." Breva smiled. Her four hands wrapped around Dorian and pulled him into a tight embrace. Rikard exhaled heavily as he tried looking at anything but the tender moment between the two of them. He whistled lightly as he watched all of the unu in the plaza stare at the three of them.

"Ok, Dorian, you can have all the fun of a reunion tonight. Right now you need to tell me what's going on: why is Terel not dead, and why am I the leader of a civilization? So move it along," Rikard whispered. Breva's eyes flashed in displeasure, but she released her husband nonetheless.

"Come, my love." Dorian wrapped his fingers in her hand. "LET US FEAST!"

"HURRAH!" the unu called out.

216

"I'm being ignored," Rikard muttered to himself as unu began to stream from the plaza towards the feasting hall. Rikard followed Dorian and Breva as they picked their way through the throngs of unu. Rikard shuffled along with the masses. He sighed. This place was so boring. The war was to the west. He had been waiting here for months. Now, the unu were just going to do more eating and drinking. Big surprise there.

"You're going to have to watch your back," Rikard said. Dorian shook his head.

"The unu are honor bound to accept the judgment of the Balance. None would dare defy it."

"Even Terel?" Dorian hesitated as he looked over to where the clanmaster remained kneeling alone. The other clanmasters had already risen and departed, but Terel remained where he was.

"I don't know," Dorian admitted. "He is a good man. Qel would have killed Breva for certain, but he gave her a chance." Dorian's face was conflicted.

"He was also going to kill us!" Rikard emphasized the word 'kill.'

"Husband," Breva urged. Dorian turned to her. "We need to go. Your subjects are waiting for you." He nodded. The stadium was rapidly depleting of unu.

"One moment, my love. Rikard. You need to go to the healers."

"I'm not going anywhere," Rikard replied. "Until we have a little chit-chat."

"Don't make me punch you in the face, Rikard."

"You aren't the boss of me, Dorian. Just cause you were born four minutes before me doesn't mean anything." Dorian slapped Rikard on the shoulder and splinters of pain jolted through his body. He grimaced visibly and audibly.

"Go see the healers. Get some treatment for your face and arm. Come to the feast and we can talk."

Rikard broke away from Breva and Dorian begrudgingly. The unu parted for him in a wave of salutes as he strode through their ranks. He limped his way through the city streets. The healer's monastery was right next to the Blue Castle. Rikard wanted to punch a wall. He couldn't run. He could barely walk. It was an effort to lift his right arm. He had only been messed up for a few hours that he had been awake for, but he was already tired of it. As Rikard walked through the city he tried to think of the last time he had been like this. The last time he had lost a fight.

He couldn't.

Rikard smiled at the thought.

Leap of Faith

Seventeen

The line between the invasion force and the natives of the underground was so clear that you would have to literally be blind not to see it. The invading army's camp was covered with red, burning torches that stood in stark contrast to the cool blue tones of the Iron Men's city. Large stone barricades were manned by thousands of Iron Men. Separating the two barricades was a long stone hill that stretched up from the tunnel leading to the Body City. If the invading army wanted to take this city, they would lose thousands just to arrive at the Iron Men's position.

"So what is your plan?" Grey asked as they stood looking over the wall.

"My plan?" Galeerial asked. Grey nodded his head.

"Of course. The whole point of my nap was to give you time to plan. You didn't sleep did you?" Grey, looked at Galeerial who shrugged,. Grey sighed. "Well, this is your show now, Galeerial. Consider this your final test. If we survive, then you pass, and we will go kill Veriel together. You fail, well, you die, and I go kill Veriel by myself. So, how do you plan on pulling this off?" *If you can't win, you aren't thinking fast enough.* Galeerial thought fast. Galeerial stared at the lines. If they entered into the kill zone they would be killed immediately. Even bearing a white flag didn't strike Galeerial as being very useful. If this army had come this far, then weren't interested in surrender; they were after annihilation. They could have the Iron Men instigate an attack and use the cover to enter the enemy lines. Stealth was not an option. There had to be some way that they could get there without being killed. Someway that would make the enemy want to bring them into their camp... Magic? No, this had to be something Galeerial could do, and the wizard had not divulged those secrets yet. He had to use his own magic. Galeerial's hand went to the Five Eye. He hesitated. He knew the gemstone was magical, but he didn't know how it worked, or even what it did. Gabriel hadn't told him anything about it when he had given it to him. Eon was just a sword, indistinguishable if you didn't know anything about the blade. *If you can't win, you aren't thinking fast enough. Fast enough...* Galeerial smiled. He knew exactly what they were going to do.

"Follow me," Galeerial said. He moved forward from their position at the back of the Iron Man battlements and pushed his way through the hard skin of the Iron Men. They regarded him with disdain and hostility, but none made any effort to seriously bar his path or jeer at them. Galeerial reached the large block of granite that served as the wall at the edge of the city, placed one hand on the top of the wall, and vaulted over. He landed in a crouch, and Grey followed with a small bit of muttering that Galeerial couldn't hear. Galeerial held his hands out and approached the army. His eyes flashed back and forth across the lines as he saw ferals and humans alike draw bows back.

"I WOULD SPEAK WITH YOUR COMMANDER!" Galeerial shouted. *Thwip.* The sound of a bowstring being let loose was his only reply. *If you can't win, you aren't thinking fast enough.* The bolt traveled in a high arc towards him. His human eyes struggled to track the arrow, but he finally picked it out as it whistled towards him. He stepped to the right and whipped his hand out in a diagonal along the approaching trajectory. He felt wood on the crux between his thumb and index finger, and he slammed his hand closed. His breathing was quick and shallow. He looked down and saw the black arrow dead center in his palm. He held the projectile up into the air before dropping it to the ground. The echo scattered through the cave to abject silence. Nothing moved for a moment, and it seemed as if the fires themselves held their breath. With a crack, wooden doors were opened in the human-feral makeshift wall, and a single feral stood within.

"You may approach!" the feral held his hand out. Galeerial and Grey walked forward. Shouts began to ring out from the Iron Men, but Galeerial ignored them.

"Nice move," Grey whispered to him.

"My teacher's done better," he replied.

"Sounds like a pretty stellar man."

"Don't push it," Galeerial replied as he stepped behind the battlements. The feral bowed as they entered, and humans surrounded them.

"My Lords, I must say, we expected your arrival some time ago...and from a quite different direction, to be perfectly honest." the feral greeted them. Galeerial's confusion manifested itself as little more than a hard tinge to his words.

"There have been complications." he replied noncommittally looking at Grey with bewilderment. Grey simply shrugged, offering nothing by way of explanation.

"Of course. The southern campaign goes well, though, I trust," the feral continued. "Please follow me; the commanders will be greatly pleased to speak with you. We have been holding here waiting for you, but I knew that their patience was nearing its end."

"Nice catch, My Lord," a man said. This caught the attention of several soldiers sitting. "I shot it myself. I wouldn't have if I had known it was you, so begging your pardon."

"It was fine," Galeerial murmured, looking around at the humans and ferals sitting together. They were gambling, talking, joking, and laughing. The man tipped his hat and removed himself. It was disconcerting seeing creatures of such different mannerisms speaking in easy, friendly tones. Some men sat around a fire brewing a stew and telling stories in quiet voices that were interrupted by furtive bits of laughter. It was the opposite of what he expected. A group of ferals were fletching arrows as some men carved them. *What is going on?* Galeerial pondered as the feral guided them deeper into the back tunnels leading away from Dynast. The crowd parted as quickly as it had gathered.

"Uh…I'm sorry, but who are you?" Galeerial hesitantly asked. *Should I know him? Does Grey know him?*

"Oh, of course, forgive me. My name is Djin. I'm Commander Setiris' son. I'm taking you to him right now. He asked that you be brought immediately to him upon your arrival."

Galeerial exchanged glances with Grey. "We…we weren't aware that anyone would be anticipating our arrival." Galeerial spoke unsurely, which he hoped didn't come through in his voice. As they walked they saw ferals and humans alike carrying weapons and ammunitions past them back the way they had come. Every man offered a verbal greeting to Djin, which Galeerial found odd. Everyone knew him: human and feral alike.

"We were told that we would know you by a remarkable feat, and that was pretty remarkable. You are magicians like the Assembler, correct?" *The Assembler?* That had to be the Dread, but this feral was not the sort that Galeerial had expected to encounter. In fact, this whole exchange was nothing like what he had originally conceived. Djin was jovial, and young and vibrant; hardly a monster, as much as his outward appearance portrayed him as such.

"Similar, but not the same," Galeerial replied, exchanging a glance with Grey. "Does your father lead both the ferals and the humans?" Djin shook his head.

"No, we joined the humans near the Eye and marched here. Commander Rayni Loras commands the humans. He will be there as well. The commanders are discussing the final push to take the city. They were beginning to grow concerned that you would not arrive in time to guide us south to join you. We were unsure of our next move, but now that you are here every question will be resolved." Galeerial nodded his head in agreement, but on the inside his mind was churning. "Does your companion not speak?" Djin gestured to Grey, who had remained silent throughout the exchange.

"He keeps his counsel until he is required to give it. Then, he becomes impossible to keep silent until he has had his say."

Djin nodded appreciatively. "I wish I had his resolve. I am so inquisitive; my father says that it will get me into far more trouble than it is worth." Galeerial found a small smile creep to the corners of his mouth, but he crushed it. As friendly as this feral was, he was the enemy. His father and the human commander would die by his hands. They twisted through the broad, well-lit corridors and finally came to a stop some ways past the last bit of encampment. An Iron Man guard tower was where they halted. At the top stood a dozen sentries who stared at them the entire length of their approach. The tower's circular shape flowed with the grain of the tunnel. To the right stood two horses tied to the tower itself. Its door was circular, and a sharp rap by Djin caused it to open. A human peered out. Djin bowed.

"The wizards are here," he said.

"Thank you, Djin. You may go," the human replied.

"Of course." He bowed once again before turning to them. "It was a pleasure to speak with you. I hope you stay with us for some time." Galeerial watched the young feral walk back the way he came. Galeerial had never met a feral before, but Djin was not at all what he had imagined them to be.

"You are free to enter, My Lords," a voice called out. Galeerial ducked down and entered into a chamber whose ceiling was mercifully large enough for him to stand erect. The entire sentry tower was a single room, with a ladder that led up to the roof. Inside was a modified Crown's table, along with a desk and several chairs spread around the room. The human himself was dressed in silver plate armor with no house crest. His breastplate contained a single golden circle on it, though, which Galeerial found peculiar. The man's face was well worn, and his hair cut short and graying. He bowed low to them. Galeerial fingered his blade, but Grey's arm shot out and grabbed his wrist. Galeerial looked into Grey's eyes.

"Wait," he whispered. "I know I said you could take this, but something is wrong with all of this. Let me do the talking." Galeerial shrugged.

"Rise, Commander Loras." Grey said. The man rose from his bow.

"Please sit." Loras gestured, and Galeerial took care to sink slowly and meaningfully into a tall backed metal chair never taking his eyes off of the commander. "We were beginning to grow concerned; we had not heard anything from Joven in many weeks. We feared that the southern campaign was going badly, but you being here assuages many of my fears." Out of the corner of his eye, Galeerial saw Grey blink repeatedly. It echoed his own disbelief. *Joven?* A sinking pit grew in Galeerial's stomach. *Is he in league with Veriel? Or is Veriel not even involved in all of this?* "What orders do you bring to us?"

"I'm…I'm sorry, you said that you hadn't heard anything from Joven in a number of weeks?" Grey asked. His voice was alight with disbelief.

"That's correct," the man affirmed. "We had anticipated this, of course, in his campaign against the unu and centaurs, but our sentries that we left posted on the far side of the mountains have reported no falcons have arrived." *Campaign against the unu and centaurs?* Galeerial reeled.

"Interesting. Well, I apologize for this lack of communication. We have had some difficulties in the final part of the first stage of the plan, but everything is proceeding as planned." Galeerial kept the incredulous smile from his face. Grey was a good liar. "My last communication with my brother was some time ago. I would like an update as to both what you last heard from him and what your last orders were, if you would be so kind."

"Of course," Commander Loras replied. "He provided us with entrance on the opposite side of the mountains. After that, we heard little from him until we had taken all of the extended cities. He came to us about six months ago and helped with our initial push into Heidrun. He told us that we were not to stop until we had taken the Iron Men apart. We have done this. Dynast is the sole remaining city. Soon they will be wiped off the board." He gestured to the Crowns board. "We have been stalled here though. The amount of troops it would take to break Dynast would leave nothing left. I am not prepared to make that sacrifice. Neither is Setiris. I know you wanted them destroyed, and given the circumstances, we have done remarkably well, but we can't take Dynast without something…extraordinary." Loras' eyes trailed back and forth between the two of them.

"Extraordinary indeed," Grey mused. Grey reached down and grasped the red piece of the human army. This was the Imperial. He fingered the design, slowly looking at it. "From this moment forward I am taking full command of this army. My companion will be taking his leave of us shortly." This time Galeerial couldn't stop the glance that he shot Grey's way. "He will need a horse that can carry him as far as Cloud Breach. Do you have such a beast?" Loras nodded.

"My steed is held right outside this tower. He is yours."

"Thank you. Commander, I need to speak with my companion, and then you and I will have much more to speak about."

"Of course," the commander said. Grey's voice was something entirely different than it had ever been before. He was in command: completely and utterly. All three rose simultaneously. Galeerial bowed before exiting the tower slowly. The sentries watched him as he exited, and so he kept walking until he was a good distance away. Grey followed a moment later.

"Listen, Grey, I have followed you this long. You can't just send me away now!" Galeerial silenced Grey before he had even arrived. Grey ran a hand through his hair and exhaled.

"I don't know. I…I just don't know. I don't know what is going on here. That mark on his armor is the Company of the Golden Circle. They are mercenaries. I can't believe this." Grey stalked past Galeerial, looking deep into the tunnel. "How could Joven keep something like this? All of this? I didn't know it existed until two minutes ago. I thought that we had all but wiped the ferals out at Long Fang, and here we find an entire

225

secondary army here attacking the Iron Men. And for what? Not only that, but Loras thinks we are attacking the unu and centaurs. What happens when he and the feral commander learn that we caused the genocide of the ferals?" Grey's voice was low. "I don't know. I just don't know. You need to get out of here, though. The dam is going to break soon, and you can't get caught in the crossfire. You have come so far. You're as ready as I can make you." Galeerial stood stunned.

"But...but what about my final test?" Galeerial grasped for something, anything.

"You passed; you passed with flying colors. Now, there are only two things left for you to do. The first is don't get killed by Veriel. You are as much one of us as my own blood. The second is you need to find out what is going on here. All roads lead south. Go to Gemport, you'll find Joven and the rest of our family there. You can trust them, but you need to uncover the truth. Joven plays things close to the chest. To convince him, you will need a phrase. Tell him that there are three glasses on a table. The third glass is blue. Do you understand? Don't confront him alone. Take Aurum or Dorian or Rayn, someone with you when you go. Do you understand?"

"No," Galeerial replied. "What is happening here, Grey? Is Joven working with Veriel? Was Veriel ever even here?" Grey ran his hand through his hair nervously.

"I wish had answers for you. I really do. I will join you in the south as soon as I can, but right now I need to solve this. You will have to go the rest of the journey by yourself." Galeerial looked at his brother. They had been through so much in the last few weeks. He couldn't hardly believe how different he was now because of this man. Galeerial bit his lip. "I'm sorry I can't offer a better explanation for you." Grey said.

"It's okay," Galeerial replied, "but if I'm leaving you here, I need something from you."

"Anything," Grey responded.

"I need you to keep your word that you will join me in the south." Grey nodded. He held out his hand, and Galeerial shook it. "Thank you-for everything," Galeerial said.

"You were a better student than I could have hoped for. Even if you were a bit stubborn at times. I am proud of you and honored to have you with us." Grey pulled Galeerial into an embrace. "Don't hesitate. Never look back. Remember what I have taught you," he whispered. Grey released Galeerial and turned away from him. Commander Loras had exited the tower and stood waiting with the reins of a beautiful white destrier in hand. She pawed the ground anxiously as Galeerial approached her.

"She'll give you attitude if you don't keep her on a short leash," Loras told him as he handed over the reins.

"Thank you for your advice. I'll keep that in mind. How will I know the way through the tunnels?" Galeerial asked.

"The passage south is manned with a skeleton crew; however, there should be sentries posted every few kilometers. It will take you two days' riding to reach the east entrance." Galeerial nodded.

"Good bye, my friend. May your skies ever be clear," Grey said. Galeerial smiled at the Skyguard saying.

"And may the winds carry you where you wish," he returned. Galeerial swung up on the horse.

"One last thing, Grey." the wizard looked up at him. "I know what I am afraid of."

The wizard smiled. "Then I was right, you are ready."

Galeerial smiled. "Heya!" he hollered, lashing the ropes. The horse surged forward in a siege of energy that carried him forward and onward.

*   *   *

Galeerial looked up at the gates. It had been an eternity since he had stood upon these selfsame doors, staring down Tenbraun. Right before Veriel had taken his wings had been the last time he had seen his home. Galeerial closed his eyes for a moment. He was terrified of what he would find on the other side of these gates. He had seen no mass of gathering Skyguard, and he feared more than anything that he was too late. What if Veriel was long gone? What would he do then? Galeerial shook his head. He would pursue Veriel to the ends of the earth and beyond the Rift itself until he killed him. That was Galeerial's purpose, of that he had no doubt.

Galeerial stared at the walls before him. He thought back to how he had been at a loss for what to do when he had arrived at Soaring, but now Galeerial saw the cracks in the stone and knew he could easily scale it. He swung down off of the horse that Setiris had gifted him with and gave the stallion a pat on the neck. It had been a good horse and had born him well across the lays. It had been a four day journey after leaving the Sparkling Mountains, and he had pushed the horse as hard as he dared. Galeerial pulled his swords from his saddlebag, sheathed the scimitars around his waist, and wrapped Eon around his back before approaching the gates. He ran his fingers along the bitterly cold stone, but he ignored the pain. He found two sturdy handholds and began his climb.

The stone gates had been worn relatively smooth by the endless winds, but that same wind had carved out divots and cracks in the rock. Galeerial was careful to make sure that he kept three points of contact at all times as he ascended. The walls stood about fifty feet tall, and Galeerial climbed quickly. As he reached the top, he realized that his muscles weren't even tired. He smiled while swinging his leg up and over the top. Galeerial looked back down to see his horse seemingly staring after him. A soft cry dropped Galeerial into a combat stance with Eon drawn in a single smooth motion. A high guard position to protect his face was immediately assumed as his eyes played across the wall, searching for the source. Inside the same guardhouse where he and Ezekiel had sat and talked for hours, and where his wings had been hewn, stood a Skyguard female. Her hair was a tangled mess and her clothes dirty. Galeerial dropped his arm down to his side.

"Jariah?" he breathed. Ezekiel's wife stood with a scimitar held out in front of her. She looked terrified.

"Ga- Galeerial? You are alive?" her voice was soft and melodious. Galeerial shoved Eon back into its sheath and ran towards her. His arms wrapped around her, and he pulled her close. She returned his gesture tentatively. "By Supremor, your wings..." she said as she slowly ran her hands over his shoulder blades. Galeerial slowly released her, and he nodded solemnly.

"Veriel," was all he said in response. He saw tears build in her eyes. "Jariah, where is Ezekiel? What happened?" he said urgently. "How did you resist the call of the horn?"

"Ezekiel warned me it would happen, right before...before..." She didn't say it, but Galeerial knew his friend was dead. Galeerial squeezed his eyes shut and swallowed against his anger. "I hid here, barring the doors. I thought I would go insane. It called to me. Veriel-" was all she could say. Her tears let out, and Galeerial once again pulled her into a tight embrace. One more thing that monster had to pay for. Galeerial wanted to stay with her, but he had to find Veriel.

"Where is he?" he whispered into her ear as her tears stained his shoulder. "Where is Veriel?"

"Gone. I-I do not know where, I have been hiding since-since then. I have been running and praying that I would find you alive. You are alive. Praise Supremor, you are alive." Jariah repeated, but all Galeerial could hear was "gone." He pursed his lips together in frustration and anger. "I thought I would never see you again."

"Where is he?" he repeated.

"I-I do not know. The Clerics in the cathedral might...what is he, Galeerial?" her voice cracked, and Galeerial looked down at her and wondered what could have happened to her to make her like this. The Jariah he remembered had been soft spoken but convicted and daring. She had been quick to laugh and slow to cry. This was what Veriel did; he destroyed innocence.

"I don't know." Galeerial slowly separated himself from her. "But I am going to find him, and I am going to kill him," Galeerial told her. Her pitiful eyes stared into his own, and they stoked the fires of rage within him. "I need you to make ready to fly south, far south." Jariah slowly nodded. Galeerial kissed her forehead and put a hand under her chin. "You can do

229

this, Jariah. First, I need you to take me to the Cathedral. Can you do that for me?" Galeerial asked softly. She nodded, and he took her hand and led her from the guardhouse.

Her wings beat with effort behind her, but they lifted the two of them slowly into the air. She wrapped her arms under his own and nestled her elbows in the crux below his shoulders. As his feet left the ground, Galeerial closed his eyes and remembered the sensation. This was the first time he had actually flown since his wings had been hewn. It was almost a year ago. The wind streamed through his face, but the cold made him feel alive rather than chilled. Her wings pumped harder as they fought against the winds towards the Cathedral of Light. Galeerial felt the way she strained. She couldn't carry him all the way to Gemport. The Clerics could, though. Usually one or two of the Clerics would remain behind to guard the cathedral when the host was marshaled.

They touched down in front of the doors. Galeerial wondered what he would say to the Clerics when he saw them. He had thought of this often, but now that he would finally face them, he was unsure.

His hands felt the smooth wood, and they barely resisted his push. As the doors opened and he entered, he was greeted with great suffering. The five clerics were hung on the walls: crucified. Chains of black fire wound through their palms, shoulders, out of their chests, and back in through their feet. Their wings were piled up on the floor beneath them. High Cleric Remiel looked up with empty eyes.

"Please save us. Please."

Galeerial couldn't move. His blood was cold, and his head spun. He had never imagined something like this.

The Willing Heart
Eighteen

Sixteen weeks.

Every day for sixteen weeks, I had tried to bleed water. Nothing. It was impossibly maddening. I stood within the Hall of Ten Thousand Rainbows inside Merhelden, the grand city of the Dreaming. Lord Alizar, the son of Supremor, had brought me here through the black door in Acheron. The Dreaming was a world entirely separate from what people here called Materia, which was Cambria and Carin and everything physical. The world here was different. I felt different. I was lighter, and the material of the world could be manipulated in bizarre ways. Space and time were openly defied here. The colors swirled around me in glistening rivers. I counted time by the swirl of the rainbows. They were random, yet once a day all the bands stood parallel to one another. It was this time of the day that I would come to this room: day after day after day. They wrapped around the white cloth of the robes that I wore. I took a deep breath and closed my eyes. Every day I said something differently, but every day it started the same.

"I believe…" no words followed those initial two. I was like a blind man groping for his cane; yet, I could find nothing new to say to this new god. Day after day, I had said something else to him, to Supremor, but it seemed to never be what he wanted to hear. From the folds of my white cloak I withdrew the dagger. It was pure white, never having been tarnished, despite being used every single day. When Alizar had brought me here he had told me that the Key to All Souls was faith. He told me that if I wanted what this land could offer, if I wanted the power to save the lives of my brothers, I would have to learn to believe in something beyond my ken.

For the 112th time, I raised my dagger of white light. I pulled the top of my white tunic down and felt the warm hum of the blade against my skin. I looked straight up. The colors were an elaborate menagerie of beauty.

"Please," I whispered. The blade slid onto my skin where the scar of every cut waited, and I winced slightly. I looked down and saw a thin red line slip down my chest. My shoulders slumped in defeat. I dropped the knife to the floor and sank to my knees. Again. Another failure. I felt frustrated anger building within me, but I breathed and let it flow through my body and out into the room itself. As I relaxed my muscles, soft footsteps made me look up. A golden archway gleamed with the reflective light. Two lions stood on hind legs, pressing their front paws together as they roared to the skies. From beneath them walked Lord Alizar. He was different, from the last time that I had seen him. His skin tone was lighter, and some of the markings upon his skin were missing. I pulled one knee up and bowed my head.

"Rise," he said. I slowly pulled myself up to my feet.

"My Lord," I said. It had been a long time since I had seen Lord Alizar. Sixty turns of the color bands.

"Walk and speak with me." I nodded in compliance. My bare feet walked along the cool pearl of the floor. I passed underneath the golden archway and out into the wide floor that was the Realm of Beauty. I didn't know how many levels this palace had, but it was seemingly endless. And that was just the palace. I had not been permitted to leave the palace itself, but I had seen the city that surrounded Merhelden and beyond that the rest of the Dreaming.

The stairs of this place ended wherever you wanted them to. It seemed like this place was endless. Each day, I would find another room that I hadn't known existed. However, I did know that there was a top and a bottom floor. The top was the Throne Room where we had arrived, and the bottom held the Pillars of Creation. The Pillars were a difficult concept for me to wrap my head around. Like everything in the Dreaming, it was a concept made manifest into physical form. Each Pillar was tied to a bloodline in Carin. Every being in Carin had a representation of themselves in the Dreaming, called their belicos. The belicos of every member of a family was connected like the roots of a tree and its branches. The Pillars then connected to these roots, and drew their strength from them. As bloodlines died out or grew too dilute, the Pillars would fall and new ones would be created. An endless cycle of life and rebirth.

We walked down the corridor, but I didn't see any doors, though I had been sure that I had seen them when I had passed by this morning.

"What happened to the other rooms?" I asked.

"I desire no distractions. Speak to me, Aurum. Tell me why."

"You think I haven't asked myself this every single day?" I asked angrily.

"Watch your tone," Lord Alizar replied calmly, but the words were cut with a slice of danger. I opened and closed my mouth without allowing any words to come out.

"Yes, My Lord."

Lord Alizar sighed as we began to ascend.

"I have given you everything that you need to access the true magic within you. My power, that of the elixis, is that of imagination itself. The elixis will save your brothers; it will save you. I have shown you the redemptive power of Supremor. Yet, still you have nothing. Still you can't bring yourself to believe. I have shown you more than any other mortal since Garen himself. Yet still you don't believe. Why?" I felt a feeling that I hadn't felt in over twenty years. I felt shame flush on my face. I hadn't felt shame since my father had been tried for treason and put to death. It…burned.

"I-I…" I searched desperately for something, anything to explain to this being that stood before me why I couldn't believe. In my mind, I understood all the reasons why I should believe. The current world around me and the power that the being walking next to me held should be more than enough. "I just don't know how." silence lingered between us for a moment.

"You use your heart," he replied. The silence between us deepened. My heart. I had buried my heart ten years ago with my wife and daughter. "You have to let them go," he said softly. I stopped walking. Lord Alizar halted a moment later. He turned back towards me.

"What you ask…don't take that from me," I said haltingly. "That is all I have left."

"That?" he replied. "Is it the memory of your family or the stone vault that you have placed around your heart that you are so afraid of losing?"

My legs were shaking. "How dare you? She is my wife!" I said through gritted teeth. "She is my daughter."

"And she dwells within the house of my father. But you are still alive, and you live a hollow life. Life is a gift, Aurum. A gift you have wasted. Man was created to love, but you live for nothing beyond the mission. Love is not merely some paltry emotion; love is imagining a better world. Imagination is the most powerful force in the universe. It is the heart of the elixis. You are alive, but you are not living. The reason you cannot believe in Supremor is because you no longer believe in the power of love. You no longer know how to imagine anything greater than what you already have."

"The power of love..." I said, "love didn't have the power to save my wife and child. Love was not what brought me here. Love has not kept me alive for the last eight years. That was will."

"And it is here and in Long Fang that your will failed; your pride, your belief in your own infallibility, in your superiority to the people here." he said quietly. "It is not your memory of them that drives you forward; it is the pain of their passing that you are running from." I turned away from him and looked at the wall of veined marble before me. My whole body was shaking. My insides were twisted together like rope into a noose.

"So that's the cost, then." I tensed my teeth together. I shook my head. "I can't do that." I looked up and saw the doorway to one of the other rooms, called Impulse, before me. I stepped in, away from Lord Alizar, without thinking. I just needed to get away from him. "I'm sorry." as I entered the room ten thousand images assailed my eyes. I knew this room. I whirled about trying to find the door, but it had vanished. All of the images were of my wife: the day that I had met her in my first year of university in the Artistry of Practicality, eating lunch on the plaza, and staring at a rainbow with her right before I kissed her for the first time. I saw fresh bread in her hands and a ribbon on her wrist. I saw her in gowns of every color. The entire world slowly began to seep into black. It started like mere cracks in some of the images, but it seeped outwards like a poison.

"No...no....NO!" my panicked voice grew louder and louder as more and more of the images were consumed by the darkness. I turned wildly back to Lord Alizar. "Where did she go?" My breathing was ragged in my ears. My limbs grew leaden, and my fingers were numb. Wild eyes darted back and forth.

"She is still there in your mind, but your heart has buried her." his black eyes somehow displayed pity. "Awake, Aurum. This room cannot lie. It showed your memories; I simply told it to show your heart instead. Welcome. Welcome to the void of your heart. There is not even compassion here; there is nothing. Only this cold depth that is destroying you. Awake!"

"I can't... I love them too much."

Hands encompassed my shoulders.

235

"I know you do. I know you do. You have just buried it. You have buried it so deep." my mouth was as dry as desert sand. I couldn't swallow. I couldn't move. "Come." his skin was warm as his hands took hold of mine. Tears stained my eyes, and the world became eclipsed in hazy clouds. I couldn't see anything. My legs were wooden, and they numbly walked forward. I looked up and saw the blackness slowly start to recede as we exited from Impulse. As we walked out, I felt my legs suddenly begin walking on open air. I tried to reach my arm up to wipe my eyes, but Lord Alizar held them firmly but gently. My chest ached. Lord Alizar released my hands, and I cleared my eyes.

Before me there was a doorway with a broad arch that lead out into a small plaza, which fell away to reveal league upon league of vineyards. In the distance, a white tower spiraled high into the sky, disappearing into the clouds. I looked at Lord Alizar, and he gestured out the archway. "Go. Go and find your heart once again."

I stumbled forward. My gait was unsteady and drunken. This place felt different. In Merhelden, the world felt like a prism. Everything was brilliant, vivid colors and a light, airy, almost ethereal feel. Here the world felt alive. It was like stepping back into the real world, though I still felt oddly disconnected-like I was a trespasser. The smell of the grapes filled my nostrils, and I breathed. The ache in my chest and the stifled breathing slowly began to abate. I looked around to see people seated around the patio. Some were simply talking; others were eating or drinking, but it was two women who sat painting together at the far end that caught my eye. I stopped when I saw them and just stared. It wasn't possible. I looked back at Lord Alizar, who hadn't moved.

"Is it really…" he nodded once. I turned back to them. I took one step forward. As coiled as my insides had been before; now the knot tightened immeasurably. I was almost paralyzed as I slowly began to pick my way between the tables that were set up there. People gave me little regard as I shuffled by them stiffly. The distance seemed to take forever for me to cross, and yet in no time at all I stood waiting behind them. Both women were wearing ornate, flowing dresses that billowed out on the bottom. Flowers adorned their hair. Each wore a sun hat with a thin wafting veil before her eyes.

I remembered the first day I saw her. It was Pure Artist's Day, and Rowen and I had been walking through the Twinala Bazaar. We had no real interest in purchasing anything. All we had wanted was to appreciate what people had made. Pure Artist's Day occurred twice a year on the day before the solstice. It was always a pleasure to see the competitions between the provinces. Veridian had crafted a new form of artwork that year called fluid portraits. I had been looking at one of a library where the books moved from shelf to shelf, spiraling ever upwards. She was the artist. I looked up from the piece to see her standing next to it. I remember what Rowen had said to me: "She's all yours." As I approached her I said, "I believe that the All is an artist, because only a painter could create something as beautiful as you." She asked me if I got that line from the inside of a Sweetheart Box. I told her it was from my younger brother, actually. It was then that she had smiled.

"Ex...ex...excuse, me ma'am, but I believe that the All is an artist, because only a painter could create something as beautiful as you." The words spilled haltingly from my lips, as if I had not spoken in ages. As I did, they turned to look at me. I couldn't place the myriad of emotions that flooded onto her face in that first moment, but I knew without a doubt that it was her, and that she could see me. It was Andusíl. My beloved.

"Aurum? By Supremor, you're here! HAHAHA." Her joyous laughter propelled her into my arms: my sweet Andusíl, my beautiful Andusíl. She felt and looked and smelled just how I remembered. She smelled of love. Her lips embraced mine, and I spun her around in my arms. A smile, a real honest-to-Supremor smile, filled my face. I looked into her eyes and saw none of the cloudiness that had colored them after her accident. She could see me. I set her down.

"You can see." I said out of breath. She nodded and smiled.

"Miracles are currency here, and Lord Supremor has given me more than I can count. Aurum," Andusíl breathed out "This is Hope: our daughter." Hope rose from her chair, slightly unsure of herself before me.

237

"You are more beautiful than I could have imagined." I said. A grin lit up her face, and I embraced her. I planted a kiss on her rich brown hair. I held on tight to my family as tears of joy streamed down my face. I planted several more kisses on my daughter's head. She laughed at me.

"I have to make up for lost time," I said to her as I wiped the tears from my eyes. "How...how is this possible?"

"This is Aeriel. This is what happens next, Aurum. After everything, all the lies and the death and the struggle. This is the end of all roads. Is it not beautiful?" Andusíl smiled. "Sit husband. We have been waiting for a long time, and now we have forever." She gestured and a third chair appeared beside the other two. *Forever.* I repeated it over in my mind. I looked back at Lord Alizar, who shook his head.

"Not forever, not yet," I said. Hope and Andusíl exchanged a glance.

"Aurum, are you...are you still alive?" Andusíl asked puzzled. I nodded in reply.

"At least I think I am. I've been through so much since I lost you, sometimes I have wondered if I wasn't dead. Has no one come here before that isn't?"

"No one has ever been brought here who has not already crossed, over to my knowledge," Andusíl reaffirmed. "Astounding. I always knew there was something I liked about you, Aurum." Andusíl offered me a sly smile. She bit the side of her lip. I loved when she did that.

"Hopefully, you more than just liked something about me," I teased. There was a small pause in the conversation.

"We have been watching you, Aurum." Andusíl said quietly. The color drained from my face and for the first time since I saw them, I pulled my gaze away from their faces and looked out into the vineyard.

"Father..." Hope began, but I held my hand up.

"When I lost you two...I lost so much of myself that I abandoned everything. I became...something terrible. I am so sorry." I knelt down and grabbed my wife and daughter's hands. "Please...please forgive me."

"Of course, my love." Andusíl sank to the ground next to me. "You are my husband. I know and love you more than anyone in this world or yours. Watching you, I could feel your every pain." She began to cry. "I wanted so much to reach out to you, to be with you. But you endured. You endured it all. And now you are here with us. I love you, Aurum." I looked into her eyes and saw the compassion that had enthralled me a lifetime ago. She leaned in close. "I love you so very much."

"I love you too." I just knelt there, holding onto them, for what seemed like an eternity. I never wanted to move. I just wanted to remain there with my family. Forget the mission. This was where I belonged. Here, with my wife and daughter in my arms, in this beautiful place.

"Father," Hope said quietly. I looked up and saw Lord Alizar approaching. I released my family from my arms and rose as he approached. My wife and daughter both curtsied at his approach, and I bowed.

"Have you made your peace, Aurum?" I looked back at my family.

"I can't stay here, can I." it wasn't a question, but he answered it anyway.

"You will return here when it is your time."

"I never believed in these things before I came here. I never believed in the soul, or gods or demons or an afterlife."

"And now?" Lord Alizar prompted.

"Now..." I gazed at my wife and daughter and then back at him. "Now I'm ready. I'm yours. What would you have me do, My Lord?"

"I would have you walk with me." I nodded. I turned back to Andusíl and Hope.

"My beautiful ladies," I said with a smile, "I will return to you." I pulled Hope into a tight embrace.

"I know, father," she whispered as she planted a kiss on my cheek. I returned it upon her forehead. I looked at her face one last time, memorizing every line and feature. I felt my interior picture of my family that I had held in my heart for ten years fade away: the picture of my wife holding my daughter for the mere moments after her birth and before she had passed away. That image slowly began to blur and crumble into dust, and a new image took its place: an image of her as a grown woman living in this wondrous place. I released her hand and held my right hand out to my wife. She looked at me without taking it.

"Husband," she said.

"Wife," I replied with a forlorn grin.

"You are wasting time. Go. We will still be here when you get back. No need for goodbyes. We are simply a dream deferred."

"Wife," I said. She tilted her head downwards and gazed at me wryly. "I love you."

"I know, and I never forgot. Now go, Aurum. Go live; be happy. Live." I knew the conversation was over now. She had that tone in her voice that told me to go. Tears stained my eyes.

"As you demand." I turned about to Lord Alizar, who stood there patiently.

"Now, you are ready," he told me. I hesitated.

"But… I have yet to bleed water," I told him.

Lord Alizar smiled. "What do you think you are doing now?" he asked as he touched the tear upon my cheek. I bowed my head. "Now come, and we will forge a Ruin out of you."

Clash of Kings

Nineteen

The wind flew from Tendra's lungs as she felt her body plummet downwards. She looked up to see Veriel's snarling face as arrows chased him up to the clouds. She felt a man's arms around her as she fell. They crashed through the roofing of a building, and she fell atop the man as they tumbled onto the wooden floor within.

"Sorry for the rough landing, My Lady," Rayn said. She managed to offer a smile as she regained her breath.

"Don't apologize. Thank you." They rose and moved to the window to gaze out on the slaughter around them. It was chaos. Unu warriors coursed across the wall with the human army launching a hasty retreat, trying to fend off the sheer power of the unu assault. The steel ceiling had collapsed due to the siege towers spilling out unu soldiers, and humans were running for cover from the steady rain of Skyguard arrows. Skyguard warriors were fewer on the ground than in the sky, though they wove through attack after attack like dancers. The steady boom of the battering ram was omnipresent in the background as the centaurs strove against the gate. Every minute or so it came again. The gates were not meant to sustain such an onslaught, and they would fall.

"Don't thank me yet. We told you to leave; now you actually need to do it. We can't protect you here, and the Skyguard are targeting you. Promise me you'll run for the docks and get out of here when I say go. We will hold the city for as long as we can, but you need to leave,," Rayn said urgently. She looked at his eyes, but they were tracking the air above them. "You dropped this." He pulled a second long sword from his back and handed Valiant to her. She took it gratefully. "Let's go," he said without waiting for an answer, urging her back from the window and towards the ladder in the center of the room.

"Not a chance," Tendra said resolutely as she swung down first. She took the rungs, quickly arriving on the ground floor in no time. The two windows in the front of the house were open and surrounded by shattered glass. The harsh winter wind furled through the ragged curtains and cut through Tendra's body. Long Skyguard arrows were scattered around the room. Rayn crossed the room in six long strides and peered out warily. He turned back to her.

"Stop acting like a warrior, and start acting like a leader!" Rayn shouted. "This city is falling around us, and you have to survive to keep humanity afloat. Please, Tendra." Rayn tore his eyes from the skies to look at her. His eyes begged her. She saw almost madness in them. She nodded. He looked back up, and she saw him go rigid. "Dreadspawn, Veriel is coming." Rayn grabbed her by the shoulders. "Keep to the alleyways. Go nowhere in the open. GO!" She leapt out the open window with Rayn by her side before turning to flee towards the docks. Her eyes shot to the skies as the Skyguard Lord Commander hurled down towards them.

Tendra sprinted in the opposite direction of the incoming Skyguard. She looked back to see the Lord Commander land on the ground and engage the wizard.

242

"Tendra! Go." Rayn screamed at her, but her eyes didn't move from the duel. Veriel's huge frame and sword dwarfed the small wizard. Yet Rayn seemed to be holding his own. His sword flashed in the grimy sunlight, catching even the smallest rays and angling them into her eyes. She was dazzled as the blades clashed a dozen times a second. They disengaged for a brief moment.

"STRIKE!" The wizard's staff lashed out and lightning sparked from its tip. The Skyguard leapt with his body seeming to curve around the electric discharge, and he landed on his feet. Then, they were back at it. The Skyguard's heavy sword sparkled with curling black ivy, and every blow launched a shower of sparks into the air. Over and over again, his heavy strikes pounded down on Rayn, who did his best to fend them off. The Skyguard began to slam against the wizard with powerful overhead strikes again and again. The wizard leapt away. He yelled something Tendra couldn't hear and fire began to pour from the staff. The Skyguard's robes caught flame, but the massive Skyguard kept coming. Rayn couldn't bring his sword around fast enough, and the broadsword impacted the center of the staff. An explosion hurled Tendra back against the wall as the staff shattered, knocking Rayn to the ground. Veriel seemed to be unfazed. The wizard leapt from his back to his feet in a single smooth motion, only to be met by an unstoppable force.

Veriel's leg looked like a tree trunk. The corded muscle seemed to move in slow motion as it lashed out, catching Rayn in the stomach and flinging him backwards towards the wall. The man slammed into the stone and was momentarily dazed.

"Rayn!" Tendra screamed. Veriel looked directly at her and smiled.

"Rayn!" Tendra screamed a second time. The Skyguard raised his sword like it was made of air and hurled it at the wizard. The blade didn't spin or waver in its trajectory as it hurtled through the air straight and true. The tip of the steel passed right through the flesh of Rayn's neck as if it didn't even exist. The blade made no sound as it slid into the stone wall and stuck there. Rayn's body was motionless for a moment as blood began to

243

fountain outwards from his neck. A thick crimson pool began to form on his feet as his cloak stained red. Tendra watched his eyes fade slowly from green to white. His sword clattered to the ground with a resounding din that echoed in her ears. Finally, his body slumped downwards, leaving his head to rest upon the blade and a cardinal streak to grow on the wall. Veriel walked slowly over to his sword and ripped it out of the wall. Rayn's head dropped downwards and landed on his body. It bounced off the corpse and rolled to the side.

"Rayn…" Tendra murmured voicelessly. Tears flooded her eyes. Everyone kept dying on her. Veriel began to walk towards her. Slowly, deliberately, like a wolf honing in on a wounded prey. Dread filled her bones, and ice flooded her veins. Yet still she couldn't move. She felt a hand on her shoulder. She turned and saw the one man she had never imagined to see standing there. It was Vizien. His cold blue eyes stared at the Skyguard Lord Commander. He held his saber at his side.

"Walk away, Skyguard," Vizien said. The Skyguard laughed.

"I just killed a magician. Do you think you scare me, human?" Veriel replied. Vizien moved between Tendra and Veriel. There was something in his left hand. Vizien wove his sword back and forth.

"I won't let you near her." Vizien proclaimed. Tendra's eyes flicked back and forth between Rayn's head, Vizien's sword, and Veriel's grin.

Lightning flashed onto Veriel's skin, and the Lord Commander was hurled across the plaza. Joven slammed down to the ground and rolled to his feet. Vizien whirled around as the wizard landed.

"Move!" Joven yelled. "Vizien, cover us!" He grabbed Tendra's hand and pulled. Tendra's legs suddenly unlocked, and she fled. They whipped through the streets of Gemport. Tendra shoved Valiant into its sheath as she ran numbly through the alleys. They twisted and turned, and Tendra lost all sense of direction. Rayn was gone, just like everyone else. She should be used to it by now; everyone would die on her…everyone. Tendra no longer heard the sounds of the war above her; all she could hear were the sounds of her heart and feet pounding in rhythm. A cobblestone struck her foot, and she stumbled and crashed to the ground. Her vision was blurred as hands pulled her up. Her legs burned from exhaustion and fading adrenaline. Her lungs burned from the cold. Her eyes burned from the tears. Still she ran until she realized that Joven's arms were stopping her.

"Tendra." A voice rang out, and her vision cleared as her tears were wiped away. "Focus. Focus!" Joven yelled at her. She stared at him blankly. "He's gone. You are not, but if you die, then humanity dies. You can't let that happen. I need you to get on this boat and sail for Terakeen. Jeric's army will be there any day. You need to take command of them, and you need to win this war. Do you understand?" Tendra became aware that she was standing on the docks, and the blurs of movement behind Joven were soldiers filing by the dozens for the evacuation. "Tendra! Do you understand?" He shook her shoulders, and she nodded.

"Yes." Her voice was a hollow croak of sound. "What about you?" she managed.

"I have my own ways of escaping. Don't worry about me; I'll make it. Take this." Joven reached around and grabbed his staff from its sheath upon his back and handed it to her. She took it carefully, as if it were a snake. The wood was coarse and wet from the snow. "You don't have to be a wizard to use some of the magic bound within it. All you have to do is say 'strike', and you summon lightning. Protect yourself, and trust no one. Now go. Be strong. Be the woman you were born as, and become the leader you are destined to be."

Tendra swallowed heavily and brought her own hand up to wipe her tears away. She strove for the center that Joven possessed after just seeing his brother murdered. That hardness of heart to continue when death so pervaded the world around her. Arrows fell around her, and she turned and stepped onto the ship in front of her.

As her foot hit the deck of the boat, sound exploded back into her ears: the scraping of wood on, wood, and the sound of hundreds of footsteps, of catapults striking the stone and battle cries echoed in her ears. She held tightly to the staff, as if it would protect her from anything and everything. A man pushed past her.

"My lady, the captain is there." The man said as he recognized her, pointing to the helm before hurrying to help the next group of people onto the boat. "Five more!" he hollered, and five people pushed and shoved to make it onto the boat. Tendra pushed her way past sailors and refugees alike to reach the captain. The cold sea sprayed into her eyes, but she paid it no mind.

"Rally up the boards, lads. We're movin' out! Get the oars going and pull them sails with the wind. Get that anchor on board, Smits!" Tendra slipped next to him. "All you dogs that aren't sailors get below deck! None o' you better be up here. You too, woman," the captain said over his shoulder to her.

"Terakeen," Tendra said.

"Nay, we sail for King's Port by the order of the Queen."

"Terakeen, good sir," she commanded, as a bit of the leadership she needed to regain echoed in her words. The captain turned to admonish her, but his words died in his throat.

"My Lady," he said. The ship cut loose from the docks, and the torrential waters began to hurl it away from city. He shrugged and turned from her to his crew. "Keep it close to the Thornes, boys, we're headed to The Iceberg!"

"THE ICEBERG" the crew echoed. The wind whipped through Tendra's clothes as she stood behind the captain. Her hands began to shake, and her legs grew weak as the high from the battle began to fade from her body. Their vessel coursed by a dozen other boats that were trying to get into the docks to help ferry people away. The oarsmen were broad, burly men, and their faces strained with every rotation of the oars. Tendra coughed heavily as a wave crashed into her face. The frigid saltwater brought a foul taste to her mouth, and she held down the vomit that rose in the back of her throat with effort.

"You might be wantin' to head below, my lady. She's not liking us much today!" Tendra nodded and began to stumble across the bridge. She grasped the side of the deck for support as she made her way towards the stairs. She took two steps before looking out onto the ocean. She saw ripples moving in a straight line through the waves. On closer look, they were less like ripples and more like arrows. They pushed through the waves as if they were nonexistent. She focused her vision as they came closer and closer.

"By Supremor," Tendra whispered. The water in front of her exploded, and a silvery blue streak flew behind her, slamming into the captain and continuing overboard. Six more blurs streaked across the ship, taking oarsmen into the ocean. Tendra's eyes flashed back to the right, and she saw six more waves coming towards her. Tendra looked back at the oarsmen. They were panicking, and the oars were abandoned as weapons were drawn. The ship began to turn beneath her feet as the wheel spun aimlessly. The second wave was less than a hundred meters away.

Tendra's hands ached, and she looked down to see her left hand gripping the railing, and her right hand gripping Joven's staff. Tendra set her jaw. This was her ship now. Three streaks leapt out of the water.

"STRIKE, STRIKE, STRIKE." Tendra screamed as she braced herself against the back of the stairs. Still she was flung back across the bridge of the boat and slammed against the railing by the force of the impact. Two of the blasts missed, but the third one slammed into the streak and sent it tumbling to the front of the ship. This was the first time Tendra had gotten a good look at it. The lizard-like mouth and lengthy body sent a chill down Tendra's spine. The telos had entered the war, and once again humanity bore the brunt of the assault. Tendra looked at her crew and realized that all eyes were upon her and the slightly smoking edge of her staff. There were twenty-two men left. Tendra's eyes looked around and saw the edge of Shining Bay. They could escape it, and perhaps they could lose the telos on the open sea, or if need be, take the ship to ground.

"Back on your oars!" she yelled. "No slacking! We need to get out of the bay and onto the Thorne Coast. GO!" The oarsmen scrambled, and she ran for the wheel. It was spinning like mad, but she threw her hand forward catching it. The force caused her to have to drop to one knee to hold it steady. She cranked the wheel upwards as the third group of telos descended upon them. She quickly glanced around and saw three or four dozen ships in the middle of coming and going. None of the telos attacked her ship in this wave, but she was braced with her staff nonetheless. She breathed a quick sigh of relief, but that sigh caught in her throat as she watched the ship next to her lose all of its soldiers in a single wave. The telos were naught but blurs as men seemingly disappeared.

"Someone who can steer the ship, bring us around!" Tendra screamed. One of the oarsmen let go of his charge and ran towards the hold. He ripped the door up.

"I NEED A SAILOR!" the man bellowed. Tendra's eyes desperately searched the water as the next wave grew closer. She couldn't hold the wheel and fire the staff, nor could she release either one. A knight was hauled out of the hold, and he stumbled up the stairs.

"My lady?" the knight said.

"Take the wheel." The words came through gritted teeth as she strained against it. The man stepped up and ripped his helmet off. He grasped the steering column with both hands and nodded to Tendra. She released her hand and slid out. The wheel held firm. "I need you to guide us out onto the Thorne Coast. I don't care where; we just need to get away from thes- STRIKE!" Tendra screamed as she swung the staff around. The telos that was flying towards them seemed to freeze in midair before being hurled backwards into the water. Tendra could feel the hairs on her arm stand on end. The knight looked at her with awe. "Get us out of the Bay, now!" he nodded and cranked at the wheel. The ship began to turn, escaping the walls of the bay. Tendra's eyes scanned the water, searching desperately for the telos.

The wind whipped through her bones as she shivered in her chain mail. The waves crashed heavily against the boat, and it rocked with every motion. Her hands were white from both the cold and the grip she held upon the staff. Tendra's mind began to grow as numb as her body. Three telos leapt on the ship, and Tendra was able to strike two of them, but only one of the next four. Her oarsmen were falling. Soon they would all be gone.

Then, they were free.

The ship burst out of the bay, and it seemed to Tendra like the sun was finally able to seep through the omnipresent shroud that had strangled it. The waters grew still beneath her as they rounded the bay walls sharply and struck west for the Thorne Coast and Terakeen. Tendra stumbled down the stairwell. Her oarsmen continued to heave in order to escape to the open sea.

"My lady, what bearing should I set her on?" the man helming the wheel addressed her. She looked up through exhausted eyes.

"Terakeen, with all haste." He nodded in reply and began to spin the wheel to take them away from the coast. The sails were unfurled, and they caught a wind. Tendra's eyes continued to scan the waters behind them for telos. But, there were no streaks in the water that would indicate their approach. She slumped to the deck. Her arms ached from the dozens of lightning bolts she had summoned from the staff. She didn't even know how she had done it, or how it had worked. Regardless, she cast a prayer to Supremor in thanks that it had.

"Heyo, Heyo, Heyo for Queen Sumenel," one of the sailors broke out. The rest joined in, "Heyo, Heyo, Heyo for the Queen O'thunder." Tendra summoned a weak smile at the oarsmen, and they took that as encouragement and continued:

Queen Sumenel walks our very decks
Good luck and blessings from the fairer sex
Lightning in hand
And thunder in grasp
She made them telos a thing of the past
With a flash and a bang
She sent 'em back where they came
To the bottom of the sea
Where they can't touch you
And they can't touch me
Heyo, Heyo, Heyo, for the Queen O'thunder.
Heyo, Heyo, Heyo, for the Queen O'thunder.

249

Tendra smiled as a blanket has brought to her. She accepted it gratefully, and the bottle of wine just as gratefully. The firewine burned as it went down her throat, and it spread through her body like its name, warming her limbs.

The harsh winter sunlight brought no warmth, and the seas were far from smooth, but they had made it out of the bay. They joined two dozen other ships that had made it out. Each of them had suffered heavier losses than her own. One ship was down to a mere two men. All of the people they had evacuated had been lost to the telos. Three of the ships were anchored and abandoned, because there were simply not enough people to crew them.

But they were alive, and they had escaped the gauntlet. Tendra's eyes looked back longingly at Gemport. The Skyguard crowded the sky, and she prayed for Joven, Wesley, and Jonathon-even for Vizien. She prayed for their safety, and for the safety of all of her people, but that was her city that was burning.

Heyo, Heyo, Heyo for Queen Sumenel!

Guilt By Association

Twenty

Humanity's soldiers had abandoned the wall and had been stationed in houses going all the way back up to the palace. The unu were moving slowly, home by home, killing every human they could find, but they were suffering heavy losses in the cramped corridors of human homes, and the Skyguard were no help in assaulting an urban environment. Despite these problems, the human soldiers were simply no match for the unu, and all but the castle had fallen thanks to the copious use of smoke fires to coax the human defenders from their posts. Vizien stood at the doors to the castle at the center of the city. There, he waited.

Vizien watched in silence and in shadow as Jeronious, Qel, and Veriel strode forwards. The three leaders had come to claim their prize. Their gait held the arrogance that their lives of privilege and power afforded them. Vizien had made and would continue to make his own power. He had

251

taken it from men like these. Vizien waited here for Veriel. It had been not quite six years since the Skyguard Lord Commander had approached him. Vizien remembered the day well.

He had just begun his tenure under Joven's tutelage when Joven had been Lord Daramont. He had received word that a man who refused to be seen was looking for him. A man who all attempts to find had been for naught. This man had intrigued Vizien. He had approached the man, and they had spoken long into the night. Vizien had plans that even Joven did not. Plans that wove through the deep passageways of the world. Plans that bound the darkest natures of men, unu, centaurs, and Skyguard. Once a year they had met. Veriel would reveal methods of manipulation and secret poisons to him, and in return Vizien would reveal the court of humanity to Veriel. This was the first time Vizien had seen Veriel in the daylight. Veriel and Joven were not such different teachers, but Veriel had never tried to stem or control him. Joven was all about control.

Veriel saw him in the shadows but did not acknowledge his presence and merely strode past him.

"-do not mistake our current understanding for anything else than honoring the arrangement I have with Clansmaster Terel, Qel. You no longer rule your people. You would do well to remember that." Veriel's comments did nothing to faze the unu, who merely carried his swagger onwards and into the throne room.

"Be that as it may, Terel understood the value in keeping me around when he allowed me to see this campaign through in exchange for the scales," Qel replied. Jeronious had a sneering look on his face as he looked around. Vizien slipped behind and slowly followed them within.

"I have been waiting a long time for this," Jeronious said. No one seemed to pay him any mind, as the response was silence.

The marks of fire blackened the polished marble of the walls and pillars. Tapestries and statues lay in tattered ruins that were unrecognizable from their former glory. The doors had been thrown open to pave the way for the coming of the kings. Blood and corpses marked the floors, and the telltale black poison of the gallowglass hissed on their flesh. Vizien could see no sign of the gallowglass. He knew every shadow in this room, and not even a gallowglass could escape his gaze.

At the end of the long room stood the Unyielding Throne, and seated within was a man that Vizien had only heard of in fearful whispers. He was shorter than Vizien, maybe five and a half feet tall and slender. He wore simple white clothing that covered his ebony, smooth skin. An Iron Man, cut off from the rest of his culture, living in the world of men. Iron Men faces did not emote or blink, but rather seemed to be permanent masks like the iron of their namesake. This man's iron face was locked in a perpetual scowl. There was no doubt that this was Corrigan. Neither Veriel nor Qel said anything as they approached, and Vizien likewise kept his silence.

"I must admit that your presence here is surprising to me," Veriel said.

"Who are you?" Qel demanded.

"Why is he sitting in our throne?" Jeronious chimed in. Veriel simply smiled.

"He calls himself Corrigan." Vizien broke his silence as he strode forward out of the darkness. "He is an information broker." Qel drew his hammer at Vizien's approach. Vizien raised his hands. "Lord Veriel?" Vizien said. He looked expectedly at the Skyguard. For a second, Vizien saw complete disinterest in the Skyguard's eyes, and he feared that the being would let Qel kill him.

"This human is one of my agents." Veriel finally spoke in his defense. Qel continued to regard him suspiciously, and Vizien slowly released a sigh of relief. "You are correct, Vizien, but Corrigan is much more than that. What is it that you want, my friend? I have been quite curious to see how long it would take until you and the rest of the secondborn entered into this conflict." Veriel finally spoke.

"You already dragged one of us into it. I'm here to speak to you about two others." Corrigan said.

"I know only of my agent. The rest are an unknown to me," Veriel replied.

"Do you want to do this in front of an audience?" Corrigan asked. Vizien watched this exchange with interest. Veriel had a commanding presence, but Corrigan...his eyes looked dead center at Veriel's. He didn't flinch.

"I believe that is my throne," Veriel replied.

"A throne is simply the chair where a ruler sits. As long as I am seated here, this is merely a chair," Corrigan countered. Qel laughed.

"For an Iron Man, you have quite the sense of humor." Qel's voice grew cold. "I have never known an Iron Man to have a sense of humor, or a name."

"You have never met an Iron Man, Qel of the Thousand Hammers, former clansmaster of the unu. Don't patronize me; it is unbecoming of you," Corrigan replied.

"How dare you speak to us in such a way?" Jeronious asked incredulously. "Do you have any idea the power we wield?"

"Peace, Jeronious; you see this is no mere Iron Man. In fact, once, it would have been called a throne at his touch. A long time ago." Veriel studied Corrigan.

"Indeed."

"What do you want?" Veriel asked bluntly.

"I want you to order the release of my two kin. I know the Wither has them, and he is not accepting my emissaries. He hasn't since he took that name and betrayed the rest of the secondborn." Corrigan said.

"I will see what can be done," Veriel replied. "What do I receive from helping you?"

"We will not enter the war against you. Also, information. A Champion is being forged to be brought to bear against you. You cannot stand against us, and the Dreaming Lord's Champion. Not only that, but a degenerate has been unleashed in Carin." Veriel's eyes widened.

"What does that mean?" Jeronious asked. "Veriel, what does that mean?"

"Silence." Veriel ordered, and Jeronious shrunk back at the harshness of Veriel's tone. "Who?" was all he said.

254

Corrigan smiled. "Swear on your name, that you will give me what I ask, and you will have your name."

"You should ask him about his relationship to the Seven," Vizien counseled smugly.

"When I want your input you will know of it, human," Veriel commanded. Vizien shot a glance at Veriel. He had not been rebuked like that in a long time. In a few long deliberate steps, the Skyguard Lord Commander approached where Corrigan sat easily in the Throne. Corrigan stood his ground. Veriel glared into his eyes, and Corrigan returned his gaze hardily. He didn't blink.

"Who?" Veriel hissed.

"Swear your oath," Corrigan replied unfazed.

"Get off my throne," Veriel hissed. Corrigan smiled as he rose to his feet. Slowly, deliberately he took each step in turn. One by one he stepped downwards until he was on even footing with Qel and Vizien. He turned back towards Veriel whose fingers ran across the markings in the arms of the throne. It was as if he had seen them long ago and was now remembering their meaning. "Alizar brings a Champion against, me, then this time I will raise one of my own." Veriel said, though it seemed to no one in particular.

"Is that a rejection of my offer?" Corrigan asked.

"Yes," Veriel replied.

"Very well then. You know better than to try and follow me." Corrigan stepped down and started to walk away.

"Wait." Corrigan slowly turned back around. Veriel looked straight into Vizien's eyes. He struggled to maintain Veriel's gaze. His stare went from Corrigan back to Vizien. "You are changed, the both of you. You have been touched by Lord Alizar's realm." Veriel looked around the room. His eyes were azure fire.

Vizien flinched.

"What do you mean?" Vizien asked. Veriel continued his searching in silence. It was as if he could see through the very walls of the castle.

255

"There," Veriel said. Vizien turned to follow his eyes: the crypts. "Take me there," Veriel commanded. Vizien strode quickly to the pillar, pressed the ring on his hand into the eye of the eagle, and twisted his fist. The secret door opened, and Vizien led the way into the darkness. No torches were lit, but Vizien had been this way many times.

The spiral staircase wound down and down, and each step echoed in the frigid air. As the torchlight dwindled, in its place came a new light, a softer blue light. Veriel walked towards the fake Heart of Fires quickly, but cautiously. He held his hand out but didn't touch it and instead ran his hand all around the stone.

"Do you know what it is?" Vizien asked. Veriel finished winding his way around the stone. He turned back to them. His face was enshrined in the light and his eyes held a manic glee. A wicked smile was emboldened by the shine.

"It's beautiful," Jeronious breathed. Vizien turned in surprise to see that the centaur had been able to make it down the stairs into the crypt.

"What is it?" Veriel paused for a moment. "A piece of heaven fallen to earth. What it means, though, is far more important."

"Which is?" Qel asked after a moment of silence.

"That I have already won this war." There was not a single waver in the confidence of his phrasing. Vizien could feel it in every word that wrapped around his spine. He had a feeling that the war that Veriel was talking about was not the same war as the centaurs and unu were fighting.

"Qel, Jeronious, Corrigan, I have business with this human. Qel, Jeronious, see about the completion of the takeover of this city. It will be yours at the closing of this campaign." Veriel said. "Corrigan, I know threats made against you are in vain, but I am sure The Wither would love to test his skills against your skin."

"Mayhaps," Corrigan replied.

"I regret that we cannot do business, but if you're right about your siblings, than I would rather they be in the Wither's care than in the wild. Surely you understand that." Veriel replied. Corrigan nodded.

"Oh, and Corrigan, did it hurt when I killed your apprentice? I know you saw it. When his body slumped to the ground and his eyes lost their sheen. Did it hurt?"

Corrigan glared at Veriel. "Every drop of blood might as well have been one of my own," he replied. Vizien watched the exchange silently. Corrigan turned and walked away. It seemed Veriel already knew of the Seven's relationship with the Iron Man. Qel and Jeronious followed Corrigan up and out of the crypts a moment after.

"You have business to attend to here?" Vizien nodded.

"It can wait. Tell me about the wizards," Veriel said. *An interesting question in light of what just happened.*

"There are seven of them with a vast variety of skill sets. The only overlap seems to be their intelligence and fighting skills. One, Rowen, was here until just before the Battle of Long Fang. He was... very blatant in his courtship of Queen Sumenel despite her betrothal. Two wizards arrived just days ago, and since then they have taken an active role in the ruling activities of the city. Joven especially, he is not the one you killed. That was Rayn. He spent a lot of time speaking with elders around the city, and Jonathon, a Brilliance in the Light Monks. We have had no word of the others since Long Fang. Though there were rumors that Qel captured one and took him to Ornus: Dorian."

"Tell me better," Veriel said. His face glowed from the fake Heart of Fires.

"Joven is an overconfident schemer. He believes in the infallibility of his plans and desires control and power over all else. He can't be used by us. He is too selfish. He wants it all for himself. I did my tutelage under him years ago when he was known as Lord Daramont."

Veriel raised an eyebrow at that. "That does not cause conflicted loyalties, I trust." Veriel asked.

"No. My loyalty remains to myself."

Veriel smiled. "Continue."

"Rowen, the other possible living one, is flaky. He is a womanizer, but he is more clever than he appears. He has some fighting ability, but his slick tongue and appearance are his true weapons. His affection for Queen Sumenel could be something that we can easily manipulate to our ends. He is overt, yet subtle simultaneously."

"Good. Two of the wizards were in Ornus when I departed. They should be dead by now." Veriel replied. His eyes were pensive, though they never moved from the stone. "Finish your business, and then move on quickly to Terakeen. That is where we will finish this. Soon, very soon, this will all be over, and you will have your crown." Veriel pulled his eyes free as Vizien focused on him. There seemed to be a weight upon him, but it was like Veriel was preparing for the last push to release it.

"Are you well?" Vizien asked uncertainly.

"Get out," Veriel hissed. Vizien offered a slight bow before slipping from the Skyguard's presence.

His heavy boots thumped against the stone as he quickly took the stairs. It would take him seven minutes to reach the dungeons on the other side of the castle, provided he didn't run into any unu who tried to question him. But Vizien was always good at walking the line through the shadows, and the bleakness of the overcast day combined with the fading of the sun meant that there were plenty of shadows for him to use.

Vizien slid back and forth, winding his way through the hallways. The sounds of battle were all-encompassing, though never specific. The Jamon's Victory had been the best and only plan for the queen to take, and it was proving to be effective in keeping the unu busy throughout the city. Vizien admired the unu for the value they placed on cunning, something humanity associated with maliciousness, but their bloodlust was distasteful.

Killing was a necessity, but it was not necessarily always the best option. Killing for perceived glory was foolishness. Killing needed to be done to make a point or to advance oneself. That was how it should be done. Vizien was on his way to do such killing. Vizien made his way quickly out of the castle and away from the sounds of fighting. He made sure to keep in the shadows. The light snow sloshed around his boots, and more was coming down every second. The bay would start to freeze soon. Vizien pulled his cloak around him for warmth. Despite it all, though,

258

Vizien enjoyed the winter. There was less movement in the streets, and it was easier for him to do his business.

Eleven blocks west from the castle gates, two blocks north, three unu patrols, and one hundred and sixty seven corpses later, Vizien arrived at the house of his choosing. He had checked thirteen times to ensure that he wasn't being followed, especially by Corrigan, that man was…dangerous.

Houses with proper cellars were hard to come by in Gemport. The hard rock of the cliff face that they were up against made that difficult, but there were a few homes that had managed to craft one. Vizien's destination was one such house that he had procured sometime in the past for use as a storage facility for people of interest. Six such people dwelt there now. Through the use of various potions and serums, as well as careful maneuvering in the last few days, Vizien had managed to acquire each of these individuals. He had kept them alive and locked away until the sacking of the city, when he knew he could safely dispose of them with no one the wiser. Making people disappear was a specialty of his, but people like this were not ones to go unnoticed in their absence. Vizien slipped quietly into the door of the nondescript brown wooden house.

Inside looked like any usual home, with a kitchen table that doubled as a work bench. Sawdust and wood shavings littered the ground, and carpenter's tools in various states of disrepair hung on the walls safely out of range of the two children who one would imagine lived there by the two small beds and one larger one. A boy and a girl, by the small wagons and ragged dolls on the floor. Vizien would come by three times a week to change things around to make it look like someone lived here- someone who was now long gone to the eyes of the unu. Vizien moved quickly through the single-story house searching for any sign of soldiers or any other rabble that may have taken refuge during the siege, but he found nothing.

Vizien returned to the bedroom, slid the boy's bed to the left, and removed the small panel that covered the iron loop door to the cellar. This door Vizien had crafted and installed himself. The original cellar door he had heavily boarded up and locked. Anyone who found it would think the

259

cellar abandoned. Vizien twisted the iron loop until it clicked, pulling upwards to reveal a bitter draft of wind. Vizien shivered involuntarily. He rather hoped none of them had frozen to death, but if they had then that was just one less death by his hands. Not that he minded. Vizien reached underneath the father's bed to pull out a readymade torch. After fishing for a few moments, he discovered the flint as well. It took only a single strike with his knife to get the torch to catch flame. The heat of the fire felt good on his face and hands.

Vizien descended the step ladder, holding the torch down before him. He heard movement. Vizien's foot struck hard dirt, and he held the torch out to view his prisoners. There were six of them: Terrance Greenhorn, Duke Salem Colfax, Duke Johan Veris, Duchess Leslin Fortnac, the Duke Berin Traenor, and Duke Traenor's son, Uran, the last two being Vizien's own father and elder brother. Each of them were blindfolded, gagged, and chained to the wall. Vizien moved to the first one. It was Duke Colfax. Vizien had never met the man until two nights ago when he had entered his bedchambers and stolen him away. Vizien slid his knife across his throat. A thin red line was all that divided men from life and death.

Terrance Greenhorn, now there was an interesting fellow. A thug with a title; it was amazing that he even had the brains to speak. A tool of some of the more…ambitious members of the Council of Elders, Terrance had been most willing to give up information once the proper torture began. Now, though, he was just another obstacle being removed. Vizien smiled. In a single day, he would remove six of the fourteen people that stood between him and the throne. Four others were already dead. The rest…well, Vizien was a patient man, if nothing else.

He slowly drew his knife across Terrance's neck. This one Vizien enjoyed. This fool had almost cost Vizien months of planning. If it wasn't for Rowen's timely intervention, Tendra would have been lost. Tendra was Vizien's ideal ruler until he stepped into the position. No one else in the line of succession would have allowed Vizien to live with all that he knew.

The next two had succumbed to the cold.

Vizien moved to stand squarely between his father and brother. Vizien wanted to look into his father's eyes as his mongrel son slew his pride and joy. Vizien wanted to laugh in his father's face when he realized that he had chosen unwisely. Then Vizien wanted to watch the light vanish from his father's eyes for what he had done to him.

Vizien undid the blindfold on Uran's eyes first. They were terrified and grew only more so as they played across the room, seeing the hanging corpses. They held the fear of a life of comfort and prestige being ripped away. They held the fear of loss. Uran would lose it all tonight. That terror changed to horror as Uran saw Vizien's face. Vizien smiled a dark grin. He then turned to his father. He pulled the blindfold and the gag out of his mouth.

"Vi-Vi-Vi-Vizien?" his father stammered. Vizien was surprised his father even remembered his name. Vizien still remembered his father coming to him when he had attained the rank of Grand Inquisitor, trying to take money and influence from Vizien's name. Vizien had laughed in his father's face. Vizien remembered being sent off to the Trading Pens when he was six years old. A school it called itself, but it was a slave trading den. Vizien had never found out what his father had been paid for him, but he had been sold like cattle to a man in the north, a thief whose only name that Vizien knew was Quick Fingers. Vizien remembered night after frozen night huddling on stone floors. His father had dared to come back to him after he had returned as Lord Daramont's ward. After he had risen through the ranks.

"Hello, father."

"What? I don't...I don't understand," Berin almost whispered.

"Of course you don't. You never understood. You never took two seconds to even try. You just sold me off like cattle and gave my inheritance to him." Vizien turned to Uran. "And you took it all. Never once daring to question. Never once searching for me. You are complicit in his every crime. Good-bye, Uran." Vizien once again slid his dagger through the throat. Uran's face contorted to become a scream as his muffled voice strained to escape from its prison, and failed. Berin was speechless. His eyes just kept sliding back and forth from Vizien to Uran. He was in shock: terrible shock. Vizien snapped his fingers in front of his father's face.

"Why? Why?" his father stumbled over his words. Vizien shook his head in disgust that this was his progenitor. He had come from this stock of man.

"Power, father, power. You tried to take it from me, and by doing so, you just made the craving that much stronger. I'm going to take every ounce of your power. I won't stop there. I will take the throne, and it is all thanks to you. So this is me saying 'thank you'."

"I didn't do this, Vizien. What have you done!" Berin veritably screamed.

"What have I done? I have eliminated the competition. Soon there will be no one and nothing left between the throne of humanity and me. One by one, I'm cutting down everyone who stands between me and the throne. There aren't many left, but I wanted your death to be special. This is the end for you, father, but before you die, I just want to tell you, thank you. Thank you from your mongrel son. Thank you from the unwanted. Revenge is a sweet thing indeed," Vizien said.

"No, don't do this! Please don't do this!" Berin begged. "VIZIEN! I'm your father!" Vizien raised his blade. There would be no thin red line this time. His father's cries fell on deaf ears as Vizien pushed the blade forward. The cries became gurgles; the gurgles became whimpers until...nothing but silence.

Vizien stared at the corpses before shrugging and turning away. Good work had been accomplished tonight, and now it was time to move on to Terakeen. He climbed up the ladder. As he did so a chill traveled up his spine. Something was wrong.

"I understand." The sound of the voice made Vizien pause, but the recognition of whose it was allowed him to relax. Sitting on the edge of the large bed was Joven.

"Understand what?"

"A father sacrificing one son for another. My own father did the same to me. He stole my inheritance and cast it aside, all for the sake of another," Joven said.

"What can I do for you, Joven?" Vizien replaced the trap door and moved the bed back to its spot covering the panel. He assumed a position on the far side of the room from Joven, leaning against the wall near the door.

"I need out of Gemport. The fighting will last for two more days at least, but there is nothing more I can do here. With your partnership with Veriel," a small pinch of tension wove its way through Vizien's back. Joven could kill him. Vizien had seen Joven kill a man without even touching him. Vizien could not win a fight with him. He prepared to run. It was the only outcome that might provide him some acceptable odds of survival, "I assume it will be no problem to smuggle me out." Joven said. There was no malice in his voice whatsoever, which Vizien found slightly puzzling.

"I can do that."

"Good. Let's go."

"Now?" Vizien asked incredulously. Joven looked at him.

"You have other nobles to dispatch?" Joven asked.

"No, but the streets are crawling with unu and centaurs. Even some Skyguard are still here. If we try to leave before nightfall, we will be accosted for certain. We need to leave under cover of darkness." Joven looked at him. His eyes bore into him, but Vizien matched them. Vizien wasn't the same man that Joven had abandoned in the middle of the night. He was something far, far different.

"Tell me about Veriel," Joven said.

"He is the Lord Commander of the Skyguard of Cloud Breach. He approached me about a year after you took me on as your apprentice."

"Why?" asked Joven. Vizien shrugged in response. It was a question he had wondered since the very first day that he had met Veriel. At the time, Vizien had thought the Skyguard had been investigating the Heart of Fires. Now, he wasn't so sure.

"I don't know. I thought he wanted a pulse on the throne and the politics of humans. I didn't know why, but that's what I thought."

"In return?"

"Various things. Information mostly, but also access to Skyguard archives, a suit of armor, and various other things. I had not heard from him in eight months. I wasn't sure what had happened until he showed up here." Vizien stopped to look at Joven, who waved for him to continue. "He is very smart. I often wondered why he needed me, for it always seemed like he knew more than me anyways. I never saw him leave any of our meetings. He's confident, but not to the point of arrogance. He's a planner, and an expert one, but he's an opportunist as well. I have no doubt that he took advantage of you and your brothers' emergence."

"What does he want?" Joven asked.

"I don't know," Vizien admitted. It had always grated on him just how little he had known about Veriel.

"I thought I taught you better than to get into business with people whom you know nothing about. Not only that, but you have been working for him for years. That is the mark of a fool. You know this." Vizien's chin jutted out, but he nodded. "What did you tell him about us?"

"A basic personality profile, as well as a little bit of history. Nothing that you wouldn't mind losing, but everything true enough that it wouldn't cast suspicions if he sought a second opinion."

Joven stroked his chin. "That's everything?"

"That's everything." Vizien replied. Joven looked at him. He smiled. "Well, I did teach you to take advantage of your resources. So what is the plan?"

"This place needs to be torched. We wait until nightfall. Use the fire as a distraction to steal horses from the unu camp outside and ride for King's Port."

Joven nodded. "Very well. It's just under two hours until nightfall. Will you be remaining here?"

Vizien shook his head. "There are things I need from the castle. It will take some time to acquire them."

"I'll remain here, then."

Despite Joven's words and utter inaction, Vizien remained tense. "I'll be back just after nightfall." Vizien turned to the door.

"No, you won't," Joven said. Vizien's breathing slowed. He would only get one chance at this. The doorway was just a foot away. Joven was going to kill him. He was so close. Vizien forced himself to turn back around.

"What do you mean?" Joven slowly rose from the bed. A crossbow was in his hand. The barbed end of the quarrel was harsh and cruel. It would tear away the flesh. Joven leveled it at him.

"You shouldn't have served two mas-" Vizien didn't let Joven finish. He dove backwards, ripping the door behind him. The bolt still managed to graze his shoulder as it deflected off of the wood. Vizien rolled to his feet and darted out the door. He didn't even look for unu. His blood pounded in his ears as he ran. Sweat poured down his body even as the cold electrified his skin. He twisted and turned through the alleys, not even caring where he was going. He just needed to get away. He took a sharp left, throwing himself through the door of the first house, and drawing his rapier in one smooth motion. He threw the door closed and slid into a small nook behind a hutch. He watched the window closely.

He waited for Joven to come.

He waited.

Slowly, his nerves began to relax. He was alive. Vizien ran his left hand through his hair. He breathed.

Oh Supremor. What am I going to do now? Joven would escape; he would make it to Terakeen before Vizien could and poison Tendra against Vizien even more than she already was. He was of no more use to Veriel. *Curse him.* Vizien gritted his teeth. This...this would not go well. Either Veriel would win, in which case Vizien would have nothing, because he had now failed him. Or humanity and Joven would win...unless Joven died. Vizien looked outside into the harsh wind as two unu strode by the window. Vizien made himself small and avoided their gaze. He needed to disappear. Corrigan...he and Corrigan had done business together in the past. They could negotiate now. Vizien just needed to find him.

He would disappear for now, but he would be back.
Oh yes, he would be back.

The Warrior Within
Twenty-One

I stood balanced at the apex of a tower five thousand feet tall.
Wind whipped around me, but I stayed rigid. Stayed focused. I closed my
eyes and followed the words of the Visionaire, one of the three viziers of
Lord Alizar and one of my three teachers. The Visionaire had taught me
how to access the elixis. I pictured a dark room: place of perfect serenity. At
the center of this room was a well filled with the fiery liquid of the elixis,
the magic of Supremor. I imagined reaching my hand down and raising the
orange liquid to my lips. When next my eyes opened, I could feel them
burning, and my entire world was seen through a red filter. I turned my
head like a hawk stalking its prey. *There.* I saw a massive human standing,
waiting for me to assault him. It was the Baroner, the second of my
teachers. He was the only man in this room, known as Vista, that I knew of
and he had been training with me for the last seventy-nine turns of the color
bands since I had seen my family. This room had been constructed to
approximate Materia, so the physics and the feel of it were much more

tangible than any other place in the Dreaming. Materia was what people in the Dreaming called Carin, Cambria, and anywhere else in what I would call the real world.

The Visionaire had shown me how to construct the visual metaphor that was the dark room and the Well, but it was the Baroner who showed me what to do with it once I had access to the elixis. It was getting so that I could access the elixis in only a couple of seconds. Compare that to the first time where it took me two hours and still the only thing I had been able to manage was slightly improved hearing. Now, I could pick and choose my abilities. I could access each one at a time, and as the Champion of Lord Alizar, as Ruin, I could access a vast quantity of abilities. It was almost overwhelming, but it seemed like just now was I finally beginning to realize the breadth of what each race had to offer. I could tap into the innate abilities of each of the different races on Carin. I could grow wings like a Skyguard, or run as fast as a centaur; I could breathe underwater like the telos and see heat signatures like the unu. It was like being in a forge and knowing where each tool belonged and how it worked.

I exhaled as I pushed upwards and outwards from the crystal tower and into open air. I had climbed it using claws that I had taken from the ferals. It had been long and brutal but worth it for the sensation that I felt right now. Flying was a dangerous proposition, especially when coming out of falling. I switched from eyesight to flight and felt my shoulder blades tingle as wings of amber fire burned up and out from my back. I grinned as I spread them out to catch the air resistance, slowing me down as I hurtled towards the earth. The sensation was unlike anything I had ever felt before. It was terrifying and exhilarating at once, and even with the knowledge that I would not actually die if I hit the ground, the base part of me revolted at the sight of quickly incoming ground. I poured magic into my wings, causing them to grow wider and wider until they were forty feet from tip to tip. I pulled up into a tight spin as I bled speed. I saw the fuzzy outline of the Baroner in the distance through eyes stained with tears from the wind. My wings beat furiously to counter the blinding velocity, but it would not

268

be enough. I was coming in too fast. I reached back into the Well to try to grab Iron Man armor, but it was too late.

Wings fizzled and died as I lost my concentration and slammed into the ground, tumbling end over end, with each impact sending jolts of pain through every limb. I came to rest on my back, shaking as my body sorted through the pain. A hearty, booming laughter behind me caused me to roll over with a groan.

"You will not survive that stunt in Materia," he called out. Materia was the name beings who dwelled in Merhelden called the physical world. "You need to switch faster and plan your movements better. We both know you are smart enough to know that you should have activated your wings before you leapt. Think, Ruin." *Ruin*...that was the name I had been given. That was who I was now. I was Ruin as much as I was Aurum. I ran my fingers along the markings that had been etched upon my body by the Libran, the third of my teachers. The long flowing script was called THE WORD. THE WORD was the language of the elixis itself. I had learned several words in the language, but I was not yet sufficiently powerful to use the words as weapons. I knew of a group of elite warriors in Merhelden called the Viceroys who were said to wield THE WORD. Chief among them was Ethios the Lightholder. I had met him once before. The being had an intense arrogance about him. I believed him to be an orpherean shard, a piece of a Materian being's dreaming self, but I was not sure. The two words on my skin read as "Ruin" and "Claimed".

I grunted with pain as he offered me his hand. The Baroner was a either a very tall, very imposing man, or a very short, though still imposing, giant. He wore no shirt, but instead had a black apron on. I wasn't sure I had ever seen him wear anything else. He had deep brown skin like he had been basking in the sun all his life. The Baroner had been a task master, but he was not without his charms. A full beard covered his face, and his eyes were the color of mirth.

"Yes, well, I will not always have full notice prior to when I will need an ability. I wanted to test to see if I could react on moment's notice. I

269

am still not there, though. I am close, but still not there." The Baroner nodded.

"No, you are not. However, since you are here, I think a test is in order." He clapped his hands, and several centaurs appeared in the room armed with full battle raiment and carrying spears, pole arms, and other long hand weapons. They approached me slowly.

"Really?" I asked.

"Indulge me."

The centaurs surrounded me with their weapons held at the ready. They were wary. I once again reached into the elixis well, and this time I pulled out the abilities of the telos.

My limbs felt…slick. The rest of the centaurs appeared to move like stilted puppets at the hands of an amateur. One raised his scythe and swung it down in almost slow motion. I easily slid around the blow, delivering a vicious chop to the windpipe, which caused the centaur to stagger back. My limbs flexed in ways that they had not been made to twist. Yet there was no pain; there was only correctness.

"Switch," the Baroner called out, and I dug into the elixis and flashed to giant strength. I felt myself grow slightly but resisted the urge to grow to the full height.

The rest wasted no time in assailing me. Two blows from behind were vaulted over, and a third from above caught between my legs. I flexed the joints and, with my newfound power, easily snapped the end off. I fell to the ground, rolled, and hurled myself up into the air, using my arms to go into a high leap. The end of the spear in hand, I flicked it at one of the centaurs and watched it explode straight through his head, leaving nothing but a pulp behind. I fell to the ground and sprinted straight at one centaur, dodging his strike, and leapt up grabbed him around the neck, coming down on the other side and hurling him into the distance.

"Switch." With four centaurs left, I considered my options. I switched to feral claws and watched my fingers extend until the orange light was razor sharp in focus at the end. I quickly used those to tear the throats of two centaurs simultaneously before moving on to the power of the unu.

The unu could see the heat that radiated off of beings and objects. After some practice with it, I learned that if I focused enough I could see pressure points and arteries that ran hotter than other parts of the body. These were points where a well-placed blow could incapacitate an enemy. My mind flinched as the briefest image of Dane came to me. I was struck on the temple, and that brought them back into focus. I was sloppy, though, in their dispatch. Once I finished, I stood slowing my breathing down as The Baroner looked on disapprovingly.

"What happened?" he asked pointedly. For the briefest moment I considered lying. I considered saying a hundred different things that would keep my guilt hidden, but they were all useless excuses. Excuses would get me killed in Materia, so I couldn't afford them here.

"I…I killed a centaur, who was my friend, with my bare hands during my trials in Materia to reach Merhelden. I beat him with my fists until he died," I said. Remorse filled my voice.

"Imagine your friend not as being dead, but as being with your family. Emotion clouded and threatened to destroy you. Imagination sets you free." I nodded. The Visionaire had taught me that it was imagination that was greatest power a man had. I had thought it surprising, for in Cambria imagination had been everything. I did not understand how we had not had a more profound connection to the Dreaming in Cambria. I idly wondered if I would ever return there before the Baroner interrupted my reverie. "You are getting faster each time switching between Aers." *Aers*, that was what the Skyguard called their soul. It had been interesting seeing the convergence of concepts in my time here. The soul was just the manifestation of pure elixis in a physical form. The Skyguard called it the Aer, and believed they were the only ones who possessed it, but every being had one. Each race's Aer was unique to them, and by touching them I could take on the attributes that made them unique. The Skyguard had a stronger connection to the Dreaming and, therefore, were reliant on the Charist, which was elixis that had been distilled into Materia in liquid form. The connections that the elixis wove in everything were staggering. The Baroner had continued to talk while my mind had wandered. I refocused.

" Eventually, it will be almost unconscious, but you are still a long way from that point. You will still need to spend more time with The Visionaire; your elixis well is neither potent nor deep enough." the Baroner said.

I nodded in compliance. My training had been split into three segments. The Baroner taught me the application of the elixis; the Visionaire showed me how to expand the length and breadth of my ability to access it, and the Libran gave me extensive lessons in history and knowledge of the elixis and the war against Midox. In my time here I had learned all about the Dreaming and its connection to Materia. I had learned about Midox. I had learned about Veriel. It was a name that I had only heard in the delusional words of Galeerial when I had carried him from Amul Kon to the Face Off.

I had learned what my purpose was in being here: I was here to become the weapon of Lord Alizar against Veriel. I had learned about the three Champions before me. I had learned about Geraldean, the second Champion of Lord Alizar. He had been named Sentry where I was named Ruin. I had learned about the Pillars of Creation, and the names of the bloodlines which kept them strong.

"What more would you have me do?" I asked the Baroner.

"Learn," he replied. His eyes flashed as he filled with elixis and slowly rose into the air with an orange aura surrounding him. He had no wings. He hovered in the air. "Though you can access any feature of the races of Carin, you are not bound by their limitations. If you want speed, you do not have to shift your body into that of a horse. Equally, your strength has been bound by your resistance to growing, though why I do not know. You are far too puny to be attractive to anyone. Nevertheless, you can fly without wings, and tap all of the strength of a giant without growing to their size rather than the paltry amount that you were taking earlier. Try it." He extended his hand.

Flight without wings. I concentrated on the wall in my mind that stood between me and my goal. I knew science, and I knew that wings were

272

what made the birds fly, and so my mind had linked the two. So I began to visualize my wings inside my body. These wings would gift me with flight, but they did not need to emerge and flap.

"Outstanding." I opened my eyes and looked down to see that I had risen to eyelevel with the massive human. "You have done remarkably well for someone that Lord Alizar needed to take to Aeriel before he would believe." the Baroner boomed with laughter. I grimaced. It had become something of a joke between his teachers-well, the Visionaire and The Baroner at least. I had never seen the Libran smile or make any kind of joke. The Libran was far too focused for any type of joy or merriment to penetrate his perfect façade.

"That will be all for today. Today is the solstice. You should watch for the harvesting of the belicos; it is something quite spectacular." The belicos harvesting was something that happened at every solstice. The bloodlines that powered the Pillars were renewed. Those who died caused Pillars to fall, and new ones were erected to replace those who had fallen in the last solstice. There were 777 right now. "First, however, the Libran requests your presence." I tilted my head. Of all of my teachers, the Libran had been the one who I had encountered the least. The Libran was dressed like a prince and had the attitude to complete the picture. He chided me whenever I did not know something, despite me not being from Carin and never having much of an interest in history beyond my readings of *The Stone*. Even that was not the most off-putting thing about him. That honor went to the fact that he wore a red mask that completely covered his face. The holes where his eyes would be were completely empty, and you could seemingly see right through his head when trying to match his gaze. The mouth of the mask also moved when he spoke, which I had initially found extremely unsettling. I tapped the elixis and rose up into the air, though I still needed wings to do it. I dropped back to the ground, focused, and felt my wings disappear. I grinned in satisfaction and rose into the air with no wings behind me.

"Ruin, I have been speaking with Ethios. You have met him before, though he comes again for you now. He has been hunting a powerful nightmare. Something stalks in Materia, something deadly and dangerous. The white-eyed serpent walks." That was what the Baroner, the Visionaire, and the Libran called Veriel. "Remember what you have learned here." There was dire caution in the voice of the Baroner. I had yet to leave Merhelden in all my days here. I did not know what lay outside its walls. I wondered if this meant that perhaps Lord Alizar or the Libran was sending me into the Dreaming.

I turned around and focused, pulling my wings inside, and drew up and away. High into the sky was a doorway made from stars, and I flew towards it. The earth receded below me as I pushed through the soft curtain that held the night sky in place around this room of Merhelden. I slowly ascended upwards through the center of a grand fountain that stood at the base of the stairwell. A tall warrior with a proud demeanor and black hair approached me.

"The Libran awaits you," the man said. It took me a moment before I recognized him.

"Ethios the Lightholder," I said.

"If you are finished stating the obvious, the Libran requires your presence. Follow me," he replied. The man turned, and I descended, touching down softly behind him. He walked not to the stairwell, but past it. I followed him through the white marble hallway adorned in ever-changing images of what I could only imagine to be past, present, and future. One week while I had tried to bleed water, I had spent days watching this wall and learning. Now, I focused on the quick, confident steps of the man. He wore silver plate armor that held the eagle crest upon each piece of his armor. He had no weapons. His breastplate was adorned with a gold star that had a single blood-red arrow pointing straight up. It was the sigil of Lord Alizar.

I had only met him briefly before, and so I took this time to study him. His face was not ugly to behold, but there was something about him that struck me-I just could not quite place it. The man reached up and ran his hand through his hair. I took my eyes off the man, leaving the mystery to remain, as I realized that the hallway we were in had no doors. Once again, I was not looking for anything but the room in which the Libran dwelt.

The man turned sharply just off the hallway into a circular room. No one was present within. Instead the man began to rise slowly in the air without wings.

"Are you...like me?" I asked him hesitantly.

"No. I am the Lightholder; you are called Ruin. I am the first in the eyes of Lord Alizar. You are...an apprentice. We are nothing alike." There was a note of disdain in his voice that I did not quite understand. Nevertheless, I continued to follow him higher. As we rose, the light faded into a series of crimson lines that wove back and forth in an endless race around the black walls. They made shapes and letters and numbers and symbols and glyphs.

I looked upwards and saw two chairs that hung seemingly in midair, as well as a pair of legs that had to belong to the Libran. We crossed the threshold of the insubstantial floor, and the Libran regarded us coolly.

"You summoned me?" I asked.

"Indeed. Good to see you have listened some of the time. Lightholder, you are dismissed." The condescending voice of the Libran rang out. His red, empty eyeholes gazed out at me from the red mask that hid his face. "It appears that you have been deemed ready to return to Materia despite my best efforts to convince Lord Alizar to the contrary. You have much to learn; you have been taught well to fight, but you do not yet know what it is that you fight. Therefore, we will need to bypass the vast amounts of knowledge that you should have, for what you need to have. Though you will need to return. Veriel is not the only shadow that is cast over your plate. Your future, Ruin, is a rondo of blood and death. There is no avoiding it; there is only the potential to curtail it. Now, you need to see the rest of the world that was. Look." The Libran pointed upwards. I watched as the domed ceiling, which was initially black, shifted and changed into white. It took me a moment to realize that it was snow. Snow covered everything in the world. I could not imagine a blizzard of such magnitude. No winter in Carin had ever been so harsh.

275

"What is this?" I asked.

"This is the dream of someone in Carin. A woman named Merian. Currently, she is within Daggerfall. This is her dream...her nightmare. Something is moving that we cannot see. This is not some idle fantasy; this is history. These are memories. She has seen the prime isterios that caused this." Isterios was the magic of Materia. It was part two of the three types of magic. Isterios had never been mentioned by either the Visionaire or the Baroner. "When you return to Materia, Veriel is your first priority, but this woman knows something. Something we cannot see. Find her, and learn what this is. Do you unde-" An explosion hurled me backwards out of my chair and against the wall. The dome snapped shut like an eyelid, and light flooded into the chamber. Something was wrong. Something was so very wrong. It felt like the elixis itself was burning within me. I clutched my chest. An instant later a gateway appeared in the air with Ethios stepping through it.

"How many?" The Libran snapped at him.

"Seven hundred and fourteen," Ethios replied.

"Seven hundred and fourteen what?" I asked.

"Pillars, you fool," Ethios replied indignantly. I reeled. *Impossible.* That was almost all of them. *How could so many Pillars of Creation fall?*

"Why, Ethios, why did this happen?"

"The war in Materia. We cannot protect lines of belicos that do not exist anymore," Ethios replied.

"Then perhaps an offensive is in order." The Libran mused. "Ruin. You need to leave now. Go to the armory to prepare, then to the Throne Room. Lord Alizar will be there, preparing for war. He will show you the way out." The Libran addressed me.

"But what about the Pillars? I can help you," I urged.

"This is not your war. It is his." The Libran gestured to Ethios. "You are of Materia; he is of the Dreaming. If either fails, the other falls." I exchanged a surprised glance with the man, who returned it with one of confidence.

"Supremor guide you, Ruin," Ethios said to me.

"And you as well, Lightholder." I felt myself fall through the once-again translucent floor and draw the elixis into me, speeding my flight down towards the main floor of Merhelden. I burst out into the artery only to find hundreds of Skyguard soldiers clad in heavy armor coursing past me. When Skyguard died, they went not to Aeriel, but here. I levitated above them, looking down. This was bad. I did not know what kind of force it would take to destroy the Pillars of Creation, but they were what held up Merhelden itself. If they fell, Merhelden would as well. I coursed past the soldiers and did not bother running up the stairs but rather shot straight up as it wound around me. Two floors up, just before the top level, I took a hard cut into the armory. The Baroner was ready for me. Laid out on the table was a suit of chain mail armor that looked remarkably similar to what I had worn under my robes in Materia. My sword, Widower's Wrath, staff, and dagger, Havoc also laid there. I looked at the Baroner and grinned. Everything looked as if it was brand new. I had not seen my weapons since I had arrived.

"Thank you," I said to him. The Baroner returned my grin. I pulled my robes off and began to don the armor, starting with the pure white underclothes.

"We added some additional...punch to the dagger. The sword was beginning to show signs of its age and so we supplemented it by treating it with elixis. Elixis is not as powerful in Materia as it is here, but your blade should hold up against all but the most fearsome of blows. The dagger is still your most powerful weapon; it is a blessed weapon, whereas I merely added a marking. Your staff...is still foreign to me. I cannot discern any magic within it," the Baroner said. I smiled as I pulled on my greaves.

"There is more to magic than just elixis," I replied with a glint in my eye. The Baroner pointed at me.

"If you are messing with axios, I will hunt you down, Ruin."

I finished strapping on my boots. "I am not; you have my word."

"Hmph," the Baroner grumbled. "I need the dagger back." I reached down to where I had laid the pure white dagger Lord Alizar had given to me in my foolish attempts to bleed water.

"I need a new one," I cajoled.

"Not this one. This one is mine. Sorry, Ruin. You will just have to make do being one short until you can find a replacement." I strapped my sword and staff to my back and slid my dagger into its sheath on my right. Everything felt right. I looked at the helmet. It was the final piece in the suit.

"I am not wearing the helmet," I said as I tested my movement. I had a surprising amount of flexibility in the armor, and I flexed my arm back and forth, admiring the craftsmanship.

"You do realize that it is just a little important to keep your face intact, right?" the Baroner asked.

"I will manage," I said, looking the massive man in the eye.

"Sure you will. You will be back in Aeriel in no time. Your kind always is, and do you know what? When you come I will ask if you died from a blow to the head. And you will say yes, and I will tell you that I told you so." His gruff tone held a lace of concern. I fired the elixis and rose to eye level with the man. I held out my hand.

"Thank you, my friend. For everything." The hand of the Baroner easily eclipsed mine as he shook it.

"Fair thee well, Ruin, and be careful." I nodded and exited the room and soared upwards. The Throne Room greeted me, as did Lord Alizar. I sunk to my knees before him.

"It is time for you to go, Ruin."

"I can help here, My Lord," I replied.

"I know, but your war is below us. Veriel assaults us on multiple fronts. My legion can hold Merhelden while you fight him in Materia. He is not the only threat, though he is the hand that guides them. This destruction is not all his doing, but one of his ally's. He is known to us, though he has been long dormant. Tread carefully. You will find him in the north. He will be a good test of your abilities before you go after Veriel. Veriel will soon assault Gemport, but your brothers and the Fallen will hold him there until you can arrive."

"The Fallen?" I inquired.

278

"Galeerial. He has chosen a path apart from us. You will have to guide him back, but not yet. His anger burns too strong for him to be satisfied by anything less than the blood of Veriel on his hands. Now go; you are my Champion called Ruin. Serve me well."

"Thy will be done, My Lord." I turned and saw the black door before me. It beckoned me, and I did not hesitate. I marched straight through and...breathed. I blinked heavily as I became flesh and blood once again. I had left this world broken, and I returned a Ruin.

A Mysterious Benefactor

Twenty-Two

"By Supremor." Galeerial whispered. Jariah stood beside him; her face a mask of irrevocable horror. She started shaking. Galeerial ripped his eyes away from the terror before him to wrap her in an embrace. He buried her face in his shoulder. Slowly, he edged her back out of sight of the interior. His arms stifled her trembling while he worked to soothe her.

"Easy, easy," he whispered. His hand ran through her hair. The smell of cedar filled his mind as he held her to him until her shaking subsided. "It's alright. Just stay out here. I'll be back."

"Do not-do not leave me, he will find me," she whispered. Fingers formed claws that clutched his skin to her. "Do not leave me, Galeerial. Please do not leave me."

"I'm not going anywhere. Veriel is gone. He can't hurt you here. He can't hurt you ever again. I promise." A brief kiss on her head was followed by his slow easing away from her clutching embrace. "I will be right back." She nodded before curling her wings in behind her and sliding into one of the nooks near the cathedral for some kind of protection. Galeerial stepped back into the doorway. The sound of steel echoed hard and fast through the cathedral as Eon exited its wrap. Galeerial crossed the room in three quick strides. Remiel was the first of the Clerics to be cut loose by a triplet of sharp slices from Eon. The High Cleric fell to the ground limply, his face leading the way. Galeerial tried to catch him, but the thud betrayed his failure to the other clerics. One by one he cut them free, this time catching each one as they fell.

All of them were unconscious except for Remiel. Galeerial grabbed the chalice off the dais and filled it in the pool of Charist. He pulled open the lips of the Clerics and allowed them brief sips that slowly brought them back from the depths. Remiel recovered first.

"What happened?" Galeerial prodded him. No response. "Veriel. Where is he?"

"We thought we could contain him. We thought we could quell the darkness. No man is bound by his birth. We hoped to save Veriel, but we were arrogant. We were unprepared. We...we lost everything. We had grown complacent." Remiel rambled. "Destruction will rain down upon us all. We have failed."

"Why didn't you listen when I came to you? We could have prevented all of this!" Galeerial called through gritted teeth. Remiel shook his head.

"We could not oppose Veriel openly. We knew what he was, and if we confronted him then, he would have killed all of us. We made a choice, and we failed." His words sounded like his throat was filled with broken glass. The long threads of shadow still hung from their bodies, and Galeerial severed off the front and back piece of the thread. Galeerial reached to where the thread had speared into Remiel's right hand like a nail. Smoke and burning flesh accompanied the blinding pain as his fingers

281

wrapped around the nail and ripped it out. Galeerial dropped it to the ground and saw his skin ripple and blister from the heat.

If you can't win you aren't thinking fast enough. Galeerial rose and grabbed the chalice filled with Charist and poured it over the black threads. It began to thrash and smoke as it dissolved into nothing. The cleric howled in pain.

"Please, stop!" he begged, but Galeerial continued pouring it onto Remiel's other hand, shoulders, chest, and feet until the air itself was filled with the putrid stench of the black thread evaporating. *Is this axios?* Galeerial knew of the magic of Midox, but he had never witnessed it. Galeerial moved to the other clerics, and one by one freed them from their bonds. Galeerial stood apart from them as they recovered.

"Fools. You had a chance to contain Veriel. Now, he will cut a bloody swath through humanity and everyone else."

"Who are you to judge us?" Cleric Ty spat out as he pulled himself up to his feet. "You can't know the weight that is upon our shoulders to guide so many while having the very snake himself in your presence. We lost Shineheart long ago, and with it our only hope of killing Veriel. It was either keep him here and docile until we could discern his plan, or have him out in the world killing at will. We bought a thousand years of peace; now you come back here seeking to deliver judgment upon us. You are as guilty as any of…" Galeerial's fist slammed into the Cleric's teeth, and the Cleric crumpled to the ground. He glared at each of them. Only Remiel held his gaze.

"Where is he?" Galeerial's voice was tinged with menace.

"Gemport, by now. He blew the Horn of Seventeen Sorrows and summoned the Skyguard to him right after imprisoning us. He told us that he would tear the rule of Supremor down brick by brick, starting with the greatest testaments to the presence of Supremor in the world: the Skyguard." Remiel's voice was even. Galeerial grimaced. He looked at each of them in turn. He could muster no more words for them. They were pathetic. He turned his back against them.

282

"You will never make it in time, Galeerial. Not in your present condition." Remiel called out after him. Galeerial heard a rumbling, and the ground beneath him shook and shifted. He stared at Remiel, who nodded to his right. The Throne of Supremor sat unblemished with a large, gaping hole in the ground before it.

"I believe His Majesty would concur," Remiel continued. "It appears that he would have words with you." Galeerial looked at the doorway that stretched underneath the altar. He didn't know what lay there, but it was obvious that it was the son of Supremor: the same son who had abandoned him. Galeerial shook his head. He had nothing to say to him.

"He can keep his words," Galeerial said. "I want none of them, and I want none of you. You disgust me." He looked to the pile of wings laying on the ground in the center of the cathedral. "Now, you are like me. I'm riding hard south to Gemport. If any of you have a speck of nobility in you, then you will follow as soon as you are able." He turned back towards the door sheathing his blade. He pulled his water skin over his head. He drank the last of the water and stepped to the Charist well, filling the skin up. Jariah would need it.

Jariah flinched as he stepped out. His heart ached every time he saw her. He remembered the beautiful woman she had been before being rendered into this terrified being by the madness of Veriel. She was as much a casualty as Ezekiel. He held out his hand and helped her to his feet.

"I'm leaving. I need to end this. I'm heading south to Gemport. You can't stay here, but you can't come with me."

"No," Jariah urged. Galeerial grimaced. *Is nowhere safe?* Gabriel would not have allowed the Skyguard of Soaring to go to war with Veriel, but that just meant that Veriel's gaze would fall upon them next. He needed to send her away.

"It's not safe. I'm going after Veriel. I will end this. There is a small group of islands, off the coast of Mesnir. The farthest one is called Parad. No one has lived there since the Mythic Age. You will be safe there." He held her face in his hands. "I will come for you. Do you understand me? I will come for you. I won't leave you alone. You just have to be strong a little while longer for me, Jariah." His voice betrayed a wild desperation. Ezekiel had left her to him. They were friends and brothers, and she was his responsibility. Jariah gulped and nodded slowly.

"How will you reach Gemport in time?" she asked. Galeerial set his jaw. He didn't know.

"I'll ride south to the river and head for the sea. I can barter for passage from Seraph to the south. I have come too far to stop, but I need for you to be safe. When Veriel had me, I always prayed he didn't have the two of you as well. You were never a part of Ezekiel's and my foolishness." He wrapped a hand around the back of her head and pulled her head up to look into her eyes. "Go, Jariah. I'll find you when this is all over."

"Something is different about you," she said. She searched his face. "What happened to you, Galeerial?"

"I...I am not the man you knew. I'm a human now. I am not a Skyguard anymore. I am not," Galeerial's resolve broke as he looked at her. "I'm not beautiful like you anymore. I'm a weapon. I'm the Eighth." Now, it was Jariah who reached her hand out to Galeerial. He felt the tears on his cheeks. He had not cried since he had awoken in Gemport so long ago.

"Galeerial," she said. He looked at her face. He had been in love with her for so long. He and Ezekiel both. Ezekiel had won her, and they had become the best of friends. For a hundred years they had been best friends, and now he couldn't be farther away from her. "Galeerial. You will always be beautiful. I cannot imagine what happened to you, but I will always love you. Do not go south if you will not return to me." She looked at him. Galeerial could see the fork in the road before him. He could run with her. With all he had learned from Grey, he could protect her wherever they went. They could find a life on the islands far away. They could escape.

"There is no escape for me," Galeerial said. "I have to go, but I promise you that I will find you again."

She pulled him into an embrace. "Do not die on me, Galeerial-not you too," she whispered.

"Be safe," he said as he handed her the skin of Charist. Grey's words echoed in his mind. *Don't give your word unless you plan on following through. A man's word is his bond, his honor, and his life. Never trust a man who has broken his word, for he has proven himself either foolish or incapable.* Galeerial held onto her hand as her wings fluttered behind her, taking her up into the sky. She was beautiful.

"Her wings are pretty." Galeerial turned to see a small human girl standing beside him. She could not have been more than ten years old. She had shoulder-length hair so blonde it was almost white. Her eyes were big and blue. A single gray shift was all she had to protect her from the cold. "What happened to yours?" Her voice was sweet: the sound of innocence. How to explain what had happened to a child?

"They were...taken by a very bad man."

"Are you gonna get them back?" She asked looking up at him. Something wasn't right about this girl. She felt different.

"Who are you? What are you doing here? How did you get here?" Galeerial went down to a knee.

"They're right, y'know. You won't make it in time, not without help," she replied with a shake of her head. Galeerial pulled a dagger out of his belt slowly from his belt. Something was very wrong with this girl. The Five Eye felt hollow on his chest.

"Who are you?" he repeated, "and who sent you?"

"That's not very nice," she berated him.

"I'm not the nicest guy anymore," Galeerial replied. "The questions stand."

"I'm a friend of a friend. Or maybe a friend of a friend of a friend. I can never keep it all straight," she said with a shrug as she threw her hands out, "but he wants to help." She gave Galeerial a big smile. "He can get you to where you want to go lickity split."

"And in return?"

She shrugged her shoulders. "He'd like to talk to you in a little while. He's kinda busy now. He'd like to be friends, and everybody can use more friends right?"

285

"Maybe, but you have to be careful who your friends are. I'll take my chances on the road." Galeerial rose up. "Do you see those doors?" He pointed back to the cathedral. The girl nodded vigorously. "Inside there are five men. They can make sure you are safe." Galeerial started jogging towards the gates, leaving the girl behind.

Memories rushed back to him as he passed familiar buildings, but everything was different from ground level. Sure, he had walked when he had been a Skyguard, but his view of the world was from above, rather than among it. Now it was a hollow shell devoid of its soul.

Soul...it had done his good to see Jariah, though it had broken his heart to see her so beaten down. His long ride here had been lonely. He hadn't realized how much Grey had given him until his voice was but a memory rather than a companion. The trip to Gemport would be even worse, but at least aboard the ship there would be people about. The city felt dead, as if it were haunted by the dust and echoes. Galeerial paused as he saw the spire that led up to his aerie. The aeries were built one atop the next, all stacked around a central pillar that stretched up almost a thousand feet. His aerie was a couple hundred feet up. He needed something from there. Galeerial began his climb. With one foot locked on a window sill, he hoisted himself up to the roof. Minute by minute, he worked his way up the stone structure. It was less difficult than climbing the wall. The architectural design of the Skyguard had always been form over function, and it provided everything he needed for the climb up. It was another reminder that the Skyguard had fallen. They hadn't created any new architectural wonders in ages. All of this had been done by the Secondborn and some of the earliest Skyguard. Now, they spun painted glass and poured over ancient texts. Now, they flew south to kill and destroy. It was a perversion of a proud legacy: a legacy that he would take back.

Galeerial reached his aerie and saw that the marks of himself and Ezekiel had been removed. He gritted his teeth and hoped it was still there. The door opened easily; there were no locks in Skyguard cities. Despite the change to the door, the inside was precisely as he had left it. A copy of *Endless* lay on the floor. Their bookshelf was covered in the dust of a year.

286

Two hammocks swung from the ceiling where they had slept. The room was spacious, with a desk in the far left corner. The bookcase was his goal, though, and it stood right next to the desk. Galeerial wrapped his hands around the heavy oak and hurled his weight to the left. The shelf groaned in protest as it slid begrudgingly across the floor. Galeerial kept pushing, straining against it. The floor beneath looked much the same as any other place in the room, worn down smooth pale gold wood. But that wasn't where Galeerial needed to access. The left side of the desk was just a slight bit longer than the right, and Galeerial pulled away the thin false end to reveal a painting.

When Galeerial had been only a couple hundred years old, not much more than a child, he had begun to paint. For two years he had painted everything he could find, ranging far and wide, looking for new things to paint. The only thing he had never painted was people. Finally, after much practice, he had deemed himself a good enough artist to attempt it. He had sat his mother and father down and had painted the two of them together. Galeerial remembered his father had never been the most patient of Skyguard, and the fact that he had sat still for those many hours that Galeerial had painstakingly gone over every brushstroke was a testament to his love for his son. The next day his parents had gone ranging in the Northern Reaches. They were both killed by a fesar: a gossamer-winged predator with a thirty-foot wingspan. A hunting party tracked down the beast three weeks later and brought back evidence of their retribution.

The second item, the fesar's horn, still hung above Galeerial's hammock. This was that painting, and he hadn't picked up a brush since then. Maybe after all this was over, after his story had been told, he would return to the brush. If he survived.

Galeerial pulled out his scimitar and hurled it upwards, slicing through the thin rope that held the horn aloft. It was rough and covered with bumps and nicks from where it had skewered its prey. These two things meant the entire world to him. They were his past, his life, and if he was going to die, then there was no way he would let Veriel have them. Galeerial laid the horn on the desk and drew Eon. The blade cut smooth

287

through the horn as he sliced it over and over again into pieces. When he was done, the horn looked like little more than rocks and dust. From his pack he withdrew a piece of flint and retrieved his scimitar from the ground. Three strikes against it sent a spark flying towards the portrait.

He watched the portrait begin to burn. The sparks swallowed the canvas piece by piece. He focused on remembering the face of his mother and father. Galeerial swallowed back unbidden tears as he watched his parents finally evaporate into a memory. The shutting of the door sent the scimitar hurling across the room, embedding itself in the door just above the small girl's head. Her body shook as her eyes blinked rapidly, staring at him in fear.

Galeerial let out a breath. The fading embers of his father's eyes tracked him as his own carefully watched the girl. He ripped his scimitar from the door and replaced it on his belt.

"How did you get up here?" he asked.

"The door was...was closed," she stuttered. Her wide eyes still stared at him.

"That's not an answer." Galeerial pulled a length of rope from his pack. He would have to tie her to his back to get her down. He opened the door and saw something he didn't expect.

There was no sound, but in a way that seemed to make what he saw before him even more disturbing. Blood flowed by his feet, and Galeerial threw his weight left as an arrow flew through the doorway and embedded itself in the wall just behind him. Three centaurs barreled by with lances drawn as humans scattered away from their charge. An unu snapped the end off of a spear and tore the head off the human who had thrust it at him. A sword cut the unu off at the knee, and he fell to the ground, his colossal fist knocking the fully-armored human into the air. He didn't land, though, as a Skyguard impaled the human at the neck between her scimitars before allowing him to fall earthbound.

"What, what is this?" Galeerial asked.

"I told you he wanted to help. That's one of the human cities. I can never keep track of which one it is. It's a big word, and I'm small. That's where Veriel is and that is who you are looking for right?"

"I told you I didn't want any help."

"Well he told me to tell you that if you don't go now, then it will be too late. That's the last human city in the south. It's where everyone is. He said if you don't stop him then nobody will. The other angels are on their way; they are almost there too."

Galeerial seethed. "Your master, what is his name?" Galeerial pried. "I will not go through that door unless you tell me his name."

"He told me I can call him Sable. Does that help? I'm sure he won't mind if you do it too."

"Why doesn't he talk to me himself?" Galeerial asked. She shrugged.

"He said you can use his services three times, as a goodwill gesture. It's like a present, or three presents, which is even better. After three times you can meet him if you want to keep using it." Galeerial set his jaw. If what she said was true, then he couldn't ride south. He pulled the Five Eye out, and it shone gray. Whatever or whoever this girl and her master were, they had enchantments beyond the Five Eye. Its magic was muddled.

"What will you do?"

The girl shrugged her shoulders. "I'll fade." She slowly began to dissolve. "Buh BYE!" She said as the last vestiges of her image faded away. Galeerial looked at the vicious battle through the doorway. He replaced the flint in his pack and grimly stepped through to the other side. The times for playing things safe were over. Safety, like time, was a luxury, and one he didn't think he would be seeing any time soon.

Old Friends
Twenty-Three

I stepped down out of Merhelden and into Acheron. The feeling of embracing the real world after living upon a spiritual plane for so long was disorienting. It had seemed like years had passed while I trained to use magic, but when I reentered the real world it felt like I had never left. I exited upon the stairwell that rose up to the gateway into Merhelden. The world felt…heavy. I had forgotten the lack of pervasiveness of gravity within the depths of the Dreaming. I looked down to see my armor had retained its color. It shone with its own light. I smiled. I looked at the second stairwell rising up opposite of mine but with a white doorway atop it. The Book of Ohm stood upon the throne of Farsight.

Welcome Champion called Ruin

"That staircase there, where does it lead?" I asked.

That is the home of the Midox. I considered this for a moment. Midox was the enemy of Supremor, but he was beyond my ability to confront at this point. Nevertheless, it was interesting how this was such a place of convergence.

"What has happened in my absence with regards to the war between humanity and the unu?"

No. I looked at the book.

"No what?" I asked.

I am not here to serve you, Champion. Your presence bodes ill for the destruction of the Garenspawn. Hmmm. Garenspawn. Every creature in Carin save the Seven of us claimed to trace their lineage back to a single man: Garen, the first man. Ohm hated everyone. He wanted all of them to die; yet, he was forced to watch all of them. What a profoundly disturbing piece of torture. I placed my hands on the book and began to flip pages. Words formed before me as always, but they were not the words of my life. These were for everyone else. One page was almost finished and as the words reached the end of the page they all disappeared leaving a blank page for the words to begin again at the top.

"Remarkable."

No. These are not your stories! The walls of the room erupted in anger.

"I will keep looking until I find who it is that I seek. Or you can tell me." I halted my turning. I didn't wish to harm this creature…he was… sad to behold. "Please." I said. Slowly the words faded from the walls as they resumed their flickering between images around the world.

The unu and centaur army has been joined by that of the Skyguard. Humanity has lost the cities of Gemport and Bicoln and have retreated to Terakeen. The army of humanity is located outside of what the humanity call King's Port. Jeric Tybius is completing the marshaling of humanity's army there. Veriel, Dorian and Rikard, and Jeronious lead the Skyguard, unu, and centaurs respectively. Queen Tendra Sumenel leads humanity. I considered this for a moment. Three things caught my interest in that statement. First, was that King's Port was north. Not only that, but Tendra was now in charge of humanity. I thought back to our plan. If Tendra was queen then Jethro and Jakob were dead. Finally, Dorian and Rikard had taken control of the unu. That boded well, though I did not know if they had complete control or if the unu were still attacking humanity. Today was the solstice which meant it was the last day of the Feast of Bejor. If everything was going according to plan then Dorian and Rikard were in Ornus. They would not catch up with the main unu force for days.

"What about the rest of my brothers?" I asked. I offered a short prayer to Supremor that they were still alive.

Joven is in Gemport. Rayn is dead. Grey and Galeerial are in Dynast.

"Stop." I cut Ohm off. My mouth went dry. Rayn was dead…out of all of us…Rayn. I buried my head in my hands as tears struck me. "Rayn…How did he die?" I managed.

Veriel. One word. One name. I needed to go…but where. There were so many places pulling me in different directions. I needed more information. I could grieve with the rest of my brothers later. When we were together again.

"Why hasn't mankind's army departed for the south?"

They have not the means to carry all the troops and supplies to the south. The ships refuse to sail. Also, a force has eliminated all reinforcements from Cirode'l. This causes Tybius great concern. The ships wouldn't sail. I could make them sail. Not as Aurum, or even as Ruin, but as something far different. As Damaen Longshore every sailor worth the tar on his boat knew me. I could make them sail. I could get humanity's army south in time to make a difference. Even with my power as Ruin, I didn't know if I could kill them all alone. Veriel would have to wait just a little longer.

"What kind of force?"

An old power: Frosh. One who will upset the balance in Veriel's favor. This was who Lord Alizar had warned me about. I needed to put a stop to him. First, more questions.

292

"Where is Shineheart?"

That I would not tell you even to save all the stories within me.

"Why not?"

Because with Shineheart you could end this war. Without it more and more Garenspawn will die. This is a pleasing result. You will have no more answers from me Champion called Ruin. I stood slightly aghast.

"You want us all dead." It was an observation rather than a question. I received no response.

"How do I leave this place?"

Up. I looked up and saw what appeared to be a glass ceiling above me that lead out into a blue sky.

"I will return to kill you for showing me my wife and daughter. Make no mistake of that Chronicler."

Please kill me now. I shook my head. *Just like all the others.* I disregarded his comment.

"One day, perhaps, but it is not my place to kill you today. Goodbye, Chronicler." I turned away, not even bothering to read his response. I gathered my strength beneath me. I breathed in and out and reached down from myself in that direction beyond space. There I found my power. It was harder to grasp it here than it had been in Merhelden. I remembered when I was first beginning in Merhelden, and I needed to use words to focus the elixis. I tried it again.

"Wings." I said. The words helped me I spread my wings inside of me and rose easily into the air. I smiled. The Baroner had taught me well. I pulsed easily off the ground upwards. I exited through the circular hole in the ceiling and was immediately dazzled by the sight of the sun. I allowed myself to bathe in its glorious rays for a moment.

I closed my eyes and breathed. I opened the bottle that held my power and allowed it to flow into me. I opened my eyes, and the world became wreathed in an orange fire. In my periphery, I could see the flames of my magic pouring out of my eyes and washing over my body down to

293

my feet. There it swelled, and I rose up into the air slowly a few feet before rotating my body parallel to the ground and then exploding out of Acheron.

The air whipped my hair back from my face and slammed into me as I burned a pathway of fire across the sky. I saw the land of Thanatos behind me. The doorway out of Acheron had also expelled me from the land itself. I roared past Sentinel and continued my northward trajectory. I was awash with power. I had never felt so free in all my life. Even training within Merhelden had not prepared me for this. Was this how Skyguard felt every time they took flight? If so then why did they ever land? I roared across the plains diving down towards the ground. I didn't even need to ride air currents. I could simply fly. My mind could almost not comprehend the majesty of it.

This was the time of winters, and I was surprised that I did not see more snow upon the ground. Still I moved on. I began to funnel more and more energy into my flight to go faster and faster. There was an audible BOOM! And suddenly there was no sound at all. I knew that I had broken the sound wall. I knew of its existence from my time in Carin, but no one there had ever broken it that I knew of. It was a marvelous feeling. I began to slow down. It was no sooner that I had before I began to see the long black thread that was the army of humankind. Warriors from King's Port, Mesnir, and dozens of other smaller cities had been marshaled to make war against the forces massed against Gemport.

I backed off on the power, more and more as I grew closer. I began to hear clarion calls of trumpets and horns as spotters took notice of the pillar of fire bearing down upon them. I circled once over head searching for the largest tent of the encampment. That would be the commander's tent. I spied it after a few moments surveying, and I began my descent. I threw energy before me in an attempt to slow down, but I came in too hard. I crashed into the ground, and the earth cracked beneath me. I fell to a knee out of instinct and rose slowly to my feet to find myself surrounded by dozens of spears.

"Peace!" I shouted throwing my arms out to the side. "My name is Rui-," I hesitated. Not Ruin, though I was indeed he. Here though and now,

I was Aurum. Aurum Guilden. My Thul was Guilden. I was no longer the Nameless. I grinned. "I am Aurum, and I am one of the Seven. I seek Jeric Tybius."

"The Seven." The words were whispered back and forth. "Alive?" Everything grew silent for a moment, and then a shout went up.

"Huzzah!"

"Huzzah!" The shout carried throughout the army as swords were sheathed and spears alighted. Dozens of soldiers embraced me and slapped me upon the back and saluted me. I greeted each one, politely, but impatiently. Three men dressed in ceremonial honor guard approached me. The crowd dispersed around them.

"Master Aurum." One said. Their armor was made up of segmented plates of gold steel. They held pole arms in their hands and golden helmets adorned their crowns. Each one also had a cape that stretched out from their shoulders and flowed down around their body of the purest white. Their armor bore a golden pyramid; it was a banner that was unfamiliar to me.

"Yes?"

"The king wishes to speak with you." I tilted my head slightly. *King?* I followed the honor guard through the hoard of soldiers with each and every one of them seeking to touch me. This spotlight and reverence unnerved me, but I held my outward composure. A massive white tent held the same golden pyramid sigil was set up at the center of the encampment. A curious look overturned my face; this was not the viper sigil of the Sumenel house. The central flap was opened by one of two guards standing in the doorway, and I ducked my head in order to enter. The interior was quite simple. A bedroll lay in the back corner, and a Crowns' board surrounded by three stools lay in the center with what seemed like pieces from at least three different boards. Seated staring at the board was Jeric Tybius. He and I had grown to be rather good friends when we had traveled from Midway to Amul Kon together. I had never asked Lord Alizar why he had sent the Light Monk with me. Next time, I would.

"It seems that the magician has picked up some new tricks." Jeric said.

"I met a mutual acquaintance that opened my eyes a little bit." Jeric cocked an eyebrow at me, but I merely shrugged with a knowing smile. "It brightens my eyes to see you again my friend."

"And it is good to have you back. We heard that you were long past dead." I watched Jeric return to his small chair beside the Crowns' board. He gestured to it.

"It seems we wizards are harder to kill than friend and foe alike believe."

"How fortunate for us." Jeric replied. "Please take a seat."

"Is this the whole army? It seems... not enough." I cocked my head back towards the entrance to the tent.

"There have been...complications that you need to be aware of." I took my seat and glanced at the board. The unu and centaur armies were marshaled outside of Gemport. The Skyguard were atop their mountains. Humanity's army was marshaled here, though it was not nearly the overwhelming force that it should have been, considering the number of humans there was compared to the rest of the races of Carin.

"This is wrong." I said. Jeric looked at me confused. I reached down and moved the Skyguard to between Bicoln and Terakeen followed by the centaurs and the unu. I removed all humans from Bicoln and Gemport. "Time is shorter than you know." Jeric balked.

"You're sure?" I nodded gravely. "By Supremor..."

"I have no doubts that this is how the board now looks, though I don't know everything. Speak to me, King Tybius." Jeric looked uncomfortable at the name.

"It will always be Jeric to you, my friend. Furthermore, it is a crown I will not wear for another two years."

"Humanity needs a king." I counseled.

"It has Tendra, and she is a more capable leader than I." Jeric replied.

"You do yourself a great disservice. Queen Sumenel is indeed as strong as you say she is, but there must be factions within Gemport, and within humanity itself, that will be resistant to the rule of a queen. Having a king would go a long way towards appeasing these interests." Jeric sighed, and I chuckled softly. "I know you are not a politician any more than I am, but this is the world that you always knew might come to pass." A moment of silence hung in the air.

"I cannot betray my vows." Jeric said resolutely.

"Nor would anyone ask you too. The men see you as their king. You are their king. By deed and person if not by title, they believe in you Jeric. I urge you to act if not for humanity then for Tendra." Jeric stared back at the Crowns' board. I needed to change the subject. "You said there have been developments. Speak to me." I said.

"We have lost all communication with Cirode'l and virtually all cities north of the Peakwood Gap. We received initial armies from Cirode'l by boat, but after those first reinforcements there was nothing. We expected seven thousand additional spears, we have seen none. I have sent scouting parties north and have heard nothing from them." My face must have made some contortion, because Jeric stared at me. "Thoughts?"

"Veriel." I answered. Momentary confusion struck Jeric's face followed quickly by realization.

"The Skyguard...the one that the Skyguard Galeerial was ranting about?" I nodded.

"In the last few weeks, I have been learning a lot." For emphasis, I drew on my magic and fire burned in my eyes. "Embers." I said. I sent that fire down into my hand like an Iron Man. "This Veriel that Galeerial was warning us about is very real. More importantly, he is a very real threat. I know he has been marshaling some kind of an army in the north. It's possible this is them, making their move while the eye of the world is upon the south. We need to investigate this." A sharp whistle caused me to crank my head back to look at the entrance.

"Enter." Jeric called. A man carrying a small slice of paper entered into the tent.

"My Lord." He bowed to Jeric. "A falcon has just arrived." Jeric's eyes widened. He handed the rolled paper to Jeric who quickly unfurled it. I watched him closely as his jaw clenched.

"What is it?" I asked. Jeric's eyes gestured, and the messenger bowed and removed himself. Jeric rose to his feet and pulled his sword belt tight around his waist. "It seems your assessment was correct." He gestured to the Crowns' board. "Gemport has been sacked. The Skyguard have joined the war, led by Veriel. The Queen has evacuated to Terakeen. We can wait no longer." I rose with him. "Aurum, I won't lie to you; I need you everywhere at once. Two wizards have been confirmed to be with us at Terakeen: Joven and Rayn." I flinched at the sound of his name. *Not Rayn any longer.* Jeric did not see it though. "First though, I need you to investigate what is going on in the north. If anyone can get in, make an assessment of the situation and get out alive, it is you. With your...brand of magic, you should be able to get in and out and still beat us to Terakeen." I weighed this request in my mind. He was right. Combined with what Ohm and the Libran had told me...I needed to end this Frosh before he could penetrate father south.

"How many ships do you have in the harbor?" I asked.

"Not enough for the whole army and many of them refuse to sail into the warzone. We have too few men who can sail to take the ships over. If we made an attempt to storm the boats, the sailors would either cut ties to the city, or simply jump overboard. They won't sail." I set my jaw.

"They will sail for me." I replied. "And word will ring out bringing more ships here by the dozens. The sailors will be pirates and thieves, but they will come if you can give me your word that your men will cause them no trouble." Jeric gave me a quizzical look. I weighed the potential benefits of telling him of my past but ultimately decided against it. Tendra's brother Jakob had spent years hunting me to no avail. I had been a most elusive prey. I did not want to cause any kind of friction between the two of us. He nodded in compliance.

"Just have your men ready to depart after sundown. I will signal you. By boat, Terakeen is only a couple of days away. We can have your army in place before the Hammer can maneuver back into position. Now, if you will excuse me, My King," Jeric grimaced as I bowed, "I need to go speak with some captains."

"You are not to bow to me, Aurum. Ever."

"Will do." I said after a moment's hesitation. "One other thing Jeric, this may sound like an odd question but…how long has it been since Long Fang." Jeric mulled this over as he strapped his sword to his side.

"About seven weeks. Where have you been, Aurum?" *Seven weeks*. I shook my head even as a small smile crept to my face.

"A story for another time, my friend." Jeric shrugged. He followed me outside, and I gripped his forearms in farewell. "Be careful. May Supremor smile upon you."

"And on you." I gathered power beneath me and pushed up into the sky gracefully, with less of an explosion than with a leap. I swung around and hurtled towards the city. I surpassed the walls and heard shouts below of fear and surprise as I wound through the stone walls towards the docks. I dipped low into an alleyway and came to a grinding halt. I knew these alleyways well. A fair share of my time during my seven years of ranging had been spent here.

I moved quickly keeping my face as obscured as possible. I didn't want anyone to see me until I was ready. I wound downwards towards the bay until the houses were made of wood and not of stone. I dusted the memories off as I moved through the streets. It had been over a year and a half since I had walked these roads, but I knew them. I knew them deep in my bones.

The home that I was looking for was really more of a shack. I kicked the door to the cellar twice, and I heard desperate scrambling within. *Skree*. Some things never changed. A small hole in the doors was opened, and I could see the flickering torchlight as Skree peeked out. *Here we go*. I infused my voice with a hard merciless edge.

"Open the door." It wasn't a request. It was difficult to return back into that persona. Damaen was ruthless: a murderer even. He had killed and maimed. He had been vicious, and men had followed him for his

299

ruthlessness. That wasn't me. Not anymore. I focused on the voice. The voice was the key. I dropped my voice lower than usual, almost a snarl, but not as raspy.

"Captain?" Suspicion laced his voice. "What's the password?"

"There is no password." I replied. Suspicion changed to elation.

"Of course it's the captain!" As I heard Skree's voice everything rushed back. The flaunt in my shoulders, the deviousness in my grin. It was like a fire had been woken that had been long dormant. I could hear Skree stumble, and I heard the sound of several latches being thrown open. The door was thrown forwards, and the big man beckoned inside. Skree was two hundred and eighty pounds of muscle that was absolutely terrified of me. I remembered when I had first met the man. I had heard that he was untamable, as likely to kill you as he was to kill the enemy: a real berserker. I had cut my mark into his chest after beating him in single combat. This made him mine in his eyes. He was the only man that had been allowed to live after I had abandoned the *Finality*. I had never had a man pledge himself to me before, and this man feared and loved me with all his heart and soul. He was my man in all things. I stepped down the three stairs into the cellar. I had to duck my head because of the low ceiling.

"Are we alone?" The man nodded. His too big nose countered his beady black marble eyes.

"It's good to see you again sir. I...I feared the worst. I haven't heard hide nor hair of you in months, but I have waited here for you. I waited...I waited just like you told me. I waited here and here and you are." The man's voice was even, but I could tell that he was excited to see me. I had asked a lot of the man. He was a fighter through and through. He was meant to be out killing and raiding, but I had asked him to stay here and wait for my return. I hadn't known how long it would be, but I needed someone, and Skree was the only man outside of my brothers that I could trust wholeheartedly.

"What is the biggest ship in the bay?"

"*Queen of Jewels* captained by Erome Tyla." He replied with no hesitation.

300

"How many captains are in the city?"

"Two hundred and twelve." I smiled. A lot of boats had fled the destruction in the south seeking refuge here and in Boaz, no doubt. It would be an excellent take this evening.

"Spread the word. Every captain will be on that boat before sundown." Skree nodded. "My effects?" He pointed to a chest that sat in the far corner of the room. "Go." I said. Skree nodded and took the stairs in one giant step and disappeared out into the city streets. I had a couple of hours before the meeting tonight. Jeric would be marshaling the troops and breaking down the camp.

I moved through the shady room to the chest and pulled it open. It was not locked. Within was my old life: my boots and cloak and hat and cutlass. A grin lit up my face. This was everything I had been for five years. I couldn't help the smile on my face. I slowly pulled my armor off piece by piece. Skree watched in awe at the armor. No doubt he thought I was some kind of high ranking soldier now. I pulled on my old life. My black coat with gold buttons still fit. My black cloak clasped easily around my neck. My boots smelled of the sea and worn water-logged leather. I inhaled deeply. I placed my current clothes and weapons into the chest. I would return for them soon enough, but now I was no longer Aurum Guilden. Now, I was Damaen Longshore: a pirate, a reaver, a cutthroat, a scoundrel.

I sat down on the hammock that Skree had set up and tried to remember the last time I had slept. It had truly been a lifetime. A lifetime ago...back at Evenfall. There was no need for sleep in Merhelden. I closed my eyes against the light from the sun and the flickering light of the fire and let myself rest.

*　　　　　*　　　　　*

"Captain?" Skree's voice instantly brought me back to awareness. "It's done." I shook my head once to clear it. It was almost discomforting sleeping without dreaming of Merhelden and Lord Alizar. Nevertheless, I swung my legs down and saw that the sunlight had faded to the last

301

flickering rays before night. I grabbed my hat and sword and put them on. It was time to work. I walked right by Skree and up into the twilight. The docks were only a few blocks away, and the smell of seawater and fish filled my nostrils. It threatened to bring a smile to my face, but I stifled it. Damaen Longshore didn't smile, or at least not when he wasn't killing someone.

My boots made a distinct *clack* as we strode through the city streets towards the shoreline. I saw the *Queen of Jewels* immediately. She dwarfed the ships around her. She was a large shipping derrick that could carry an incredible amount of cargo. She would be a prize in the open ocean. I knew she was too well guarded for any of the most dangerous pirates to attempt to take down. Pirates like me. The captain would be none too pleased to have all of these other captains on his ship, but I didn't really care. I walked forward and up the gangplank where a woman stood glaring at me.

"Captain Longshore, I want to know what in Supremor's name you think you are doing holding a meeting aboard my ship?" This must be Captain Tyla. A woman: interesting.

"I needed a ship, and yours was the only one that could hold all the people I needed to talk to. Now, get out of my way." I pushed to walk past her, and I saw steel flash to my throat. I held my hand out to stay Skree from making a motion. My eyes looked her up and down. She was dressed in completely practical clothes, which even then did little to hide her curved body. Her face was soft, but her eyes were hard. A gold loop hung from her right ear. I ran my tongue along my teeth.

"Permission to come aboard, Captain?" I asked. Where in another's voice there might be a tone of mocking, in mine there was only droll severity. I felt Skree give a start. It had been a long time since a human had stood up to me. It was refreshing.

"And if I deny you?" Erome replied.

"That would be unwise." I almost began to draw upon magic instinctively, but I refrained. I was still the best at what I was. I looked into her eyes. They were blue as the sky. She probably hated them because they

302

were beautiful. I could tell that she was that kind of woman. She hesitated. She had gotten more out of me than she thought she would. Now, she was playing with me.

"Denie-" She didn't finish the word. I whipped my head backwards and down. My left leg swept out and knocked her feet out from under her as my own dagger flashed into my hand and onto her throat as I perched on top of her.

"You were saying?" She licked her lips. Her eyes sharpened, almost cat like as they penetrated deep into my own. I was a predator, but so was she. We recognized that in each other.

"Welcome aboard, Captain Longshore." I rose to my feet and stepped off of her.

"I have killed for less." I told her.

"But you have never been challenged for so little." She replied. I mulled this over in my mind as I moved onto her ship. "The others are down below." She pointed to the steps that led down to the main hold. I gestured for her to go ahead. This woman was no trader. She had stolen this ship, of that I was certain. It only cemented her boldness in my mind. A ship this big was hard to hide, and as a pirate ship it would be so slow as to be almost useless. This was a reaving ship. It was designed to be the most powerful vessel in the seas. No matter what the royal navy sent against her, the amount of weapons on the vessel meant that she could withstand anything less than an armada. Her presence here betrayed her arrogance.

"You should kill her." Skree whispered.

"I rather like her actually."

"That's why." He muttered. "Women bring nothin' but trouble." I said nothing in reply. Tyla climbed down the stairs to the hold. I heard hushed voices from within as she struck the deck. I looked down. It was fifteen feet. I didn't bother with the ladder.

"Stay here." I told Skree as I dropped down into the hold. My boots crunched on the deck as I fired a little bit of magic to slow my fall. I stifled the usual fire that accompanied it, and instead landed flat on my feet.

303

Silence filled the room. My eyes played over the assembled captains. Two hundred and twelve men and women watched me.

"Welcome." I said simply. "You are all here because of two things. You either fear me or you owe me. For most of you, it is both. So with that being said, I am calling in all debts. Every ship in this harbor will, at the conclusion of this meeting, prepare to weigh anchor and sail with humanity's army south to Terakeen." Murmurs of dissent and outrage filled the hold, but no one dared speak out directly. "You are each of you human: whether you be pirate or thief, smuggler or honest trader. I don't care. Any ship that doesn't do as I say will be burned along with her crew. For those of you who know me or know of me, you know I don't make threats; I make promises. Are there any questions?"

"Yeah," a voice called out. A mountain of a man pushed through the crowd to the empty space before me. "I'm my own man." He thumped his chest. "I don't care if you are King Jethro himself, you don't tell me what..." My knife thudded into his forehead, and he fell to the ground. I walked forward and ripped it free. Brains and blood dripped off of the blade.

"Are there any other questions?" I asked. Silence encompassed the cabin.

"M-...M-...Mr. Longshore?" A tall wiry man with long sloppy hair that wrapped around his head in an unkempt wave stepped forward hesitantly.

"What?"

"M-...M-... My ship holds herbs and salves...medicines for Cirode'l. We only arrived this afternoon. We leave in the morning. I swear it." I regarded the man darkly.

"You would not lie to me..." I approached the man standing a mere foot from his face. Sweat ran down the bridge of his nose, and he fidgeted under my glare.

"N-n-no." He stammered.

304

"Stay after the rest leave. If you are telling the truth, you will be permitted to continue your northern course. If not, you will be burned with your ship." The man nodded vigorously.

"The rest of you get out. Get your crews; soldiers will be arriving in an hour. Don't fail me or try to run. I will know. Go." I said. The captains streamed by me as they raced away to retrieve their crews from the brothels and the bars and the alleyways. Only the thin captain and Captain Tyla remained.

"My associate Skree is on the deck." I told the thin man. "Escort him to your vessel. He will inspect it. You will know if he is satisfied or not." The man nodded and scurried up the ladder. I turned to Erome.

"What?" I asked. She smiled thinly at me.

"You're a man of power. I like that." She traced a finger along my chest. I gripped her wrist with my hand.

"Good for you." I pulled her hand away and turned from her. I heard the crack of a whip, and my eyes tracked the thin cord as it snapped over my right shoulder. I didn't turn my head back. "You may be a shark in these waters, Captain Tyla, but I am hurricane. Test me, and you will be destroyed. Make no mistake." I climbed the stairs deliberately.

"What a positively delicious man." I heard her say to someone as I ascended. I felt a tingle run along my neck. It had been a longtime since a woman had tried something like she had, but Erome didn't know the fire she was playing with. Skree was gone, and the night air held a chill. I walked down the gangplank and began to move through the city. The night was a riot of activity as sailors spilled drunkenly out of the bars as their captains pushed and shoved them back to the ships.

I began to head for the city gates, but I felt a flicker in the shadows and knew that Erome was following me. She was becoming bothersome. I briefly wondered what she would think if I suddenly just rose into the air and flew away. Once again, I almost smiled at the idea.

"Captain Tyla. Do you have a death wish?" I stopped and turned slowly around to look directly into the shadows where I knew she was standing.

305

"I'm following you aren't I?" Her voice echoed out of the darkness. It was sharp and seductive.

"What do you want?" She stepped forward and into the rising moonlight.

"You've been gone a long time, Damaen. I have heard stories about you. The greatest pirate that ever sailed vanishing with his entire crew leaving his ship abandoned on the Thorne Coast. I heard you were a man as cold as the ice herself; but that you never let your men harm a woman or a child, even though their husbands and fathers were slaughtered before their eyes. What kind of a man believes that to be mercy? What kind of a man kills a woman's betrothed before her eyes and then offers the comfort of his cabin all the way back to King's Port. What kind of a man serves that woman wine yet never enough to get her drunk and never takes advantage of her. What kind of honor does this man have?" I had no look of sorrow or apology in my eyes. The mission had been everything. I had been a pirate; it had all been for a purpose.

"I make no apologies." Her so-red-they-were-almost-black lips curved upwards. She swayed her body as she walked towards me. I made no move as she trailed her finger along my neck as she walked around me. My eyes followed her progress. She was only a half a hand shorter than me.

"I hated you for depriving me of that life of happiness, married to a wealthy merchant. It was every girl's dream. He was sweet and charming and...weak." She came back around to stand uncomfortably close to me. "But you. You were so strong. So wildly calm. It was intoxicating. Now daddy's little princess is something far more dangerous. She plays with fire and loves getting burned. Tell me Damaen, do you want to burn me?" She came in towards my neck and traced her tongue along it. It was warm, and I struggled to suppress a shiver that played down my spine. I made no motion at all. "You really are just as cold as I remember, but every man has warmth somewhere." I pulled two fingers up to her lips and pushed them slightly away so that I could once again see her face. Her tongue played along them. Shadowed flame played in her eyes.

"If you touch me again, I'll cut your head off and mount it on the city walls." I breathed. She blinked twice heavily. "Now, get out of my sight." I turned away from her and stalked back into the night streets. As soon as I turned, the corner I whispered to focus the elixis to burst softly up into the air and landed on the rooftop. I peered back over at her. She was staring in the direction that I had just left.

"I'll have you Damaen." I heard her whisper to the wind. "Oh yes I will." She turned and vanished back towards the docks. I exhaled heavily and collapsed to the ground. I was surprised at just how...draining that had been. It was not like I had never dealt with women before, but she had exuded power and ferocity. My hands shook softly as adrenaline poured out of them. I took several deep breaths before rising up and circling back towards Skree's cellar. I was able to call up the flight elixis without words this time. I smiled. In mere moments, I arrived at the safe house, and I descended rapidly and changed back into my chain mail and robes. I wrapped Widower's Wrath around my back. It felt good to have its reassuring weight upon my shoulders. I left quickly. Skree would ensure that things occurred as I had planned them. After that Skree would join up with a crew since he had fulfilled his obligation to me.

I flashed up into the air and looked down into the encampment for Jeric. The camp was in a flurry of movement as the army made ready to enter the city and head to the bay. I saw Jeric amidst a dozen warriors musing over a Crowns' board. I descended quickly landing easily next to them.

"It's done. The ships are being prepared as we speak." Jeric nodded.

"And the other matter?" He asked.

"I'm leaving now." I replied.

"Thank you. Supremor go with you." I extended my hand outwards in agreement towards them and nodded. I marshaled my power for a smooth leap but decided to abandon it.

"Wings." I exploded upwards in a stream of orange flame and cheers erupted as I blazed a fiery streak in the night sky towards Cirode'l. I looked back towards the bay and saw a single ship ignite. I shook my head. I hated slavers almost as much as Skree. I smiled as I flew towards the north and towards the war that waited.

Line in the Sand

Twenty-Four

"The main problem is water," Retren said to her. He was in charge of all the cities supplies, and his analytical mind was a godsend. "The stores here are not sufficient. In Gemport we could pull water straight from the river, but here it must be distilled from the sea or brought in from outside sources. We can't distill it fast enough to account for all the additional people here. Food supplies are short enough, but without water we won't last the week." Tendra sat hunched over the broad stone table of scrolls filled with expenses, supplies, and troop strengths in the Merchant Hall. Her eyes flashed back and forth between Retren, Merinam, and Wesley. Wesley had arrived just after she had. He had been unable to find Jonathon, and her gallowglass hadn't yet returned from Gemport.

309

"Supply problems aside," said Merinam, "there are greater issues afoot, namely that someone is performing sorcery. In the last seven days, almost sixty people have fallen asleep and won't wake up. After three days, they die. No one knows what is causing it, but the people are afraid. It is happening within bloodlines. The families Diren and Calpraith have been completely wiped out. The Birel and Pran are on their last legs. It was happening in Gemport and reports say in Bicoln too, but people hadn't noticed it as readily because of all the confusion in the evacuations. People feel it is a second coming of the White. There is fear here, My Lady," Merinam said quietly. "There is great fear." Merinam was but a boy of thirteen. Yet his words were haunting. Tendra didn't know what the boy had seen before retreating from Gemport, but it had changed the very fiber of his voice.

"I still don't understand why we are here instead of at King's Port," Wesley broke in.

"Because here we have the Star Tower, which eliminates the Skyguard's principle advantage." Merinam replied. "The main body of our troops will be planted there. What remains of our cavalry has already been put out to sea and is even now hiding in Bloodstone Cove on the edge of the southern Rift Mountains. As soon as the Hammer breaches the city, the ships will put forth to flank them from behind. The Star Tower is our greatest advantage. We will have heavy archer emplacements on the upper levels of the towers with infantry, specifically pike and spearmen, holding the line at the bottom. A firewall will be set up at the lowest entrance, which will hold off the ground troops for a time."

"That can't be enough to ensure a victory," Wesley said.

"It isn't. In fact, baring a stroke of divinity, this battle has already been lost. Even with the arrival of all of humanity's reinforcements from the north the likelihood of a defeat of the Hammer's forces is no greater than 0.7%." Merinam replied. A gloomed quiet fell over the room. "Sorry," he said. "Honesty is a habit."

"Then it is lucky for us that we have a stroke of divinity," Tendra said. The other members of her counsel looked at her. She reached over to the side of her chair and pulled Joven's staff out and laid it on the table. "I have this. And the wizards have a plan."

"The wizards are dead, My Lady," Retren said. "I saw one die with my own eyes the same as you. Nothing has been seen of Joven. We cannot count on whatever plan they had, and don't forget it was their recklessness that got us here in the first place." The wiry man's tone was laced with rage. "If it wasn't for them, none of this would have happened. If you were to ask me, every one of them should be hung for war crimes."

"Then it is a good thing that it is not up to you," Wesley said. "The wizard gave his life defending Her Majesty. Yes, they started this war, but I'll be damned if I waste a second throwing blame around when I could be trying to come up with a plan to survive."

"Think about it Retren, the wizards destroyed the ferals in less than a year. Do you honestly believe that they wouldn't have planned for something like this?" Merinam said quietly. "While the wizard Rayn was alive I spoke with him. These men are planners of the highest order. They knew this would happen. All we have to do is guess what their plan is."

"Did they plan for Long Fang as well?" Retren shot back. "Because the last time I checked, at least two of them died there. I wouldn't call losing a quarter of my manpower a victory, would you, O Master Planner?"

"No, I wouldn't. You are a man of numbers, Retren. Not a man of people. The world is not an equation, and variables exist in far too many fashions to ever be accounted for. What you see as folly, I see as delayed gratification. We know for a fact that one wizard is dead. That is all. Everything else is by secondhand account. This means that there very well could be six of them out there right now."

"Or none," he shot back.

"Enough," Tendra said. "Throwing blame around will do us no good. Retren, as soon as the ships arrive, I want you to take your staff down and immediately take a census of troop and weapon strength. Then water and food rations. Lord Jeric should be with them. Speak with him and see what you can come up with."

311

"My lady."

Tendra turned to see a young man in leather armor standing timidly several paces away.

"Yes?" she replied.

"You...uh...you asked to be... they're here. The boa...ships. The ships are here." Tendra turned back to her council. She grinned but didn't wait for them to say anything. She just turned and ran. Her footfalls pounded in her ears. The guards couldn't get the doors open fast enough, and she herself pushed to open a gap wide enough to slip through.

She took the stairs down four at a time with reckless abandon. Her ornate steel boots clanged against the stone. Every step brought her closer and closer. Soldiers stared at her as she hurtled past them, but she paid them no mind.

Please be here. Please be here. Her breathing was trapped in her lungs as she sprinted through the cold and snow. Her legs slipped out from under her, but she kept her footing as she ran. Her breath grew labored and her lungs burned with icy air. She couldn't stop. She didn't stop. Her eyes tracked ahead of her, and she saw a most beautiful sight. A thousand ships were in the harbor: ships of every shape and size. They would have taken her breath away had it not already been lost. A legitimate smile broke onto Tendra's face. This was an army. Tendra hadn't stopped running.

She lost sight of the bay and fleet of ships for a moment as she passed behind buildings on the winding road down to the docks. All roads led to the docks. As she pushed forward, more and more people became obstacles. She pushed her way through them. The throng was curious. They wanted to see the soldiers. Not her...she was desperate.

She needed to see him. As she pushed her way through the crowds, they began to part for her as people recognized her and calls went out as to her identity. She didn't know how she would find him...she just needed to find him. Her eyes searched the first boats as the strokes of the oars brought the boats into shore. As the first vessel touched down, the first boot onto shore was the one for which she was searching.

312

"Jeric?" Tendra looked into her betrothed's eyes for the first time since…all of it. She just couldn't…she couldn't believe he was really here. Tendra didn't understand her tears. She didn't understand them, not one bit, as she saw him step off the lead ship onto the wooden dock. His white armor with the golden pyramid shone. He was an angel. Tendra wiped her tears away and swallowed heavily. Jeric's eyes widened as he saw her, but he maintained his composure. He strode towards her carefully and confidently.

"My Lady, I come bearing humanity's army, and my own regrets that I could not have brought them sooner." He paused a moment. "I am so sorry I wasn't here sooner." Jeric went down upon one knee, and slowly a ripple spread out and every soldier on the docks followed suit, as did all the people. Tendra reached down and wrapped her hand around his chin where the makings of a beard scarred his skin.

"You came just in time." She held her composure. "You came just in time." With her hand, she guided him upwards to his feet. His empathetic eyes searched hers, and she knew that he would find only fear and need.

"I missed you so much," he whispered. "I'm so sorry." His pained voice was choked with tears. "I'm so sorry I wasn't here for you, but I'm here now. I will never leave you." A pitiful smile graced Tendra's lips as she caressed his face. Until this moment, she hadn't realized just how much she needed him. She had been running for so long, and now he was slowing her down.

"Army of humanity!" she called.

"AHOO, AHOO, AHOO," they echoed.

"You have entered a time of war." With every word her iron shield returned. It comforted her. "You have entered a land of blood. Our enemies surround us. They attack without mercy, and without remorse. Their goal is the annihilation of man. You are humanity's sword and shield. This is where we make our stand. This…is where we fight. This is our victory!" she screamed. Cheers rang out through the docks that were carried far out into the bay. Tendra realized she was shaking.

"Laten," Jeric called. An old man with a long black beard rose from just behind Jeric.

"Yes, My Lord."

"Find the men food and water. I am going to meet with the Queen and the captain of the guard. Tell the men to prepare for war. There will be no drunken revelry this night."

"Yes, My Lord." Jeric had not taken his eyes off of Tendra since he arrived. Tendra shied from his gaze. He would see through her walls. She turned from him and began to walk back towards the Merchant Hall. She heard Jeric's heavy boots behind her as the docks sprang back to life.

They walked in silence for a few moments as Tendra caught her breath.

"I missed you." they both said at the same time. They stopped walking, and Tendra found her eyes caught in Jeric's.

"Do you remember eating strawberries in Deren's Aviary at Illuvium?" Jeric asked her. "As I was sailing here, I couldn't get that image out of my mind. The way you laughed, every man in Illuvium knew when the princess was there because every hall was brighter. You brought me those strawberries, and the elder monks let me eat them with you."

"I remember," Tendra replied.

"In return, you made me promise that I would write to you once a week." Jeric reached into a leather satchel that hung around his neck and pulled out a bundle of letters. "I wrote to you every day that I was apart from you." He handed them to her sheepishly, and she pulled her gloves off to take them with her hands. The coarse, folded paper was marked with dates. There were over dozens of them wrapped in twine. She could see tears in his eyes. "I'm so sorry I wasn't here for you." He pulled her into a hug, and she grew stiff at his embrace. No one had hugged her in as long as she could remember. She slowly raised her hands up around his larger body. He smelled like sea water and iron. She could taste the metal in her mouth, but he felt like comfort. Tendra closed her eyes, and for an instant, she let her burdens fall away. Her shoulders collapsed as if a weight had been cut free, and her legs went limp. He held onto her. Her breathing became shallow as dry tears welled in her eyes. It was only for a moment, but it was a moment where she went back to being the girl he had left. An instant later and it was gone. Tendra found her feet again and pulled her arms free, disentangling herself from her betrothed.

"Things...things have changed. I am changed," she said haltingly. "Jeric...we will talk later." She breathed. *Good, that was good. Push it to later. Business now.* "We need to focus on the war."

"Of course, of course," Jeric said after a moment. They continued their climb upwards and through the city.

"The Hammer is even now in the final days of taking Bicoln. They split their forces with the arrival of the Skyguard and were breaking down the walls there while Gemport was being taken," she said. "Our reports say that the first wave of the Hammer is half a day out. So we have a little bit of breathing room to shore up defenses, but not much."

"Time is ever our enemy, is it not, My Lady?" a voice rang out. Tendra turned to see Joven approaching the two of them from the direction they had just come. The elder wizard looked more or less the same as when she had last seen him shoving her on board a ship, but bereft of the manic gleam that had shown in his eyes then. "Joven, did you arrive with the army?" Tendra asked with surprise.

"Merely fortuitous timing, I assure you. I managed to acquire passage on the last ship out of Gemport. I was on my way to the city center when I saw the two of you. May I walk with you?" he asked.

"Of course," Tendra replied.

"I don't believe we have been introduced," Jeric held out his hand. "Jeric." he said.

"Joven." Joven said as he shook Jeric's hand. The two men stood awkwardly facing each other in silence for a moment before Tendra cut in.

"Tell me about Gemport." she said.

"The city is a smoldering ruin. There was a small bit of sporadic fighting left, but the city was all but taken when I departed. Although, I regret to inform Her Highness that I spied Vizien not only working with the Skyguard Veriel, but he seemed intimately familiar with him."

Tendra blinked heavily, but kept her emotions to herself. Vizien had saved her…but that had been a lie too. She had known he was a snake; she maybe hadn't realized how deep his venom had penetrated. She would need to replace him, though. She didn't have anyone in mind, but right now she had a war to fight.

"You didn't see Jonathon, perchance?" she asked. Joven shook his head. "Very well," she indicated with her head back towards the Merchant Hall. "The rest of my cabinet are gathered there. We should join them."

"Of course." The rest of the walk back was awkwardly silent. Tendra didn't mind the silence; they reached the Star Tower in no time. Tendra enjoyed seeing the look on Retren's face as the wizard came into view. Tendra grasped Joven's staff in her hand one final time before passing it back to the wizard. He wove it back and forth a few times, spinning it in the air.

"You took excellent care of it, My Lady," Joven said.

"It served me well and saved many lives."

"Excellent."

"If you are finished with your self-congratulatory waxing, there is the little matter of the defense of this city that needs to be dealt with."

Joven smiled at Retren's indignant tone. "Have faith, my good man. This is all part of the plan."

"Told you," Merinam whispered.

"Perhaps you would care to enlighten this body as to what the plan involves, mage." Retren ignored Merinam's comment.

"In seventy-two hours, this war will be over, and the Seven will control the unu race. If we can stay alive until then, we win. If not, then we will all be dead, and it will not matter one way or the other." Joven peered at the map of Terakeen where the figures of archers and swordsmen were placed. "This is good work. Yours?" Joven gestured to Merinam, who nodded. A three-dimensional open sculpture of the Star Tower had been created, and Joven peered within. He grasped three of the archers and placed them on the ground level. "Place archery units here as well. We can create choke points of bodies at the entrances. The Skyguard will still be able to breach the upper levels, but they aren't strong enough to carry unu or centaurs. We can strangle their offensive here. Where will you be, My Lady?" Tendra pointed to the upper spokes of the Star Tower. "Is there any way I could convince you to take cover in the Rift Mountains with your naval forces?"

"No," she replied.

"I didn't expect as much."

"Where do you want me?" Jeric asked.

"Right beside me," Tendra said. Jeric smiled.

"No place would I rather be."

Retren stood from the table. "You just expect us to trust you that there is some majestic scheme in the works?" Retren asked incredulously.

"Yes," Joven replied. "I created a plan that destroyed a civilization in six months. What more do you require to show you that I know what I am doing?"

"Six more just like you," Retren replied. Joven stiffened.

"You would do well to never speak of my brothers again." His voice was cold and hard.

Retren flinched backwards. "With…uh…with your permission then, Lord Jeric, I would like to speak with you about the supplies your army brought. As soon as possible." Retren fumbled through his words.

"Of course," Jeric replied.

"Rojen." Tendra gestured, and a young boy scampered forwards. "Accompany Lord Jeric, and show him to his chambers when he is finished."

"Yes, M'Lady," the boy said.

"I need to go meet with the Merchant's Guild. They are refusing access to their blacksmiths until we render payment. Joven, I want you to work with Merinam some more. As soon as you have any changes to his plan worked out, I want the two of you to accompany Wesley to start working on maneuvers with the army."

"Anything you need," Joven said. Tendra considered his words. Having this man close would be a boon.

"Also, it would appear that I am in need of a new Grand Inquisitor." Tendra addressed Joven. He bowed his head to her. Out of the corner of her eye, she saw Retren start.

"I would be honored," Joven said.

"I don't care if you are honored. I care if you can do the job," she replied sharply.

"Of course," he said. There was nothing but confidence in his voice.

"Good. You are all dismissed," Tendra said. As they slowly dispersed and went their separate ways, Tendra felt an overwhelming sense of relief to be alone. She was finding solace more and more in silence. She sat in her chair, staring at the map before her. This was it. She prayed that it would be her final battle. She hated this war. She hated all that it had stolen from her, but she was deathly afraid that it wasn't done with her. She wondered who or what would be taken from her next. A gallowglass shifted back and forth in the corner, staring at her from behind its hooded cloak.

*   *   *

Bodies. So many bodies. Tendra let loose with another arrow as a Skyguard whipped past her, and she watched as it slid right through its helmet and sent the Skyguard into a freefall. She had already nocked her next one and whirled about, searching for her next target. There were six humans in her entourage standing upon the Watcher's Spike, the highest spoke upon the Star Tower. It was one of three dozen such platforms that extended out from the massive metal body of the tower. She saw Jeric bat off a spear thrust from a charging centaur before cutting through its front legs, sending the centaur hurtling off the edge.

Tendra's arms were like lead. They had been fighting for some three hours by this point, and a snowfall chilled her bones even as her heart sent pound after pound of warm blood coursing through her veins. The floor of the spike was slick from water and blood. Zechariah, Na, and Jeric were her Light Monk guards, and the rest of the men around her were veteran

318

warriors. She had started with nineteen. One of the others, Dregen, let loose with his crossbow, firing round after round.

Tendra saw the telltale blur of an arrow shaft just in time to jerk her head back. The wind whistled in front of her as the dart passed just inches from her face and embedded itself in one of her companion's heads. The force of it pushed him forward to the ground. Tendra put her boot upon his side and shoved, sending him spiraling down to the ground before much blood had a chance to seep out of the wound. They needed room to maneuver, and corpses would restrict them. Tendra let loose with her arrow but saw it fall short. She was so tired. There was no end to them. She reached for another arrow in her quiver to find it was her last one. A quick look around told her that they all needed another round.

"Tower!" she called. A Skyguard dropped to the spoke between them and the entrance. Jeric was on the other side of them fighting against an unu warrior. Two men moved to engage. The Skyguard's scimitars worked hard and fast as the two attacked at different angles. The Skyguard was totally fluid as it parried their every blow. Tendra nocked an arrow.

"Three, two, one." she said. On one, two of her companions let fly with their arrows as well. The Skyguard's blades whipped upwards to intercept two of them, but the third slipped through and into his left eye. An instant later, the swords cut through the Skyguard's armor, finishing him. They had learned quickly that a Skyguard at the ready could easily handle one or even two arrows. Overwhelming force was their only option. A lightning bolt flashed in the distance, and Tendra knew that meant the fleet had arrived at the coast and engaged the enemy. A flicker of relief flooded her.

As they reached the inside of the tower, Tendra looked down to see piles of human, unu, and centaur corpses covering the base level of the Star Tower. Small flames still burned from earlier when they had covered the floor with oil and set it aflame.

Thwip, thwip, thwip. In rapid succession, Tendra heard arrows take out the three of her companions who were watching the spoke. She whirled around to see three Skyguard advancing at a sprint. Tendra threw her bow to the side and whipped Valiant out of its sheath. The first two blows almost wrenched the blade from her grip, but she held strong, launching into her own counterattack. The other two Skyguard broke to fight Jeric and the Light Monks. She saw Dregen on the ground with blood flowing from his torso. Tendra disengaged after three blocked blows spinning back out of range. The Skyguard's wings billowed out behind him, and the red eyes of the Skyguard's helm burned into her. She circled him warily. She kept a slight profile as she searched for Dregen's crossbow. She spotted his body and slowly began to edge towards it. The Skyguard didn't let her get far as he engaged her yet again.

She spun her blade back and forth, and sparks flew from each parry that she made. She threw her long sword forward in a deep lunge. The Skyguard caught the blade in his own, twisting around and ripping it from her grasp. Tendra let it go. She knew that she couldn't best the Skyguard's strength. Instead, she dove to Dregen's body, grasping his saber in one hand and the crossbow in the other. In one motion, she pulled it free from its sheath, brought the blade up in a high guard to defend from the double overhand blow while stepping in close to the Skyguard. She brought the sword all the way over her head, catching both blades while raising the crossbow up beneath the Skyguard's head and firing it. The quarrel shot right through the bottom of his mouth. The Skyguard collapsed backwards.

Tendra turned to see the others just finishing with their own Skyguard. Tendra looked out over the edge and felt despair well up within her. Despite the choke point that the entrance to the Star Tower gave them, the unu and centaur forces had still managed to press inwards. Fighting was now occurring on all levels. The Skyguard had been able to run enough interference to allow the unu to make it all the way up to the level below them.

"Tendra. We need to get you out of here," Jeric urged.

"I concur," Zechariah said.

"No. This is everything-right here, right now. Humanity either dies here or lives. There is no middle ground. There is no surrender. There is no other day to fight," she said vehemently as she retrieved Valiant.

"Proud words." Tendra turned to see a one armed unu approach, flanked by six unum. "Most befitting a queen. Unum, take the others. The queen is mine." This was Qel of the Thousand Hammers. She still had Dregen's blade in her other hand. She raised it high and hurled it forwards. The blade sunk into one of the unum's chests with a thud. Qel simply smiled as the unum ripped the blade out, stumbled two steps and then collapsed. "Seems this viper has a bite to her." Tendra very deliberately pulled her empty quiver from her back. She needed a moment to rest. She rolled her shoulders.

"Stay close to me," Jeric whispered.

"I don't need your protection," she said in return. She slid a quarrel into the crossbow that she still held and raised it, firing at Qel. The bolt hit him square in the chest. He reached up and pulled it out casting, it to the ground.

"Are you ready?" Qel asked. The unum rushed forward as her human companions struggled to maintain their engagements against the raw power of the unu form. Tendra turned and walked out onto the Star Tower, grabbing Valiant as she walked. Out here, her smaller form would give her a greater advantage, whereas Qel would be forced into limited maneuverability. The unum kept the human forces inside as Qel followed her. He had a hammer in hand. He was like a bull. A mass of rippling muscle covered in the barest of garb, all coiled and ready to trample her. She swung her sword back and forth twice before leaving it in a point guard. She hastily reloaded the crossbow, but abandoned it as Qel came at her. Qel stormed forward, and Tendra dove forward under his overhand blow, lashing out with her blade and cutting into his flesh. His hammer swung back around, catching her in a glancing blow to the shoulder that sent her spinning backwards.

Qel lashed out with a heavy kick that connected with her chest. She felt as if her rib cage was going to collapse into her heart as she hurled backwards. She peered over the edge and saw the spoke just below it. It was only about twenty feet down. She could make that jump if she needed to. She threw herself to her feet. Hammers were hard to fight. She had never really learned techniques for defeating them. Instead, she just relied on instinct. Tendra dodged two blows, carving her blade into Qel's offense. She managed to land a small slice on his right arm, but otherwise her attacks were ineffective against his expert maneuvers. Qel growled at her. Something was wrong. She should not have had this much of a chance against the unu. His balance was off. The loss of an arm had dramatically affected him.

She was patient as she watched for an opening. The clansmaster stepped forward with a pounding overhead slam. The blow just missed her, but it hit the tower and sent heavy reverberations through it, causing her to lose her balance as she lunged forward for a killing blow. His knee caught her in the stomach as she fell, and she crumpled to the ground seeing stars, unable to breathe. His hand wrapped around her head and shoved her onto her back. She groped for her blade, but Qel kicked it away as his boot crunched down on her chest. Tendra went for the discarded crossbow. Qel brought his hammer up as her hand coiled around the grip.

"A valiant effort," Qel breathed. His breath could be seen in the air.

"Let's end this." She whipped the crossbow out and took aim.

The New Balance
Twenty-Five

Burning ruins had greeted them at both Gemport and Bicoln, but
that didn't matter to Rikard. What did was the head of Rayn. As they had
ridden towards the city, a pike had greeted them outside the gates with a
single black feather hanging from Rayn's ear. It was a message: a message
from Veriel. He knew that they would see it. He hadn't even needed it
confirmed by the few dozen unu who had been left to secure the city. Veriel
knew they were coming for him. That had made Rikard angry, and every
ounce of that anger was directed at Veriel. Not only had he humiliated him
in Ornus, but he had killed the best of them. Rayn was the conscience of
their family. He had stopped them from walking many a dark road in the
past. Now, he was gone. Rikard felt Rayn's broadsword on his back. He had
found it stuck in the ground before what remained of Rayn. He preferred his
daggers, but he would make an exception in this case. Rayn's sword would
bleed Veriel; it would bleed him deep. He would be Rayn's dark avenger.

The Hammer was moving extremely fast. The unu had used a leap tactic. They sent the bulk of their forces to Gemport but had an auxiliary unit move on the cities of Ferum to Bicoln. As resources were siphoned out of Bicoln and Terakeen to prop up Gemport; the defenses for the other cities grew weaker and more lax, which was what the unu were apparently counting on when they fire-bombed the city. Women and children had made no difference to the unu. Bicoln was a tomb, though Gemport had still been racked by sporadic fighting. Dorian had left a single clanmaster to call the clans to order. The siege of Gemport was supposed to have waited until the Clansmaster had arrived, but the unu at Gemport hadn't received word that Qel wasn't in charge anymore, and so the order had been given. That was where Qel had gone: sneaky bastich.

The Skyguard had rendered the idea of city walls affording some semblance of protection an utter joke. If the reports that Rikard had managed to gather were true, Terakeen was where humanity was making its stand. The human army was already there, as was Queen Sumenel. Now, Rikard just had to make it in time. Dorian was driving the unu hard. Their horses had been exchanged at Gemport, but even their new mounts were at the point of death. However, Rikard knew they were almost there by the black skies, compounded by the massive stone city that stood tall before them. Their troop consisted of the clanmasters as well as the unum, whose ranks had been replenished after he and Dorian had taken command. There was also Terel. Rikard glanced back at the former clansmaster.

He had taken his fall from grace with a stony face, but Rikard knew he was just waiting to stab them in the back. Despite the unu's strict code of honor, Terel had a chip on his shoulder the size of the Rift, and he wouldn't let that go easily.

Rikard felt a tingle of anticipation begin to grow on his spine. It had been a rough few days' journey, but the healers in Ornus had done good work. He gingerly moved his arm, which hung in a sling. He sunk his heels into his mount and urged the poor beast forward to catch back up with Dorian. They would be at the city within the hour.

"I'm fighting," Rikard said.

324

"Rikard, we've been over this. You have one arm, and one eye," Dorian replied serenely.

"You're hardly the epitome of good health, yourself." Rikard shot back.

"I have full muscle control. Just give it two weeks, Rikard; you know we heal fast. You will be right as rain in no time. In the meantime, you need to stay alive. I want you to coordinate retaking control of the unu."

"I don't know them, Dorian. You do. You are an unu; I'm just the guy who's along for the ride," Rikard argued.

"Why do I even bother talking with you? I should content myself with the fact that you managed to listen to me at Ornus and didn't go off half-cocked on the unu," Dorian replied.

"You should, which means that you owe me the chance to go off half-cocked against the Skyguard and everyone else. It is only fair-" Rikard paused for a moment, "-and balanced." he added. Dorian flashed him a dubious look, which he returned with a wide grin.

"You may do what you wish, but Qel is mine."

"I can work with that," replied Rikard

"Also, I don't want you going anywhere near Veriel. I know you're angry. So am I. The others can't see it, but I know you can." Rikard nodded again. Dorian was usually the epitome of serenity, but his face was taut, and his hands were rigid. "What..." Dorian paused, "what he did to Rayn, he'll pay for, I swear to you, but if he took Rayn down in single combat...then I don't want either of us going near him without serious backup. Hopefully, the rest will be there, specifically Grey; he knows how to fight Skyguard better than anyone alive. If he isn't, then we take him together. Find Joven; he'll be with the queen; I need you to find both of them. Veriel will be wherever the blood runs thickest."

Rikard looked at his brother. "He came and saw you."

It wasn't a question, but Dorian nodded anyway. "He's dangerous. I didn't realize how dangerous until I saw Rayn...I want to feel his heart bloody in my hands as much as you, but savagery isn't going to cut it. We need to be smart fighting this. You find Joven, while I take care of Qel. Then we take out Veriel. Understood?" Rikard didn't like being ordered around, but this sounded like something resembling common sense, and since becoming the clanmaster of the unu, not a whole lot had been making sense. The unu stared at him- a lot. It bothered him.

"Who is going to call off the unu?"

"The clanmasters will disseminate through the city spreading the word. Also we will be wearing the standard of the Sentinel of the Scales. The unu will be confused, but they will not hesitate to stop fighting if they think the Balance has changed."

"What about Chuckles back there?" Rikard gestured to Terel.

"What is most precious to you, Rikard?"

"Excuse me?" he replied, taken slightly off balance by the question.

"What do you value most in your life?"

Rikard thought about this. He felt like no matter what he answered it would be wrong. "A challenge," he said hesitantly.

"Imagine you just spent the last ten years of your life pursuing the greatest challenge in all the world, and just as you are about to achieve it, it is taken away from you. That is how Terel feels. I have a deep respect for the unu, and I am saddened that it had to happen this way. So don't degrade him."

"When did you start giving me orders?" Rikard replied.

"Since you stopped thinking about anything other than killing people. You were brilliant once, Rikard."

"Hey." Rikard shot him a glance accompanied by a finger. "I'm still brilliant."

"That's not what I mean, and you know it. I know we drifted apart in the last few years, but when you are ready to tell me what happened, I'll be ready." Rikard considered this for a moment. Dorian really had no idea what Rikard had sacrificed for him. He looked into his twin's face. The greatest secrets are between family. They had drifted apart, because that was the price. They had drifted apart because Dorian had abandoned him

326

for his wife. He knew it; Dorian knew it, but he had refused to accept the proclamation of the Orrery of Words back in Cambria. Rikard was not so foolish. After Rerem and Carin, there was no doubt that the Orrery would not be denied. Dorian seemed determined to vex it. Rikard accepted the inevitability of the Orrery's proclamation. He had no problems with it. His father had been the keeper of the Orrery, after all, and Rerem had never lied to them. There was no reason to believe the Orrery had either.

"You know why we drifted apart," Rikard said pointedly. "You found a wife, and I didn't," Rikard lied. "It's as simple as that. Always has been, you just have always wanted to make things more complicated. You have always wanted more than what we could give. You ignored the Orrery," Rikard replied, looking dead ahead. He felt the lie in his heart. It wasn't a complete lie, but it was enough that Rikard felt a twinge of guilt.

"You are right," Dorian murmured. Silence lingered between them.

"What did Terel say about Frosh and the Skyguard?"

"He won't talk to me," Dorian replied.

Rikard snorted. "I can make him talk."

"Like you made Desmond talk?" Dorian shot back.

"Don't act like you were blameless in that, Dorian. You voiced no objections. We did what needed to be done to protect the family," Rikard said.

"That's why you were always better than me, Rikard. You had no boundaries. No limits," Dorian said quietly.

"You are going to preach to me about limits?" Rikard asked incredulously. "Maybe if you had smarter limits, father would still be alive," Rikard seethed. "This is war, Dorian. You know that better than anyone. He knows things about Veriel. Things we need to know. When you are ready to stop pretending to be so noble and to take care of your family, come find me." No more was said, for Rikard pushed his horse to gallop ahead of his brother. He rode in silence with his thoughts. He hated being that way to Dorian. He loved his brother more dearly than anything else in the world, but he couldn't deny the agony that Dorian had caused their family, and himself in particular.

327

The sounds of battle were no longer muffled. They could hear catapults and ballistae, thunder and screams. There was lots of screaming. Rikard pushed his thoughts of his brother away to soak up the situation into which he was throwing himself.

Terakeen was first and foremost a port town, and so the town was built primarily as a waypoint between Gemport and King's Port. The city walls were built for defense against raiders far more so than an actual army-not that it would do any good against the Skyguard in any case. The city itself was laid out in a slanting pattern that had everything leading to the docks, since that was the city's reason for existence. The land stretching up to the town was littered with massive stones, javelins, and bodies riddled with arrows.

A fleet of ships had landed to the south, and there was a massive amount of fighting down there as the human forces made steady progress up the beach to flank the unu and centaur forces. It was a decent idea. The execution needed to occur faster, though, for it to make a difference. Dorian didn't bother going for the beach. The real action would be inside the city. Namely, at the Star Tower.

They thundered through a makeshift campsite where Rikard saw several physicians caring for wounded soldiers away from the battle lines. Dorian pushed his horse into a sprint towards the gates. The clanmasters and the unum knew their tasks. They were to stop all fighting. The clanmasters didn't like the order, but they had acceded to Dorian's wishes. It wasn't like they had much of a choice in the matter regardless.

The sound of their cavalry parade thundered through the air as they charged to the open gates. A massive group of centaurs lingered at this access point. Rikard wished he had his staff; a lightning bolt would get them out of the way in a hurry.

"MOVE!" Dorian thundered, which caused the centaurs to rush to make a gap for the tight line of unu warriors that punched into the city. Dorian leapt off his horse, and Rikard followed soon after.

"CENTAURS, THIS BATTLE IS OVER!" He bellowed. Rikard was already moving. His ankle screamed in pain as he jogged through the city streets. He wished he wouldn't have been so quick to abandon his horse, but the tight streets were slick with blood and covered in corpses. He rounded a corner and saw a group of unu moving down the street entering buildings searching for soldiers. They saw his royal colors and gaped at him.

"Dorian?"

"No, I am his brother, Rikard, and we are the clansmasters of the unu now." The group of eight saluted him.

"Where are your unum?" the lead unu asked.

"They are spreading word through the city, all fighting with humans is to cease immediately. I want you all to spread this message as well. Is that understood?" Rikard said. The stunned unu didn't speak for a moment before they all nodded and saluted once again. "Do any of you know where the queen of humanity is?"

"Clansmaster…clanmaster," the unu corrected himself, "Qel and his honor guard have pursued the queen into the Star Tower." The unu pointed past Rikard, and he turned and cursed silently.

"Find Dorian; tell him what you told me." Rikard pulled Rayn's sword from his back-Vengeance, he had decided to call it. The unu saluted before dispersing in multiple directions in pairs to spread the word.

Rikard stared at the Star Tower and debated whether it was worth it. The Star Tower stretched high in the sky in an attempt to reach its namesake. The Star Tower was the only reason one would come to Terakeen. Almost a thousand feet high, the tower wound upwards with multiple spokes stretching out from it. It had been built as the Southern Watchtower by Garen himself. As such, the tower was made not of stone, but of some unknown metal. Rikard had spent some time researching it when they had first arrived in Carin.

The spiral nature of the tower made assaulting it difficult, even though that had not been the builder's intent. Rikard once again took off at an easy jog, but one that favored his uninjured leg. The humans passed him over as they continued hunting unu while watching the skies. Rikard's eyes searched for Veriel through the hazy winter sky, but his lone eye could see only masses of wings and the glittering of dim sunlight off of steel. Rikard struggled up the heavy marble staircase that led up to the base of the Tower. It was a daunting figure, and Rikard felt a chill brought on by the light snow that had begun to fall around him as he passed into the shadow of the structure, picking his way towards the entrance.

The broad doorway leading in was a massacre. The unu had led with centaurs wielding long shields. The hope had no doubt been that the shields combined with momentum would let them work through the first few layers of archers and establish a foothold. The reality was much different. The humans had smartly placed their archers on the upper tiers and placed barricades all the way up the lowest ramps leading upwards. All momentum had been lost, and centaurs and unu alike had been slaughtered. Piles of the dying called out for help as arrows dipped in poison struck from all manner of angles. Rikard kept his head down as he slid through the corpses.

He couldn't move save by climbing atop them. His footing was uneven, and the ground up flesh was slick with blood and loose clothing, but still he managed to move through the bottom floor without attracting attention. He soon found out why that was the case.

The Skyguard had crashed in through the upper spokes and distracted the archers long enough to get the bulk of the unu force through and up into the upper tiers. The barricades had been cast aside, allowing a clear pathway for centaur cavalry to storm through. Rikard had to crane his neck to see to the top. Three levels from the highest he saw a group of unum. They were guarding a one armed unu: Qel.

"Sorry, Dorian. Priorities," Rikard muttered to himself.

Rikard flashed back down to his own level as his eyes tracked the different fights going on. Centaurs, Skyguard, and unu fought against what seemed to be an endless supply of human corpses. Humanity's army had arrived. That meant that hopefully Grey would be wandering around somewhere in this chaos. Despite his injuries, Rikard managed to maneuver through the warzone, but with some difficulty. Rikard relished a challenge, but despite his blustering before Dorian, he knew that he shouldn't be in a place like this when his body felt like it did. Skyguard circled the Star Tower like moths around a flame.

He entered into a cacophony of reverberated sound that echoed harshly through the massive structure. He looked up and craned his neck to see all the way to the top of the building. A bronze spiral staircase, made of the same metal as the rest of the tower, ran along the walls, stretching in a serpentine pattern that wound all the way to the top and was broken up by long platforms every thirty feet or so. A large bell was placed at the height of the tower. Along the way there were numerous rooms and spokes that were little more than bridges, leading nowhere. Rikard began to slide up the stairwell. He sheathed Rayn's sword and drew Bleed from its sheath. With one arm useless, a broadsword was never going to be his first option.

A Skyguard soared through one of the portals leading to the open air, and Rikard whipped his dagger forward, catching the Skyguard in the right wing. The Skyguard's momentum instantly ceased, but it almost jerked Rikard off the tower. The knife sheered through the feathers and cartilage of the wing, and the Skyguard went tumbling to the ground, desperately trying to retain control as he crashed with what Rikard had to imagine was a crack. He peered forward and outside, scanning for any additional Skyguard. Satisfied, Rikard moved forward. He continued this process through the first two levels of the Star Tower. At the third level, the fighting began in earnest.

Rikard scanned his pathway through the battlefield. His eyes charted a way through the mass of bodies and warfare like they would a cliff face. There was no possible route that would allow him to reach the other side without a fight. Unlike outside, the majority of the fighting here was between humans and Skyguard. The humans fought in groups of three or four, desperately trying to keep the Skyguard isolated from one another, but the Skyguard were having none of it. They kept up fluid movement patterns, using their wings to outmaneuver the gravity-bound humans.

The Skyguard were an extraordinarily well-disciplined force-always attacking, always advancing, and never from the same angle. Rikard glared at his wounded arm and cursed it silently. The Skyguard worked their scimitars close and kept their wings folded close behind them. The Skyguard's biggest weakness was their wings. They had to keep them safe, and, by natural instinct, they would protect them even at the cost of their body.

 If he got into a fight here, then he would be bogged down all the way to the top. Besides, these Skyguard weren't the one he was after. The song of steel called to him, but he prepared to sprint through.

He shunted the pain of his ankle out of his mind as he wound his way through the mass of moving flesh. He kept his head on a swivel and his blade on the defensive. He deflected two blows from a Skyguard before rolling away into the crowd of humans who had circled up in a phalanx to defend against the Skyguard.

"Who are you?" one of the humans shouted.

"No time to talk, gotta run." Rikard backpedaled through the center of the circle and slipped through the back of the lines. A Skyguard warrior was waiting for him. Rikard blocked a blow with his dagger and leapt into the air, blocking a second strike while head-butting the Skyguard in the face. Rikard felt a satisfying crack. The Skyguard stumbled backwards, but Rikard was already running again. He cast a furtive glance back as he began ascending again, but the Skyguard were more concerned with the group of humans than a lone wolf like him.

Rikard gritted his teeth against the pain in his leg. It was deep and throbbing when he put no pressure on it, and sharp and angry when he did. He was able to maneuver past the next three levels without as much as a block before he had to stop for breath. This wasn't working. He was traveling too slowly. He looked back down the way he came and saw Skyguard come bursting in through the outer portals to skewer humans with their swords before sending the lifeless bodies tumbling into the ground. Rikard smiled at the idea. He looked up the staircase and saw the next doorway not too far up. He hobbled forward the last few steps against the pain. He stood in the doorway and waited. Outside the sky was a flurry of movement as Skyguard armed with bows fired arrows down into the city and others dove down towards the docks. He saw his mark.

The Skyguard wore a dark red breast plate with two white strips extending down from his shoulders. The Skyguard pulled a tight curve around in the sky and angled towards him. Rikard tried not to be too obvious that he was waiting for him. He fingered his dagger and spread his legs out. He tensed his muscles as the Skyguard grew closer and closer. The Skyguard's arms were close to his body until just before he hit the doorway. His scimitars flew out in front of him with his hands to catch Rikard in the chest.

Rikard leapt, not out of the way, but straight up into the air and kicked his legs out flat. He threw his hand out and buried the dagger in the surprised Skyguard's back in the flesh right between his wings. The Skyguard jerked upwards in response, carrying Rikard spiraling through the tower upwards. Now he just had to get off. Rikard searched right and left for his exit vector. The Skyguard swung his right blade backwards, and Rikard threw his weight to the left. Bleed ripped out of the Skyguard's back, and Rikard cut the strap on his sling and threw his right arm up to grab the ledge.

Rikard screamed in pain and felt blood on his tongue. He gasped for breath. His whole body shook as he started to go into shock. His fingers bled as the metal bit them deep. He hung there for a second. He was going to fall, and it was a long way down.

"I thought I told you not to do anything stupid." Rikard was so paralyzed by the pain that he couldn't even look up. He felt hands wrap around his arm, and he almost passed out from the pain as he was yanked up by an unum.

"I…I don't remember you saying that," Rikard gasped. Rikard could barely breathe, and he huddled on the ground, shaking. The pain was excruciating. Rikard almost succumbed to the blackness, but he regaled against it. Dorian knelt down next to him.

"Can you walk?" Dorian put his shoulder under Rikard's arm and helped him slowly to his feet. "Take him back to the gates."

Rikard grabbed Dorian with his left hand.

"I'm… going… to finish this." He gritted his teeth until they dug into each other forcing the pain away. He stared Dorian in the eyes.

Dorian shook his head.

"Alright, let's go." The unum handed Rikard back his dagger. "There isn't much higher that we can go, and I haven't seen Qel or Queen Sumenel." A human warrior leapt towards them with a spear aimed at the unum. The unum reached around to the tip of the spear and snapped it off the wood. Fear gripped the human's face as he stumbled backwards. Three unum were fighting other humans around them.

"Kill it!" he screamed at them.

"Peace, man," Dorian barked back. "The unu are laying down their arms around the city. This battle…this war is over. Where is Queen Sumenel?" The man's eyes flashed back and forth. "Where!" Dorian thundered. The man spat at him.

"I ain't telling you nothing, traitors." Dorian nodded. One of the unum wrapped his fist around the man's throat, lifting him over the edge of the pathway.

"If you value your life, then tell me now!" Dorian commanded. Fear gripped the man's eyes. His defiance fled with his breath.

"She's out on the Watcher's Spike," he whimpered. "Please…please don't kill me." The unum threw the human to the ground, disgusted at his groveling. Dorian brushed by him, and Rikard hobbled along in pursuit. The Watcher's Spike was the longest spoke in the entire tower and also the broadest; it stretched out a hundred feet into the air, and was broad enough for six men to walk abreast. There were only two people on the arm: a woman who was quickly sliding backwards on the ground towards a long sword that was obviously too far out of reach, and Qel. The one-armed unu wielding a battle hammer sent his booted foot crashing down on the woman's chest.

"That's the queen." Dorian took off running as he pulled his broadsword from his back. "QEL!" Dorian bellowed sprinting forwards.

"What are you doing?" Rikard said to himself. Then he saw it. He watched in slow motion as Tendra whipped a crossbow up. She had been reaching for it, not the sword. She aimed it at Qel. *She's going to hit Dorian.* An instant before she fired Qel was knocked backwards by Dorian's reckless charge.

"He wants Qel for himself," Rikard muttered. "He better not get himself killed."

"Have faith, clansmaster," the unum replied. Rikard grimaced; Joven was nowhere in sight. That was bad, but his musings halted as he watched Dorian go to work. Qel recovered from the shoulder check in time to stave off a flurry of blows from Dorian. Dorian's blade was all broad, arcing sweeps that sent the unu reeling backwards to escape the flourishes. Tendra scrambled toward where Rikard stood.

"Who are you?" Tendra asked as she rose to her feet. She still held the crossbow in hand and, she raised it up to take a shot.

"No." Rikard raised his hand to the crossbow. "My name is Rikard; I'm one of the Seven. That's Dorian. This is his fight," Rikard said absentmindedly. His focus was on Dorian and Qel. Qel's balance was off. Losing his arm made his movements unsure. This would have been close to a fair fight under normal circumstances, but with Qel so incapacitated it was barely a contest. Dorian swept his blade up and around the rim of the hammer and ripped it backwards. Qel stumbled as he tried to maintain his hold, but the hammer spun out of his grip and off the side of the Watcher's Spike. Dorian hooked his foot around the unu's knee and kicked off the unu's chest into a back flip. Qel slid towards the edge of the tower. Rikard moved forward so he could hear their words.

"Yield," Dorian offered.

Qel snarled in response. "You think you can stop this, my son? Will you kill your father to satisfy your thirst for power? The fire has been ignited; you can either burn with it or feed the flames. Join me, Dorian, and we can rule this world. We have the human queen, and the centaurs will follow wherever we lead. We can take this world. Together it can be ours."

"Yield," Dorian said in reply.

"You can't hold the unu without me, Dorian. They won't follow a human forever."

335

"Yield."

"Are you even listening to me!" Qel screamed at him. "I spared your life at the water's edge; I brought you into my family. Now, you are trying to take it all away." Qel spat at Dorian's feet.

"If you yield, you will retain your position as clanmaster of the Thousand Hammers. All you have to do is say a single word." The massive unu rose to his feet. He was easily two feet taller than the man, and his bulk was double that of Dorian's.

"My pride is worth more than my life. You know that. I will not bow to you, Dorian Shamesword." Qel reached down and grasped Tendra's sword. He stood back up. "You will have to kill me." Dorian stared at his father figure. Seconds seemed to stretch into agonizing minutes as Rikard tersely watched the exchange between the two men.

"Go." Dorian lowered his blade. "You spared my life. You took me into your family. You were like a father to me. I am offering you your life; take it and go. I don't care where, but if I see you again, I can't guarantee your protection." Rikard's mouth dropped open. He couldn't be serious. Qel would be back to kill both of them. Letting him live was dangerous and stupid. Neither of them moved. Rikard's eyes kept flicking back and forth between them. "Please." Rikard almost wasn't certain of the word as the wind kicked up around them.

It seemed like an eternity; the Skyguard seemed to fade out of view as the two iron wills focused on one another. Rikard slowed his breathing and readied his dagger; he eyed his shot. He could hit Qel square between the eyes at the slightest hint of provocation. He slowed his breathing as the seconds stretched on and on. Rikard didn't like being exposed, but it felt like they were at the center of the maelstrom. A hurricane of violence swirled around them, but it couldn't touch them.

Rikard blinked as the unu's left foot moved. The proud unu took a step to the left. He drew square with Dorian as he moved around the motionless wizard. Rikard saw Qel's lips move to whisper something, but he couldn't hear it. The unu took another step forward. He was now between Rikard and Dorian. Qel and Dorian stood back to back now. Qel

336

seemed to be looking far past where Rikard stood, but Rikard dared not take his eyes from the unu to follow Qel's gaze. Qel's face betrayed no emotion, which was how Rikard knew that he was going to strike. Qel's grip hardened on his sword, and he whirled around spinning his blade in a wide arc to separate Dorian's head from his body. Rikard's wrist snapped as he sent his knife flying through the air, but it was already too late. The blade soared into the unu's shoulder, but it wasn't enough. Yet, the unu stopped mid spin and slunk to the ground. A broadsword stuck out of his chest like a banner proclaiming ownership.

The queen's sword rolled from Qel's grip, but still Dorian didn't move. He just stood there staring out into the city and the ocean beyond as Qel sunk to his knees, and then the ground. Rikard slowly approached his brother. Blood spurted from Qel's lips as he struggled to breathe through flooded lungs. His eyes held the same mixture of contempt and pride they had in life. The unum and the queen attempted to follow, but Rikard held his hand out. They stopped.

Rikard didn't know what to expect as he finally drew flush with his brother. He saw Dorian's usual stoic face, but he also saw the tears that grew in his eyes. Dorian's neck pulsed as he tried to will them to recede back into his body. Yet one after another they rolled out and down his face. He made no move to wipe them away. Rikard held his hand up to his brother's shoulder. He pulled him into a tight embrace, but he knew Dorian's eyes were vacant. Rikard knew they were no longer as close as they had been, but Dorian had lost a brother and a father. Rikard knew what that was like. Dorian's body was tense in his arms.

"He brought it on himself. It wasn't you that killed him; it was his pride," Rikard whispered in his twin's ear. "It wasn't you. This isn't like dad." Rikard felt Dorian's hand on his chest as he pushed his brother away. He met his brother's eyes, and he found them to once again contain life. Dorian breathed in a shuddered breath.

"I know," he replied. "I...I know, but it is still my fault. I have killed both my fathers now. How many others will die due to my actions?" Rikard had no answer for him. Everything died; such was the way of the world. Dorian reached down to place a kiss on each of Qel's eyes after closing them. Dorian stood back up from his knee and pulled his blade from Qel's chest. He wrapped his hand around Qel's thick braid of hair and began to saw through it. With each cut, Rikard could feel Dorian's emotion pouring out of him. Rikard worked to remain impassive as he watched. With one final stroke the braid came free, and Qel's head fell back to the ground. The braid would be burned, as was tradition. Dorian tucked the braid into his belt, and, with his now-free hand, he retrieved Tendra's sword. The human queen and the unum approached them on the edge of the Watcher's Spike. Her astonished gaze greeted them.

"By Supremor, your faces…" the woman said.

"Queen Sumenel, my name is Dorian of the Thousand Hammers clan, and this is Rikard of the same. We are the clansmasters of the unu. We are here to protect you and to end this war."

"That would be a godsend," the queen replied. "But how do you plan on stopping them?" The queen pointed behind her to the mass of Skyguard who hovered behind them. Their eyes were upon them as a single Skyguard floated into view.

"Well now, isn't this just perfect?" Lord Commander Veriel's voice made Rikard's eyes go red with rage. "I get to kill you all at once. Shall we begin?" Rikard snarled, took three steps and leapt, pulling Rayn's sword out in a single smooth motion to skewer the Skyguard where he flew.

He missed.

A Dish Best Served Cold

Twenty-Six

Galeerial had never seen a true war before. At Long Fang, he had been so blinded by his need that he had acted on pure instinct, hurtling through the city. Now, as he looked at the symphony of steel and the rondo of blood around him, he shuddered. The audacity...the atrocity of the destruction vied to defy comprehension. Even though the sun shone brightly in the sky, the world seemed glazed over like the weather itself understood the grim pallor of the hearts and minds of the assembled warriors. Snowflakes began to fall around him as he watched. Galeerial looked back at the doorway from the shop that he had just vacated and saw only the interior of a store whose tables had been broken and glass shattered.

"C'mon!" a human soldier in heavy plate armor grabbed him by the shoulder. "We have all been recalled to the Star Tower. Let's go,

339

soldier!" he yelled at him, pulling him along. The roofs. Galeerial looked up. He needed to get to the roofs. He had to find Veriel. Ignoring the human, he grabbed the slats of the roof of the store and began to pull himself up. "What are you doing? That's their territory. Stupid…" The rest of the human's comment was cut off as an arrow pierced his gullet, sending him to the ground in a fountain of blood. Galeerial surfaced on the roof and took off running.

A three story building was next to the one he was on, and he leapt over, crashing through a window and tumbling inside. A ladder led up to the next floor, and Galeerial took the rungs quickly as he hurtled upwards. He cut his pack free. It would only slow him down, and nothing in there would help him kill Veriel. He would keep his scimitars in case he ran into trouble with unu. The roof was slanted, and Galeerial climbed on top of a dresser before leaping up to one of the crisscrossing braces. He swung up and kicked out three of the slats. He hoisted himself up and onto the roof.

Balancing carefully, he moved along the rooftop. The city was an utter mess, and the bay itself seemed to be on fire as the ships burned. There were hundreds of ships in the bay; Galeerial knew that meant that humanity's army was present. The skies above the city were awash with Skyguard. Tens of thousands of his brethren rained arrows down on targets with no means to defend themselves from the onslaught. The largest mass hovered around a large metal tower that stretched high into the skies. This was the Star Tower. Galeerial had never seen it, but he knew it well from the old books. Galeerial's heart skipped a beat.

He needed to get the attention of a Skyguard, but how? Galeerial looked around. An arrow spiked to the ground next to him, and he frantically searched for the shooter. It seemed he would have their attention easily enough, but making it nonlethal would be the trick. Galeerial ran across the rooftop and leapt through the glass of the window to the house next door. He felt an arrow slice through the skin on his neck. Blood seeped out of the wound, and he pulled open the drawers of the dresser, locating a dark brown shirt that he wrapped around his neck like a scarf to stem the bleeding.

340

Galeerial looked around the room trying to find something to bring the Skyguard down to his level. He was surrounded by birdcages. He was in a falconer's den. The birds eyed him dispassionately with an occasional cry. He looked at each of the birds. They all had labels on the cages. He saw the names of cities on several before he came across one that read 'hunting.' Galeerial smiled. He grabbed one of the heavy black gloves that rested near the outside of the cage and opened the cage of the white-and-brown falcon. The bird cocked its head, staring at him. Galeerial reached his hand into the cage. The bird obediently walked out upon his hand. He had experience with falconing. He brought the bird to the window and peered out. A Skyguard circled the rooftops near him.

"Release." Galeerial cast his arm forward, and the falcon leapt from his arm. It hurled toward the Skyguard. Galeerial pulled the Five Eye out from his tunic and unsheathed Eon. He grabbed the windowsill and pulled himself out onto the ledge, leaping across the alleyway to the rooftop he had previously vacated. He watched as the falcon's talons grabbed onto the Skyguard's wings, tearing into them. Galeerial winced. He didn't want to harm the Skyguard, but he needed the Skyguard's attention. The Skyguard whipped around, skewering the falcon with his scimitars, and instantly his eyes came to rest upon Galeerial standing with Eon in one hand, arm out, pointed toward the ground, and the Five Eye in the other. The gemstone shimmered as it caught the light of the sun. The Skyguard approached with caution.

"Identify yourself, human." The red lenses on the crest of the Skyguard's helmet gleamed in tandem with the gold in his armor.

"My name is Galeerial Starheart, and I am the Supreme Cleric of the Skyguard. I am searching for Gabriel Highflight. Do you know of him?" The Skyguard came to rest on the ground in front of Galeerial. He pulled his helmet off.

"Aye, my name is Uriel Windborne. I flew with Gabriel hear from Soaring. He told us to be on the lookout for one such as you." Galeerial was struck by this. *How could he possibly know I would be here?*

"Do you know where he is?" Galeerial asked urgently.

Uriel nodded. "He searches for Veriel Stormrise to try and quell this madness."

Galeerial looked up at the Star Tower. "I am going there. Find Gabriel; see if he can lure Veriel to that point. Do you understand?" Uriel nodded.

"Thank you," Galeerial replied.

"Supremor guide you, Supreme Cleric." The Skyguard wheeled, about taking to the air, as Galeerial took off across the rooftops. The Star Tower was like a beehive with Skyguard fluttering around it. Fire belched from one of the openings, sending a Skyguard screaming to the ground, his wings burning. As he impacted, a thin silver light shot away towards the north. His SoulSong would sing through Winter Crest or Cloud Breach, but Galeerial didn't know if anyone would even be there to hear it.

He raced across rooftops, leaping across gaps as fast as he could towards the Star Tower; finally, he reached the edge before the courtyard, and Galeerial stopped dead at that edge.

His black hair streaming in the wind, his skin marred with the blood of his opponents, his steel pointed toward the ground at the ready. Two men assaulted him, but to no avail. He was like an artist, making broad strokes of red and silver within the canvas of the world. Two swipes of his brush and the men were dead upon the ground.

Veriel.

It had been over a year since he had seen the creature; yet Galeerial would never forget his face: the rigid jaw, the malicious eyes, the self-aggrandizing grin, the confidence in his every step. It was all there. Veriel cast his eyes about and passed over Galeerial at first, but his gaze returned, and all motion stopped. Veriel waited. He waited for Galeerial. Galeerial focused on his breathing. Slowly, deliberately, Galeerial climbed downward, hand over foot. Every lesson that Grey had ever taught him came rushing back. He remembered every move, every ache and pain of the last few weeks. As he reached the ground, he turned to see Veriel watching him.

342

"Galeerial," Veriel laughed. "I thought it was you. Well, this is unexpected to say the least. Looks like you have grown up." *When fighting an opponent who has an obvious advantage, it is imperative that you control the terrain. This isn't necessarily the land, but others fighting on that land. If you can force your opponent into having to defend on multiple fronts, then you control the flow of the fight.* Grey's words returned unbidden to his mind once again. Galeerial's eyes flashed upward to see the Skyguard mulling around in the air. He saw the humans battling the unu around them. One charged Veriel, but his sword slipped through the man's ribcage, and he collapsed to the ground. There would be no one to help him. He was on his own in this fight.

Every warrior moves essentially the same way by the sheer limitations of the craft. If you watch his hips, you can see the changes in balance and motion that indicate where he will strike.

"Nothing? No banter...no, not for you. You have found a purpose in this life that was nonexistent in your previous one." Ripper was held loosely by Veriel's side as Galeerial approached up the white stairs, slowly drawing his own blade. Galeerial felt the heat on his chest. He looked down to the see the gemstone begin to glow as if in reaction to Veriel's presence. He couldn't worry about that now. Galeerial paid little attention to Veriel's words; all his focus was on what Veriel's body was telling him. Galeerial was ten feet from his opponent.

If you can't win, you aren't thinking fast enough.

"Shall we begin?" Two steps closed the distance between them, and their blades cracked like thunder. Galeerial didn't flinch. His eyes caught Veriel's, and Veriel smiled. "Indeed we shall." Veriel slid his blade along Galeerial's and disengaged in a pirouette. Galeerial followed with a quick thrust that spun into an upward slash before stepping back to ward off three of Veriel's own strikes. Veriel's weight balanced on his left foot, and he brought Ripper up in a massive overhead strike. *Don't block when you can dodge. It's much less painful and gives you better positioning.* Galeerial leapt backwards as the sword crashed into the ground. He leapt forward, slashing back and forth in a diagonal pattern at Veriel's chest. Veriel spun backwards, hauling his sword with him and blocking the third strike. His sword flashed upwards, and Galeerial deflected the blow while leaping left into a roll that carried him down two stairs before he was able to scramble to his feet. Veriel didn't pursue him. Instead, he waited.

Galeerial rose back up to even footing with his opponent. He held the blade loose with his left hand and whipped a scimitar up and out. Veriel whipped his shoulder back, but it wasn't fast enough. The blade buried itself into his right clavicle. Three quick stabs at the head were desperately blocked as Veriel was forced to switch to his off hand.

Relentlessly, Galeerial pushed forward. Strike. Slash. Parry. Riposte. Two to the head, one to the chest. Veriel blocked each one with the precision of a surgeon. Galeerial worked the right side of his body, pushing hard to force Veriel into positions of poor footing, but no matter how hard he pressed the elder creature seemed always half a step faster. *Don't get angry if you can't fight angry. You aren't a berserker; you are a spring coiled at the ready.* Galeerial disengaged with a half turn and retreated three steps to reacquire his breath and reassess, but Veriel was having none of it.

Veriel launched forward, hacking at his blade with almost unbearable strength. Galeerial slid his blade back and forth in the weave. The muscles he had developed as a human worked well for him still. His blade was a blur, and Galeerial felt like he could keep it that way as he searched Veriel's assault for a break. He parried a low blow and saw an opening. He took two long steps forward, penetrating Veriel's guard on his right side where his arm had hung useless for the fight and hurled his blade forward at his foe's stomach.

Stars erupted in Galeerial's vision as a gauntleted fist struck him in the temple. He whipped his blade back and upwards on instinct and heard a metallic clash as he struggled to regain his sight. Galeerial felt fingers claw around his neck as Veriel held him up into the air. Veriel started laughing.

"It's you? It is you. Corrigan spoke truthfully. It seems my father, Lord Midox, has quite the delightful sense of humor. It was a valiant effort, and you are to be commended for it, but it was ultimately futile. Go, Galeerial. I spared your life once, by delivering you to The Wither. It was

344

not my choice but rather my best option. It had to be done. Now, I spare it a second time because you are the degenerate." A glint of something that Galeerial couldn't identify flashed in Veriel's eyes. "How deliciously ironic."

Blackness encroached onto his vision. He had to do something fast. Galeerial allowed his whole body to slump, and his eyes to close. He allowed Eon to slip from his fingers. He stifled the intense desire to fight for air that screamed through his every muscle. A second later, Veriel dropped him to the ground. Air rushed back into Galeerial's lungs, but he made no motion that acknowledged the fact. He waited for several moments before slowly opening an eye to see Veriel rising up the outside of the Star Tower. For half a second, despair filled him.

He had failed.

That was all the pity Galeerial allowed himself. He didn't know what it meant to be a degenerate or why it meant Veriel had let him live, but he knew that he would never stop going at Veriel. This was twice Veriel had failed to kill him, and Galeerial would take advantage of Veriel's mistakes. One way or another, one of them would fall. Galeerial sheathed his blade. *If you can't win, you aren't thinking fast enough.* Galeerial thought fast and ran faster.

He took the rest of the stairs leading up to the tower quickly, coughing as he went. Every breath was labored as the icy air filled his lungs, and his head still ached. The entrance was stuffed with bodies. He scrambled atop the mound and slid past limbs into the tower. That combined with the sporadic fighting meant that it would take him far too long to reach the top. Straight in front of him there hung rope tangled within the masses of corpses. Galeerial's eyes followed the rope upwards to see that it connected to the bell at the top of the spire.

That would work.

Galeerial sheathed Eon before taking off running. The corpses were slick and squishy beneath his feet, and he struggled to build any kind of momentum before his leap. He grabbed the rope and started to climb. Hand over hand, foot over foot he climbed. He prayed no one took notice of the human in the center of the room, for he was paying no attention to them. Most of the fighting was confined to the lower levels. If he could climb the rope to a level above it then he could run the rest of the way. His arms and shoulders burned, and he struggled to ignore their protests. Up, up, up he climbed. Thirty feet, fifty feet, eighty feet, one hundred feet. Another twenty feet and he would be above virtually all of the fighting.

Galeerial's muscles rippled as they stretched, trying to break out of his skin. A flash of motion caught Galeerial's eye as a Skyguard flew through one of the many portals that honeycombed the tower, and Galeerial threw his weight to the side. He swung back and forth as the Skyguard pulled up his scimitars drawn. He was going to cut the rope. Galeerial flung his body back and forward. At the apex of his swing, Galeerial released his hands as the tension in the rope went slack, and he hurtled towards the ledge. He didn't make it. The next level was over ten feet below, and Galeerial swung his arms to slow himself as much as possible. Unforgiving stone met very forgiving flesh and bone as he instinctively fell into a roll, coming up onto his feet in a single motion. Scimitar sprang into hand as the Skyguard landed in front of him. Sporadic fighting on this level was far away from him. It was the two of them. Galeerial pulled the Five Eye from his jerkin.

"I'm the Supreme Cleric of the Skyguard. Stand down." Galeerial said. The Skyguard's eyes went wide.

"How dare you defile the holy gem? You will burn, heretic." The Skyguard's scimitars flashed into his hands. Galeerial dropped his own and drew Eon, which drew another hiss from his opponent.

"I said stand down, Raptor!" Galeerial bellowed as he fended off the Skyguard's blows. He didn't want to kill him, but he couldn't delay. Galeerial kept the Skyguard at a distance where his scimitars couldn't be used except to block as he worked the Skyguard back towards the edge. Galeerial worked his blade right and left before he smashed the Skyguard's right arm hard with the flat of his blade and kicked out, hitting the Skyguard in the chest sending him reeling back off the ledge.

"Sorry," Galeerial whispered. He pulled out one of his scimitars and hurled it into the Skyguard's right wing as he plummeted downwards. The Skyguard beat his wings, and Galeerial knew he would be able to shed enough speed that he wouldn't be seriously hurt, but he wouldn't be able to follow him anytime soon. Galeerial looked up. He was three floors from the top. He started running. He avoided the two conflicts that had erupted between unu and humans on that floor and kept a steady pace as he ran, ever upwards. He stopped a floor short of the top and sprinted out onto one of the spokes.

He looked through the sky, scanning rapidly for Veriel. His weak eyes made it difficult, but he spotted him hovering in front of three humans and several unu only two levels down. Galeerial pulled Eon back out from its sheath. He saw a Skyguard furiously pounding his wings towards where Veriel stood. Galeerial focused on him, and his eyes widened in recognition. It was Gabriel. A plan formed quickly in his mind.

He backed up and leapt off just as one of the humans below threw himself from his spoke. Galeerial's eyes widened as the human flew through the air at Veriel, who in a furious pulse of wings hurled himself backwards. The human flew under him towards the ground, and Veriel turned his back to watch. Galeerial's eyes widened, but he kept his focus angling his sword and body on an intercept vector with Veriel.

Galeerial's body was an arrow as it shot through the sky. Seconds seemed to stretch into hours as he approached his target. Veriel seemed entirely unaware of his second attempt. Underestimating him would be this monster's fatal mistake. Veriel turned his back on the humans to watch the one who had attacked him fall. Galeerial focused squarely on the being's back. He saw his target: right in between the two wings. Galeerial's blade slid easily into Veriel, who hissed in pain as his skin started to smoke and burn away. Their bodies crashed together, and they both plummeted earthward.

"You fool! You will die too!" Veriel screamed at him, but Galeerial smiled.

347

"No, just you." Galeerial pushed off of Veriel's body as Gabriel came soaring down to grab his hands. Galeerial saw a second Skyguard holding onto the human. He watched as Veriel tried to push Eon out of his chest, but he didn't have enough time. The Skyguard impacted the ground with an force that sent dust and stone swirling into the air. Stone stairs crushed under the impact of the Skyguard, and Veriel lay defeated on the ground.

"Good save," Galeerial said as he caught his breath.

"Supremor must really love you, Galeerial," Gabriel replied.

"Take me down." Gabriel circled downwards, keeping his eyes fixed squarely on the adversary. Skyguard by the thousands followed them downwards.

"I am the Supreme Cleric, and you will stand down! THIS. WAR. IS. OVER!" Galeerial bellowed as his eyes traced around the sphere of Skyguard. When it seemed that no one would move, Galeerial turned back to his enemy. Veriel had landed hard on the steps with his body broken. His arms were sprawled out to the sides and cracked at disgusting angles. His legs were crunched up into each other. He was dead. Of that, there could be no doubt. Eon was stuck through his chest and still the flesh smoked as if it was being burned.

Galeerial breathed a sigh of relief. It was over. It was finally over. A laugh drew his eyes back to Veriel's corpse. He was laughing. He made no motion as if to move, but somehow the creature was still laughing. Ripper lay by Veriel's side, sticking upwards from the stone steps that it had cut through.

Galeerial wrapped his hand around the hilt of the blade.

"Veriel Stormrise, I hereby judge you guilty by the powers of the Supreme Cleric of the Skyguard. Your sentence is death. Your madness is at an end." One strike to the head is all it would take. He could hardly believe it was happening. This...he was going to actually do it. Galeerial drew it forth, and turned to stare at Veriel. He grew blind to all but the point on his neck where he would sever his head.

348

"Wait!" a cry went out. Galeerial turned sharply to see Gabriel staring at Veriel's corpse. "By Supremor," he whispered. Galeerial followed Gabriel's gaze.

"No," Veriel cackled beneath him. "No, it is just beginning." Galeerial watched as long thin tendrils of shadow began to seep out of where the sword had pierced Veriel's flesh. At first they were few in number, but more and more poured from his flesh until one final burst of torrential black shadow hurtled out of Veriel's chest upwards into the sky. Galeerial's eyes followed them as they wound towards the sun.

"No," Galeerial echoed. He watched as a shadow appeared on the sun and slowly began to spread. The darkness looked like cracks as the middle of the sun faded. The world grew colder as the corruption spread through the star until only a black disk remained in the now night sky. *Darkness will be speared by time; a ruin will befall the light.*

"The black sun rises: my sun," Veriel sneered as he gasped from the ground. "This victory belongs to me. It always belonged to me, but now this world will die for your insolence." Galeerial wasn't listening; his eyes were fixed on the sun.

What have I done? I am the Dawn of Darkness.

United We Fall
Twenty-Seven

Much had happened in the four days since Veriel had fallen and the sun had gone black. Since Qel had been killed by his own son. Since the entire world had changed. Since the war had ended. The war was over. The war is over. The last eight months had seemed to eclipse the entirety of her life; yet it seemed like the end of that era had finally arrived. For Tendra, it couldn't have come soon enough. A shiver traveled up her spine as she looked out the window to behold the black sun bearing down upon them. When she was honest with herself, it terrified her. Whatever Veriel was…he was some evil she could not comprehend. He had poisoned the sun itself. Who knew if there was any cure for it? Perhaps the rest of their days would be spent beneath it. The world had grown cold since the black sun had risen. The winter seemed doubly harsh, and she had cold bumps on her arms despite the heavy furs she wore. A blizzard had coated the world in snow, and people throughout the city huddled about bonfires to keep warm in the endless night. There was no celebration while the black sun held sway. For it brought with it the most important question of all: what now?

In less than a year, the map of the world had been redrawn and in the place of the two kingdoms and the provinces of humanity there stood only a burnt smear of ink. The Hammer controlled virtually the entirety of the South. The Light Monk Army had vanished without a trace. By some scattered reports, the halls of Illuvium had gone dark. Only a single Light Monk woman had arrived two nights ago to supplement the two dozen or so that had made it out of Gemport.

She had asked Jeric about her, but he had been unusually silent in regard to the woman. Though he had confided in her that she was there representing the Radiance. She thought about Jeric. He had occupied far too much of her thoughts lately. She thought about what she was to do with him. She was scared for him. Everyone who had ever been close to her in the last eight months was either dead or missing: her father, Jakob, Rayn, Rowen, Jonathon. All of them. Despite the warmth and comfort of their initial meeting, since then she had kept Jeric at arm's length. Too many people were dying. She couldn't bear to lose him too. She was so different now than she had been when her father had sent him to rally the banners in the north. Everything was different.

Gemport and Bicoln were in ruins, and villages and townships across the lays had been razed. Not to mention whatever was happening in the far north that Aurum was currently investigating on Jeric's behalf. Despite the war being officially over, there was still so much left to be done. So many mysteries left to be uncovered.

In the meantime, though, Tendra readied herself for a very different kind of Council of Five Pillars than she had attended those long months ago. This had been the first time she had been able to get these very different pillars together. Only two of the rulers who had attended the Council at Midway still stood. Jeronious had been deposed and was even now in chains as a criminal of war to the centaurs. Meanwhile, a young captain named Lotius had taken control as the new Herdmaster. Rikard and

351

Dorian of the Seven were the joint rulers of the unu, and Gabriel and Galeerial represented the Skyguard. The other ruler was Eferven of the telos who had arrived by boat this morning to open hostility. Two members of his royal entourage had been killed by dockworkers before soldiers could restrain them.

Tendra stood stiffly outside the doors to the Hall of Merchants preparing to enter. She felt someone behind her, and she whirled about, dagger instantly in her hand. Jeric held up his hands defensively before him. She rushed to hide the dagger. It was the one that Rowen had given her.

"Tendra." Jeric's eyes searched her own, and she saw concern grow within them. "It's just me. You're safe." He told her. His hand cupped her cheek, and he leaned in and kissed her, which she stiffly returned. Jeric retreated slowly looking into her eyes all the while. "What's wrong, my love? Why are you avoiding me?"

"I..." Images came unbidden to her mind: images of her brother's funeral pyre, her father's corpse lying on the throne room floor, and Rayn's head perched on Veriel's blade. Images of Rowen handing her the dagger that she even now held in her hand raised against her betrothed. "I am queen now," she replied, her voice hard as the stone around her, "my time is in high demand." She had just shuffled these thoughts away not moments ago, and now Jeric was bringing them back even stronger. She needed him to back off.

"That's not an answer," Jeric sharply, before pausing regretfully. "I'm sorry. I...I should have come. I don't know what you have been through. You have shouldered all of this alone. Let me help you."

"NO!" Tendra said far louder than she meant. She tempered her emotion back down. "You do right by staying as far away from me as possible. You would do well to continue this course of action." Tendra took a sip of water before brushing past Jeric, whose stricken eyes bored into her back as she moved to the merchant hall. He followed behind her a respectable distance; he would be present as the highest ranking member of the Order in the city, though she imagined the woman would join them as well. Tendra swallowed heavily and balled her fists, letting her nails sink

352

deep into her skin to regain her composure. Curse Jeric for dredging these things up right before the council meeting. She needed focus.

Jeric was right about one thing, though. He didn't know what she had been through. She was not the girl he had left behind. Jeric stepped up next to her at the entrance and wrapped her hand in his, squeezing it for comfort. She made no motion to acknowledge the gesture; she simply pushed open the doors, where inside stood a round table. The merchants of Terakeen ruled the city as equal partners. There was no elected magistrate, no hereditary duke, and no lord.

Lords, that's what they all were. No, not lords, but players in a grand game of Crowns; a game in which each piece was a living being. Tendra had made mistakes in the past, but she could handle this now. She was Queen Sumenel of the line Sumenel, and she was the queen of humanity. Her crown of vipers rested perfectly upon her head. She pulled her hand free from his and entered to see that everyone else was already seated. They rose at her approach, as was customary. Beyond the round table, there were three steps that led down to a wide open platform. That was where the lower merchants and criminals alike would make their pleas, offers, bargains, and deals. Now, once again, criminals would enter, though this time they would sit in the chairs at the table.

The rest of the assembled were standing at her approach and took their seats only after she had taken her own. It seemed like the only constant were the quartet of gallowglass that shifted silently in the corners of the room. She barely even noticed them anymore as they followed her everywhere, and Lotius and Eferven each had a gallowglass as a bodyguard as well. She glanced uncomfortably at Dorian and Rikard; their shared face unnerved her, but she refused to allow that to show.

"For those assembled who do not know me, I am High Queen Tendra Sumenel, forty third in my line, and this is my consort, Jeric Tybius. We are here to discuss three matters: the terms of an armistice between the races assembled here, the reparations by the unu, centaur, telos, and Skyguard races towards humanity, and the fate of Veriel Stormrise." Moments of silence embraced the assembled.

"First, the unu people will make no reparations, nor should the centaur or Skyguard races," Dorian opened. "The only reason humanity is not an endangered species is because of leadership coups. The corrupt leaders have been deposed. We will make no concessions beyond admitting that we have overstepped our bounds as a civilization after being held hostage and blackmailed by overly ambitious leadership. We will return the lands taken from humanity, but our conquest against the ferals gives us first right to feral lands. Therefore, we claim them as our own in the creation of the first unu nation. As for Veriel, we kill him." A brief period of silence followed before Galeerial nodded in agreement.

"The Skyguard have long ignored the happenings of the ground states, but no more. My race contributed in no small part to the destruction of countless human lives, but we have no gold or material goods with which we can offer. We can, though, offer knowledge, and in speaking with the Clerics we are willing to offer the reintroduction of the Tolomin as a peacekeeping force in Carin. We are a people of few material resources, but as teachers and peacekeepers, we have much to offer." Galeerial spoke.

"Do you really think that having Skyguard attempting to police Carin so soon after they tried to annihilate it is a good idea?" Jeric inquired.

"The Tolomin were recognized far and wide as arbiters of wisdom and justice." Gabriel took over from the Supreme Cleric. "We have forgotten that we are all the sons and daughters of Supremor. We have allowed ourselves to be divided along petty lines of racism and distrust. The Tolomin can change that. It would be foolish to expect any kind of integration overnight, but through the creation of such a joint force wherein which each race will pledge even just ten men or women a year, by which we can break down the old bonds of mistrust, we can avoid the kinds of mistakes that brought us to where we now stand."

"The recreation of the Tolomin, while an interesting idea, is not what we are here to discuss," Tendra cut in. "There is plenty of time for that when tens of thousands of my people aren't starving and freezing in the streets, because there aren't enough rooms to house them."

"My lady," Lotius said, "my people, like Dorian's and like Galeerial's, began all of this for a cause. Our cause was our feud with the ferals that has stretched back so far, that, to be perfectly honest, most can't even remember what began it. That is our curse, the knowledge that we killed for no reason, because we always had. After that we acted out of fear, fear of your father, fear of yourself, fear stemming from the Heart of Fires. I won't apologize for what has happened; that is not my place. What I will say is that as the new Herdmaster, I intend to cast off the chains that have bound my people for so long. We will pay whatever price this council deems necessary for our actions. Under two conditions: the Heart of Fires is given up to this ruling body, and the wizards give us answers."

Tendra hesitated for the moment. The idea of keeping the illusion of humanity having the Heart of Fires was a powerful one. Yet, the wizards themselves could destroy the story in an instant, and peace could only come from that revelation. At the end of the day, however, she really had nothing to bargain with. If these negotiations failed, humanity would perish. She was walking a razor's edge.

"A compromise is necessary," Jeric proclaimed.

"The idea of fair compromise is appealing to this one." The telos Imperial spoke up. "We would be willing to aid in the reconstruction of human cities."

Lotius looked angrily at the telos.

"I can only speak for the first of those demands." Tendra said. "Humanity doesn't have the Heart of Fires; we never did, to my knowledge. A blue stone was in fact discovered within Thanatos by my own brother and brought to Gemport under the auspicious guise of being the Heart of Fires, when in fact it was nothing of the sort. I have touched it myself and stand before you no more a wizard than a juggler. That stone was yet another mad delusion of my father's-nothing more, nothing less. These men are of no machinations of mine or any among my line. The Heart of Fires remains lost."

"We have intelligence reports from agents that infiltrated your castle that this is untrue," Lotius said.

"Regardless of what your intelligence says, the fake Heart of Fires that lies within the crypts of Gemport is nothing more than a curious glowing blue stone. I myself have touched it, as has Vizien, my Grand Inquisitor, and nothing has happened. It is a fraud, something that my father designed within his mind to rationalize his control over the Seven, which he never had. I would be happy to show you the stone once control of Gemport has been turned back over to my people." Tendra reinforced.

"If you would be so kind," Lotius interjected. Tendra nodded in acquiescence. One demand down, and now hopefully answers would come that she had desired for some time.

"If the wizards would care to explain themselves to the rest of us, we are very interested in your story." The two brothers exchanged a glance, the one she thought was Rikard shrugged, and the other rose.

"My name is Dorian of the Thousand Hammers, and I will tell our tale, but not in front of him," Dorian said, pointing at Eferven. Tendra cocked an eyebrow in surprise.

"Explain yourself," Tendra inquired.

"Of course, after the Council of Five Pillars ended, I followed the Imperial back to the Spire, where his people transported tens of thousands of ferals northwards." Tendra saw Lotius' eyes widen, but he was too disciplined to show more than that. "In speaking with Lord Galeerial, I am now supremely confident that the telos are implicitly in league with this creature Veriel and are here even now to spy on our activities. I will not speak a word in his presence unless the Imperial can explain to me where those feral warriors went, if not to join the enemy of this entire world."

Tendra glanced over to see the unnerving serenity on the faces of the Skyguard as they regarded the telos Imperial. Eferven blinked sideways.

"That was simply part of our deal. We were to provide a delaying action at the Heart and transport the ferals to the north. We knew of nothing sinister, only the deal. We did what our business deal required of us, Mage of Two Faces."

"That's not good enough," Galeerial cut in.

"The Lord Commander of Wings is in chains in the lowest dungeons humans may dig. How were we to know what the Lord Commander of Wings was doing?"

"Ignorance is not a good excuse."

"Neither is condemnation," Tendra interrupted. "The matters of this council stay in this room. The word of honor still holds true for all assembled. Is that understood?" Tendra made sure to rove her eyes across everyone assembled, lingering only on the Light Monk woman. Her hair was long and bleached blonde, and her eyes were a dark brown that was flecked with red spots. Iona was her name, and she met Tendra's gaze perfectly evenly. It was almost as if she was paying as much attention to her as she was to the words being spoken.

"I am required to report back to The Radiance. It is my function," Iona finally spoke up.

"Where is the Lady of the Light?" Eferven inquired.

"Otherwise indisposed," Iona replied curtly.

"She has more pressing matters than the fate of the world?" Gabriel inquired.

"Indeed she does."

"Then Supremor be with her. Nevertheless, Dorian, will you continue on with your tale? Not all of the assembled know you like I do." Gabriel replied. Dorian gazed evenly at the telos.

"How is it that you know the wizard so well, Gabriel?" Lotius asked.

"I knew of the Seven far before today. For several years now I have held company and counsel with them. I know that they are unaware of the Heart of Fires."

"A strong show of support," Lotius replied. Gabriel said nothing.

"I would have your word that my story will not reach another's mind by your doing." The telos blinked twice before waving his hand.

"I give my word," the Imperial replied.

Dorian looked at Rikard. "You know what I would do." The second brother said.

"That's why I do the talking." Dorian hesitated as Tendra leaned closer in anticipation. "My name is Dorian, son of Rerem and Sera. I was born the sixth day of the third month of the year in the Jerichain Province in the land of Cambria, a nation that exists west of Carin across the Rift. My brothers and I arrived here almost eight years ago and have spent those years preparing for the inevitable war that was to come."

"A war that you started," Tendra interjected.

"A necessary war. I spent the better part of my life studying the mechanisms of warfare and the types of social and political landscapes that breed such conflicts. This world was primed to explode; all it needed was a catalyst. We directed that explosion in the manner that resulted in the most productive end we could manage. It was either the entire world burned or only a piece of it. We did what we had to, as all here have done in this last year."

"Tell us about your magic," Jeric inquired.

"It is not from the Heart of Fires. I can tell you that much. It is related to certain words that are accompanied by inner focus and sometimes with focusing objects such as our staffs. We have never seen the Heart of Fires, nor do we know where it is. Our magic was brought with us from Cambria. We have experienced no magic in Carin like what came with us." Dorian paused, staring directly at Jeric and Iona.

"And what kind of magic is that?" Iona asked.

"I'm not sure I know what you mean," Dorian replied.

"There are three types of magic, or so scripture has told us: the isterios, the magic of the world; the elixis, the magic of Supremor; and the axios, the magic of Midox. Tell me, wizard, which do you wield?" Iona asked.

"In Cambria, there are no gods. Our magic, I suppose, is what you would call isterios then. We have no such name for it, and you, what of your magic? Is it from your Heart of Fires?"

"What are you implying?" Iona replied.

"That you either have it or at the very least know where it is."

"Why would they know?" Tendra asked confused.

358

"Because they are Light Monks. Of course," Rikard cut in before Dorian could respond.

All eyes now focused on Jeric and Iona. "Of course not," Jeric said.

"He's lying." Rikard interjected.

"How could you possibly know the veracity of any statement I make?" Jeric challenged.

"I'm a magician; I used my magic truth telling spell." Rikard waved his hand at Jeric. "It doesn't matter anyway, because anybody could tell that you are lying."

"That's enough." Tendra sharply cut off the wizard. "If the Light Monks do have the Heart of Fires, then at a later date we can bring the Radiance herself before us, in chains if need be, to tell us."

"The Radiance in chains, the Tolomin resurfacing, two sharing a single face; it is a time of change indeed," Lotius murmured.

"Things are changing more and faster than you know," Galeerial said quietly. "There can be little doubt now that Veriel is beyond any mere Horror, much less a Skyguard. I believe that in the presence of the black sun, we have only one conclusion to make. This truly is the end of days. The words of the last prophecies of the Book of Arestephan are coming to pass. Veriel either is the Dread reborn, or some new kind of enemy come with power of equivalent measure. I speared him through the heart with one of the Cardinal Swords, and he neither bleeds nor dies. Darkness was speared by time. Whatever he is, those chains cannot hold him. The Skyguard have," Galeerial exchanged a glance with Gabriel, "…ideas on how to contain him, and Lord Gabriel will be searching for methods with which to kill him."

"What about Shineheart?" Tendra asked. "Isn't the white sword capable of destroying any evil?"

"The Sword of the Spirit is no longer in our custody. There can be no doubt that Veriel was responsible. His machinations have culminated in this war. Veriel used the Seven as a flashpoint to send the Skyguard to war and to ruin the races of Carin, but his plans are not complete. An army of

359

vast proportions has marshaled in the north. I spent time at Dynast with the Iron Men and the wizard Grey. Their civilization is almost destroyed by this force. A force supplemented by ferals that the telos helped to ferry north."

"That explains much," Lotius interjected. Tendra's eyes turned to the centaur. He looked hesitant for a moment. "We have sent multiple emissaries to Dynast to request aide from the Iron Men, as laid down centuries ago by Harin himself. We heard nothing in reply. We would have gone to investigate, but, with the war in full force, we had no one to spare."

"Whatever the results of this council, one thing must be made clear. There is no walking back to your lands. There is only more death, more war, and more blood," Galeerial continued.

"It's true. The centaurs are bound by duty to aid the Iron Men in any danger. We will ride north at first light. All of us, and, even if not a single one of you join us, we will fight," Lotius said. His words were heavy, but resolute. The remainder of the council exchanged glances.

"The Skyguard will fly north as well," Galeerial announced, "but not before imprisoning Veriel at Soaring, far from his army and any strength he draws from or provides to them. He is the reason we are here, and it is his poison that has caused the death of so many with the power he wielded as a Skyguard. The Burning Host will descend upon Veriel's armies from the skies. We will fight until there is nothing left of either us or them. No quarter can be given to such darkness." Galeerial and Gabriel moved to stand beside Lotius, placing a hand on his shoulder. "We will kill them all." Gabriel nodded as well after a glance at Galeerial. Imperial Eferven's tongue slithered out of his mouth once, twice.

"The Swimmers in Water will follow to repair what the Pillars of Life see as their error." It was as close to an apology as she had ever heard from one of their kind.

Tendra was yet again at a crossroads. She knew that humanity would speak last as was tradition; yet she was torn. The centaurs and Skyguard were duty-bound to follow their courses, and the telos would go because they couldn't afford not to. Everyone believed them to be traitors, but humanity had no such chains. They could walk away. No more war. No more death. No more brothers and friends and fathers lost. The Skyguard and centaurs could destroy any threat imaginable now that the power behind the threat had been neutralized.

"I cannot speak for the Light Monks, but I have no doubt that the Radiance will give whatever aid she can to fight this," Iona spoke up. "As she has been fighting in the east."

"What lies in the east?" Dorian asked.

"The remainder of the Light Monk army desperately trying to hold back the black tide of Veriel's army. That is why I am here, to tell a tale of sixty thousand ferals, human corsairs raiding up and down the coast, and mercenaries attacking every settlement they can find. The east is being raped while all the armies of the world exchange blows wholly unaware."

"Not wholly unaware," Dorian said quietly. "Why do you think such haste was made to arrive here? The unu have claims on the former Kingdom of Fangs. We will fight in the east to protect our claim if nothing else."

"And humanity?" Galeerial asked. "What will the Template decide?" Tendra was silent for a moment.

"I have looked into Veriel's eyes," she said with slow deliberate words. "Within them, there is naught but the abyss. Whether he be the Dread Reborn, or something else entirely, he represents a grave threat to this world; of that there can be no doubt. However, this is not humanity's fight." Stunned silence swept the council. "Veriel has been removed from the equation. There will be no war march for mankind."

"You cannot be serious!" Galeerial exclaimed. "You are a part of this world. Veriel is not an animal to be caged. I have seen but a fraction of his force at Dynast. Who knows what else lies in the north? You are a fool if you choose to stay."

"Then call me a fool," Tendra replied. "Humanity has suffered at the hands of unu, the hands of centaurs, the hands of Skyguard and telos, and we survived. Our suffering is complete. My men want to return to their families, to their farms. They want to return home, and so they shall. Go fight in the north. Humanity is done."

"You are going to pillage our lands while we fight for the survival of Carin," Lotius proclaimed.

"Peace, Herdmaster." Gabriel held his hand up to calm the centaur. Lotius rose to his feet.

"Is this your plan?" he asked her. "Feign unity for your own profit? Your father would be proud," Lotius spat.

Tendra maintained her calm.

"My Lady, if I may," Iona began. "What of the human cities of Boaz and Seraph that are being assaulted by Veriel's army? The Light Monks cannot hold them there forever."

"Volunteers and members of the standing army will be sent to aid them, but the local militias and banner men will be liberated from their duty. All save those who remain to guard Veriel who will be held here."

"Veriel is ours," Galeerial said sharply, interrupting her. Tendra glared at him with daggers in her eyes. "We cannot trust his imprisonment to anyone else, regardless of race." Galeerial said.

"You are not seriously suggesting that we turn this being over to the same people that allowed him to run rampant for centuries, do you?" Lotius said incredulously.

"How dare you presume to judge me by their folly? I am not merely a Skyguard. I am the Supreme Cleric."

"Then where are your wings?" Lotius asked.

"They were cut off and burned before my eyes by Veriel," Galeerial answered. Lotius swallowed hard and was a bit taken aback. "I know what that monster is capable of more than anyone. I leapt off of the Star Tower to bring him down. I would do whatever it takes to see that his head is on a stake." Galeerial seethed. His blue eyes searched her own. "You are searching for someone to blame for the deaths of your family. You think because you lost them that makes you something? All that makes you is a victim. Veriel is a threat to us all, but he is the responsibility of the Skyguard. We carry the guilt of his machinations. This is a fool's argument."

"Beyond that, the Light Monks are past their twilight." Iona and Jeric's heads turned sharply to stare at Gabriel. "Though we live apart, we see much that goes on in this world. The Light Monks, though strong, have lost the spark that caused their order to bloom. They have withered like a tree deprived of water. They cannot hope to hold him," Gabriel continued.

"The Radiance herself is coming to take Veriel into her custody. You would defy her?" Jeric challenged.

"I would. As powerful as she is, she understands what this kind of power is and what it means. You don't, young Monk; you have yet to walk the Shaded Path. You don't understand, Jeric. But she does." Gabriel gestured to Iona.

"I understand enough to know that you are guests in my house, in my kingdom. He is my prisoner, and I will do with him what I will," Tendra said sharply. "The Skyguard have all but vanished from this world for hundreds of years, and now, the moment you return, it is with steel in hand and war in mind. Forgive me if your legacy has been tarnished by your present actions. Thirty thousand Skyguard showed up on our doorstep and killed tens of thousands of my people. Meanwhile a force of ten thousand comes to try and stop them. It looks like you are on the losing side of your people's loyalty."

"I am entirely in control of my people now that Veriel has been excised. He is like a parasite that has been flushed from the body but still lies patiently waiting for his next victim." Tendra looked at Galeerial. She remembered when she had borne him with Rowen to Soaring in search of Charist. He had been so weak then. A hollow shell of a creature, but now he was something far more regal. He was hard and callous.

"How do you hope to contain him, then?" This exchange was getting out of hand. Tendra's eyes stole away from the Supreme Cleric for a moment to view the others. Rikard was grinning wildly, while Dorian looked concerned. Lotius looked unsure of himself, and Jeric was uneasy. Eferven was as inscrutable as usual. "What do the wizards have to say?" Tendra looked straight at Dorian and Rikard.

363

"Why don't we just kill him already?" Rikard asked. "Why risk imprisonment, or waste time with it? We won; he lost; war's over. I'll take his head off myself."

"It is not that simple," Gabriel and Galeerial replied in unison. They exchanged glances.

"I have yet to meet a man who doesn't die when you cut his head off."

"You are welcome to try," Galeerial replied. "But the only weapon that can hope to kill him is the sword Shineheart."

"Which leaves us nowhere because you lost it. So where is it?" Rikard asked. "We glossed over that little point earlier in the discussion. So why don't you explain to the council how the Skyguard lost the most important weapon in the history of the world?"

"We gave it to Geraldean to strike the Dread down in the Dread War. He failed, and the weapon was lost. Geraldean took the secret of the sword's location to his grave," Gabriel replied. "We did not lose it."

"Is there no way to find it?" Dorian asked. His eyes searched the room.

"No," Gabriel replied. "Not that any of us know. We could petition Our Lord, but one does not make demands of a deity." Gabriel regarded the room. "But until that time, we have no way to kill him. Eon seems to have affected his magic in some way. Containment is the best that we can hope for, and even that is more than humanity can hope to do. You invite disaster with every second that you hold him in your dungeons."

"What are your plans for containing him? What can you do that humanity or the unu can't?" Dorian inquired.

"We do what the first gathering of the Radiance did with the Dread; we drown him in Charist. Keep him submerged, in chains, with Eon through his body at the bottom of the well in one of the Cathedrals. Skyguard live forever, and we never forget," Galeerial replied. Tendra looked at Jeric. She couldn't give in to the Skyguard, but she couldn't deny any of his claims.

"And the Radiance? You brought your petition for his fate to me before this council, but you never explained what she had planned for him. Do you know?" Tendra asked Iona.

"The Radiance has power beyond that of other people. Though she believes she can contain Veriel, she would not be opposed to discussing his future with the Skyguard. She should be here in the next two days," she replied.

"When the Radiance arrives, we will reconvene. As of right now though, Veriel will stay where he is. Is that understood?" Tendra looked around the table and everyone nodded. "The unu and centaurs will vacate the lands taken from humanity during this war. The former Kingdom of Fangs will be divided among the centaurs and unu as they see fit. In addition, the centaurs, telos, and unu will provide supplies to assist humanity through the winter. That is what has been decided." No disagreement was forthcoming. She rose, and the others accompanied her. She turned and departed, leaving the leaders of each race talking amongst themselves. She heard footsteps behind her. That would be Jeric.

She exited the chamber, and Jeric reached out and caught her hand. He pulled her back to him.

"Ten-" She silenced him with her lips. Her tongue played along his lips, and her hand wrapped around his head. He pulled away as soon as the surprise wore off.

"What...what is wrong with you?" Jeric recoiled. Tendra breathed heavily at her own impulsiveness.

"We are free, Jeric. Humanity is free from the war, from the fighting. I'm free from it all. We can be together without..." Her voice trailed off. Jeric held her shoulders hostage against the wall. Tendra looked desperately at him.

"Without what?" he asked. She dropped her gaze. "Without what?" Every word was pronounced slowly. Still she said nothing. "Tendra! Without what!" Finally some harshness leaked into his voice.

"Without dying!" The words escaped her lips before she could stop them. Her mouth went dry. "You aren't going to die now." She bit her lower lip as Jeric took a step back. He shook his head.

"Tendra...I..." He looked at her, and it seemed like it was the first time she had truly seen him in a long time. He had a façade that was strong, but it broke at this point. He became the man she had known for years. "Tendra, everyone dies. It...it isn't your fault that they died. It's no one's fault but the one who raised the blade. I swear to you that I am not leaving you. I am back now. I am back, and I am not going anywhere." He pulled her into an embrace. She was stiff in his arms.

"You don't know that. Everyone is gone, Jeric. I can't lose you too. I can't lose you too." Tendra shuddered, and her hands felt numb. She pushed herself back from him. "I love you, Jeric. Now, we can be safe. We can be safe together." She pleaded with him.

"We can't live our lives in fear," Jeric said. "You...you did this for me. You pulled humanity out of the war for me?" He said the words, trying to learn how to believe them.

"Yes!" she exclaimed. "I did it for us. I did it so no woman has to watch her lover die. No sister has to see her brother die. No daughter has to see her father's body lying on the ground lifeless." Tears welled in Jeric's eyes. Sadness grew on Jeric's face. Tendra sunk to her knees. Jeric knelt down beside her.

"I am so sorry. I wasn't here for you. I wish I was. I wish with all my heart I could have stood beside you through everything." She wrapped his hand in her own. "Tendra. I know you need to be safe...but this is bigger than us. This is bigger than all of us. You have seen what Veriel has done, what he is capable of. Whatever he is doing in the north, it will change everything. I love you, but I can't let you use me as a reason to run." Tendra looked him in the eyes. "You are stronger than that. You are braver than that. I have always known it. You know it too. I watched you in the Star Tower. I watched you with the council. I know how strong you are. You can surpass everything that has been thrown at you. You will survive this and so much more."

366

"I have survived too much already, Jeric. I'm ready to live my life."

"This is our life now, Tendra. Whether we like it or not, this is our life. You and I, we are living it. We can't just run from it."

Tendra turned her head in shame. "I know...I know," she said in tired resignation. "Just so much has happened in so little time. It is like a lifetime has occurred in the last year. It is just too much. I need time, Jeric. I just need some kind of peace. A day, just a day without a thousand people and a thousand worries and a thousand problems. So much more has changed than you could know. I can't do this anymore. This fighting, this war. I can't keep fighting." Jeric squeezed her hand.

"Just don't shut me out. These last five days I have never felt farther away from you. You are not alone. I am here. I am here for you...always. You can always talk with me. Okay?" Tendra nodded. She rose slowly to her feet. Jeric followed her. "Can we have dinner together tonight?" Jeric asked. A choked smile came to her lips.

"I would like that. I would like that an awful, awful lot." She said. Jeric leaned in and kissed her on the cheek. "Sunset?"

"Perfect," he replied.

"Well, then, I had better go get ready," she replied. Jeric shot her a confused glance.

"You look beautiful."

"Well, that may be the case, but I am also thoroughly exhausted. I'm going to sleep for the rest of the day and you?"

"I'm walking my betrothed to her rooms," h e said. She smiled. He extended his arm, and she took it. They walked silently through the castle, but for the first time since she could remember she didn't mind the silence. It was comforting in a way. They arrived at her rooms, and she turned to face him.

"Thank you," she said. He touched her cheek and gave her a soft kiss.

"I love you," he said.

"I love you too," she replied. She slipped into the room. She moved over to the writing desk, slipping out of her shoes. She pulled the center drawer on the desk and pulled out a small bundle of letters. She strode to the lamp and ignited the flame within as she slipped into the bed. She unwrapped the tight cord that bound the letters together. They smelled of salt and the paper cracked as she touched them. She drew one at random and unfolded the paper.

Dearest Tendra,

It has been forty-seven days since I last saw your face. I have spent all day upon the vessel Sea Spray. She is a fine craft, but short on amenities. I fear my sea legs are starting to sink in, as today I did not have to rely upon the supports once while the boat rocked through the waves on the trip from Cirode'l to Mesnir. Tomorrow, I should be back in King's Port. I cannot wait to see how Halfen and the others have done on rallying the banners. I hope to set sail for Bicoln as soon as two days from now. I miss the feeling of your hair on my shoulders. I have a beard now, but I will shave before I return. I know how much you dislike when I have one. I miss you, and I think of you every time I see a bird in the sky. You are what sets my heart to be as free as they are. I miss you and love you.

-        Jeric

Tendra finished reading the letter, set it aside, and started the next one, and after that the next one, and the next.

Black Sun Rising

Twenty-Eight

Galeerial stood outside the rusty iron cell that bound Veriel in the depths of Terakeen. It had been two days since the council, and Galeerial was ready to face Veriel. The creature sneered at Galeerial's approach. Galeerial regarded him coolly; Veriel's arms and legs were bound by heavy chains and pulled taut so that he could not move. The Sword of Time, Eon, was pierced right through the center of his chest, angled downward with the hilt gleaming from between his shoulder blades. The only light in the chamber came from flickering torches on the wall, nonetheless Eon seemed to catch the red light and reflect it back making the sharp metal sparkle with a radiant sheen. Galeerial felt the Five Eye burn his breast as he walked; its light barely concealed beneath his armor. Galeerial was startled by the power of the reaction of the gem to the presence of the being that stood bound before him. He had never felt anything like it, even when he had fought Veriel before. He looked down and saw it glowing even through his chain mail. Its light was pure white.

"Come to gloat, Galeerial, over your...victory?" Veriel smiled. Galeerial nodded to the human Light Monk who escorted him here with the key. The Light Monk inserted the key, and the gate to Veriel's cell creaked open. The old iron groaned against the stone. Galeerial heard the click of the lock as the guard shut him in.

"Leave me. All of you. Stay at the top of the stairwell. I will call for you when I am finished."

"My Lord, my orders come from Queen Sum-"

"I am the Supreme Cleric. Does a queen overrule a deity?" Galeerial asked severely. The Light Monk seemed conflicted but nodded. Galeerial waited as they filed down and out of the hallway. There were six prisoners in the cells that had lined the hallway. They wouldn't be a problem.

"No, I have come for answers." Galeerial said simply. Veriel regarded him coolly.

"And why should I be forthcoming?" Galeerial reached back and pulled a sword from his back. Veriel chuckled. "That will do nothing to me. Your sword of time has frozen me in my present form."

"Indulge me." Galeerial swung down hard, but the blade made not even the slightest dent in his skin. Galeerial felt the jolt in his shoulder but shunted the pain to the side. "Let's try again shall we."

"Is there a point to all of this?" Veriel asked. "If you really want to cut me, just pull this blade from my chest, and you can cut me to your heart's content."

"If that is how subtle your manipulations are, it is a wonder that you were ever able to fool the clerics." Galeerial interjected.

"No, my manipulations are much more subtle, I am just trying to see what your plan is. You've grown Galeerial, grown smarter, grown stronger. When I last saw you, you were but a child, but now look at you...the Supreme Cleric." Galeerial held his face in stone, but Veriel still smiled. "You have risen high and far thanks to me."

370

"You sent me to hell." Galeerial said calmly, Veriel smiled.

"So that is what all this is about then. Vengeance over how I wronged you. Fine then, let's do this."

"I want to know everything, and you are going to tell me." Galeerial pulled a second blade from his back and saw Veriel's eyes flash in recognition. He knew this sword. The Cardinal Sword of the North, Ripper, the Sword of the Flesh, cut cleanly through Veriel's shoulder, and his arm fell to the ground. A harsh growl contorted Veriel's face, but he made no sound. There was no blood, it was as if he actually was a Skyguard, but Galeerial knew better. He regarded his bisected limb coolly, "or the next blow takes your head." Veriel clicked his tongue.

"What do you want to know?" Veriel regarded Galeerial with a gaze of sordid indifference.

"What are you?" Veriel smiled; it was a smile that Galeerial knew would have sent a chill down his spine had he seen it all those months ago. Before he had become what he was.

"You know what I am. I am the terror Arestephan of which wrote, I am the white-eyed serpent coiled about your throat. I am the darkness that spawns the night. I am the shadow that drowns out the light. I am the name that strikes men dead. I am the name of every... secret..." Veriel allowed the sentence to trail off. Galeerial regarded him.

"Where is he?"

"He?" Veriel asked. "I'm not sure I..." Veriel froze as the blade touched the base of his neck. "What day is it?"

"Why does that matter?"

"Because depending on what day it is, will tell me which city he is in the process of tearing down brick by brick." Veriel snorted. "How foolish you are, Galeerial. Do you honestly believe that anything you do could jeopardize my plans? I have been laying the groundwork of this for generations. I control the fate of this world." Veriel lowered his chin, and the shadows covered his eyes. "I have already won, as we speak The Wither sits within the ruins of Cloud Breach. Your city lies dead at his feet while he drinks from the skulls of the Clerics. He's waiting for you. The Maw

371

waits for you. The Pillars of Creation are falling, and the Skyguard fall with them. The Divide between the Dreaming and Materia is weakening. Merhelden will fall just like the kingdoms of Carin. Midox has already won. Even if I remain trapped here, there is nothing you can do to stop this avalanche. You have lost." Galeerial stared at him.

Veriel mocked him. Somehow he mocked him with his words. He knew what was happening even locked in the depths of the earth. Somehow he knew. Galeerial gazed at the object of all of his hatred.

"You want to kill me. I can see it in your eyes, but the funny thing is that no matter how small the pieces Ripper cuts into, I cannot be vanquished by swords such as those anymore. Maybe in the first war, but now? Only Shineheart can kill me now, and that blade is long gone. I cast it away after drinking Geraldean dry. Imprisonment is the best you can hope for, and even that is but a temporary solution." Veriel boasted. "There is nothing left in this world that can vanquish me. You have been fighting a losing battle since the beginning. You are a lot like Geraldean in so many ways. You were both fallen, both consumed by vengeance. He couldn't stop me, and neither can you. It isn't your fault; it is just how it had to happen." Galeerial was careful to make sure no emotion played across his face.

"You spoke of the Maw." Galeerial said quietly.

"Of course. Everyone knows that the Twilight of Ages is followed by the Dawn of Darkness within the pages of the Maw. Arestephan's book of prophecies relied heavily on the final book of *The Stone*, even if people choose to ignore it. The Ravishing of the World is at hand.

A black sun rises over a broken plane,
a new day dawns in night.
Darkness will be speared by time;
a ruin will befall the light.
Gods speak from on high,
a human burns with might;
magic stands revealed,
as the world succumbs to blight

You have given me my victory, Galeerial. Darkness has been speared by time. Now a black sun rises. My sun. It feeds me…gives me power, power that will make this all be over soon. It feeds me just like your fear does. Just like the fear that drips through this palace. Just like the fear that Ezekiel had right before I smashed his body into the ground. Right before I reduced his flesh to a mass of bloody pieces."

The Five Eye hummed at him in its harmonic din, and Galeerial pulled it from beneath his armor. Its light exploded like a sun within the room, and Galeerial heard Veriel scream. Galeerial's eyes were blinded while his ears were deafened. It was the most unearthly sound he had ever heard. It was like teeth being ground across brick or glass being scratched by glass. It slammed into Galeerial's head, and he dropped the Five Eye from his hand to clutch his temples, but half a second later it was gone. Galeerial was able to see Veriel's body despite the blinding light.

Veriel pulsed in agony; his whole body thrashed against the chains that bound him causing them to shake and rattle. Galeerial strode forward to Veriel's surging body and pressed the Five Eye to his chest. The flesh rippled all across his body. Galeerial watched, as it seemed like something was trying to push its way out of Veriel's skin. Veriel's mouth was open in a silent scream. The flesh seared as if burning, and a circular brand was etched in the rippling skin.

Galeerial pulled the gem back beneath his shirt, and the light vanished leaving him momentarily blinded. His eyes slowly readjusted to the weak light. He looked at Veriel's body, which looked like a corpse it hung so limply. Even his arm was now in a different position from when he had cut it off just a moment ago.

"Perhaps, it is I who feasts on your fear." Galeerial whispered. "Now, you will tell me everything. Do you understand me? Everything. Or by Supremor I will make you burn." Veriel's eyes opened, and he looked up at Galeerial. The saliva from his mouth struck Galeerial in the neck, and he reached for the Five Eye again.

*   *   *

By the time, Galeerial called out to the guard to open the gate, the human guard's face that held the key had been so drained of blood from the sound of the agony induced screams that his hands shook, and he dropped the keys twice before finally managing to unlock the door. Galeerial stood there patiently waiting. He had everything that he wanted, except the question that bothered him the most: why didn't Veriel kill him the second time. Veriel had merely laughed even amidst the pain when Galeerial had asked him that. Galeerial knew that Veriel had lied about one thing though. He would find Shineheart, no matter how long it took. No matter how far he had to search. He would find it, but first he had business to the north.

He pushed through the gate and felt the Five Eye cool against his breast. Galeerial strode confidently past the wildly differing gazes of the guards who returned to their watch in the cells. A legion made up of unum, Skyguard and humans stood guard over Veriel's cell and their eyes told their feelings: disgust, admiration, fear. Galeerial didn't care about their judgment. He pushed by them all.

The narrow winding stairwell that led up to the surface was stifling. He needed to get out of this prison. His every footfall sent reverberations cascading throughout the stairwell, and he walked faster to escape them. When he reached the surface he was breathing heavily. Standing there watching him escape the cells was a lone Skyguard. Galeerial didn't shirk Gabriel's gaze in the slightest, and Gabriel rose to the challenge.

"I need to get back to Cloud Breach immediately." Galeerial said. He didn't stop to acknowledge the other Skyguard but rather just kept walking past him forcing Gabriel to walk quickly in order to catch up as he walked across the central plaza outside the castle.

"Let me see it." Galeerial glanced back at his friend.

"No." Gabriel grabbed his arm firmly and pulled Galeerial back to face him.

374

"Galeerial, let me see it." Galeerial looked at Gabriel nonchalantly as Galeerial pulled the gemstone from his tunic. It was black. Gabriel's grip loosened as horror filled his eyes. "What...what have you done?"

"What needed to be done." Galeerial replied. "The Wither is at Cloud Breach, and Veriel's army marches south from the Burning Waters. I did what needed to be done." Galeerial shook free of Gabriel's grasp. The quickest way to the stables was through the cathedral.

"Stop." Gabriel commanded behind him.

"I'm the Supreme Cleric; you have no authority to command me to do anything." Galeerial shot back.

"I am not commanding you as anything other than your friend." Galeerial stopped and turned back to look at Gabriel. "You have crossed a line. I will not pretend to know the depths of the pain that was inflicted upon you, but you are more than just a human now Galeerial. You bear two of the only magical items left in the world after magic was bound into the Heart of Fires. You are dangerously close to losing that right."

"Will you take it from me, Gabriel?" Galeerial challenged looking back at the elder Skyguard.

"Yes." Gabriel met his gaze. There was a time when he would have shirked from the stare, but Gabriel was right, He wasn't just a human. He was one of the Seven, and as such Galeerial was more than prepared for the challenge.

"You are welcome to try, but I have my purpose, and it lies with the blood of The Wither on my hands and then Veriel's. There is nothing else. I will do whatever it takes."

"At what cost? Galeerial, I cannot know your past. I can only know what you do now. I will not judge you, for that is not my place, but I will stop you from destroying yourself. You once told me that you would learn to kill a thousand to kill one. But you have crossed a line. Rather than learn, you *will* kill a thousand to kill one. If the cost of victory is your soul, then the cost is not worth it. You know this as well as I do."

"Do I?" Gabriel, reeled stunned.

"You know not what you say." He breathed.

"Don't I?" Galeerial didn't flinch from the Skyguard's desperate gaze and instead bore down upon him with his own. "For months, I was bled, burned, cut, frozen, beaten, scarred, and sliced. For months, I called out to Supremor and his son, for help, for strength, for aid. For six hundred years, I dedicated myself to the worship and study of them. Their voice rang through the Clerics week after week, but the one time I needed them. The one time their voice needed to be heard. They kept their silence. They ignored me."

"*Yea though I walk through the Valley of the Shadow of Death I will fear no evil for your sword and your hand lie around me.*" Gabriel quoted from *The Stone*.

"*Call out for your Lord, and he will answer you, no matter the darkness.*" Galeerial shot back.

"*It is not our place to know the mind of Supremor but to accept that everything is in his plan.*"

"*I will never abandon you; I will never place you in so deep a darkness that you cannot see the light.*"

"*Only when you close your eyes, will my light vanish from your heart.*" Gabriel matched Galeerial's barbs.

"*Faith, hope and love are the good things he gave us. Keep any of these in your heart, and I will be with you.*" Gabriel shook his head.

"Which one of those do you have in your heart now, Galeerial? Lord Supremor never abandoned you. You abandoned him. I will pray for your soul that you might see reason before the end."

"I have not changed so much since Soaring. Still you made me Supreme Cleric. You are complicit in what I have become Gabriel. You set me in this path. I walked it, but you showed me the way."

"I did not show you this. I showed you a way to live through your own despair. You would have killed yourself if I had not done this. You were on the path to self destruction, a path you still walk though it is hidden by 'purpose'." Gabriel spat. "You will kill yourself, Galeerial, and your soul will suffer when it stands before Supremor. I renounce you as Supreme Cleric. I will always believe in you Galeerial, but I will not follow you as

376

long as you follow this path of destruction." Now, it was Galeerial's turn to reel. "You truly are fallen." Galeerial set his jaw.

"I've made my choice." Galeerial turned away from the Skyguard crossing the rest of the plaza without looking back. He could feel Gabriel's harsh gaze upon him. He pushed at the first door he arrived at to escape it. The door resisted his push. He pushed harder and harder, and the door slowly gave way inch by inch until, finally, he was able to slip in.

He was startled to see the shiftstone statue bearing down upon him; its image of a flame seemed to dance in his eyes. He stalked around the edge of the cathedral towards the exit. Every step seemed to grow more and more weighted. His eyes rove back to the image of the flame.

"What do you want from me!" Galeerial screamed at the stone fire. Silence filled the cathedral. "That's right. You keep your silence, just as you do whenever we need you. This war won't be won through prayers. It will be won with steel and willpower."

"Yes…yes it will." Galeerial's eyes flashed, and he saw one of the Clansmasters of the unu seated near the front of the church. He rose from his knees, and slowly made his way back to where Galeerial stood. It was Dorian; he could tell because the other one had a scar on his eye and was perpetually either shouting or mocking. This one's tone held neither contempt nor outrage. It was one of his brothers.

"Supreme Cleric." Galeerial remembered what Grey had told him.

"Dorian." The man nodded. "I bring a message from our mutual brother. There are three glasses on a table; the third one is blue." An eyebrow cocked on Dorian's face, and he nodded.

"Hello, brother. Grey, Rowen or Aurum?" He inquired.

"Grey." Galeerial replied. A smile came to Dorian's face. It looked to be the first one in some time that had graced his face. "Though Aurum was alive in Cloud Breach not three weeks ago."

"It brings joy to my heart to hear they are alive. Please sit, if you have a moment." Dorian gestured to the pew before him. Galeerial hesitated before moving to come to rest beside Dorian. "Where is Grey?"

"Dynast." Galeerial replied. "I sent Aurum to Thanatos." Galeerial confessed. He expected Dorian to balk or react with some surprise. Instead, he simply nodded. "He has a destiny. I've known it since he went before the Orrery and emerged changed. Do you know what that land is?" Galeerial shook his head. "Neither do I. This land is full of dark places."

"And dark people." Galeerial added. "How well do you trust Joven?" Dorian considered this for a moment.

"I trust him because he is my brother, and as such he will never do anything to harm us. Beyond that, his machinations stretch across the length and breadth of Carin. Why do you ask?"

"The leader of the army that assaults the Iron Men told us that they were raised by a human named Joven."

"But you said at the counci-" Galeerial held his hand up to silence him.

"I know what I said, but when we met with the leaders of the opposing army they said that they were assembled by a man named Joven." Dorian sighed. "Is there a possibility that your brother is in league with Veriel?" Several emotions flashed across the wizard's face as he struggled before replying.

"We spent the last eight years doing such things that should have gotten all of us killed long ago. We survived, all of the original seven. That changed just over a week ago when I found the severed head of my youngest brother impaled on a spear at Gemport. He was killed at Veriel's hands. If Joven was in league with him, then their bargain no longer holds that I can promise you. And as much as I would want to tell that there is no way that Joven would even think about working with Veriel, it wouldn't be the first time he has made a deal with the devil." Silence lingered between them as each considered the ramifications of his words. Galeerial had embraced being one of the Seven, but if that group was compromised then he wasn't sure if he could ever trust anyone again.

"I'm leaving soon. Very soon." Galeerial said finally.

"May I ask where?" Dorian replied.

"Cloud Breach. A being called The Wither is there. I don't know if you know anything about me, but I was a Skyguard once. The Wither took that away from me. I'm going there to kill him: in as painful a way as possible."

"Will it bring you peace?" Dorian asked. Galeerial turned from the flame to look at him.

"I don't know." Galeerial admitted. "But I do know that I have no choice." Dorian nodded.

"Necessity is something I know all too well. My father died when I was young and...and foolish. When we came here, a new father was given to me. I was taken in by the unu and the Thousand Hammers clan. It was a second chance. Six days ago, I killed my surrogate father. I plunged my sword through his heart." Galeerial looked at the wizard whose head was bowed in shame. "and...and the last thing he said to me before he died," the wizard's words grew choked, "he said, 'I'm proud of you' right before I killed him. 'I'm proud of you.' Qel was not a good man. Not like Rerem my real father. Qel was everything he wasn't, and yet he was so like him. Qel lied; he manipulated; he stole and murdered and...and...and he was my father. He treated me as his son. I killed him for his graciousness." Galeerial saw tears roll down the man's face and was stricken by them. Even when Grey and he had born Aurum across the breadth of Carin he had never seen this kind of emotion from one of the wizards. They were always in control. They were always reserved in their emotions to the point of frigidity. It was unnerving. "I used to believe in what we were doing. I used to believe that we could guide this world down a different better path than ours went. But now? Now, my soul is heavy with my sins."

"Why are you telling me all this?" Galeerial asked slowly.

"Because I have no one else to tell. I betrayed Rikard twice in the past. He forgave me the first, but the second knife... he has never fully healed from the wound it inflicted. He has become a base mercenary wanting nothing more than to keep killing: never looking back. Joven is too arrogant to admit weakness. My wife...she tries but I know she doesn't understand my anguish. I used to speak with Aurum and Rayn, but now

379

Rayn is dead and Aurum…is gone. I don't know. I just don't know."
Deathly quiet came over them.

"I tortured Veriel." Galeerial said quietly. Dorian's eyes fell heavy on him but contained not a hint of judgment. "He is the worst evil I can imagine, and yet, still I felt dirty when I had finished. It was necessary, but I burned him over and over again with light. Grey taught me how to handle fear, but what about doubt? I feel like I need to keep pressing onwards for if I stop then I won't have the strength to go on." Neither man looked at one another, but instead they both gazed upon the stone fire.

"In Cambria, there is no god. The words 'believe' and 'faith' have all but vanished from our vocabulary. I wanted something more than the unstoppable thirst for knowledge and human perfection that seemed to content my contemporaries. I came here for him." Dorian gestured to the flame. "Do you believe in what you are doing? Is your heart right?" Galeerial looked up at the statue. "I'm not judging you, but doubt is the ultimate destroyer. To be one of us is to believe in yourself unconditionally. If you couldn't do that then Grey would never have welcomed you as the Seventh."

"Yet you doubt yourself now." Galeerial replied.

"No, I am shamed by my actions. I don't doubt in their necessity. We are a step above and a step apart from most humans, but we are still humans. We feel, and we regret. But we don't doubt. I'm sorry that I killed my father, but I know…I know that it was right to do so. My heart is just catching up with my head. Rayn and I always had that problem. Aurum used to, but then… well that is not for me to tell." Dorian's hand rested on Galeerial's shoulder. "Thank you; you aren't alone. It may seem to the world that all we do is fight and kill and wield magic and play with power, but we're a family. That family includes you now. I'll pray for you brother. Go where your heart takes you, and though it meanders, like it does even now for me, it will never steer you wrong." Galeerial looked him in the eyes, and Dorian held his gaze. It was one of the things he appreciated most about them; they never shied away from your eyes. "And speaking of my heart, my wife will be expecting to wake up beside me." They rose together, and Dorian pulled him into an embrace. "Take care my brother. I just lost one, and I would hate to lose you now that I have just found you."

"Th- thank you." Galeerial said hesitantly. A thought sparked in his mind. "Don't let Joven anywhere close to Veriel." Galeerial whispered.

"I won't. Make your peace, Galeerial; it is all we can ask for in this life." He whispered back. Galeerial watched as Dorian made his way out the back of the church the same way Galeerial had entered. Galeerial stood and walked to the door of the cathedral. He reached for it and pulled it open. On the other side he saw the guards' quarters atop the battlements of Cloud Breach. *It will happen three times.* Someone up there believed in him; someone wished his quest for vengeance to succeed. Galeerial wouldn't deny him.

He stepped through and beheld the room were his wings had been hewn. On the ground there was a single wilted feather. Galeerial bent down and picked it up. He ran his fingers lightly through it. It was his. Somehow, someway he could sense it. He tucked it into his tunic. He turned and closed the door on Gemport and opened it again to behold ruin.

The gates had been reduced to rubble, and it was a wonder the guard tower still stood. Stone and wood blended together to create a portrait of destroyed beauty that stretched from the gates throughout the city. That wasn't everything. The Cathedral of Light…it was gone smashed to pieces of broken glass and stone. Galeerial gaped at the destruction before him.

"This is impossible." Galeerial whispered. *How could this be possible?* He blinked over and over again as if the world was simply a mirage put forth to confuse him, but the world persisted.

"No, no, no nonono." Galeerial swung down onto the ledge and climbed quickly down to the ground. He took off running and leaping from shifting rubble to shifting ruble. He barely got his feet down before he was off onto the next piece. He was manic in his search around the wreckage of the city. As he worked his way through the city he realized there was only a single place The Wither would be.

BOOM! Galeerial heard the echoes of thunder as he approached his destination and towards his final conflict with The Wither, and he began to focus his fear. He reached deep into the cold grip that wound from his stomach to his spine and ripped it out. He took that icy emotion and hurled it into the flames of his rage. The fire ignited inside of him. He didn't feel any of the frosty grasp of the snow that peppered his skin. He was an arrow outside of time, beyond feeling. He was focused will: a spear prepared to shatter even the greatest of shields.

Galeerial slowed his approach and pulled Ripper from its sheath on his back. *Fight first with your mind. If you can win that battle, then you will never lose.* Grey's words came to him unbidden. Galeerial picked his way towards the shattered cathedral.

Galeerial watched the steam from his breath rise into the air. He was struck speechless by the desolation before him. Massive metal pipes from the organ were bent and twisted and cut by some ragged blade. Stone gargoyles that had watched Carin for ages were but rubble strewn amidst thousands of pounds of glass.

"What could have done something like this?" He murmured. The Wither was created to destroy and kill, but this was beyond even him. This tower had stood for fifteen hundred years despite the best efforts of the Dread and the natural world. Something was wrong. Something was very wrong. Once again fear started to wind through his bones.

He strode forward. *BOOM!* Ripper felt good in his hand. Galeerial felt uncomfortable about holding it though. This was the blade that had sent him spiraling into despair. But this blade had once been called Justice. Now, it was to be reclaimed for that purpose.

Galeerial worked his way around a miraculously still intact stone wall and instantly stopped. Before him he beheld the Throne of Supremor. It was a chair that was seated immediately to the west of the Charist pool in all three cathedrals. Sitting in the Throne was The Wither.

Rain of Darkness
Twenty-Nine

"Enough." Veriel said. He had sent the fool Galeerial away with the greatest weapon they had against him. Soon Galeerial would be back in the hands of The Wither, and everything would be as it was supposed to be. Veriel marshaled the power the black sun fed him, even buried as far away as he was. He glanced down at his arm that had been hewn from him by the blade Ripper and smiled. When Galeerial had cut it off, the limb had been severed from him. He would never be able to reabsorb any piece of it into his flesh. However, it was no longer bound to Eon, so he could control it. The fool was so eager to prove himself: to prove he wasn't a victim. Galeerial had played right into Veriel's hands. The flesh began to grow black and swirl together into a pool of darkness as Veriel focused his will upon it.

Eon made it difficult. The blade smoked against his skin, and it burned him at a fundamental level from the elixis woven into its metal. He pushed. Sweat poured down his face, and his every muscle tensed and rippled as the pool of shadow slowly took the form of a massive hand whose arm stretched up into the air. The fingers reached around the handle to grip Eon. It burned.

Veriel felt the fingers wrap around the cold steel and slowly begin to pull. The blade scrapped his insides and pulled flesh with it as it emerged. Veriel licked his lips. He thrived on pain. Pain was bread and rage, wine. He snarled and brought the full power of his mind to bear ripping the sword from his back.

Veriel screamed.

Instantly, his body collapsed into a pool of black ink which thrashed upon the ground. Screeches of pain echoed through the cell. It was like knives scraping against shale. The death hails of a thousand dying infants. The pool stretched and squeezed: waxed and waned. Shapes began to coalesce in its depths and loops of blackness hurled forth from its nadir.

It curled and flayed about on the ground. Spikes of shadow speared towards the sky, and the pool began to grow upwards. Not out from the epicenter, but up into the air. Slowly a head began to form it grew apart from the swirling mass of obsidian, extending from the center. From there a snout grew from its ovoid shape, and it opened into a soundless scream. Great jaws extended, and teeth grew from the top and bottom. Its form collapsed again into a pool of darkness and then rose just as quickly.

The cries of pain turned into the gnashing of teeth as he strove to maintain form. The head reappeared followed quickly by two arms extending from its sides. They were bulges at first, and then, they grew long and thin: insect-like. The pool of darkness grew smaller as the shadow grew taller and grew into humanoid form.

Great wings spread out from the darkness. These were the wings of nightmares, and they slowly folded back in to form a long flowing cloak. The face of the beast grew taut and stretched as the featureless form slowly came into focus. The mitts for hands grew fingers and those fingers grew fingernails and fingerprints. This spread farther and farther up the arm. Details drew in like a portrait being painted one feature at a time. As it grew up the arm, it also grew up the legs, all coalescing in the body, where it swirled like rapids. The stomach and breast forged into shape, and finally, it grew up to the face. The snout withdrew back into the rest of the face, and the teeth grew smaller. His dark materials had recreated the Lord Veriel.

He fell to a single knee, grunting with exertion. He put his hands on the ground and pushed himself up to his feet. He was weak, and the pool of axios that was his arm lay on the ground in defiance of his efforts to draw it in to him. Before him lay Eon. His skin was gaunt, stretched across his body.

"Ahhhhhh." he screamed in triumph and pain. A smile crept across his face, "Yessss." He looked down and spread his arms out from his side, and then brought them together in front of his chest, exhaling. He was weak, so weak. The power of the black sun had enabled him to accomplish that feat, but he needed more.

From his sunken eyes he saw the blood drain from the human guards' faces. The unum and Skyguard though, were made of sterner stuff, and he couldn't acquire the taste of their terror. The humans though, were so sweet in their emotional outpouring. Veriel drew strength from the raw emotion emanating from the men. He needed more. He needed flesh and blood. He didn't have time to draw strength from the ambient emotion. He needed to be free. Whistles of alarm rang out, and Veriel snarled in answer to their challenge.

Thin tendrils of shadow began to shoot out, and whipped across the humans' necks. Heads slid off shoulders amidst fountains of blood as the bodies collapsed to the floor with a satisfying thump. The Skyguard and unu had their weapons out and posed ready to fight him. Veriel smiled as he seeped through the bars of the cell and out into the long hallway. The shadow of his long cloak flowed out over the body of a human. It only took a moment to leave nothing but dust in place of flesh. The white-eyed serpent would not be bound. Let darkness rain.

"GO!" The Red Man screamed, and Tendra felt a chill of fear flow through her body. She awoke screaming in her chambers, without even realizing that she had fallen asleep. Her heart was pounding at what she had just witnessed. That dream…was no dream. Veriel. She reached up and grabbed Valiant before hurtling out of her room. The two Light Monks sprang after her.

"My Lady!" they called after her.

"It's Veriel! Raise the alarm. He's free!" She screamed back after them. She leapt down the stairs three at a time. Her adrenaline and fear belayed all weariness she felt. The Seven were being housed in the West Tower. She crashed down onto the lower floor and glanced outside to see fires burning. It was then that she heard the whistles.

That was when the screams began. She needed armor, she knew, but she had to rouse the others. Tendra sprinted through the hallways. Soldiers flowed around her as they rushed to see what the commotion was outside. She knew they were all dead. She had seen the darkness that was Veriel, and it filled her with terror.

Tendra skidded around the corner that led upwards to the West Tower. She took the stairs three at a time hurtling higher and higher. She tried to rip the door open, but the locks held. She slammed on the wood of the doors. A moment later the door was wrenched open to the groggy eyes of Joven who wore only a pair of trousers, and his bare chest was completely shaved.

"What's happening?" He muttered.

"It's Veriel!" She breathed through her exhausted breath. The sleep vanished from his eyes. Rikard pushed his way through the door. He held a staff in hand and a dagger in the other.

"I can hear screams through the stone. Veriel is free." Rikard said. "Dorian isn't in his room. I'm going." He bolted out before either of them could get a word in edgewise.

"Get to safety." Joven already had his chain mail on and was lashing his boots. He grasped his sword while wrapping his belt around his west. He grabbed his staff from where it stood at the door. "The Skyguard

386

are being housed on the rooftops, you need to find one of them, and get out of here."

"No. These are my people." She said through gritted teeth. "This is my home. I will not run."

"We can't afford to protect you, and we can't afford to argue with you. This isn't a request. Leave now." He pushed his way past her and took off down the stairs. She waited a moment before following him. He was scared. He was trying to hide it, but he was scared. That terrified Tendra more than the dream. Three unu came hurtling down the stairwell.

"Where is the clansmaster?" One thundered at her.

"Follow me!" she yelled at the unu. She took off running descending the stairs rapidly. The stone hallways began completely quiet, but as they coursed through them a steady din began to rise in the background as everyone was roused.

"My lady!" She saw Wesley standing at the doorway holding her armor and sword at the ready with heavy boots laying on the ground. *By Supremor, how does he anticipate me like that?*

"How did you know I would be here?" She said as the unu coursed past her. She grabbed Valiant and cut a slit into the legs of her evening gown so she could pull on her greaves. She pulled her chain mail over her head.

"Please, as if you would be anywhere else." Wesley said. She slipped out of her evening slippers and pulled the boots on.

"Thanks." Wesley held the door open. "Is everyone roused?"

"Working on it." He replied.

"Get it taken care of. I'm going out there."

"Of course you are." He muttered. She pushed by him to emerge in the far side of the plaza. She charged around the end of the castle and reached the front. The doorway to the dungeons emerged along the castle wall, and it had been blown outward. The black sun gave off no light, and torches had been lit all along the wall. Tendra watched in horror as a man went flying from the doorway and sailed over the wall on the other end of the courtyard. The four wizards slowly approached.

387

"My Lady!" Out of the corner of her eye, she saw a Skyguard zoom down to her. He held a massive ornate sword. It was Iris, and this was Gabriel.

"I'm not leaving." The four wizards waited outside of the doorway, behind them stood hundreds of warriors wielding all manner of weapons. The walls were lined with archers. It was as if a breath had been taken before the exhale that would blow the house to the ground. *Wait, four?* Tendra's eyes widened as she realized that Jeric stood with the wizards.

"Here," he handed her a bottle. "It's Charist. Douse yourself in it. The Dread will not be able to harm you if you do."

"Thank you." Gabriel nodded. She raised the bottle over her head and felt the thick liquid pour down her body. She shivered.

"He's coming." Gabriel said. He took off flying towards the doorway as shadows began to emerge. Tendra could barely make them out but they looked like humans, only featureless and formed entirely from the deepest shadows she could imagine. Their faces had no distinguishing features and were instead just smooth and round, almost like a helmet. However, in each of their hands the shadow men held a sword. They poured out of the dungeons by the dozens sprinting forward to engage the humans, centaurs, unu, and Skyguard that stood marshaled against them. Skyguard crisscrossed back and forth holding barrels of Charist that they poured down upon the warriors. The shadows couldn't harm them, but steel could.

A shade hurtled towards her, and she met his swing with her blade. She felt a jolt cascade up her arm. The creature was strong. She disengaged and launched into a flurry of attacks driving the shadow back towards the hole.

"Strike!" The shadow before her exploded as the lightning bolt struck it, causing the sword to clatter to the ground. Suddenly calls of "STRIKE" began to echo everywhere as lightning shot through the plaza. But that wasn't what Tendra's gaze was focused upon. That was focused upon Veriel.

The being known as Veriel emerged from the darkness of the dungeons atop a flowing cloud of ink. His form had coalesced into the same

388

form he had worn as Veriel only completely black, with blue fire defining his edges. His eyes were white. Small tendrils of shadow extended off of his skin.

He looked at her.

Despair engulfed her. She fell to her knees as he descended upon her. She could do nothing. The sounds of battle raged around her. Shadow fought flesh, and the living screamed as the dead silently fought. A hand coalesced from the darkness. The fingers were long talons, dripping with blood. A blue flame ignited within his palm as he reached for her.

"You won't touch her!" A voice screamed from the darkness surrounding her. The sound of sanity broke the spell of despair surrounding her as white steel sliced through the hand. She leapt to her feet bringing Valiant to bear as she saw the face of her rescuer. It was Jeric.

"Light Monk. You are beyond your station." His voice was hypnotic. Tendra gripped her sword tighter. She strode to stand beside Jeric. He looked her in the eye and nodded. This was them: together. This was how it should be.

"I will shatter your darkness with my light." Jeric's voice rang out strong and confident. Veriel simply looked amused.

"Do you truly believe you can stand against me?"

"There is nothing we can't do." Tendra replied.

"You can't win." Veriel smiled. His teeth were black. His hand shot forward growing larger as it grabbed Jeric around the waist barreling forward to hurl Jeric up and over the outer wall.

"NO!" Tendra screamed. Her face drained of blood as she watched her betrothed hurtle to his death. She felt a hand so cold it burned her flesh, curl itself around her shoulder. Tendra saw his darkness hiss and burn as he touched the Charist on her shoulder. She swung her blade around, and the metal cut through the hand only for a new one to instantly take its place.

"You have taken too many from me." Tendra said through gritted teeth.

"Don't worry. I will take care of you." His voice hissed into her ears.

"Over Supremor's dead body." Rage burned her eyes. She had no technique, no finesse, just rage. Her sword slashed over and over, but every time Veriel slid around it or deflected it with his own. He kept smiling at her.

"That's the idea." Suddenly Veriel froze in mid-air before exploding.

"How about over yours?" Tendra saw a Skyguard behind him as Veriel reformed an instant later in front of them. Veriel snaked to the ground to scoop up his blade in time to stop an onslaught of strikes by the Skyguard. They took to the skies, and Tendra watched in awe at the furious exchange before defending herself from two shadow demons. She pirouetted around between them slicing her blade through the knee of one and back up through the top of the second's head. They collapsed into a pool of ink. She hazarded a glimpse over towards where the wizards were fighting. Dozens of human and Skyguard warriors were fallen, and the humans lay bleeding upon the ground. Two of the wizards stood holding off hordes of shadow warriors. She saw the third hurtle off the wall towards Veriel. It was one of the twins. She wove Valiant back and forth, just like her uncle had taught her.

They were relentless. They just kept pounding away at her. She kept cutting them, but they simply reformed over and over again.

Then, they vanished. Tendra's eyes flashed upwards, and she saw the wizard clinging with his legs locked around Veriel's head as he brutally hacked away at Veriel with his daggers. The shadows flowed back up into Veriel, and he grabbed the wizard and hurled him down to the ground. The man struck with a hollow thump and was slow to rise. Veriel's fist flew out and slammed into Gabriel. The Skyguard hurtled backwards.

"STRIKE!" Half a dozen lightning blasts slammed into, and through, Veriel, courtesy of the wizards.

She saw Gabriel recover and then soar back at Veriel. The wizards and assorted warriors who were left gathered to watch the aerial ballet. Gabriel's blade swirled and twisted impossibly fast.

"Can't you do something?" Tendra called out to the wizards.

"We might hit Gabriel." Dorian said.

"I have a shot. Gabriel can disengage." Rikard called.

"They're too close." Joven said.

"I'm taking it." He replied. "Strike!" The bolt shot out. Tendra held her breath as the electricity arced towards the two opponents. Gabriel slashed downwards, forcing Veriel's sword downward before disengaging. The lightning bolt threaded right into the end of the sword. A howl that echoed of desolation and destruction pierced her ears as pain wracked Veriel's body. Gabriel dove back in, stabbing Iris into his body causing Veriel to erupt into a shower of black rain drops that coalesced before they even made it to ground forming into Veriel's humanoid form. Veriel snarled as he scooped his fallen blade up with long thin tendrils. Joven leapt forward at Veriel's threads slicing at them with his blade. He severed several dozen, but more took their place with others combined into a single massive rope that slammed into the wizard and sent him sliding across the plaza. Tendra could make out blood on his forehead. The aerial ballet between Gabriel and Veriel continued, and Tendra watched helplessly with the other members of the army standing beneath. Even the Skyguard watched in awe of Gabriel's prowess. Tendra struggled to track the exchange of blows, but in an instant she saw the same small opening that she had seen right before Rayn had been killed. A moment after she saw it, Gabriel's sword was knocked high by a vicious blow and was followed up by a ravaging kick that lashed out sending Gabriel hurling towards the ground. His wings beat furiously, but he still landed hard. His body was covered in cuts and burns.

"Help." She heard him whisper. Veriel slowly descended to the ground to confront the wizards. Joven limped next to the other two.

"Enter the famed wizards. I have seen your magic, and I am not impressed." Veriel's arms suddenly became a battering ram of shadow slamming down into the ground sending them flying. Tendra felt her stomach rise into her throat as she tumbled end over end. She sprang to her feet as Veriel once again took human form.

"Take the Imperial, and the Crown becomes mine." Veriel said reaching out and grabbing her around the throat. Veriel grew in size as she clawed against his hands. Shadowed tendrils flew out to engage the soldiers who rushed in to try and retrieve her.

"My people will never be yours." Tendra said through gritted teeth. She gasped for air as his fingers closed around her wind pipe.

"So they always say." A lightning bolt sparked past his face. "Those staffs are quite the annoyance." Tendra watched as he launched a flurry of tendrils that wrapped themselves around the staffs of the wizards and ripped them away. "Much better."

"Why don't you just kill us?" Tendra spat.

"You have a choice Tendra here and now. Surrender, allow me to find and kill the ones I need. Then I leave, never to return or death will come. Such a death as you cannot imagine. My Will shall steal the last vestiges of your soul, right before I steal your life."

"My soul is my own!" Tendra screamed with all the fury she could manage. Her vision was going black. She could barely see. She heard a crash.

She felt herself suddenly falling. The sky looked so far away. She thought that she might be able to hear the wind whistling by her, but she couldn't be sure. There was a cloud that looked like a horse. She felt herself falling. This time Rayn wouldn't be there to save her. She heard a voice that was so far away, she wasn't sure if it actually even existed. She hit the ground hard and felt her shoulder pop.

"You want war?" A voice rang out above all others as silence enshrouded the plaza. It sounded slightly familiar, like she had heard it in a long ago dream. She could barely hold onto her consciousness though she struggled to do so. "I will give you war. Are you prepared for the consequences?"

Swordstorm
Thirty

For two days, the darkness had held the sun captive. For two days when I had gone to sleep, I had been greeted by darkness with no sign of Lord Alizar. It was an odd feeling to have spent so much time in the dreaming world of Merhelden only to now be deprived of it. I felt like a piece of me had been cut off. The black sun did not help my already dour mood. It gave the entire world a pale shadowy din that was not helped by all the clouds covering the world. I stepped away from the doorway to the small house with my eyes closed. I looked at the scene of death before me and felt rage begin to swell within me. My eyes began to burn with orange fire as I viewed the horrific scene around me. This was the sixteenth village I had found with the same scene of massacre. Each body cut to pieces, and no one left alive. This was not the work of a warrior, but of a surgeon.

Each cut was at precisely the same spot on every corpse: one to the neck severing the head, and one cutting each of the limbs from the bodies. It was almost beautiful in its mathematical precision, and its complete and utter slavery to exactness. Yet the empty murky eyes of children not older than two years old which vacantly watched my every move ensured that I would never see this as beautiful. It was terrifying in its brutality.

I had been following the trail of this creature for three days, always arriving in the aftermath. Somehow he was staying inexplicably ahead of me, but the trail was now clear. I had overshot him in my haste to arrive at Cirode'l.

The devastation in the city had been horrific. The buildings, the houses, the structures, all of it had been intact. Only the people had been harmed. I had spent hours searching through the city for some kind of clue to what had happened. Anything… but there was no one left alive in the city, or in any of the surrounding farms. Whatever had attacked the city had swept through killing everything around it as well. There had been signs of obvious struggle: shattered swords and bloody streaks but no enemy bodies. Whoever or whatever had done this had been unbearably thorough.

For three days, I had searched through the northern reaches trying to find this creature. I had flown along the southern tip of the Burning Waters and along to Bastion and down to Shezon. Luckily, those men had neither seen nor heard anything of this creature. So I had flown along the northern boundary of Whisperwood. Now, I was near Visir and once again I was too late.

No more delays. Whatever this was could not be allowed to make it to King's Port.

I felt the power build in my feet, and I exploded from the ground into the air, a trail of orange light forming a tail in my wake. The wind flew through my face and hair as I surged forward. I passed by two more devastated villages, but I refused to stop. I had to make it to King's Port. That was where our confrontation would occur. I followed the coast down just to the breaking of the Beak and exploded into the Gulf of Crowns.

Seagulls flashed by my face as the water formed a hemisphere around my flying form. The high gray walls of King's Port rose in my view. I angled my body upward and skimmed close to the stone and hurtled up and around the walls before descending hard and fast into the plaza.

I was too late.

I cursed. I had started following him at Cirode'l, and now here a second fortress of mankind had fallen. Mesnir had been strangely left alone, but here, they hadn't been so luckily.

"Let me hear as they do." I whispered. I felt the fire flow into my ears, and I listened for any sign of life. A small shift of stone caused me to whip my head around just in time to see a massive sword come flying at my face. I dropped to the ground, whipping my sword and staff from my back and rolled to the left exploding backwards across the ground. I eyed my opponent carefully.

The man before me stood in armor so black that I could scarcely comprehend its lack of color. His sword all but cackled with the same shadow. My chain mail rattled on my arm as I swung my sword carefully. He bore a helmet that obscured everything but his eyes. They were of a deep and resounding blue whose vibrancy contrasted heavily with everything else about his body, which screamed death.

Even from ten meters away, I could see that his sword was an absolute marvel in craftsmanship. I had never seen a sword as beautiful and perfect as the one that I beheld right now. Its steel shone despite the lack of light, and the brilliancy of its edge was as remarkable as it was deadly. This was a sword that today had killed hundreds; yet it looked as if it was newly wrought from the forge. Its hilt seemed to flow right into the metal of the blade and was of the same dark hue as the armor. The fearful visage of a wolf adorned the sword with the blade emerging from its mouth.

"Who are you?" I asked as we warily circled each other. He was completely silent. I couldn't even hear the creak of his armor as he moved. "Very well then. Strike." Lightning cascaded from the tip of my staff and slammed into his armor. My eyes widened as the black metal shuddered for a moment as the electricity coursed through it, but the man made no motion that he felt the impact. I cast my staff to the side. This battle would begin and end with steel it seemed. Inadvertently, my mind flashed back to my fight with The Wither.

It was at that moment, he struck. He crossed the distance between us in three strides. His blade came across at a strike at my neck. I met his blade with mine, and sparks flew from the metal. I poured speed into my limbs and sent a flurry of blows at him. High, low, left, left, right, high, I pressed hard in a furious effort to drive him back, but he didn't give an inch. I studied his body as Rikard had taught me so long ago. The black knight's every move was done with absolute purpose. There was not a single wasted motion in his parries and counters. This wasn't art to him; it was math.

I sent a crippling blow at his right leg, and he blocked and slid his blade off of mine before sending a blow hurtling towards my right arm. Steel collided for the hundredth time as we disengaged for the first time since our battle had begun. I struggled to control my breathing. Supremor help me.

"Might of giants." My eyes flashed with power, and I felt strength refill my limbs. I could feel my arms and legs growing larger as the muscles expanded with the power of the elixis. I limited their expansion. If they grew much larger, I would burst free from my armor. The black knight stood at ease before me. I couldn't beat him technique against technique. *Let's see how you handle strength.* I looked at him. His posture was impeccable, and his back impossibly straight.

"Who are you?" I asked again. Once again there was no answer. He held his sword easily in front of him, blade pointed towards the ground. He didn't seem concerned at all by me or even curious. It was almost like he felt nothing at all. I held my sword in my left hand and carefully worked Havoc into my right.

"Wings." I once again pooled the elixis into my wings and flew from the ground towards my opponent launching Havoc towards his left hand while bringing Widower's Wrath down in a hard strike.

"Might!" I threw my entire body weight behind the blow along with the momentum from my flight. I shifted to strength and added it to the force of my blade. The force of his resistance almost stopped me in midair as my entire body was jarred by the impact for a half a second before that resistance shattered. There was a shriek that threatened to shatter my ears.

396

Shards of metal flew through the air, and I tumbled to the ground behind him. I looked down at the sword in my hand and saw only a broken fragment. The red lines of the elixis faded from the blade until only steel remained. I pushed myself up to my feet and saw my opponent doing the same. I had knocked him down, but at the expense of destroying my weapon.

I glanced around frantically for Havoc when I saw something that gave me a brief instant of hope. Havoc had pierced his armor. The black knight raised his left hand and stared at the dagger that had slid through the glove on one side, and jutted out from the palm of his hand. He casually reached down and pulled Havoc from his hand tossed it aside. His glove, which had previously been pure black now held a streak of silver where Havoc had been. I held the broken remnants of my sword in my hand. I had to get to my dagger. I shot up into the air and descended behind him while he watched. I lifted my staff from the ground.

"I am Ruin." I said through gritted teeth. "Strike. Strike. Strike!" Three pulses shook my staff, and I watched them slam into the black knight. The armor absorbed the first one with merely a shudder, just like before. The second one caused him to take a step back, and the third one threw him across the plaza. His body was crushed into the stone of the outer wall at the opposite end of the plaza.

The metal of his armor cut deep into the stone wall and left an indentation. *By Supremor.* The man pushed against the wall and pulled himself up. He seemed unfazed by the lightning. I slowly walked over to where Havoc lay on the ground. I dropped my staff to the ground. It was steel that hurt him, and it would be steel that killed him.

The shards of Widower's Wrath were cast around me as I lifted Havoc off the ground. Widower's Wrath was a small stump of its former glory. It had a sharp ragged edge and was about a quarter of its original length, barely longer than Havoc. I held my knife in my right hand and my blade in my left. It was time to take this fight to the next level.

397

"I will give you war. Speed!" I shot forward, my legs pumping as I sped towards where he lay on the ground, and I leapt into the air flying above him launching a volley of strikes.

I spun in the air to the ground throwing one blow high at his ear and a second straight in at his torso. He ducked down low, using his helmet to slam against the flat of my blade driving the blow towards the ground. At the same time, he threw his own sword at me in a thrust at my stomach, but I leapt twirling in the air slipping around it and pulling my dagger back scratching a deep scar into his armor.

A blinding light momentarily emerged from the scar, and my vision splintered into a fountain of stars. I instinctively took to the sky to avoid being struck while my eyes recovered from their wound. I blinked heavily.

My vision slowly returned from the white, and my opponent was gone. I frantically scanned the plaza but saw nothing. I whirled around and saw him sprinting along the wall towards me. The gash in his armor from the dagger looked like it was bleeding light almost like the armor was skin. He took a step onto the shelf on the interior of the battlements and hurled himself into the air at me. His sword gleamed in the starlight. This time I was the one who stood calmly watching his flying approach. I raised my twin blades as if preparing to meet him.

I admired the man's courage and quick thinking. Five seconds faster and he would have been able to skewer me easily. His sword was gripped in his left hand and poised to strike it through my heart. The blade was already moving to puncture my flesh when I dropped from the sky.

I let my burning aura of the elixis fade from me, and I dropped towards the ground. The man held his composure as he flew through the air and crashed onto the roof of one of the nearby buildings. Havoc gleamed in my hand, and I could almost feel the hunger of my blade.

"Wings!" I proclaimed. The words kept me focused on the switch. I alighted again and gave myself a quick burst towards him.

I landed on the rooftop and immediately was assailed by a swarm of metal taps. He was trying to wear me down. He knew that strength alone

398

wouldn't beat me. I could almost see the respect in his piercing blue eyes. He had never fought someone like me, and the feeling was mutual. Even fighting The Wither was nothing like this.

Left foot, right foot, left hand, right hand, he echoed my every move with iron diligence. His movements were the most beautiful thing I had ever witnessed. Here we stood upon the edge of death with only the briefest hint of steel keeping me upon this mortal plane.

My thrust met his forearm, and his strike met my sliding parry. The telos were masters of this form of fighting. They were like gallowglass in their speed. They slid around the battlefield with their little scratches of swords.

"Flexibility of telos." I whispered through bated breaths as I called upon the gifts that Supremor had given them. I would endure.

We were getting nowhere, and he showed no signs of stopping while I was being forced to pull more and more from the well within my soul. I had to end this now or else it would not end in my favor. Then I saw it. The scar that I had scratched into his armor had begun to spread. Little cracks had seeped across his chest plate with the rivulets reaching even so far as his greaves. I couldn't believe I hadn't seen it before. Impossibly enough, he hadn't seen it either. Or at least he didn't acknowledge it. His black armor was growing whiter by the second.

I back-flipped down off of the roof we had been fighting on, while slowing my descent. I landed lightly on the ground and watched as he descended. I coiled my knees and burst upward slamming into the other man's body. I grabbed his wrist as we grappled skyward. I rammed his body into the wall of the house, but his hand didn't loosen his grip in the slightest. I angled us towards the high bell tower. I dragged his body along the gray rocky wall towards the top.

"Strength!" I screamed the instant before I whipped him around and threw him with all my might slamming him into the bell. I felt myself falling, and I struggled to reactivate my wings and barely caught myself as I hit the ground. The bell's tattered moorings shredded upon impact, and the two went toppling towards the ground. I watched them fall, and fall, and fall.

The bell hit first, and I grimaced at the sound of the metal clanging against the ground. I clutched my hands to my ears to try and muffle the awful noise. The clatter made a symphonic tone that coincided with the impact of the black knight's body a second later. Upon impact, he seemed to almost sink into the ground as the dust flew into the air, obscuring my vision.

I staggered to my feet clutching the wall behind me for support. My legs wobbled with every step, and my head was spinning. I descended gingerly touching down at the base of the crater. I peered into the hole where his limp body lay. His sword was stuck in the rock above him. I watched as the cracks in his armor grew more profound. I stepped down into the crater and reached down for his helm. The flesh of my fingers had just barely tipped the metal when I was hurled backwards to the edge of the crater. I groaned as I found myself on my back staring at the sky.

The sun was black as it found a breach in the ceiling of clouds that covered the winter sky, but its darkness was refuted by the brilliance of the light that emerged from his glistening armor. The light was not what caught my eye though. What I focused on was the hand.

My brain almost couldn't comprehend what my eyes beheld. The black knight lay on the ground defeated and from the scar that I had carved into the metal came the form of a hand bursting from the black knight's chest. The inky darkness of the armor fought hard against the coming of the pure white hand that was seemingly made from crystal.

"What in Supremor's name?" I whispered as I circled the body of the knight. The shimmering white hand was open like it was reaching for something. To my surprise, the hand was perfectly smooth and the fingers were not those of a warrior or even those of a man. I knelt beside the body staring at the hand. I wasn't quite sure what to make of it. I pulled my gauntlet off my right hand and reached out to touch the skin of the hand. The fingers curled around my wrist squeezing tight. I tried to pull away, but the hand was latched on firmly. I pulled my other gauntlet off with my teeth and wrapped both hands around hers.

I slid down into the crater as the dirt gave way beneath my feet, but I braced them against the heavier stone foundation as I straddled the black knight and pulled. I strained against the unforgiving grip of the hand. I gritted my teeth. It was like trying to draw a tree out of the ground. I pushed upward with my legs and arms and back giving my every effort into this singular task.

"MIGHT!" I poured the strength of giants into my body, and I felt the hand slowly begin to emerge. My muscles bulged with the effort as I drew more and more strength from them. I felt my clothing strain as I grew taller, and my muscles grew larger.

Sweat poured down my body, and orange flame swept around me. My eyes burned with intensity as I drew the hand out of the prison of the black knight's armor.

Slowly, the hand became a wrist, and the wrist became a forearm, which revealed an elbow. Still I pulled. Weariness filled my bones. My pursuit and subsequent fight with the Black Knight had pressed me to the point of exhaustion, and now I felt my back begin to strain as my muscles tore. I tried to let go, but the hand held fast to my own.

I couldn't stop. I tried to stop my legs from pushing, but they seemed to act on their own accord. I was committed. I would either die, or I would pull out whatever, whoever, was imprisoned here.

My feet dug into the stone and dirt beneath me as I pushed towards the sky. I felt my arms seem to elongate, and my temples screamed from the exertion. I was not going to die. I was Aurum Guilden.

"I am Ruin!" I screamed, and the armor erupted from beneath me. I was hurtled skyward. I was so dizzy that I could not move. As I hurtled through the air I saw tens of thousands of faces shrouded in a beam of light erupt towards the heavens. *BOOM!* The sound of ten thousand lightning bolts echoed through my ears as the ray of light evaporated. I couldn't breathe. I just fell, and fell, and fell towards the ground.

Blackness threatened to engulf my vision but I struggled against it. I would not fall. Not yet. By sheer force of will, I fought the darkness away. I triggered the elixis for flight just before I hit the ground. My body ached from the impact. I lay there for long minutes bereft of the ability to move. Finally, I pulled myself into a sitting position looking around dazed. The crater from the black knight was a hundred yards away. I slowly pushed myself unsteadily to my feet. I stumbled back over to where the black knight had been. I saw pieces of the armor littering the ground. I reached down and grasped a shard only for it to dissolve burning my hand as I dropped it to the ground. As I reached the center of the crater, I saw the source of the light.

A woman sat shining: a beacon of light as the revenant of the black knight.

She radiated light. Her skin contained a soft glow, and her blonde hair was golden and shone brightly. I almost had to shield my eyes she was so radiant. A star gave less light than this woman who stood before me. Her hands were elegance combined with her skin most delicate. Her face was like silver glass made of the most precious silk. It was then that I realized that she was naked as well, As I did so obscured light wove around her body covering her in a long sash that wound around her body like a vine.

She was kneeling on the ground shivering despite the heat that poured from her body. Her entire body rocked back and forth as she mumbled incoherently. I carefully slid down the stone and dirt walls of the crater towards her. I raised a hand up to protect my eyes.

She turned her eyes towards me, and the light began to dim around her so much so that I could see the green of newborn grass within them.

"Who…who are you?" I breathed. I felt like I was in the presence of majesty, the presence of royalty and that I should be on my knees. The power was astonishing. It wasn't what I felt with Lord Alizar but perhaps equal to the Libran. I almost felt my feet being pressed into the ground, as if her very gaze was pushing me back. Her eyes never left my body. She rose unsteadily to her feet almost gliding towards me. As she approached, I

402

found myself standing straighter. Her hand reached up to touch me; her fingers were like clouds ethereal and surreal.

"Please…I beg of you…please be real." She whispered. Her voice was a bell in the hushed din of the dead city where we stood. It tolled out clear and melodious, a beauty of which I could not describe with thoughts but only with emotion. She reached her hand out to me and scraped her fingers upon my eyelids. I did my best not to flinch, but the moment her flesh touched my own I felt like I was going to die.

I saw childhood. My father's cane laid to rest atop the mantle after his death. I saw my school in the Artistry of Practicality, and the first time I saw a Crion. I saw the Orrery of Words, and what it said to me. I saw my wife when I had first met her. She had been seated amidst her artwork, and I had felt as if I had been struck, so amazed was I by her beauty. I saw the first time I touched her skin, and the blue fire of her eyes. I saw my drafting board. I saw the accident that had robbed my wife of her sight. I saw her in labor and the doctors pushing me from the room. I saw a thousand empty bottles. I saw their graves. I saw the Infinity Helix. I saw the gallowglass and my ship the *Finality* fully crewed upon the open sea. I saw Merhelden and The Baroner, The Visionaire and The Libran. I saw Lord Alizar. Then, I saw the woman still standing in front of me.

I blinked and stumbled back to the ground gasping. I scrambled backwards finding my broken sword and dagger upon the ground. I grasped them desperately rolling onto my back facing her.

"What in Lord Supremor's name was that?" I said through gritted teeth. "What are you?" The woman looked at me. Her eyes held the touch of innocence.

"I had to be sure." Her every word was hesitant, half an apology and half an assertion. It was as if she was speaking for the first time in a century. "I have been locked within the Koriandr for a thousand years watching each piece of butchery by Frosh. For a thousand years, I have been bound to him. Every stroke of his sword stole another soul to be woven into the Koriandr. I had to be sure you weren't another one of them. Thank you, thank you so much." Tears began to flood from her eyes as she sunk to the ground. "Thank you." She grasped my hand and held it desperately, as if the act of letting go would cause me to vanish. "Thank you," she whispered again. I knelt down beside her.

"Who are you?" I repeated softly for the third time. Her glistening eyes looked up to behold me. She closed them and breathed deeply. She made no move to wipe the crystal clear tears from her cheek. "What is your name?"

"My name?" Struggle was evident on her face. "It…it has been so long. In a life long ago, I was called… The Bloom." She nodded uncertainly. "Yes, The Bloom. That was my name, so very long ago and now. I suppose it is so now." She looked up into the sky for seemingly the first time, and her voice stuttered. Her breathing became labored as she stared upwards. I followed her gaze to the black sun.

"No…No….No," she whimpered. "Such cruelty I could not know. Speak to me, Champion." She grabbed me by the shoulders with desperation in her voice. "Speak to me of what has happened. Of the darkness that has swallowed the light." Snowflakes began to fall around us. They hissed into vapor as they touched The Bloom's skin.

"I don't know." I admitted. "It happened two days ago."

"You don't… know? But you are the Champion. You can see the natures of things." I titled my head questioningly.

"I'm not sure what you are talking about. The Visionaire never mentioned anything like that." The Bloom shook her head.

"Give me your eyes, Champion." she held out her hands and looked at me expectedly. I stared back at her. I shrugged.

"I don't know what that means." The Bloom smiled at me.

"Such innocence. I pray it doesn't kill you. Don't blink." She held out her middle finger and touched each of my eyes. I recoiled but not before a feeling of fire coursed through them up into my mind. I felt my chin being pushed to stare at the black sun which was low in the horizon, just dawning. Suddenly, I knew. I didn't know how, but I knew.

"It has been poisoned by Lord Veriel fulfilling a prophecy from the book of Arestephan. The second part of the Dawn of Darkness. *A black sun*

404

rises over a broken plane. He was pierced by the Blade of Time, Eon, and the prophecy was fulfilled. It happened two days ago in Terakeen. We have to go." I tore my gaze away from the sun back down to the earth, and my mind became flooded with information. The bell from the tower had been forged in 782 by Josef Camelon. It had taken him one hundred and seventy one days to complete on behalf of the human king Tiwon Estranen, the Conductor King. My eyes fell upon corpses on the ground. Ytir Stronsbard, son of Utir Stronsbard a baker, born 1844, never married, a gambler. Jesray Benzel guardsmen, born 1850 in Shezon family migrated here to escape a death warrant on his sister's head. Heronimus Rexus, Killian Set, Pioter Greeves, Victoria Sol, Hurin Nezbil, name after name and life after life filled my head as I saw the bodies of dozens of people. I tried to shut my eyes, but I couldn't. I screamed as my whole body shook.

"Shhh." The wind whispered in my ear, and finally my eyes slammed shut. I panted heavily as I fell to my knees.

"What…what happened to me?" I gasped. "What did you do to me!"

"As Ruin you have the power to do so much beyond simply the access of the Aers of the other races. Though that is where your training by the Baroner focused, it is not limited by that. We have what we need though. I need you to relax. Now instead of drawing from the elixis, I need you to pour into it. You have more of it than you can handle right now. That is just fine. You will learn. I did not realize just how new you are to this role." I slowed my breathing down and found the calm black room where all that existed within was the well of elixis. The serenity of the room filled me, and I envisioned pouring elixis back into the well. I felt the fire that burned the blood of my eyes slowly, slowly begin to subside. I breathed and pulled back out into the real world. I opened my eyes slowly and beheld The Bloom before me. No flood of information entered my mind. I sighed in relief. She offered me a smile.

I felt parched and hungry. I looked to see the sun just start to peek over the horizon. That wasn't right; it had been fully on display just a moment ago.

"What happened?" I asked. I was flat on my back, and I rolled over to try and rise, but dizziness overcame me.

"You have been unconscious for almost four days." She replied. I blinked heavily.

"What?" I clutched my temples with my right hand.

"I guided you to return the elixis, and then you blacked out. Here drink this." She handed me a glass of dark colored liquid. I drank it, and the taste of the indigo firewine filled my throat and stomach with warmth.

"It seems like only a moment passed after I returned the elixis to the well." The Bloom shrugged.

"Time passes differently in the mind than in the world." I struggled to my feet. This time the dizziness passed quickly.

"We need to get moving. Lord Veriel is in Terakeen; I need to end him." I saw the black knight's sword on the ground. I bent down and picked it up. It felt...wrong, but powerful. The sword regaled against my touch. It burned my hand as I touched it.

"Iron Man armor." I said. My hand grew enshrouded in a fiery gauntlet. This sword was dangerous. As I held it in my hand I could feel it almost yearning to fight. It felt hungry. "This sword, do you know its name?"

"Forlorn. The presence of the blade bodes ill. It does not belong here. It was forged in the Dreaming. For the use of the viziers of Lord Veriel. It is primarily axios, and this is why it burns. It also contains a vein of elixis necessary to survive in the Dreaming. That means it can hurt Lord Veriel., but if he acquires it he can purge the elixis from it." I nodded. As I held the sword I began to see what looked like flow lines around it. It took me a moment to realize that I was seeing some foreign form of the elixis around the blade. It was peculiar though, it was almost anti-elixis. This was what axios looked like it was a ice cold blue. I reached down and grabbed Havoc and instantly saw the same thing, only different. Havoc's was smooth and red like a river; Forlorn's was more like rapids: jagged and splintered. I blinked rapidly and the sensation ceased. I looked over at The Bloom. I replaced the broken shard of Widower's Wrath with Forlorn on

406

my back. I dropped the remnants of my old sword to the ground. The symbology was not lost upon me. I regarded The Bloom.

"When you touched me, the elixis flowed through to me so easily…more easily than ever before. How did you do that?"

"I unlock the potential within things. It is the isterios that I wield, and why I was imprisoned by Frosh and The Wither during the Dread War. I make people the best they can possibly be." She replied. I was conflicted. I didn't know who or even what she was. All I knew was that she was powerful, and that she could help make me powerful enough to take Veriel down. I knew I would need every advantage I could get, and I couldn't leave her here, she was too valuable and potentially dangerous.

"You will have to come with me." I told The Bloom. She nodded.

"I have been absent from this world for a long time. I am ready to rejoin it, even if that means rejoining it as a soldier." I didn't know whether to believe anything of what she said or not. I had no reason not to take her at face value, but there was too much that I didn't know. Her beauty was…intoxicating. "But time is of the essence. Veriel will not be contained for long. Shall we?" She asked. I picked her up in my arms. As I touched her I felt my skin crackle almost as if a charge had been placed upon my body.

"It will take hours to reach Terakeen." The Bloom smiled knowingly.

"I don't think it will take that long." She reached her head up and kissed me on the lips. As she did it was like liquid lightning was being poured into me. It flowed through my lips and down into my body. I felt like…I couldn't describe it. I felt like I was on fire…like I was power incarnate.

Everything becomes vivid and sharp. As she pulls away, I stand stunned.

"I'm married." I say blinking still shocked. The Bloom just smiles.

"You are wasting time, my dear." I shook my head as she turned away from me. The elixis came to me easily, and as I called upon my wings, I burst into the air. The elixis flows into me, and my body feels supercharged by it. I whirl through the air as a comet spins through the sky leaving a trail of fire in my wake as we hurtle southward. The sound wall explodes as I surpass it, and still I am picking up speed. The Bloom smiles in delight as the land flows past us like water while we streak through the early morning sky.

I blow past Sentinel with the tower being only a brief flash of grey. We curve around the outer arc of Thanatos, and I can feel eyes upon me as Ohm furiously writes in his book. I grin. The second guardian tower Evenfall is a blur, and from there it is a straight shot to Terakeen. The entire journey has taken only minutes. I can scarcely believe how fast we are flying. It had taken me days to patrol the north searching for Frosh, and I have covered an almost equal amount of ground in twenty minutes with The Bloom. I hit the brakes as the city came into view. Sound returns in a rush of wind through my ears that threatens to deafen me.

The city below us is dark with the flickering of torches as the only indication of life, besides the screams. My eyes rove searching and finding what looks like dozens of shadows moving and lightning bolts hurtling through the sky. I see a man hurtle through the air towards us. I descend quickly lining up an intersect trajectory.

"Drop me. I'll catch him. You go take down Veriel. He draws his power from the darkness that has overcome the sun. The longer you stay out of contact with me the weaker you will become, but he will stay at the same strength. Fight him quickly. Now GO!" she urges. I let her go, and she flies through the air towards the human.

I weave around the city towards where I had seen the lightning bolts trying to find the center of the maelstrom below me. It is a torrent of fire and smoke and death.

There.

A strike of thunder is eclipsed by a shadow that is surrounded by almost a hundred warriors. They are being slaughtered: Skyguard, centaur, unu and human alike. I angle my body and slam into the ground right before the massive shadow that I knew to be Veriel. I see three of my brothers standing around it with Gabriel and a score of others who are unknown to me.

The shadow eclipses over me and seems to draw strength from the sun in shadow. It is a massive creature of storm and fury. The ground swirls around me as I impact the stone plaza. I draw my weapons in a single smooth motion.

"You want war?" I say to the shadow. "I will give you war. Are you prepared for the consequences?"

The Once and Future King
Thirty-One

My very body itself is shaking. The supercharge that The Bloom had given me makes it hard for me to keep still. It is intoxicating how much energy I have. I feel like I have suddenly become two hundred percent of myself. Twice as good as I ever had been, twice as powerful. As I stood there the whole world began to wash away. Now, there was just me.

Just me and it.

In the flash of an instant, my mind memorizes the positions of everyone around me. I see Gabriel's body sliced to ribbons, and my brothers in not much better shape. My brothers are scattered about bleeding from dozens of wounds. Joven is prone as if dead, and Dorian is knelt over him. I can tell that Rikard's shoulder has been dislocated, and there are dozens of other injuries that plague them. Not to mention the hordes of dead soldiers scattered around the plaza. Tendra Sumenel struggles to rise at the creature's feet or rather, the shrouded cloak where the lower half of its body vanished. Galeerial is nowhere to be seen; neither are Grey, or Rowen. There is no help for me. This is everything. I hold the sword I had taken from Frosh by my side.

"Finally, someone worthy of death." Veriel says to me. "What title has Lord Alizar bequeathed upon his Champion?"

"Ruin." I reply.

"No doubt Lord Alizar believes it to be a fitting title. Or such is his hope. Though perhaps Intrepid would be more fitting still for you are bolder than your predecessors. They had more respect." Long white teeth protrude from Veriel's face. Our voices are calm and collected. We are the center of a ballet crafted from hurricanes.

No one can defeat this creature but me. No one has the power, the skill and the will. No one else believes that they can. We slowly begin to circle one another. The last of the shadow warriors is absorbed into the source at Veriel's behest.

I watch the way he flowed. It will be like fighting air. The black sun above us makes every shadow appear to be a part of him, and in a way, it is. His powers are weakened by the sun, and so he destroyed it. Now the only light besides the torches, which did a poor job of illuminating the courtyard, is that which burns crimson around my form. In Veriel's hand is a broadsword that I know isn't one of the Four. My own sword, Forlorn rests easily in my grip. The sword is powerful. It will give me a much needed edge. This is what I had trained for. Veriel's Ruin is what I had been forged into, and I will let neither Lord Alizar nor my family down. I can feel their presence upon me.

"Let us end this."

"Come, and let a ruin befall the light." Veriel snarled. I burst forward in three strides before leaping into the air as fiery wings erupt into the air behind me. The world explodes into light as Veriel raises his sword to meet my own. Forlorn flashes back and forth and is met with two dozen blades guided by shadowed arms. Each blade splinters after only a couple blows from Forlorn.

410

The quickness of the telos fills me, and I slide between blades, deflecting as much as I dodging. I feel half a dozen strikes slip through my defenses and slice against my armor. I vault backwards into the air. My right hand bursts into white flame, and the fire carries up my blade. I close my eyes and blinked. The world becomes clear before me as if it was daylight. I am seeing as the unu can. I watch Veriel waiting for me.

I have an idea. I feel like I have a mainline into the elixis. I don't need the words. In fact, I am going to try something I never have before. I start with the agility of the telos to add onto the eyes of the unu that I have already active. I feel like I can do more. I pull on the strength of giants. I can go farther. I start layering enchantments: the wings of the Skyguard, the endurance of the centaurs, the hearing of the ferals, and the Iron Men's armor. Crystalline red light begins to fountain from my chest. Glowing opaque plates stack one on another across my skin from my feet to cover my head which gives the entire world an orange tint. Sweat is pouring off me, but I know I can maintain. I have never tried something like this before, but I feel invincible with the pulsing energy of The Bloom.

I rise slowly into the air until I come to eye level with the monstrosity that is Veriel. I look into Veriel's pure white eyes. Within them, I see naught but void. A shiver of fear stretches up my spine. My feeling of invincibility begins to waver. It isn't the power that is floundering, merely my belief that it will be enough. I see within his eyes the last moments of my wife's life. I see within his eyes my stillborn daughter. I see within his eyes my severed head hanging high from the battlements of a burning tower. By looking into those eyes I come to a single unavoidable realization.

I could not win.

The realization struck me like a blow to the face. I didn't want to accept it, but I knew that I must. Even with all this power, all the training that Lord Alizar and The Baroner had infused within me, I could not kill the beast before me. Something was blocking the last push of power that I needed. I didn't know why, but something was holding me back. Now, I needed to figure out how in Lord Supremor's name I was supposed to win a

411

fight against a foe that couldn't be beat. *If you can't win you aren't thinking fast enough.* I thought about the axios running through Forlorn. It was time for a gamble.

I brought my sword level with his chest and dropped it. As Forlorn left my grip, a second breath fills my lungs, and my armor shifts to volcanic red. That is it. I have a plan now. I have the will; I have the power; I can take him out, but first things first. I need a new sword. I see Gabriel slowly inch towards a particular blade. I just need a distraction.

"What will it take for you to leave, right now?" This causes Veriel to pause. Once again a grin lights up his face: a brilliant, awful grin. Once again we circle each other. I work to keep him focused on me as I maneuver into position near Gabriel.

"You truly are worthy of your title, Ruin. You're smarter than your predecessors. I want the rest of the Pillars. That is all I have ever wanted. If you give them to me, I will leave for the north. No one will ever see me again. That is my offer. I can either kill everyone or just those few who have been drafted against their will by Lord Alizar's machinations. Choose Ruin, and choose wisely."

"Are you afraid, Lord Veriel?" I ask. This time the shadow doesn't smile. His eyes narrow. I become aware of the air around me. It is so still. Everyone is holding their breath, just waiting for what we titans will do.

"Always, but that has never stopped me in the past. You know what I want. Still you stand in my way. You would sacrifice yourself and everyone else for nothing. Do you even know why Lord Alizar chose you? Not because you were righteous, honorable or true. He chose you because you were the best warrior this world had to offer that he could get his hands on. You are only as good as your sword to him. I could care less about that. You serve my enemy, and for that I will not lie; I desire your death. You don't understand the agreement you have signed though, and for that I pity you. You have been searching for peace for a long time. I can give you peace."

"I have found my peace, and I am not interested in your own. I saw what your warrior did in the north." Veriel tilts his head.

412

"He eliminated the Pillars of King's Port and Cirode'l." Veriel replies.

"He butchered thousands of innocent people all across the Northern Reaches. Were they Pillars as well?"

"No, I imagine they weren't. I have eliminated all the Pillars that weren't concentrated within the cities of humanity and unu. I am not responsible for his actions outside of the orders I gave him." I see Rikard raise his staff, but a quick flash of my eyes tells him to back down.

"This battle will kill everyone here, and still I will walk away. Your weapons are not strong enough to kill me." Now, it is my turn to smile. "Your soul will bear the weight of their deaths."

"Or you can walk away right now." I reply.

"I have nothing beyond my purpose. I have waited generations for this; I cannot stop now."

"Neither can I."

"Then this is the way the world ends." Veriel's eyes narrow as he glares at me. I blast from the ground sweeping Forlorn up with my foot into my hand and hurling it straight at him. Once again as soon as the blade touches my skin I feel the shadow flicker across my soul, and when I release it, the shine grows unfettered.

Veriel howls as Forlorn slices a ragged hole in his shadowed body, and a blue energy flows from the hole like blood. Havoc flies into my hand as we meet in a cascade of blows.

My blade meets his own in a shower of sparks. Shadow tendrils creep outward from Veriel's back and whip towards me like snakes. I jet backwards disengaging towards Gabriel.

"Aurum!" A blade whips through the night towards me, and I catch it in an icepick grip. The sword glows as it touches my skin with a fiery red light that feels more right than any sword I have ever held. I twirl it in my hand into a traditional grasp just in time to fend off a flurry of strikes from a dozen different angles. My armor holds up well against the impacts of the crushing blades as they strike me everywhere I can't block. I drop all pretense of blocking and thrust the long sword forward forcing Veriel back.

413

As it connects with his flesh it explodes outwards. The blast throws me backwards as a dark rain flies around me. The droplets become a tornado as they whip back towards center mass and an instant later Veriel reforms with a snarl before me. But a few pieces of his shadow strike Havoc and hiss and burn as they dissolve. I grin a black smile. This is my victory.

My sword swings with mighty blows as my body contorts against the coming shadows. My eyes track each and every one of them with the speed of the predators that the ferals inherently are. My body instinctively begins to contort to impossible angles as my bones become flexible far beyond human ability, and I warp around the shadowed tendrils while pouring strength and speed into my every blow. I am an amalgamation of the greatest of everything that Supremor has built.

Swords and spears hurtle towards me, but the sounds give them away. Havoc works in overtime striking with fury around me as I spiral in a tight loop shattering steel to fragments that rain down on the human soldiers below. A second time Iris touches Veriel, and I have just enough time to see him scream as his form dissolves. I work Havoc back and forth as fast as I can, burning away as many pieces of shadow as I could. The air becomes choked with a foul stench as Havoc burns away his taint. Then he is back. Still we fight.

I can win this fight. A grim smile emerges upon my lips.

He is everywhere at once. He casts his form outwards and around me swallowing me in a bubble of absolute darkness that threatens to drown the light of my armor. I burn upwards, releasing my wings and hardening them into razors cutting a swath through the cloak of black that was Veriel's form. I didn't even know I could do that, it is instinct. He snarls in agony as I burst free. Hundreds of tendrils swarm me and even as I dodge and cut a thousand, still more wrap my arms and legs trying to bind me. I shoot up higher into the air and begin to spin winding Veriel towards me as I become almost cocooned in the black. I fight to stay both conscience and oriented. I shoot out over the walls and down into the ocean. The water seeps through the thin lines of the darkness. As I breach the surface of the water I feel the hold Veriel has on me decrease ever so slightly. It is just as I suspected.

414

I need to break his power. This sun is feeding him more energy than I have. The only way to destroy a shadow is to either eliminate the light or drown it in light. I have to take this fight somewhere that he can't access the black sun. Under the sea is working but not enough. Underground, then. That left two options: Illuvium or the Sparkling Mountains. I tunnel through the sand and stone at the bottom of the bay shedding layer upon layer of Veriel as he is torn off piece by piece.

"You will fall." Veriel snarls through the ocean water. The tendrils tighten against my armor and slowly cracks begin to form upon it. I need to not be underwater in a few moments. I grit my teeth and pour the last of The Bloom's energy into the armor praying that it won't fracture.

I angled my body upwards and shot towards the surface with all the speed I could garner. As we emerged into the air, my face broke free from Veriel's grasp. I saw the shadow clinging onto me like a horrible monster being brought thrashing into being.

A white sparkle caught my eye as I struggled for altitude. It was The Bloom. Good, she had made her way to the plaza. This was going to be a race. Illuvium was closer. I knew from the maps that Rayn had made when he had been with the Light Monks that there was an extensive network of tunnels underneath the city. If I could lure Veriel down into them, then just maybe I could gain the upper hand.

I swept Havoc down and severed dozens of tentacles which hissed as my blade touched them. It wasn't enough. I needed to lose Veriel immediately. I flicked off the Aer of the Iron Men causing my armor to evaporate and Veriel's foothold to vanish. Veriel collapsed momentarily falling back towards the water before he was able to reengage his own power of flight. That was all the time I needed.

I burst high into the air searching the city desperately looking for the light of The Bloom. I saw her at the edge of the plaza. I exploded towards The Bloom with Veriel in hot pursuit and gaining. It was a race. The Bloom stood approximately two hundred meters from the two of us, yet that distance may as well have been inches.

If any person would be watching they would have seen a comet, and its shadow racing for a star. We shot over the wall and down into the plaza. I glanced over and saw Veriel straining towards the light. I didn't know what would happen if he got hold of The Bloom, but I knew that there was no way I could let that happen.

We were less than ten meters away. I whipped out Iris and hurled it towards Veriel's forehead. The blade struck square in the middle of his face. As the blade hit him, Veriel's form shattered across the plaza and hurled me ricocheting across the courtyard. I bounced twice on the ground before skidding to a halt. My mail screeched in protest as it carved deep gashes into the stone plaza.

"STRIKE!" The echo of a dozen lightning bolts thundered into the spot where Veriel had quickly reformed, and I saw The Bloom rushing towards me.

"I NEED A CHARGE!" I screamed at her as I took off at her. She nodded, and her hands ignited in the same light as when he had met. I didn't have time to stop and instead grabbed her by the hands and felt life roar back into my weary limbs. I whirl around and hurl her down towards the ground as I take off westward. I need her away from Veriel, and I know she will land safely and that Veriel will follow me.

My body becomes an arrow through space and time as I rocket towards Illuvium. I can't let him reach me. If I can get him underground where I control the light, then I can banish this creature once and for all. I don't look back.

Veriel catches me outside the blackened ruins of Harin's Dale. I had poured as much speed as I could into my body crashing through the sound wall near the border of Kana, but it hadn't been enough. I clutched hard onto Havoc as I flew. I stole long claws from the feral race that began to grow out of red light as we plummeted towards the ground. My claws tore gaping holes in his shadow form that tried to eclipse me aided by Havoc in my left hand. Still claws of his own dug into my legs, enshrouding them in darkness that weighted me down pulling me towards the ground. We dropped like a stone. I flung the lower half of my body forward hurling

416

Veriel in front of us as we hurtled down. I pulled every ounce of power I could from the well and dumped it into armor to shield me. The impact on the wood and thatch roof of the Hall of Triumph barely registered, but the second impact on the stone floor caused me to nearly bite my tongue off.

The shadow exploded before me and around me, but I landed with a thud that sent reverberations through every ounce of my body. I couldn't feel anything. Not a single thing in my body beyond the iron taste of blood in my mouth. I tried to breath, but I couldn't. The roof caved in around me with hay and oak sending dust and birds hurtling up into the air. I couldn't see anything. The dim starlight wasn't enough to halt the encroaching blackness around the edges of my eyes.

Slowly, I became aware that my chest was rising barely perceptibly. A long thin snake of black smoke wound around in the air above me and slowly began to coalesce. I followed its movements with my eyes as best as I could, but I still couldn't move a single muscle. I grasped desperately for strength, but I couldn't focus on the well. My mind was abuzz with small explosions of light that caused any cohesive thought to quickly dissipate. I tried to stand, but my legs wouldn't respond. I looked down to see that they were still there, but I couldn't feel them. *Oh Supremor, my legs.* I felt choked. I could barely breathe. I couldn't feel my legs. I tried to scream at them to move, but no sound escaped my lips.

A sliver of smoke formed into a face that pooled downwards into a long cloak of night. Veriel. He was impossible. He grinned at me maliciously, but the grin was pained. He was hurting…but it wasn't enough. I had not been good enough. His form was more gray now than black. He was gaunt, and his form faltered. His breathing was labored. He was in pain. This had hurt him almost as much as it had me. As he stood within the shadow of the black sun I could see him grow stronger by the second. Not by much, but by enough that in minutes he would be strong enough to kill me. *Oh Supremor, he is going to kill me: right here, right now.*

"A…A valiant effort, Ruin. You do your predecessors proud, but like Geraldean, you lost, and now you lie here broken: just like him." Veriel hefted an axe in a hand that formed from his cloak. "And just like him. I will kill you. I have not had to fight like that in a thousand years. You almost undid everything today. A thousand years of planning my revenge, my victory undone by a new Champion. Lord Alizar chose well in you. You should be proud." His hand faltered, and the axe slid through to the ground. "You truly are worthy. We could have been allies. Good bye, Ruin. Enjoy your time in Aeriel." He reached down to grasp the axe again in hand, but I was no longer looking at my executioner. I thought at first my vision was blurring the lines of the stars, but then I realized that a new star was arcing through the sky. A smile came to my face.

"Lord Alizar be praised." I whispered. Whatever... whoever that was would break Veriel's hold on the sun of that I had no doubt. Veriel turned and beheld the racing star.

"NO!" he snarled. I saw him work to gather up the energy. He flexed down to the ground shooting up slower than he had before. I desperately searched for my elixis for something to stop him as he raced towards that being hurtling through the air. But there was nothing. My armor around me flickered even as a glint hurtled downwards from Veriel.

SHING! The axe embedded itself in the armor above my neck with the front of the blade piercing down almost to touch the skin. My armor pulsed weakly one final time and then collapsed. The hatchet dropped nicking my neck, and I involuntarily winced. I could still feel my neck. I couldn't feel my legs, but I felt the cut of the axe and the weight of the blade as it lay on my throat.

My eyes flashed back upwards as I watched the green star pulse farther and farther away. My prayers urged him onwards and upwards towards the sun. *Please make it. Please make it.* I forced him upwards by sheer force of will. Despite the distance I could still see the star rising. I dared not blink for fear that it would go out. Up, up, up it went...out. I blinked fervently focusing my vision desperately trying to see whatever it was, but all I could see was darkness. Veriel had caught him, and I felt hope drain from me.

We had lost.

I had lost.

418

I had failed, and now the whole world would know darkness.

Predator and Prey

Thirty-Two

Galeerial said nothing as he watched the blasphemer desecrate the sanctity of the Throne. He merely watched as a long smile curled onto the face of hatred.

"Do you like what I have done with the place?" The Wither threw his arms around him. "I used Amul Kon as my inspiration. Just wait until you see be receive my designs for the other cities." The Wither's voice was the same as had been etched into the hallways of Galeerial's memories.

"I don't think so. This is where you die." Galeerial responded, "by this sword and by my hand." The Wither sneered.

"You think that tooth picker can kill me? I. AM. DEATH! And she is I." *BOOM*! Galeerial heard a clap of thunder but saw no lightning. "You can't kill me. I broke croak choked you. I showed you what you really are. I stole you and withered away your false dreams and hopes and gave you something far better. I gave you strength."

"Don't talk like Veriel." Galeerial felt the rage seep into his words and checked himself. "What you did was for your own sadism. Your lies hold no power over me."

"Yet still with will, you will try to kill your fill of me." *BOOM!*

"I may have left your presence broken, but I come now for justice." The Wither's smile momentarily vanished.

"Then what are you waiting for?" The Five Eye began to smoke against his chest. Galeerial walked slowly forward. *Make a mistake attacking and you might survive, make a mistake in defense and you won't.* He refocused his attention on The Wither. He brandished his blade in a high guard. Still The Wither sat. He was six paces away.

In the blink of an eye, Galeerial dropped his left hand to the satchel and whipped out one of the throwing knives that Grey had given him and hurled it at The Wither's forehead. His eyes watched the blade fly straight and true as he leapt after it. The Wither vanished the instant before the blade struck his flesh. Galeerial threw his sword out in a wide slash but found himself slicing empty air. He pin-wheeled on his feet but felt cold hands grasp his collar. He was propelled backwards off his feet and over The Wither's head. Galeerial whipped his blade back and forth as he flew. A flash of gray entered his periphery, and Ripper bit into decaying flesh.

Galeerial threw himself to his feet in a single smooth motion just in time to hear a howl erupt followed quickly by a vice grip encircling Galeerial's neck throwing him back to the ground. The Wither's body contorted impossibly so that his torso was facing him with his left leg encircling Galeerial's neck. A dozen blows impacted Galeerial's face as The Wither snarled at him. *BOOM!*

"You're better, but I have broken the best." Galeerial cast his blade upwards through The Wither's back, but once again the creature had vanished. He took a ragged breath searching desperately for his foe.

Galeerial rose slowly to his feet with his head on the swivel and blade working back and forth in a weaving defensive pattern.

"You're braver, but I am the leech that saps your soul." A boot heel sent reverberations throughout Galeerial's body as it impacted his chin. Stars exploded into his vision.

"You're faster, but I am speed incarnate." A kick to his stomach was deflected by Galeerial's flailing hand, but he missed the blow to the neck and the third to the left leg. It instantly went numb. Galeerial staggered.

"You're stronger, but I wither strength to ash with a touch." Galeerial whirled his blade around in a desperate attempt to make any kind of contact. The Wither was so fast. Impossibly fast. Arms encircled Galeerial, and he was whipped around hurled backwards. *BOOM*! He slid across the rough ground, and his back slammed against something unyielding. Galeerial gasped in pain.

His body was a mangled mess. The Wither was nowhere to be found. This wasn't how it was meant to happen. It couldn't end like this. He ran his hand up the stone and felt carved markings engraved on the side. It was the Charist fountain.

"You're smart, but I am the darkness that swallows all brilliance." Galeerial saw The Wither stalking slowly forward with malevolent glee in his eyes. Galeerial pulled himself up to the lip of the well without taking his eyes off of The Wither.

The Wither was only three paces away. Galeerial lowered his hand into the well. The liquid eclipsed his arm, but it wasn't the cool silvery light feeling of the Charist. This was heavy and dense. Galeerial slowly turned his head and glanced down.

The pool was entirely black.

The Wither's mocking laughter engulfed Galeerial's world as he stared at the pool with disbelieving eyes.

"Now do you understand, Galeerial?" The Wither sneered hatefully. "All you had to do was just stay, play, be okay with me. But no. Now, the Twilight of Ages will come to pass. And every one of you little

422

birdies will wither away. Skin turns to water, bones to dust, and it is thanks to you." Galeerial just stared at the well of ink before him as the words snaked into his ears. *How could this happen?* It meant one thing and one thing only, the Son of Supremor had abandoned them. He had abandoned not just Galeerial, but the entirety of the Skyguard.

Galeerial refused to believe it. This was the death knell of his race. This was the Twilight of Ages: the twilight of the Skyguard. Galeerial's left foot slipped underneath the blade of his fallen sword. The Wither was right behind him. Even if the creature was telling the truth about the Charist, he would take him down. Galeerial threw his elbow back at where he knew The Wither's face to be, but, of course, he vanished.

Your instincts never steer you wrong. Except when they do. Galeerial went on instinct as he kicked his sword up into his hand and hurled it at the throne. The blade slammed into the wood as The Wither materialized in the same spot. An explosion of light erupted as The Wither screamed.

Galeerial's eyes bled tears as the beautiful light bathed over him. He couldn't see anything as the flash of light was accompanied by the return of the sun from behind its shaded veil. The Wither seemed to become nothing more than a black mark before vanishing altogether as his screams echoed in Galeerial's ears. As his vision slowly returned, Galeerial saw naught but a sickly green puff of smoke.

Galeerial sunk to the ground not taking his eyes off of the spot.

It was over.

He had won.

The Wither was dead.

He had won.

It was over.

"No, not yet." He murmured staring down at the Charist, which held its black hue. Galeerial was at a loss for what to do now. He approached the throne and pulled Ripper free from its post in the back of it. Veriel was imprisoned within Terakeen; The Wither had been destroyed. Galeerial looked up to the black sun, that was his fault, but he would fix it.

423

He didn't know how yet, but he would fix it. Everything was going to work. Galeerial grabbed Ripper…no Justice and pulled it from the Throne. It had more than earned its name back.

Galeerial made his way through the ruins of Cloud Breach. He saw the half-buried body of the High Cleric Remiel. His lifeless eyes stared up at Galeerial, and Galeerial closed them. Despite it all, the Clerics had been his constant companions for centuries. He imagined the rest of them were buried beneath the rubble. Now, they were dead. He wondered how many other of his friends were dead. *BOOM!*

Galeerial's eyes flashed as he realized the sound came not from the skies as would thunder, but rather from the west. He started jogging, scrambling over the rubble as feelings of dread slowly began to grow in the pit of his stomach. As he crested the mountain, he looked down to behold a sight that chilled his blood. The Wither could not have destroyed the city on his own. Galeerial knew now how he had.

Giants.

He saw at least a hundred of them marching across the prairies away from Cloud Breach towards King's Port. Galeerial couldn't believe his eyes. Giants had entered the war, and they marched with Veriel. Galeerial scrambled back towards the gates. Tenbraun was the only road leading up the mountain. The rest of the peak was a treacherous maze of cliffs that no sane creature would dare try to climb. He vaulted over rubble flinching with every step as his left leg groaned in protest. He shunted the pain away. He couldn't afford it. He needed to get to Cirode'l as fast as possible. He slowed his run. *What good will that do?* They couldn't be warned. The giants would be seen from miles away; there was no potential for a sneak attack. *Think with your mind.*

Galeerial started thinking. He needed to get to Grey. He didn't know what was happening beneath the Sparkling Mountains. Falcons would alert the southern armies about the giants. As soon as they found out that Veriel was defeated than they would face justice, but the army in the caverns in the Sparkling Mountains needed to be dealt with. Galeerial moved deliberately through the remainder of the ruins towards the gates stopping at the doorway with which he had arrived here from.

"It will happen three times." Galeerial grinned grimly. He didn't know who his mysterious benefactor was, but he would use what was given to him to the best of his ability. Galeerial focused on the sentry tower where he had left Grey. That was where he needed to go. He opened the door and saw only blackness within. Perhaps he was outside the city in the caves. Galeerial stepped through. He left the door open, though right after he stepped through the door swung shut. Galeerial pulled his sword free. The cave wasn't completely devoid of light but rather there was an almost pure white torch being held on either side of the free-standing door. Galeerial reached up and pulled one free. This was…not what he expected. The door led nowhere, and he cocked his head in confusion. This place felt different. Something about all of this was…off. Out of curiosity, he held his hand up next to the flame and felt no heat whatsoever. If he wasn't so sure that he was awake, he would have thought that he was dreaming.

He stopped walking and started observing. The very air around him flowed with an ease that betrayed just how massive this cave was. Galeerial slowly turned around holding the torch high to cast the light as far as it could go. Behind him was a wall of gray stone that seemed almost featureless except for a pattern of what looked like waves rippling in smooth lines that stretched evenly spaced as far up as he could see. Galeerial looked to the right of the wall and beheld the stone path he was on extending forward.

A displacement of air beside him caused Galeerial's eyes to divert back to the gray wall which began to ripple and move. It was not a wall at all.

It was scales.

Galeerial stumbled backwards a step. As it cascaded away from him Galeerial held the torch out in front of him and felt fear. A dread welled up in his stomach, and his hands shook.

A dragon stood revealed.

Towering at least a hundred feet tall, Galeerial gaped at the being that stared at him. In the Far Away Times, a great war had been fought between the nations of Carin in the south and the dragons in the north. The War of Unending Flames had lasted for thirty years and had burned the sky black with ash. The Burning Waters had been created from the death throes of the Dragon Lord Nephilim. Only a single dragon, which had walked with the Dread, had been seen in Carin in a thousand years. His blood ran cold as he fell to the ground. Fighting Veriel, The Wither, they were nothing compared to this creature. He couldn't breathe.

The dragon's face was as gray as its body, and its eyes were a deep sparkling blue that sought to entrance him in their majesty. They were unto the most beautiful stars in the night sky. Galeerial tried to close his eyes, but he couldn't. He could only marvel at their sparkle. Galeerial began to see flashes of images in the dragon's eyes: each and every one a memory from times past. They flew by so fast he couldn't pick out any individual one, until the flow stuttered at the time when Veriel cut his wings off. Galeerial didn't feel anything; he only watched unblinking. More and more the dragon saw everything up until his fight with The Wither. Finally, the dragon's eyes closed, and Galeerial's eyes watered as he blinked a hundred times to clear them as he fell to his knees gasping for breath.

"What…what is happening?" Galeerial wheezed as he brought his breathing to control and rose slowly to his feet. With the dragon's eyes closed he was able to see the rest of the creature. Its long neck curled back and around into a body hundreds of feet long with wings so large they passed out of view of his torch's meager light. The gray wall had been the dragon's neck. Smoke slid from the dragon's snout. The dragon slowly opened his eyes again and as Galeerial watched began to shrink. The towering creature slowly grew smaller and smaller before his eyes. It was not extraordinarily noticeable at first but within a minute it had become a scant thirty feet in length.

The dragon took flight and came to rest on Galeerial's path as it grew smaller still. The scales of its skin began to withdraw to reveal flesh. The snout pulled back into a man's face, though the wings stayed attached

426

to his shoulder blades like a Skyguard. They were leathery with clawed tips at the angles. The man was on his hands and feet and rose without his knees touching the ground. The scales for the Dragon's skin had become chain mail upon his form, and the claws twin gauntlets that ended each finger tip with a wicked spike. A scaled tail extended down from behind him, and it flicked back and forth. The man's face looked well worn, though was clean shaven. His hair was white, though he possessed those same brilliant blue eyes of the dragon, though their luster had diminished enough that Galeerial was not hypnotized by them.

"Who...what are you?" Galeerial breathed. Galeerial grasped Justice, though he had no idea what even the Cardinal Sword could do against a creature like this. The man offered him an easy smile as he looked around.

"I'm not a what, Galeerial; I'm a who." The man said chuckling. "And I'm the man responsible for your speedy jaunts around Carin. I'm sorry you had to see me like that. I don't get many visitors, and usually the ones I do get are not as welcome as you." The man said offering him an easy smile. "I have to take the necessary precautions to protect myself and my charge."

"Are you Sable?" The man nodded. "You may be a who, but there are few who can wield the kind of power that you do." Galeerial slowly pulled the Five Eye out of his mail. It shone the same gray as it had when he had been in the presence of Hope. The man seemed to weigh this criticism in his mind.

"Indeed, but you don't truly believe Supremor has only a single son do you? Not all have positions as glamorous as being Lord of Merhelden, but each has their own place. This is my domain. Welcome to Corinth. Now, let there be light." The man drew in breath and expelled it as a blue star that shot upwards into the sky illuminating the cavern for the first time. The stage around where Galeerial and the other man stood was elevated high above a basin that surrounded them. The entirety of the world below instantly took in the light and shone as radiant silver that radiated with an inner fire. It took Galeerial's breath away. "Beautiful, isn't it?"

427

"It's the Aer." Galeerial whispered. It was like a river passing smoothly around them flowing to somewhere that he knew not.

"That's correct. Skyguard have a more concentrated dose, which is why their Aer is more potent. It flows through here and out into the world where a single drop is enough to fill a mortal vessel." Galeerial breathed. "The reason you are human is that you lost some of your soul; it bled out as you lost faith. Here you can reclaim it. If you so chose." Galeerial tore his eyes away to look at the man. He chuckled. "Just because you want nothing to do with beings like me, doesn't mean we don't want something to do with beings like you. You're bitter, but you have come far. Your anger is no longer the potent driver it once was, but it still burns strong. The wizard Grey saw to that. You have great will within you, and it grows stronger every day. You just need a task to focus that will. You can't kill Lord Veriel. Not without Shineheart, which has been lost. Therefore, that job has now passed on to the Lord Alizar's Ruin though his ability to do his job is somewhat questionable at this point in time. Lord Veriel is his burden to bear. You want to save your people. Despite it all you are still a Skyguard. You still hold their nobility close to your heart. There is an artifact called The Spirit of Lights. It was taken from this world some time ago, by a human named Desmond. With it he fled across the barriers that separate this world, from another."

"Cambria." Galeerial replied after a moment's hesitation. The man nodded.

"Your friend Grey can take you there. Together you can save your people from the machinations of The Wither, and Lord Veriel." The last word was said with disgust. Galeerial eyed him carefully. "If you so choose."

"What do you want in return?" Galeerial asked.

"The Skyguard have fallen far. I would see them rise again. I would see you redeemed. You rejected a chance at the hands of Lord Alizar. I'm offering you not so much a chance, as an opportunity. I have given you the key, but you must unlock the door. There is the door." Galeerial turned and saw a simple wooden door to the left of him. The man held out a key.

428

"If I don't take it?"

"The only other way out is to swim. You already denied Lord Alizar that option; though that choice is always open to you. Something you have realized far faster than Ruin, is that you always have a choice. Right now you punish yourself over and over again for what has happened in the past, but you refuse to allow yourself to be controlled. I don't want to control you. Far from it. I want you to fly free. The only question that remains, is will you?" Galeerial looked at the man, and then down at the key with a star shape built on its head that he held out. Galeerial reached out and took it. He backed slowly away inserting it into the doorknob. He turned the key, and the door opened to reveal the familiar vistas of Dynast. He saw Grey meeting with the Skull of the Iron Giant and the human commander he had met before departing. He looked back at Sable. Something was wrong here. Galeerial pulled the key out of the lock. He crossed the distance to Sable in three strides and held Justice up to Sable's throat.

"Here's the deal. I already told you that I want nothing to do with you or your kind."

"Yet you used what I offered when it was convenient for you to do so." Sable shot back.

"No more."

"And if it is Jariah's life on the line next? Or Gabriel's or one of your new brothers? Will you deny my gift then? Will you let one of them die because of your distrust of me? You feel like Lord Alizar and Lord Supremor abandoned you into the hands of The Wither. Regardless, there are things you can walk away from, but the meddling of powers with your life will continue. Whether you like it or not, you have been singled out, and we will haunt you whether you bury yourself in the far reaches or ingrain yourself at the center of this maelstrom. You think you are anything but one of the Chosen? You are the Supreme Cleric of the Skyguard. You just defeated a prime isterios and inflected the most amount of anguish that creature has ever experienced. Whether you like it or not you are a piece on our Crowns board. You can either accept that, or you will be running in circles for the rest of your life. You were chosen for a reason. So what will it be Galeerial? You have the potential to be the keystone of this conflict. Or you will abandon everything and be hunted down like a dog and killed in your sleep. There are no other options. The only escape from this is death, and for that I am truly sorry. Now, you must choose. Choose wisely." Galeerial looked dead into Sable's eyes. He didn't blink. There was no fear whatsoever in them. There was firm resolve. "I don't need you, Galeerial. I want you, but there are a hundred thousand Skyguard who would leap at the chance to save their people." he added. Galeerial slowly drew his sword back and released the man's collar.

"Then why even bother with me, when every other is so willing?" Galeerial asked.

"Because you can survive what Cambria will throw at you. I don't believe any of the others can. I understand your distrust. I really do, but you are wasting time. Veriel's army is preparing to march south. The road through Cambria will be difficult. It has changed much since Grey left."

"You don't understand me." Galeerial replied.

"Perhaps not, but regardless I wish you luck. That is Aperio, the Skeleton Key. It will open any door and take you wherever there is a door to be opened. Take it. Think of it as a gift, not a debt waiting to be repaid." Galeerial once again grasped the key and looked to see Grey still arguing with the assembled parties. Galeerial stepped through the doorway without another word. He looked back at where Sable stood. Galeerial expected a smirk of victory, but instead he got only a small nod. Galeerial saw him mouth the words "Choose wisely." Galeerial didn't know what the raw feeling in his bones was about, but regardless of what Sable said, he didn't trust him. He didn't trust anybody except for the human standing before him. Galeerial closed the door behind him.

"Hello, Grey." Galeerial said. All conversation stopped as the assembled turned to stare at him. "I hate to interrupt, but you're needed to save the world." Grey looked back and forth before pointing at himself.

"Finally! Something worthy of a man as handsome as myself. I knew there was a reason I put up with you for so long. You guys," Grey pointed to the two opposing forces. A feral was revealed to be standing behind the human Commander Loras, "figure it out. Cause I'm tired of dealing with your nonsense. Either kill each other, or come with us, final offer." His gaze worked back and forth between them. "I don't have all day." Neither party said anything. "I'll make it simple. All in favor of killing each other raise your hands." Nobody moved. "All in favor of not being stupid and killing the sucker responsible for this disaster raise your hands." Again no one moved. Grey sighed. "Fine, I'm outta here. Galeerial lead the way." Grey rose from the table and walked towards Galeerial who smiled at his approach.

"Wait, you can't be serious." The Head of the Iron Giant protested.

"Yep I was, and you blew it. So see ya in another life. Hopefully, you aren't as stupid then. Did you kill Veriel yet? What are you doing here? Why are we saving the world, and what from? Shall we?" The questions came fast and furious. Galeerial smiled. Grey gestured towards the door. Galeerial nodded in acquiescence. He inserted the key into the lock.

"How do you feel about Terakeen?" Galeerial asked as he opened the door.

"Ambivalent." Grey replied as he backed through it still chuckling at the incredulous faces of the commanders. "Whyyy?" Grey's letters slurred together as he beheld the Star Tower of Terakeen before them. The gaping look on his face was priceless. Grey's eyes wove around and then back to Galeerial.

"We have a lot to talk about I see." he said. Galeerial smiled. He enjoyed the reversal in power position.

"You have no idea."

"So where to, Oh Captain?" Grey asked.

"We need to find Gabriel. Then, on to Cambria." Galeerial said. Grey cocked his eyebrow.

"I really don't have any idea what is going on in that head of yours." Grey replied. "It's quite refreshing actually. Let's do this thing." Grey started to lead the way. "Oh and Galeerial, it is good to have you back." Galeerial smiled. It was good to be back.

431

The Secret History of Carin
Thirty-Three

Rikard watched as Aurum burst into the sky leaving a trail of crimson fire in his wake carrying the glowing white woman westward with Veriel hot in pursuit. Rikard's eyes flashed as he saw a Skyguard sprinting towards the cells. It was Gabriel. He would know what was going on. Rikard dropped his still smoking staff to the ground as he finally felt the heat burning against his palm. Rikard took off running after the Skyguard. He needed answers. Stunned soldiers surrounded him still staring at the blazing trails that had been left behind in the wake of Aurum's path. Rikard burst through the doorway and took the stairs three at a time. He could hear Gabriel's steps just ahead of him. The frigid stone sent cold bumps running up and down his arms, and it made his shoulder ache. He ignored the pain as he ran. The flickering lights of the torches sent shadows jumping everywhere. The ground was covered in corpses of armor. Rikard held his daggers at the ready. Whatever Veriel was, he could manipulate the darkness for his own purpose. Rikard didn't plan on dying from a shadow. His eyes flicked back and forth. A resounding clash drew Rikard's eyes to where Gabriel had smashed open the steel door at the end of the hallway that led into Veriel's cell.

"Gabriel!" Rikard hollered at him as he scrambled through the hallway. The Skyguard didn't even turn around. The chamber beyond held a pile of chains that had once bound Veriel. Rikard didn't know how Veriel had gotten out, but Rikard would kill whoever it was that had helped Veriel to escape. Rikard saw what looked like an arm lying near the chains, but it was the sword which caught his attention as Gabriel grasped its handle.

"Gabriel, what is going on?" Rikard slowed to a walk as he entered into the chamber. The air was frigid and open as the chamber ceiling stretched thirty feet into the air.

"Aurum needs help. If he is going to kill Veriel then he is going to need the sun back, and I am going to give it to him. Iris will scatter the darkness of Veriel, and Eon will trap the form of the sun in its present state." Gabriel voice was utterly resolute and yet heavy. He twirled the blades in his hands. Each carved a clean arc through the air.

"You'll die." Rikard said. Rikard believed in a glorious death, and this…this was glorious. Rikard envied the man. Gabriel strode towards him with literal fire in his eyes. They burned green. "You too? How?" Rikard asked, but Gabriel pushed by him. "Gabriel, how!" Rikard called as he followed the Skyguard.

"You will understand soon enough. I need a boon, Rikard." Gabriel didn't stop as he stalked through the empty cells. Rikard kept pace with him. "I need you or one of your brothers to save Galeerial. He is walking down a road that will bury him. That cannot be allowed to happen. Can you do that for me, Rikard?" *This was Gabriel's death wish?* "Redeem him."

"One of us will." Rikard replied in earnest. They reached the stairs, and Gabriel's pace quickened as the resolve in his voice hardened.

433

"Thank you." They emerged into the night, and Gabriel pulled his other blade from his sheath. They hummed as Gabriel erupted into the same kind of fire as Aurum though this fire was green. Shouts and murmurs ignited around them as all eyes turned towards them. Light poured out of him illuminating the entire courtyard. "Goodbye, my friend. Pray for me." He was gone. The trail of emerald light led straight upwards towards the sun. Rikard joined the masses as they stared upwards. Dorian ran up next to him.

"What is he doing?" Dorian asked out of breath. One hand clutched his head which was still leaking blood.

"He is going to reignite the sun." Rikard said. They stood watching together as Gabriel arced towards the sun. The flame burned farther and farther away. Rikard felt helpless as he watched Gabriel burn higher and higher into the heavens.

"By the Balance, he's going to make it." Dorian whispered. "Just let Aurum hold Veriel for just a little longer." Gabriel's fire grew smaller and smaller as he moved farther and farther away. Rikard saw it first and Dorian a split second afterwards: the darkness. It was hard to tell with so little actual light up in the stars, but this seemed blacker than black. "No." Rikard said nothing. He just watched. He watched as the light of one of his few friends vanished.

The flash of light was so profound that Rikard thought that he had been struck. The yellow rays of the sun poured through his vision like water, blinding him with their brilliance. Unlike the remainder of the rabble, Rikard knew better than to move. Instead, he listened for the sound of some idiot soldier stumbling towards him with a sword just waiting to skewer him. Rikard stared into the red of his eyelids as he waited patiently for his eyes to accommodate the rapid influx of light. As he waited he began to hear something besides the usual screams. He heard the call.

It felt like a whisper, and Rikard turned his head until he could hear the whisper louder. His eyes slowly came back as he searched for the source of the voice; however, he kept them closed so that he could better focus on the sounds. He could hear it in his mind. He couldn't make out any

434

words, but rather only the incessant murmurs. It was like the entire rest of the world had taken on a hushed din, and all that existed was the whispers. He could vaguely hear Dorian calling out to him, but he was focused on whatever was speaking to him. He opened his eyes and began his hunt. His gaze roved over the bodies on the ground. As he made his way toward the wall at the far side of the courtyard, they grew louder and louder. That's where he saw it. The blade shone with an inner darkness, like it was filled with an insatiable hunger. This was a sword of power. Rikard could feel it; this was one of the remnants that Rayn…Rikard swallowed at the thought of his brother…for which Rayn had always searched.

He wrapped his fingers around the hilt, and instantly the whispers formed into a single word whispered over and over again. *Forlorn. Forlorn. Forlorn.*

"Forlorn." Rikard murmured aloud. The name came to his mind unbidden. It seemed to fit the blade perfectly though. He stared down at it in his hand. The handle was wrought with concentric circles of gold on a black steel base. Leading into the blade was the mouth of a wolf with two blue diamonds for eyes. Its claws stretched out in black around the sides of the blade in a cruel hilt. The tips of the claws were blood red rubies that seemed to hold fire captured from the sun. Rikard reached back to his scabbard for his own blade. He looked at his own long sword, Break. He had never really cared for long swords; they were too bulky. He liked the quick precision of the knife, but this new blade, it called to him. Rikard dropped his old sword and sheathed Forlorn on his back. The world seemed to bleed back to life, and Rikard started looking around.

The first thing Rikard saw was the bodies. This was not a plaza anymore, it was a graveyard. Close to a hundred and fifty bodies littered the ground. Veriel had done quite the number on them, and he had just been getting started. Swords and spears littered the ground from the shadow warriors that had vanished when Veriel had pulled them into himself to fight Aurum. Most of the warriors in the courtyard were human, with a half dozen unum, and a scattering of Skyguard and centaurs. His head snapped right as he heard the bellow of an unu.

435

"How dare you human! How dare you accuse us of betraying the Balance itself?" The unu reached his hand out to grasp the human around the neck, but three other human soldiers marshaled around the human with their weapons drawn. The unu snarled in response.

"How else could he get free? You just wanted any reason to kill more humans!" The human shouted in retort.

"Enough!" Joven's voice cut through the air as the elder wizard stepped in between the unu and the group of humans that had rallied around the first instigator. Rikard rolled his eyes at the entire affair. He saw Dorian making his way through the ranks of the dead kneeling by each one. Rikard figured that Joven could handle this squabbling. As he observed the world he saw a cloaked figure swiftly and easily navigating the maze of bodies towards the dungeons. Something was wrong about the way that he moved. Rikard followed him maintaining a bit of a distance studying the man as he walked.

Rikard picked his way slowly through the mess of bodies. He hadn't realized just how badly Veriel had torn through them. Centaurs, unu, human, Skyguard, and telos had all felt his wrath. Bodies were strewn on the battlements as well.

Rikard saw the queen stumbling around in a haze. Her right arm hung limply at her side, and she held a great sword in her left hand dragging it behind her. He made his way towards her. He would follow the shadowed man in a moment.

"Queen Tendra?" He approached her hesitantly. At first, it didn't seem like she even recognized him. He saw the ball of her dislocated shoulder protruding from the top of her armor. Rikard grimaced.

"Clansmaster," was all she said.

"Tendra, I need you to hold still and try to relax." He reached down and grasped her arm in one hand and her shoulder in the other, and pulled. For an instant there was silence as the shock hit her.

Tendra's scream echoed through the courtyard as a Skyguard came to rest next to them. Instantly, all eyes turned to him and half a dozen weapons were brandished against him. Rikard had to force himself not to

436

draw his own blades. Instead, he held his hands out to show he was unarmed.

"Stand down." Tendra said through haggard breaths. "Stand down." She repeated more forcefully, and begrudgingly the soldiers lowered their weapons. Tendra looked at Rikard. "Thank you." She said. Her wits seemed to be returning to her more and more every minute.

"Still think humanity can sit this one out?" Rikard asked. Tendra said nothing in reply. She just looked at the desolation before her as if seeing it for the first time.

"Have you ever wanted something so bad that you would do anything to get it?" Tendra asked. Rikard nodded. "Well I want to be gone from this war. It has taken everything from me. It has taken my family, my innocence, my life. All I have left is my life. My life which has been cast about like a branch in a storm." Rikard considered her words. She was not like him. She was not a warrior. She needed other people. She was not independent.

"Then maybe it is time you stop believing you are the branch and start believing you are the storm." Rikard replied. "You stood against Qel and Veriel. You are standing here now: alive. More than they can say." Rikard gestured towards the corpses on the ground.

"Tendra!" They were interrupted by a shout before she could reply. Rikard saw Jeric running towards them. Tendra's gaze lingered upon Rikard for a moment before looking at her consort. Jeric embraced her, and Rikard recused himself and made for the dungeons. The queen was an interesting woman. Selfish...but interesting. She was stunted by her mindset. It would be intriguing to watch her in the coming weeks.

Rikard retraced his steps to the dungeons. Once again he found himself at the entrance to Veriel's cell. This time though he really noticed everything around him. The guards had become nothing but a mass of armor. Rikard wondered briefly if Veriel had eaten them. Rikard shivered involuntarily...from the damp cold of the dungeons, not fear. Rikard didn't fear anything: never would. That had been the one of many gifts his father had given him. Rikard touched a hand to his heart and then to his head in honor of Rerem before continuing farther downwards. He finally came to the long hallway that led into Veriel's cell. A man was hunched over the chains. He straightened at Rikard's approach.

"I can hear your sword, Rikard. It is a cursed blade. Have a care whom you kill with it." The voice was gravely and deep but familiar.

"Who are you?" Rikard asked. "What are you doing down here?"

"I'm…a stranger. I walk in the shadows between the lines of good and evil that the world defines. Now, I am here to find information. That is the true power of this and all worlds." The man raised his hand to his face, and Rikard heard him sniff. He approached the human, circling around him. He lowered his hand back down to the ground.

"Do you know how Veriel got free?" Rikard asked. The man shook his head. A heavy hood was hung high on his face blocking it from view.

"No. Eon's enchantments were strong; it is enough to get the blood boiling though: the mystery." The man stood up. "So you're the new Sufferer. Interesting." Rikard eyed the man.

"What's that mean? The new Sufferer?" Rikard asked. Rikard was directly in front of him now, but still the hood obscured his visage.

"It means you bear that sword, nothing more sinister than that." He replied. Rikard could almost hear the sound of a smile on his voice. Rikard pulled Forlorn out and slipped the point under the hood and flicked it up and off. As the man's face came into view Rikard's eyes widened. He stumbled backwards at what he saw losing his breath as he tripped and collapsed to the ground. The metal mask of Corrigan glared at Rikard.

"Rayn?" Rikard could scarcely breathe. "You…you're alive."

"Unfortunately not. Your brother is dead. He was merely a steward of my face and name for some time. I am a stranger to you and to all. Make no mistake. Now Sufferer, you have other business to attend to, as do I." Corrigan turned from Rikard.

"I don't think so." Rikard threw himself to his feet as Corrigan turned back to him. "I want answers, and I want them now. Now, I am going to ask, and you are going to answer. Understand?" Corrigan's eyes stared hard at him.

"Do you truly believe you can stop me?" Corrigan asked.

"Without a doubt." Rikard replied. "Now there is an open cell door to your right. Walk in there." Corrigan didn't move. "Do it, or I will cut you into tiny pieces and feed you to the crows." Corrigan's feet moved ever so slightly. Rikard locked eyes upon his hands. They were unclenched and rested easily at his sides. Corrigan's mask was as inscrutable as the rest of him. The ground protested as steel heels ground into them as Corrigan pivoted and strode into his cell. The rusty iron grated backwards and flecks of rust splayed off of the joints. His gloved hands pulled the door closed behind him.

"There's a good man." Rikard played his daggers back and forth upon his fingers as he approached where Corrigan stood impassively. "Why are you wearing my brother's face?"

"It was a loan to your brother. The face and the name were mine long before I allowed him to borrow them." Corrigan replied. His voice was eerily calm. Rikard was unfazed.

"You're an Iron Man?"

"Aye."

"Yet, you have a name."

"I gave you that information out of respect for your brother's death, and because the Imperial was in his hands. Now, the standing is neutral. Your brother and I had a very profitable relationship. If you would like to deal, then we may renegotiate the terms of the contract to suit your...animalistic nature." An animal. That's what this Corrigan thought he was. Rikard played his tongue under his upper lip. *Very well then, I can act the part of the animal.* Rikard ripped open the door and lashed out with his good leg hurling Corrigan back against the wall. Rikard's dagger flashed into his hand, and he held it to Corrigan's iron throat.

"You like information, well here's a piece." Rikard growled. "This knife can cut through your metal skin as easily as it would butter. There are only two kinds of animals in the world, predators and prey. I'm a predator, and I'm at the top of the food chain." Corrigan was unfazed.

"Come now, one such as yourself should well know that there is a third kind of creature, the symbionts. Your brother and I had a symbiotic relationship. You and I can have one as well if you so choose." Rikard glared darkly at the man. There was no fear in his dim eyes: only calculation. This man was different from the rank and file. He wasn't afraid. Rikard smiled. He dropped Corrigan and stepped away from him.

"What do you have to offer?" Rikard asked over his shoulder.

"Information of course." Corrigan replied as if it were the only thing in the world worth bargaining for.

"And in return?"

"My relationship with your brother was fairly simple. I gave him information on matters of import to him, and he returned in kind. With you however, I am presented with some unique opportunities. You are the Clansmaster of the unu, and quite the warrior. Therefore, I will trade you information in exchange for actions: contract killings, troop movements, force shaping and things of that ilk." Rikard considered this for a moment.

"Who decides how much information is worth, or how much my services are worth?"

"We bargain for it of course." Corrigan's voice finally held the note of an emotion: impatience.

"I want to know two things. First, I want to know everything about what is going on with Aurum. Secondly, I want to know how to kill Veriel." Corrigan's fingers began to trace out motions in the air. It was as if he was calculating the worth and value of each individual piece of information. His eyes flicked back and forth, while his head remained utterly stationary. It was like he was writing and conducting a symphony simultaneously.

"In return, I want to know your Thul." Corrigan replied simply.

"Not a chance." Rikard shot back. Corrigan grinned.

"Something simple then, I want you to use that sword, and kill six humans by the next whole moon. It doesn't matter who they are; they just have to be human. I'll know when you have done it. As a show of good faith though, I'll answer your questions all beforehand. Do we have a deal?" Rikard considered this for a moment.

440

"Six random humans?" He repeated. Corrigan nodded. "Why?"

"Does it matter? Those are the terms of the deal. The deal can't be changed once agreed to. If you fail to fulfill your end of the deal, then the terms of our contract will be nullified. Neither I nor my colleagues will ever do business with you again, if we don't put a knife in your back. The question remains Rikard, do we have a deal?" Corrigan held out his hand, and after a moment Rikard took it. "Excellent. We will meet again when you have fulfilled your end of the deal. Then the card will flip. You will perform your action, and then I will supply you with the information. In answer to your first question, your brother Aurum has been chosen by Supremor to be his Champion in this world. Your brother has been gifted with a type of magic separate from what was bound in the Heart of Fires. It springs purely from his belief in Supremor: nothing else. There have been three Champions before him. Aurum's one and only mission is to protect Supremor's people, in this case, that is from Veriel. To actually kill Veriel, in the wake of what I saw today, I would say you need to acquire a weapon of extraordinary power. Aurum used that blade you have, and it seemed to cause Veriel pain. That would seem to indicate that Forlorn could be used to kill him. Obviously, since Veriel isn't dead, I can't be sure. That is an old sword that doesn't belong here; it has a small piece of elixis forged within it. It needed to in order to survive within the Dreaming. The running odds state that there is a fourteen percent chance of success in using that blade. I can't give you a better answer than that. Save Shineheart, but you already knew that." Rikard's head snapped as he heard trumpets sound. That was the sound of the unu army preparing to leave. Heavy footsteps impacted the stairs as an unu squeezed down the final steps of the not so narrow staircase. The unum had long loops in his ears that stretched them into a hole so big Rikard could fit his wrist through.

"Clansmaster, your other face requests your presence. The clans are prepared to march north with your leave."

"Where?" Rikard called out.

"For King's Port." The unum replied.

"Not where are we marching, where is my brother?"

441

"Outside the city gates, at the command tent of the Thousand Hammers Clan." the unum replied.

"Six humans." Corrigan reiterated. "Then we will meet again." Rikard stepped out of the cell and closed it. He turned to the approaching unum.

"Keep him here." He spoke quietly but urgently.

"If you leave, I won't be here when you return." Corrigan called out.

"Don't let him leave. I'll be back in an hour." The unum set his jaw and bowed. Rikard could see that the proud warrior was disappointed. He believed he was being left behind but was duty bound to obey. Rikard had no doubt that obey he would.

"Yes, Clansmaster Rikard."

Rikard moved quickly through the passageway and emerged into the courtyard to find it still a mess of bodies, though the Skyguard and human soldiers were the only ones that remained. The Skyguard moved amongst the people praying over each one. The unu bodies had all been scalped. The unu didn't believe in burying the dead. They simply burned the braids. Rikard strode through the masses of humans with little regard for them as he headed away from the castle and began making his way through the city.

Indeed as soon as he arrived at the city gates, he was greeted with the sight of the unu packing up their tents and loading the herds of bulls and horses. Siege towers had begun to pull away from the city and turn painstakingly to the north. Dorian would abandon them. They were useless in a field battle, which was where the majority of the coming battles would take place. That and they were dreadfully slow. Two city guards stood gazing down at the slow procession of unu preparing to leave.

"Can you believe the Queen just rolled over for those scalers?" One said.

"Barbarians, we should kill them all. Show them that you can't fight humanity and walk away." the other replied with false bravado.

"Maybe they are just running from us." The first man said. "Cowards."

"How many have you killed?" Rikard asked as he stopped momentarily beside them.

"What?" The two turned to regard him. No recognition colored their faces.

"How many did you kill in the war?" He repeated.

"Oh. Uh, we are just castle gu-" One stammered over himself in an attempt to make excuses for his spinelessness.

"Then you should hold your disrespectful tongues you cowardly curs." Rikard cut him off. "Neither of you are worthy enough to lick their boots. Now go hide in your holes like the rats you are while the men prepare for war." Rikard didn't bother to wait for a response from either of them.

Rikard favored his left leg as he moved across the no man's land that led towards the unu encampment. It took him far longer than he would have liked to reach the edge of the camp. He searched for the banner of the Thousand Hammers upon the top of the command tent. Unu stopped their motions to greet him over and over again, and Rikard returned their salutes each time but remained silent. Their adoration was something he hadn't felt in years, not since he had been in the Artistry of Flesh in Cambria. He heard Dorian's voice inside, and he stepped in to greet it.

Dorian was surrounded by several of the clanmasters seated in a circle. A pile of weapons stood in perfect order at the door. Dorian looked up as Rikard entered and nodded to him.

"It is not a choice. It is a necessity." Dorian finished.

"Clansmaster." The sentiment was echoed around the circle. They rose at his entrance.

"I know you are all busy preparing for the northern march, but I need five minutes of my brother's time." The clanmasters bowed respectfully and retrieved their weapons as they stepped out of the tent. "What was that about?" Rikard inquired.

443

"The clans are concerned about this new alliance with humanity. They believe we should set out on our own to engage Veriel on our own terms." Rikard smiled. That sounded vaguely familiar.

"You don't agree?"

"This morning we had the three of us, a dozen Light Monks, the unum, a Skyguard Lord Commander and fifty human soldiers, and still Veriel took us apart. It wasn't until Aurum showed up with that magic display that is far beyond what any of us can do that the tide even remotely began to turn. On top of that, now we have lost Gabriel, one of the most knowledgeable beings I have ever encountered." Dorian rubbed a hand against his temples. Rikard considered telling Dorian about Corrigan but decided against it for the moment. "Veriel will not have an untrained army at his disposal. Our men are warriors. The humans aren't, but they have numbers on their side. Even with the centaurs, they outnumber us eight to one. We can't win without them, but fighting with them puts our own forces in jeopardy." Dorian sighed heavily. "But you aren't here to rule, you're here because you agree with them. You are going after Veriel."

"He killed Rayn," was Rikard's only reply. Dorian looked sad for a moment but quickly grew pensive.

"Was there anything you could have done this morning that you didn't?" Rikard shook his head after a moment's deliberation. "Then what are you going to do different when you find him?" Rikard displayed Forlorn in his hand. Dorian stared at the sword uncertainly.=

"What is this sword, Rikard?" He reached his hand out to touch it and immediately withdrew it. "It's cold."

"It was the blade Aurum cast away near the start of the battle." Dorian started.

"Get rid of it Rikard. Take it to the Rift and throw it off. There is something very wrong about that sword. No good will come from that blade."

"Use the enemy's strength against them. Isn't that what we were always taught? This sword is a gift." Rikard hesitated for a moment. "You know I don't believe in most of the stuff people here do, but if this blade can hurt Veriel when others can't. Then my course is clear. This sword made him bleed. I don't know why or how but it did."

"Aurum was also using magic. He...I don't expect you to care or understand but he has become something greater. He has a destiny."

"Destiny? You are going to talk to me about destiny? You who despite the Orrery's words have turned your back on us over and over again? You fight your own preaching, Dorian. I know my course. I know the path the Orrery set down for me. It is the path I chose for myself. This is what I have spent my entire life doing. What is the point of all of this if all the rest of us do is provide a distraction?" Rikard's frustration bled into his voice. He slowed his breathing down.

"Okay." Dorian replied.

"Excuse me?" Rikard asked.

"Okay. Go after Veriel, but find Aurum first and do it together. Whatever magic he has found it is powerful. However well he wields it, I know you can wield it just as well."

"Better." Rikard cut him off.

"Better." Dorian corrected himself. "Start in Harin's Dale. That was near where I lost his trail in the sky. He fell somewhere over Kana."

"I can find him. If he's alive, then I can find him."

"Just promise me you won't do anything foolish. If you have a clear and sure shot you take it, but nothing less." Rikard stepped forward and embraced his brother. "I have already lost one brother; don't you dare make it two." Rikard stepped back and emerged to find a human waiting for him amidst the clanmasters.

The female was small by human standards and looked positively miniscule in comparison to the massive unu that surrounded her staring at her with a mixture of curiosity, contempt and interest.

"Rikard?" her voice was high and clear. It rang out with some measure of authority.

"Do I know you?" Rikard asked.

"My name is Iona. We met at the Council of the Pillars." *Ah yes, the annoyingly vague and noncommittal woman.* Rikard didn't like her. "The Radiance would like a few minutes of your time."

"So she finally decided to show up, huh? What does she want?"

"I don't know anything other than that she has some kind of proposition for you." Rikard grimaced; he didn't have time for this.

"Tell her thanks, but no thanks. I neither want nor need anything from your tired order." Rikard had almost no respect for the order itself. It was a shadow of what it had the potential to be. He pushed past her and headed back towards the city. He needed a ship.

"May I walk with you?"

"Whatever floats your boat." Rikard replied casually. He kept walking without waiting for her to catch up. A ship could take him to Bicoln, and he could pick up Aurum's trail from there. He would steal a horse and head into Kana. The centaur borders would be scantily defended if at all.

"You are going to assassinate Veriel." Iona said matter-of-factly. "What if I told you that the Radiance could get you the same kind of power that your brother wields?" At this Rikard did take notice but still didn't stop.

"I would ask why her own people don't." Rikard replied. He took another long look at the woman. She was smaller than him and had hair so blonde it was almost white and green eyes.

"You used to have brown eyes." Rikard commented. Her eyes reminded him of the diamonds on Forlorn's hilt.

"You don't remember me, but you remember my eyes?" She challenged. Rikard suddenly knew who this was.

"We missed you in the battle against him, your Radiance." Rikard hated these silly games with people that thought they were so smart. "Maybe if you would have bothered to show up then he wouldn't have gotten away." Rikard continued. He turned and kept walking through the city. Everywhere people had abandoned their swords and spears for wagons and wheelbarrows with which to collect the bodies for burning. The city

446

was in a desolate state. The unu had burned or destroyed a good chunk of the city through their bombardment; the roads were a labyrinth of rubble, broken glass and burned wood. The stench of death was so pervasive that Rikard barely noticed it anymore. The cry of hundreds of crows in the sky was the loudest noise in the city. The light snow had made the world into a hushed casket of winter. It was like a coffin surrounded the city.

"I had other concerns during the battle."

"Well right now I have other concerns than you." Rikard pulled ahead of her only to run square into a wall of green energy. Rikard stumbled backwards a step. The wall stood just over seven feet high and stretched outwards into a square. The wall hummed almost outside of his ability to hear. He reached out and touched it. The wall was cool, almost as if it was made of ice, and yet entirely solid. He regarded The Radiance. "How did you do that?"

"Your brother isn't the only person in the world with access to magic." She replied. "Am I your concern now?"

"What do you want?" He replied ignoring her question. She smiled. It was a victory smile. Rikard wanted to slit her throat. She wouldn't feel quite so enthusiastic then.

"A slight change of plans. You want to kill Veriel. You have the sword; you have the skills, but what you don't have is the power necessary. I know where you can find it."

"In exchange for what?" *The unu, Corrigan, now the Radiance.* Rikard couldn't remember the last time so many people had wanted something from him.

"The death of Veriel," she said simply.

"Don't play games with me." Rikard spat. "I don't care if you are the bloody Radiance; you bleed like everybody else." That same smile appeared.

"Very well, if we aren't playing games. I want an army. The Light Monks are soldiers, but you are a warrior. You have no fear. That is something we need. My people are few and well disciplined, but our greatest swordsman is not as good as you. They sit in Illuvium and pray and

447

study, but too rarely do they put steel to flesh. I need that. So here's the deal. If you survive, then I want you to come and work for me. I want you to be my blade master." Rikard chuckled.

"You got me confused with someone that cares about you or anybody else on this rock besides me, my brothers, and the man who is going to kill me. Nobody else matters. Period." She eyed him carefully up and down.

"So that's it?"

"That's it." Rikard replied.

"It must be hard living for nothing but to die." She coldly rebuked.

"Must be hard not being able to do everything yourself." Rikard replied. The wall disappeared as the sound of her footsteps refused to follow him. "Giving up that easily?" He crowed.

"I know when I am wasting my time. I had heard different of your brothers. I heard that they were great men. I had hoped you were of the same breed. It seems however that I should search for one of the others. Perhaps one who is confident enough in his abilities to teach others."

"You can't bait me woman. I'm the best, and I know it. So do you, or else you wouldn't have come to me first. I don't have an ego; I have a spine. I know precisely who I am and what I am capable of."

"The best," she cut in with a bark of harsh laughter, "not anymore. There is a Champion in the world now. You are a predator, Rikard. I am offering you a chance to stay on top of the food chain."

"Keep your offer. I have made it this far on my own. If Veriel kills me, then I am fine with that. I made peace with death a long time ago. I don't need your pitiful offer at a legacy."

"Rikard," she called out, "for someone so eager for death, you have yet to fight a gallowglass. Perhaps you should cut your teeth on one of them before taking on this new Dread." Rikard kept walking through the drab cityscape. He didn't bother looking back. It was true that he had never fought a gallowglass. *How had she known that?* He idly wondered before pushing the thought out of his mind. He had more important matters to occupy his thoughts. He slid down a pile of loose gravel and pushed by a

448

man in a tattered cloth who walked in front of him carrying a bucket of some foul smelling liquid.

It would be good to find Aurum. It would be good to have the brotherhood back together mostly. He wondered about Grey and Rowen. No one had seen or heard from Rowen since Long Fang. Joven had played it off like it was part of his plan, but Rikard had learned a long time ago how to see through Joven's slick talk. Dorian had mentioned that Galeerial had told him that Grey was in Dynast. That would be an interesting story no doubt. Rikard missed Grey. The man was maybe the only one of the brothers who understood how big of a joke so much of what these people considered to be important actually was. Especially back in Cambria, Grey had recognized the absurd nature of many things. Grey had helped Rikard to realize what was truly important in life. In many ways, his younger brother had been nearly as influential as Rerem in shaping his perspective.

"Rikard?" The sound of a familiar voice shook Rikard from his reverie. He looked to see his brother's grizzled face approaching with Galeerial beside him. "Speak of the devil." He muttered with a grin. "Speak of the devil."

The Round Table

Thirty-Four

"Rikard?" Grey called out to a man who seemed lost in thought as he trod the streets of Terakeen. Galeerial saw one of the unu clansmasters approach them with a smile cracking through his grim demeanor.

"Grey? Where in Rerem's name have you been?" Rikard pulled his brother into a firm embrace while Galeerial hung off to the side. A smile shone on Rikard's face. Galeerial had never seen the man smile. When they disentangled, Rikard turned to Galeerial.

"Rikard, I'd like you to meet the eighth. Eighth, meet fourth." In the past, Rikard had taken Galeerial's measure, but now it seemed like the man looked at him with a different pair of eyes entirely.

"He's not Eighth anymore." Grey looked crestfallen. He swallowed hard.

"Who?"

"Rayn." Rikard said quietly after a moment.

"No…no." Grey squeezed his eyes shut as his shoulders slumped and tears rolled down his cheeks. "Not him." Rikard placed a firm hand on Grey's shoulder as he buried his face in his hands. "How?"

"Veriel." Galeerial's heart skipped a beat, "in Gemport." Galeerial breathed a sigh of relief. Veriel was still imprisoned, but this was just another reason why death was too simple a punishment.

"Then seventh, meet fourth." Grey's voice cracked just a little as Galeerial stepped forward to the man.

"Fourth?" Galeerial asked.

"Fourth oldest. Grey is fifth. It seems I may have misjudged you. Welcome to the Brotherhood." Galeerial nodded and offered the man his hand. Rikard took it.

"Awwww. It's so nice when all the kids get along." Grey's voice was strained as he tried to make the joke; his heart wasn't in it though. His voice still held the tones of sadness. Galeerial had never met Rayn, but Grey had called him the conscious of the group, that his sense of wonder was legendary. "Where are you headed, Rikard? Besides an early grave, I mean you look terrible."

"You're hardly going to win any beauty competitions yourself." Rikard ribbed trying to bring some levity back into the conversation. Galeerial had to admit that Rikard looked to be in pretty bad shape. One arm was in a badly torn sling, and he had half a dozen visible cuts. He favored his left leg as well. "I don't know how much you know, but the war as it was is over. A cease fire and a new tentative alliance are in the works between humans, unu, centaur and Skyguard. This morning, Veriel broke free of his imprisonment in the cells. Gabriel's dead." Galeerial almost missed the second part of Rikard's statement. *Escaped? How could he have escaped? He couldn't have… not without help. But who?* Galeerial's mind reeled, *and Gabriel dead.* This was a nightmare. Everything was so close to being right. He had destroyed The Wither, and Veriel was imprisoned. He was on his way to find the Spirit of Lights to save his people, but now?

Now, Veriel was free. Galeerial thought of Gabriel's last words to him. *You are truly fallen.* Galeerial would never get the chance to prove to Gabriel how wrong he was. How everything he did was to save his people. Rikard was still talking, but Galeerial couldn't hear him.

"ARGH!" Galeerial bellowed and slammed his fist against the wooden boards of one of the houses. The steel gauntlet on his hand cracked the wood as Galeerial struggled to get his breathing under control as Rikard went silent.

"Are you okay?" Grey asked.

"Fine," Galeerial replied as he seethed. "I want to know what happened, everything." He said pointedly.

"Go talk to Joven. He should be at the merchant's palace. I'm going to try and find Aurum. He came blazing in here with some pretty strong magic and managed to take Veriel on for a lengthy fight. Last we saw of them, they were flying over Kana headed towards Gemport. I'm going to head towards Harin's Dale and try to pick up the trail."

"Galeerial can get you to Harin's Dale right now." Grey replied. Rikard cocked an eyebrow.

"How?" Galeerial held up the Skeleton Key.

"It can open a door to anywhere I want as long as there is a door where I am going and a door that I can insert the key into on my end. It seems I can reach just about anywhere."

"That's convenient. Do it." Galeerial nodded. He turned around looking for an intact doorway. Terakeen had been hammered hard, but he spotted one not far from them.

"Follow me." Galeerial nodded his head in the direction of the door. "Keep talking."

"There are three of us here, Dorian, Joven and myself. We were asleep last night when," the streets were littered with rubble, and the three of them picked their way through it towards an intact shop, "I heard screams through the stone. The queen was already awake and in Joven's room. She knew Veriel was loose. We reached the courtyard outside the entrance down to the dungeons as shadows in the shapes of men carrying

452

weapons began to fight us. They had arms and legs but no faces. They spawned from Veriel and returned to his body when Gabriel engaged him. I killed dozens, but they kept reforming until a group of Skyguard flew over the top of us pouring out barrels of Charist down on the soldiers. The Charist covered my knives, and it burned them." Galeerial felt his heart sink at that: barrels of Charist ruined. He needed to spread the word to begin rationing it immediately after they got Rikard on his way. They arrived at the door, and Galeerial slipped the Skeleton Key out from his belt and inserted it in the lock. A quick turn opened the door to a cold burned out husk of a city.

"Very useful indeed." Rikard murmured. Grey and Galeerial followed Rikard into the destroyed city. He flinched at the smell. The door fell from its hinges broken, and the gateway between cities vanished.

"Looks like we are going to need a new door." Grey said.

"Your grasp of the obvious is impeccable." Galeerial replied more sharply than he meant. It was utterly desolate. Galeerial had flown over Harin's Dale many times in his youth and remembered it vividly as a sprawling city of long houses and wide roads. Now, it was a scorched remnant of its former glory. The centaurs used the plentiful lumber that was sent south by the giants to build their entire city out of wood and thatch. Once the fire started, there had been no hope. This was an old fire though. This hadn't been caused by the fight between Veriel and Aurum.

Rikard began to pick his way up towards the only building that was still even remotely intact, which seemed to be the main hall. A great statue lay in ruins upon the ground as they picked their way forward.

"Hmm." Rikard murmured as he passed through the ruins into the mead hall. The doors had been destroyed, but the walls had been made of stone and so while they had been scorched black, they still stood. Interestingly enough, inside there was not a single centaur body, but there was one...a human.

"Aurum?" Grey whispered. "By Supremor." Grey vaulted over the rubble sprinting towards his fallen brother. Rikard was only a second behind, and Galeerial kept pace. Aurum was in bad shape. One arm was twisted at an abhorrent angle and cuts and deep bruises enshrined his body like a second skin whose tone was more black and blue than white. His muscles were tense even though he was clearly out cold. Grey was knelt down tapping Aurum on the face. "Aurum." No response.

"Let's get him back to Terakeen. Joven will know what to do." Rikard said. "Find something that we can use as a liter so that we can carry him without damaging him too much." Galeerial continued to stare at Aurum as Grey and Rikard scrambled around searching the room. He stepped closer and knelt beside the man. It was the first time Galeerial had seen him since Galeerial had left him with the centaur at Winter Crest. Galeerial started roving his hands over Aurum's body. Two of his ribs seemed to be cracked, and there was a fracture in his right arm.

When he had fought him at Terakeen, Veriel had easily dispatched him and had barely seemed concerned. Aurum seemed to be a much different sort of problem, perhaps he was even the Champion that Galeerial had believed him to be. Galeerial wondered what sort of luck had stayed Veriel's hand, because he should be dead. Galeerial tentatively turned the man on his back and felt his intact shoulder blades and down to his back. He reached about two thirds of the way down when he felt a strange perturbation in the bone. A feeling of dread coursed through Galeerial's body. Galeerial blinked heavily and confirmed what he felt by pulling Aurum's chain mail jerkin up.

"Grey, Rikard." Galeerial said heavily. The two wizards looked up from their pursuits. "His back is broken." Galeerial could hear the breath catch in each of them. They didn't believe it, but neither could muster up the words to say so.

"No...no...no." Grey whispered as he ran back to where Galeerial stood over Aurum's fallen body. Galeerial didn't have to gesture, Grey began to feel down the back, and he stopped at the middle of the spine. His shoulders slumped. "No...no...no." He murmured over and over again. Rikard just went back to searching. Tears began to run down Grey's face, and Galeerial reached down and put an awkward hand on his shoulder.

454

"I've got something." Rikard called to them. "Galeerial give me a hand." Galeerial looked over to Rikard who had his jaw set hard. "C'mon. Aurum's not going anywhere unless it's with us, and the faster we get him to Terakeen, the faster we can get him some help. So, let's go!" Grey didn't move, and Galeerial pulled his hand from Grey and made his way towards Rikard. The wizard had found a piece of the roof that had escaped the fire and collapsed with a piece of a crossbar covered in bound bales of thatch. Between the two of them, they were able to drag it over to where Grey was kneeling over Aurum.

"Grey, go find a door. It just needs to have a lock." He didn't move. "Grey!" Rikard shouted.

"It's not supposed to be like this." Grey said. "We are supposed to be invincible." He whispered as he stepped out of the way as they brought the liter flush. Grey vaulted over some debris and took off running unsteadily down through the hallway.

"You know anything about being a doctor?" Rikard asked.

"What Grey has taught me and through books." Galeerial nodded. He had read books about it. There wasn't much call for doctors in the Skyguard. They were able to heal quickly from injuries, and there wasn't much that didn't kill them that could be treated.

"Then you know he will never walk again." Rikard said. That thought dominated his mind even as they eased his corpse…body onto the liter. Aurum didn't look peaceful. He looked sad, like his last thought had crushed his hope. Grey called out to them from down the hall.

"One. Two. Three." Rikard said, and they hoisted it up onto their shoulders. The hay stuck into his face and splinters of wood pierced his hands, but he ignored it. His face was hard and impassive, just like Rikard's. Galeerial felt an odd sense of kinship with the man. He hadn't interacted much with him, but his brush with Dorian meant that he felt like he knew the man: though Rikard was harder by far. They made their way back towards where Grey was. He gestured them inside to a room that didn't look much better than the hallway.

455

"Where's the door?" Galeerial asked looking around. Grey pointed down at a kitchen cabinet with pots and pans held within it. Galeerial blinked to be sure that he understood. "Are you serious?"

"Of course I'm serious." Grey snapped. "There are no other doors. So you shove him through this cabinet so that we can get him the help he needs, or I'll snap your neck and take the key and do it myself." Galeerial looked at the large cabinet doors. He inserted the key and turned it focusing on Terakeen. It opened, and Grey went down into a crouch and slipped out into the drab of the grey sky of Terakeen on the other side. He gestured to Rikard and Galeerial, and they pushed Aurum's body through to the other side. Grey, and a woman Galeerial didn't recognize, pulled the gurney through to Terakeen.

"Friend of yours?" Galeerial nodded to the woman.

"It's the Radiance." Rikard replied. The tone of his voice led Galeerial to believe that Rikard was not her biggest fan. Galeerial cocked an eyebrow as Rikard crawled through the doorway. The Radiance. Galeerial knew all about that storied line of individuals. The Radiance had been part of the group that had killed the Dread. It was a name as much as a title. When the individual took on the station of the Radiance, he or she forsook their name. They became the role. Galeerial pulled the Skeleton Key out of the cabinet door and slid through to the other side.

They were on an utterly deserted street within Terakeen. The sounds of movement and voices could be heard, but none within the vicinity, but he could feel something approaching. He stood up as the Radiance bent over Aurum's unconscious form. He recognized her now as the Light Monk who had been at the Council of the Five Pillars just days before. Strange how they had happened upon her out of all the doors in Terakeen it seemed power was drawn to power. Galeerial stiffened as he felt a humming in the air around him. Galeerial didn't know how he could feel it, but his whole body felt like it was vibrating, and the hairs on his arms stood straight up. Galeerial reached up for his sword and pulled Justice from its sheath. He looked down at the Five Eye on his chest, and it gleamed with a soft green hue. He had never seen that color.

456

"Whoever you are, show yourself." Galeerial called out.

"You may put your blade away, Supreme Cleric Starheart." Her voice was like a flute, and it came not from any of the streets but from above. Galeerial looked up as did his companions to see a woman clothed in white descend upon them slowly as if floating on a cloud.

"My...my Lady?" Galeerial turned his head to behold the Radiance prostrate upon the ground. He turned back to regard the woman who descended to the ground touching down as lightly as a feather.

"May I pass, Supreme Cleric? Ruin needs my assistance." The woman said.

"Not without knowing who you are." She smiled.

"You fool. That is the Lady Bloom." The Radiance scolded him. "The Bringer of Life." Galeerial didn't replace his blade.

"I'm afraid that I am unfamiliar with her Ladyship." Galeerial replied pointedly. "What and who are you?"

"I am The Bloom, and if you will allow me, I can perhaps heal Ruin's shattered spine." Galeerial locked eyes with her. The Bloom...the name seemed familiar, as if he had read it long, long ago. He reached into his cut up and dirty tunic and pulled out the Five Eye.

He pressed it against her skin and the light of the Five Eye begin to wrap around the entirety of the gemstone at the end of its golden necklace. The gold of the chain ignited into quicksilver that spread down around his left hand. It burned so hot it froze the skin on his wrist and hands as the metal flowed from his neck like water and around his hand forming sharp talons along his fingers. Galeerial's eyes widened with fear at the transformation before him as the gold began spiraling in a triple helix along his arm forming a wicked gauntlet with the Five Eye searing into the back of the palm of his left hand. The Five Eye blinked once and the gold turned into shimmering silver, then went quiet.

"What...what did you do?" Galeerial demanded as he stared in a mixture of terror and awe at the cold silver of his hand. He was paralyzed as he held the gauntlet before him. *What was happening?* He could no longer feel his fingers but rather he felt the hand as a whole articulated before him.

457

His fingers touched each one with a clear *clink* like that of a bell toll. His right hand shook as he grasped his pointing finger and pulled. Nothing happened. He clawed at the points where flesh met metal trying to pry it off, but nothing happened. He couldn't get a firm grasp on it. The Five Eye had been welded onto his hand. "What did you do?" Galeerial bellowed grabbing her around the neck. An instant later, Galeerial was on the ground with the Radiance blade at his neck, and her boot on his chest.

"You will not touch her." The Radiance hissed.

"Get off of me, right now." Galeerial said calmly staring at her.

"You will not touch her again." The Radiance repeated.

"Aurum's back is broken!" Grey screamed at them. Silence descended.

"Radiance, please release the Supreme Cleric." The Bloom touched her on the shoulder, and the Radiance stepped off of him. The Bloom reached down to pull Galeerial to his feet, but he rose of his own accord. "I revealed the potential within your gemstone. It was hiding its true power, and I unleashed it." She replied calmly looking him right in the eyes without flinching. "You are much more than your meager flesh, Supreme Cleric. I see your potential, human-once-Skyguard. Look at you. You are becoming a veritable nexus point of magic. However, that is irrelevant at this point in time. Will you let me see Ruin or not?" Galeerial licked his lips before stepping gingerly to the side. The Bloom brushed by him and moved to where Aurum lay. "Radiance, I need you to take that one," she pointed to Rikard, "and rally the other wizards. It is time for a gathering, a gathering of those with potential: a gathering of powers. I need the remainder of his brothers, Tendra Sumenel, a boy named Hallen Retin, and a being named Corrigan. You should be able to sense them if you focus."

"Yes, My Lady." The Radiance rose to her feet. "Shall I bring them to the Hall of Merchants?" The Bloom looked uncertain.

"If you think that the best meeting place."

"I'm not leaving, Aurum." Rikard said. "I don't care what you are. I don't get ordered around like a school boy. I will cut a woman."

458

"Rikard." Galeerial stepped in close to where the wizard stood over Aurum's body. "Whoever she is, she can help us. You want vengeance against Veriel. Look at my hand." Galeerial held up his gauntlet. "She has power. Power we can use. Go find these people she desires, and maybe we can gain some of that power." Rikard looked grimly at Galeerial.

"Send Grey." Grey's head cocked at the sound of his name. His eyes were bloodshot from the earlier tears, but he cried no more. Grey nodded and rose.

"Let's go." Grey said simply. Galeerial watched his brother amble off. His stride was different. It had lost some of the levity. His footsteps echoed heavily on the cobblestones as he and the Radiance made for the Star Tower.

Galeerial watched as The Bloom knelt besides Aurum. Rikard had his daggers held loosely at his sides. Galeerial hadn't even seen him draw them. Working quickly and expertly, The Bloom pulled off Aurum's mail and tunic clothes to reveal a series of intricate line markings up and down his chest.

"Why do you keep calling him Ruin? His name is Aurum." Rikard questioned.

"See for yourself." She gestured to lines that had been etched in his skin in red ink.

"He has been Claimed." Galeerial murmured in revelation. "That is THE WORD, the language of Supremor. I was right. He is the Champion." Galeerial's eyes trailed along the lines as they curled and wove their pattern that was the language of Merhelden. "Ruin." A shiver inadvertently trailed down his back. "That is his new name."

"What does that mean?" Rikard asked.

"It means that Veriel is something far worse than we could have imagined." Galeerial said.

"The runes declare that he has picked a side. Every being that I am now gathering will do so at one point or another." The Bloom spoke quickly. She rove her hands down Aurum's spine until she reached the obvious contusions. Galeerial could see her grimace as white light began to

459

stream from her hands down into Aurum's flesh. The deep discoloration fought against the flow of the light, but slowly the deep purple and black began to crack and vanish pushing backwards and slowly disappearing altogether. Galeerial watched in wonderment. There was so much magic present in this city. For it to have lain dormant for so long only to all explode now at once. Galeerial glanced down at his new hand. It felt cold, and he fought off a second shiver in his spine.

Aurum coughed twice as he shook awake from his slumber. He groaned in pain as Galeerial watched his back spasm as it tried to reconcile what was, with what is. The Bloom pulled her hands away and tried to stand only to collapse wearily back to the ground. Galeerial knelt next to the man.

"Yes." Galeerial looked to see Aurum staring upwards at the sun. "It is alive." Aurum whispered. "How?"

"Gabriel. He...he didn't make it back." Rikard said quietly.

"I...I can't feel my legs." He whispered. "I can't feel my legs." Rikard looked at The Bloom.

"You lied." He said darkly.

"His back has healed, but his mind is still fractured from the trauma. You need to draw on the elixis for strength, Ruin. I healed your body, but your mind has yet to understand what has happened to you. It felt your back break. Even now your body says you can walk, but your mind regales against it."

"I used so much of it fighting him." Aurum's voice was hoarse. "I used so much, and he was so strong."

"Aurum, focus," Rikard said, "like I taught you. Focus. Focus on your feet. You can move them. Be confident that you can move them and you will." Galeerial saw Aurum's face relax, and the ink on his body began to glow.

"Help me sit up." Aurum said. Rikard leaned forward and pulled Aurum into a sitting position. Aurum held his hands out, and they pulsed with a soft energy. Galeerial watched fascinated. He pushed his hands down onto his legs. The light began to spread into armor around his waist, legs and feet. At first the armor was loose, but slowly it began to tighten around

460

his legs until it was like a second skin. Then, it sunk into his legs disappearing entirely. Aurum closed his hands. Now, his face did grow tense. His teeth were gritted hard, and Galeerial could almost hear them grinding together. Slowly...oh so slowly Galeerial saw Aurum's right foot quiver and bend. Sweat poured down Aurum's face as relief poured through his body. "Help me stand brother." Galeerial reached down with Rikard, and Aurum looked quizzically at Rikard.

"We have a new seventh." Aurum nodded. They slowly pulled Aurum up to his feet supporting his arms on their shoulders. He was unsteady and his legs seemed like boards they were so stiff. He took several long breaths before turning to look unsteadily at Galeerial. His eyes drifted to Galeerial's hand.

"Much has changed since we last met." Aurum said eyeing the Five Eye gauntlet on his hand. Galeerial almost laughed at the sheer inadequacy of the comment.

"You really have no idea how much." Galeerial said, "and it seems as if I am not the only one who has gone through a transformation. When last I saw, you were barely alive, and now you are a Champion."

"I'm still just as amazing as I have always been, in case you were wondering Aurum." Rikard said. At this Aurum actually laughed. With that it seemed like the dour mood surrounding them broke.

"I don't think I ever got the chance to say thank you for rescuing me from Long Fang, Galeerial."

"My debt to you is hardly repaid considering what you saved me from at Amul Kon." Galeerial replied.

"In my eyes, we stand on even ground." Aurum said.

"Ruin, we should be going." The Bloom cut in to their conversation. "How did you get back to Terakeen, and what happened with you and Veriel?" She asked. Galeerial didn't know who he wanted to know about the key outside of his brothers. Galeerial looked sideways at Rikard and slipped him the key as Galeerial reached up and put a hand on Aurum's chest to stabilize him. Aurum looked at them quizzically.

461

"I brought him back: with magic." Rikard replied. "I'm a wizard remember?" The Bloom looked at him dubiously.

"Do you know the way to the Merchants' Hall?" She asked. Rikard nodded. "Then let us be off." It was at this moment, that Galeerial noticed that a large crowd had gathered around them watching. All work had stopped in their small singularity of existence. Some recognized Aurum from earlier. Some recognized Galeerial from his actions at the Star Tower no doubt. They were all curious. It was as if they realized something important was happening with important people, but they didn't quite know what.

"You got him?" Rikard asked. It took a second for Galeerial to realize he meant Aurum.

"Got him." Rikard moved over to the door with the key. Galeerial wondered if it would work for anyone but him. Sable hadn't exactly been forthcoming in that respect. Rikard marched up to the door. Galeerial watched close trying to see how Rikard would do it. The wizard simply opened the door. Galeerial couldn't even see him slip the key into the lock, and he was looking for it. Despite all that Grey had taught him, Rikard was still better than he was. He could learn from this man. The door was pulled open, and the same room where their council had met was laid bare before them. A shockwave of whispers erupted amongst the crowd. They were still awed by magic.

"Let's go." The Bloom entered first followed by Galeerial and Aurum. Rikard pulled the door closed behind them. Aurum hobbled forward on stiff legs, and Galeerial helped him to slide into one of the chairs. By the time they arrived Aurum's breath was heavy. The man was exhausted. His knees shook with the effort, but he never said a word in complaint.

"Who are you two, anyways?" The Bloom asked. Rikard exchanged an incredulous look with Galeerial.

"I'm Rikard. He's Galeerial. We are Aurum's brothers."

"Galeerial is not a human name." She replied.

"That's because I'm a Skyguard."

"A Skyguard without wings. A wizard who can open doors…"

"And you are?" Rikard cut her off.

"A woman."

"Fantastic, because I obviously don't have eyes." Rikard said drolly.

"If you would let me finish." The Bloom said. "I am the sole keeper of potential isterios in Carin." Their conversation was interrupted by the sounds of doors opening. The Radiance led the procession of wizards, royalty, and men. The queen walked beside her consort and Joven. Dorian and Grey kept together and a young boy shuffled along somewhere in between them. Bringing up the rear was an Iron Man. Aurum rose to his feet at his brothers' approach. Rikard moved up to support him, and they moved together to greet their brothers at the far side of the chamber. Galeerial hung back as they embraced, and hushed words were exchanged. Rikard looked over Aurum's shoulder and gestured to him with two fingers to approach.

"You are family now." Rikard said. Galeerial was overwhelmed with a true sense of pride…of belonging.

"Where have you been?" Joven asked Aurum.

"You would not believe me without the whole story. Tonight perhaps, over a really big bottle of wine." Aurum said with a smile.

"It will take more than one." Grey said.

"Ahem. If you are done…" The Radiance cut into their reunion.

"We will be done when we are done." Rikard said sharply.

"We can catch up later, Rikard." Joven said. "We are ready to begin. I think introductions are probably in order as there seems to be some new faces since the last time we all convened." Joven gestured for them to take seats at the round table. There was a chair for everyone and one additional that stood empty.

"Or ummm…why I am here, My Lords and Ladies? I'm just a bookkeeper." The boy spoke nervously betraying his obvious intimidation by everyone present.

"You are here, Hallen Retin, because you have great potential within you." The Bloom replied. "As does everyone standing here. You asked for introductions. I am The Bloom. I am a prime isterios who was imprisoned during the Dread War by two beings: The Wither and Frosh." Galeerial started.

"It should please you then to know that he is dead." Galeerial said. All eyes turned to him. "I fought The Wither in the ruins of Cloud Breech. I killed him with this blade." Galeerial gestured to Justice on his back. The Bloom exchanged a glance with Corrigan.

"It is certainly possible that you killed him. A Cardinal Sword is strong enough. I tell you that my joy would know no bounds to hear of his death."

"Yet you doubt the truth of it?" Galeerial asked.

"I'll believe he is dead when I see his corpse before me. I have fought him for far too long to accept anything less than that." The Bloom replied. "Corrigan?"

"I'll look into it." The Iron Man said.

"You better have a real good reason for wearing that face." Aurum's voice was ice cold and sharp as a razor as he addressed Corrigan.

"Rayn has been borrowing mine. Not the other way around." The man replied. "My name is Corrigan. I...knew your brother well. We had a working relationship. He was allowed to use my face and reputation, and, in return, I was given access to certain information." This answer didn't seem to please Aurum.

"You and I are going to have a real long discussion then, because in all the years Rayn used your supposed name, I never heard once of you.

"Perhaps, it is because you weren't meant to do so." Corrigan replied.

"Do not try and play games with me." Aurum warned. "You are a variable. I don't like variables."

"All of us here are variables." The Bloom cut in. "The people here are those who can disrupt Veriel's plans. Look around you: five magicians, a human Supreme Cleric, the first queen humanity has had in eight hundred

464

years, the leader of the Light Monks, a boy whose destiny holds the power to define our own, and an Iron Man disconnected from the Iron Giant. Each and every one of us is unique and outside of the ken of the rest of the world. We are the ones who will keep Veriel from tearing down everything that makes this world work. He tried once already, and it took better men than we to stop him. Those gathered here are the powers of this world. It is up to us to decide what we do next. Make no mistake, the entire world is the prize in this game of Crowns." Silence was exchanged by the assembled. Galeerial began to speak but was beaten to the punch by Tendra.

"I would know of the Light Monk army that never arrived to support us." Tendra asked pointedly at the Radiance. "We lost Gemport and Bicoln, and if it weren't for the intercession of Galeerial and Gabriel then we would have lost Terakeen as well."

"Cause we didn't help at all." Rikard drolly added.

"That army is the reason there was a Terakeen left to defend. The durandal are on the march." The Radiance replied.

"Durandal?" the boy asked.

"Giants." Galeerial translated. "The Wither didn't act alone at Cloud Breach. Giants marched with him there too."

"The Light Monk army has been attempting to delay their approach. There have been heavy casualties."

"When were you planning on informing the rest of us about this?" Queen Sumenel broke in. "When the durandal broke down the gates of King's Port?"

"They will not have to." Aurum said quietly. "King's Port is a mausoleum. One of the warriors of Veriel got there first. Every last soul in the city is dead." Silence rippled through the room.

"Things are worse than you know." Galeerial said.

"Things can get worse?" Rikard asked. "How delightful."

"Rikard." Dorian cut his twin off.

"The Skyguard's supply of Charist has been poisoned. I have been…conscripted by a being called Sable with a mission to save our people by finding an artifact called the Spirit of Lights. To do so, I must

465

travel beyond the Rift," Galeerial hesitated as he watched the others, "to Cambria." Startled looks were passed around the chamber. "I will need a guide though to cross the Rift and navigate through the land."

"You will not be welcomed into Cambria." Joven answered. "You will be identified immediately as an outsider and the Torrentials, the soldiers of the government; they will bring you forward for questioning. A questioning you will not survive." The wizard's voice was calm, yet apologetic, though it sounded entirely calculated.

"This isn't an optional quest. I would rather not storm through your streets with an army, but if need be every Skyguard under my command will march with me, and we will take the Spirit of Lights by force." A sliver of anger crept into his voice, but Galeerial checked it.

"We will give you whatever you require." Joven replied. "I merely wanted to impress upon you the magnitude of what you are attempting."

"I understand. The only other option then is stealth: myself and Grey slipping in undetected to acquire the artifact. Can I acquire what I seek with only having Grey as my companion?" Galeerial asked simply. The wizards looked back and forth among each other.

"It'll be tricky, but I know my way around. I can get him wherever he needs to go." Grey said.

"Do you think your marker will still work?" Dorian asked. Eyes turned to Joven.

"There is no reason for them to deactivate it. Then again, we are a unique case. You should still be able to gain access to the archives, even the ones in Iron Heights." Joven nodded.

"Do any of you know anything about the Spirit of Lights, what it looks like, where it can be found?" Galeerial asked.

"No, I have never heard of such an artifact, none of us have." Joven said. He looked to the others who gave similar signs of negativity. "If any such item existed though, it would be at the Artistry of History, or in Iron Heights, the Torrentials' base of operations. Grey was a member of the Artistry of History, which means that he should be able to gain access to the archives there. You will not, but Grey does provide you with the widest

466

range of options for finding that which you seek. A more important question than all of this is that you are the ruler of your people. If you leave, then who will lead the Skyguard?" Galeerial hadn't thought of that. He hadn't thought of a lot of things. He was no longer just a Raptor; he was the Supreme Cleric. He tried to think of someone he trusted absolutely. The list was small; the list of those still living was even smaller. There were two, and one was in no position to do anything. He needed Grey with him to acquire the Spirit. Furthermore, the Skyguard wouldn't follow a human.

"I'll speak with the High Clerics and appoint someone to act as Sentinel in my absence." Galeerial said begrudgingly. He didn't know how much he trusted any of the Clerics, but those at Soaring had expelled Veriel from their ranks. They had not joined his army when the Horn of Seruvia was sounded. The force of will that it would have taken to counter the call would have to have been immense indeed."

"Good, next?" The Bloom pushed.

"The unu and centaur forces are ready to move out under our command. I have sent the towers ahead already." Dorian gestured to himself and Rikard. "I assume the human forces are as well?" Dorian asked. The queen said nothing. "Queen Tendra, you can't run from this." Dorian said. Her eyes trailed around the room. A look of confusion came to Aurum's face.

"Humanity is not going to war?" Aurum asked.

"Humanity has already been to war." Tendra replied. "It has been to war with Skyguard and unu and telos and centaurs. Humanity has been to war."

"I was sent here by the son of Lord Supremor himself from the heart of the Dreaming Kingdom." Aurum said. "This war is being fought by mankind whether you wish it or not." Galeerial watched her closely. She was struggling with this decision. He didn't know much about the young woman, but it was obvious that she bore her burden heavily.

"It may be that we have already been fighting it without anyone knowing." Tendra said quietly. "Over the course of the last three weeks people have been dying in their sleep...by the hundreds. No apparent cause, they simply don't wake up." All eyes turned to Aurum.

"The Pillars of Creation..." Aurum said. "It all makes sense now. Everything they said to me."

"Care to enlighten us, Aurum?" The queen's consort asked.

"Veriel. This is his plan all along. That is what this war is, he is attacking the Pillars in Materia and in the Dreaming." Aurum stopped talking and smiled. "My apologies, the parameters of my world have changed much in the last few weeks. Allow me to start at the beginning. As you all know the world is divided into the Dreaming and Materia. At the center of the Dreaming is Merhelden, the great city of the son of Supremor. It is held aloft by the strength of eight hundred bloodlines throughout Carin. When a bloodline dies, the Pillar falls. Veriel has been destroying them in Carin and his Champion in the Dreaming. That is why people have been dying in their sleep. Because Veriel is killing them in the Dreaming."

"How do we stop it?" The Queen asked.

"In the Dreaming? I do not know. I will find out though. In Carin, we stop Veriel." Aurum said.

"These Pillars as you called them, what happens when they all fall?" Grey asked.

"Merhelden falls."

"Which means what exactly?" Grey asked. No one had an answer. "Another question for you to take to your new friends, Aurum." The Champion nodded.

"Which brings us back to the question." Galeerial said. "Will mankind stand with us, or will you stand alone?"

"In the wake of the devastation wrought by your peoples," her eyes shifted between Galeerial and Dorian, "we are struggling just to keep our people fed. You may have access to vast stores and resupply from Kana, but we had to abandon much of our supplies in Gemport when we evacuated. We sent ships to try and scavenge anything that you didn't burn. The first ships should be arriving tomorrow with some of those cached stores." She said.

"That's still not an answer." Joven said. Galeerial simply waited in silence as she stalled. She was justifying it all in her mind. She had to believe it was not just the only thing that she could do, but that it was the right thing to do.

"The soonest we can move out is next week." It was like a collective exhale filled the room. Her lips pursed into a thin line as she waited for their attention to return to her. "We can use the ships that Jeric acquired from King's Port to move a good portion of the army into position there before advancing north to Mesnir and beyond to wherever Veriel's army is stationed. I am concerned about King's Port though. Communication with them has been nonexistent for the last few days."

"That is because King's Port houses naught but the dead." Aurum said. "Every man, woman and child was slaughtered. Before I arrived here with The Bloom, I fought one of the lieutenants of Veriel in King's Port. By the time I arrived, everyone was already dead." Silence filled the room. Rikard laughed. Everyone stared at him.

"Don't all of you see? It is like your god is building two piles of sand. Galeerial defeats The Wither, but at the cost of Cloud Breach being destroyed. Humanity says it will march with us, only to find out that one of their main cities is massacred. It truly is enough to make one believe in the unu's balance." Rikard finished with a chuckle.

"I'm glad you are so amused by the slaughter of thousands." The queen said bitterly.

"Better to be amused than distraught. It's a sunk cost. Nothing you can do about the dead any more. Now, let's talk about this." Rikard pulled out Forlorn and set it on the table, "and how we can use it to kill Veriel."

"That blade shouldn't be here." Galeerial's voice was hard. "How is it here? It belongs in the Dreaming." Confusion laced his words. "That is one of the Forsaken Weapons. How is it here? It should not be here. It shouldn't have been able to cross the Divide. How can it be here?" He looked at Aurum. "Aurum?" The Champion was at a loss.

"I know of the Forsaken Weapons, but I didn't realize this was one of them. Axios doesn't feel like I thought it would." Aurum said.

469

"The Divide between both worlds is weakening." Corrigan spoke up for the first time since Aurum's confrontation with him. "There is an eighty-four percent chance that the Divide between the Dreaming and Materia will collapse should all the Pillars fall. No one can be sure, but it was heavily speculated to be so by Corug and other members of the Legion of Light. They believed that to be what Veriel fought for in the Dread War, and there is no reason to that that his motivations have changed now."

"So Veriel is the Dread?" Queen Tendra asked.

"Yes," The Radiance spoke up before anyone else. A quick glance occurred between her and Corrigan. Galeerial almost missed it; she was hiding something.

"I still don't understand. I saw this sword hurt Veriel. If Veriel is an agent of Midox, then why would a sword using his own magic hurt him?" Dorian inquired.

"That sword is poison." Galeerial spat out. All eyes turned to him. "The Forsaken Weapons work as the Cardinal Swords do. Four blades were forged from the void beyond the Dreaming: Forlorn, Sword of Suffering, Tempest, Sword of Savagery, Blaze, Sword of Malice, Abyss, Sword of the Void. Those swords were never supposed to enter the real world, just as Supremor's swords are never meant to enter the Dreaming. It's a balance of power, but now that scale has been tipped in axios' favor. You would do well to bury that sword far away from everything, The Rift perhaps." Galeerial's voice rang through the chamber. The Bloom and Corrigan were the only two whose faces remained emotionless.

"It still doesn't answer the question as to why it hurt Veriel." Rikard asked.

"The blade had to be forged with a vein of elixis within it otherwise it couldn't exist as a freestanding artifact within the Dreaming; it would have to be tied to a belicos, an individual's specific dream state. I would speculate that when it was being used by Aurum, as he is the Champion of Supremor, he amplified that shred of elixis until it overcame the axios of the blade." Corrigan said.

"Can it kill him?" Rikard asked.

470

"Maybe, or the concentrated axios could make him stronger. There is a seventy one percent chance that it will augment his own power and make him stronger, a fourteen percent chance it will kill him, and a fifteen percent chance of neither outcome." Corrigan replied.

"How do you know all of this?" Galeerial asked.

"That is not what we should be worried about." The Bloom interjected. "If one of those swords has fallen through into Materia, then it means that Veriel is only the beginning, and things are about to get much worse. He needs to be stopped quickly, which means we have but a single recourse. I will reignite the Drowned Flame at the heart of Illuvium. Then we will take the fight to Veriel." *The Drowned Flame? The Iron Men had asked them about the same thing.*

"The Drowned Flame?" Grey inquired.

"She's talking about the Heart of Fires." Joven entered into the conversation. Tendra started, and Galeerial's eyes widened. "The Light Monks have had it, or a piece of it, for almost a thousand years I would imagine. Since the Tolomin dissolved at least, maybe before that."

"For an outsider, you know much about the secret history of the land." Corrigan's voice was harsh yet even.

"That's how you used magic." Rikard said. "Gabriel too?"

"Not..." The Radiance looked to The Bloom before proceeding. The Bloom nodded her assent. "Not precisely. We have half; a half whose magic has been inert since the sealing of The Bloom in the middle of the Dread War. The other half lies in Daggerfall with the gallowglass. Gabriel, I and six others broke into Daggerfall to try and reacquire the other half. We failed, but three of us managed to touch it, and escape with our lives."

"Who were the others?" Galeerial asked.

"They are all dead." The Radiance replied quickly. Silence descended upon them.

"Then it is settled, the Drowned Flame will burn again." The Bloom said. "Galeerial will take Grey across the Rift and recover the Spirit of Lights. As for the rest of us, we march now to a war that must be won."

471

A Time for Reckoning

Thirty-Five

"Did all of you know?" Galeerial asked pointedly. He stood with the icy winter wind whipping through his heavy cloaks. His bones themselves were chilled, but he refused to allow any sign of pain or weakness to creep into his demeanor. Assembled behind him were the High Clerics of Soaring and Winter Crest, who had arrived as per Galeerial's order just that morning. In addition, there was Sevitel Starglass the Lord Commander of Winter Crest. The powerful Skyguard had abandoned his post when the sun turned black. He had given his Cardinal Sword, Iris, to Gabriel, and it was now lost. It had been the right thing to do, despite Galeerial's order to remain guarding the Clerics. He needed more men like that: who would think and not blindly follow. It was by his actions that the sun was no longer engulfed in shadow.

Galeerial looked down from the top of the Star Tower. It was poetic, he supposed, that this was where they met, but Galeerial just wanted to see everyone down below. He wanted to see all the people who were going to die. He didn't look at the assembled and instead stared south out at the city, and the sea beyond that, and the Rift Mountains beyond that, and the Rift beyond even that. Those mountains and the Rift surrounded the entirety of Carin...like a prison. "Did you all know who Veriel was?"

"Yes." Cleric Rayner of Soaring replied. He looked remarkably similar to Gabriel, which fit due to him being his brother. "Not at first. He came to our Cathedral, a couple hundred years after the Dread War, wearing the skin of a Skyguard. We knew immediately that he wasn't one of us, of course, though we welcomed him as if he were. We were curious, I suppose. The Dread had maintained his constant form for the entirety of the war, so we knew nothing of his ability to steal skins. About a week later, I was granted an audience with Lord Alizar. I knew Veriel was evil. He has a taint to him that made me sick, though I have always had an overly perceptive Aer. Lord Alizar commanded patience. I waited three days before forcing him out."

"Lord Alizar said nothing else?" Galeerial asked. Rayner shook his head.

"At least not to me."

"And you?" Galeerial nodded to the Clerics from Winter Crest.

"We don't know why, but when one becomes a High Cleric of Winter Crest their connections to the Dreaming merge together. It gives us glimpses into the future, and it is why we speak together. Perhaps it has something to do with Horizon being destroyed, but since the Dread destroyed the Tower of the Skyguard, the joining process has occurred. When he arrived, our dreams grew troubled. Every pathway was rife with casualties. The path we chose was an effort to minimize casualties and collateral damage." They replied together.

"Minimize casualties." Galeerial mused. "Every single Skyguard dead is on your hands."

"You have no idea what the other pathways showed us." They retaliated angrily. "Ten thousand dead? At most? A pittance. There were paths that lead to the extinction of all life in Carin."

"We still have a war to fight."

"A war we have a chance of winning!" they proclaimed. "We have the Seven, the Five Eye is awakened, and The Bloom has been found. There is a new Champion. We have a chance now."

"And the Skyguard are a step away from extinction. The Charist has been poisoned in all three Cathedrals. The well itself has been corrupted. The Five Eye," Galeerial pulled off the glove that he had been wearing over his left hand to unveil the metal sheath upon his hand and forearm. He held it up so that they could see the Five Eye on the back of his hand "has somehow been bound to my hand by The Bloom's touch. I can't take it off. Gabriel recovered the sun but at the cost of two of the Cardinal Swords." A deep silence spread through the Clerics. No one but him had known that all the fountains were bereft of Charist. Their meager stores were not enough. Galeerial had less than a two weeks, three at the most, to find the Spirit of Lights within Cambria. If it was truly even there.

"So that is it then? I refuse to accept that." Cleric Rayner replied. A grim grin threatened the corner of Galeerial's mouth.

"The prophecies o-" Cleric Tevorin began.

"I do not care what the prophecies say." Rayner continued. "I will not go quietly into this night. Supremor would not so abandon us." Galeerial snorted which brought forth startled looks of displeasure.

"Supremor will not save us, but perhaps I can."

"Oh?" Cleric Apel asked. "Since when, human, did you grow more powerful than a god?" Galeerial ignored the admonishing tone.

"What do you know about the Spirit of Lights?" Galeerial asked the gem on his hand glowed a soft white. Cleric Rayner greeted him with a blank stare, but one of the other clerics spoke up.

"It is an old legend. It talked about how when the Heart of Fires was born the Spirit of Lights was born to accompany it. It was said that it was a pure representation of the spiritual resolve of the people of Carin, and of the Skyguard specifically. It was said to have been forged from the elixis." Cleric Tevorin answered. "Legends of its whereabouts have been all but nonexistent for centuries." He continued.

"You think it is real?" Cleric Apel asked.

"Not only do I think it is real, I think I know where to find it." Galeerial answered, "and I think it could be the salvation of our people."

"You are leaving us." Cleric Rayner inferred.

"Yes." Galeerial replied. "I was approached by a being who calls himself Sable." No recognition lit up the faces of those assembled. Galeerial grimaced. It had been too much to hope for he knew, but regardless…he had hoped. "He gave me this key." Galeerial withdrew the Skeleton Key. "It opens any door to anywhere that I want to go…instantaneous travel." Cleric Eli murmured something incoherent, and the clerics of Winter Crest got a glazed over look in their eyes. "He's the one who told me where to go searching for the Spirit of Lights, namely Cambria, the land of the wizards." Galeerial gestured with his eyes to where Grey sat behind them with his back to them. "Grey has agreed to take me there, but I need someone to act in my place. I need a Sentinel." The clerics exchanged glances.

"It is a mission of fools to cross the Rift and further deny us the power of the Five Eye. Can no one else go?" Cleric Apel inquired.

"No one else would be able to identify the artifact. Watch." Galeerial held up the Five Eye. "Spirit of Lights," he said. The Five Eye gemstone hummed, and a hard light ignited in the corner of the stone. Galeerial turned until he was facing northwest, at which point the light stopped its motion around the outsides of the gemstone. "It's a compass. Whatever the Spirit of Lights is, it is not just real but it is powerful enough that the Five Eye can sense it across the Rift. Not only that, but Grey has informed me that Skyguard don't exist in Cambria." Rayner flinched at Galeerial's words. Galeerial hadn't really thought about it too much, but the idea that in another land not only was your species extinct but had never existed in the first place was a hard glass to drink. He saw Aurum land shakily near where Grey sat. He was still unstable on his legs. "It has to be me; so I need someone to take my place, and the eleven of you are probably the most knowledgeable beings on the planet. I need counseling. I want to take you all to meet Sable to speak with him and to determine if his motives are genuine. The Five Eye goes a dull gray when I am near him; so it offers no insight. Ruin and Grey will accompany us." The Clerics turned around to see Aurum standing wreathed lightly in orange fire. "When we reach Sable's…lair, don't provoke him. When I first met him, he took the form of a gray dragon, and his skin shifted into that of almost a human. Do not underestimate him." Galeerial let his words sink in for a moment. "Let's go."

Galeerial pushed through the throng of Skyguard back to where Grey was scrambling to his feet, and Aurum was looking at him approvingly.

"Leadership suits you, Galeerial." Aurum said softly, with a small smile at the corner of his lips.

"I disagree," Galeerial replied, "but we do what we must. How is your back?" Aurum tilted his hand back and forth indicating it was more or less fine. One floor down was a weapons' locker that had a door on it where he could use the key. The clerics and Grey followed silently behind the two of them.

"I have to maintain a constant flow of elixis to it, which is difficult. When I woke up this morning, I could not move my legs. It was…terrifying, but as long as I maintain a flow, it seems to be fine. The Bloom has examined me again and so did Rikard. In Cambria, he was a member of what we called the Artistry of the Flesh. He knows bones and muscles. He said everything is more or less healed, but my mind cannot reconcile the disparity between what it knows happened and what exists. Rikard said all it takes is time." Galeerial nodded.

"Good, the coming days will be difficult, you will need men like your brothers."

"You are one of those brothers. Though I would imagine you are far far older than the fifty one years that I have seen."

"I don't know how many years I have seen. To immortals like us, what use is there for age?" Galeerial said.

"A fair point indeed. Though the question then is, are you immortal still?" It was an interesting question and not something Galeerial had considered. He enjoyed speaking with Aurum. There was almost a sense of balance to their interactions. The first time they met, Aurum had saved him, and then he had paid back the debt. Now, they walked side by side. "I must confess that I am not entirely sure why I am here, Galeerial."

"You're here because if I have to kill Sable, then I want someone who knows how to fight. Besides, as of this moment you are the most powerful magical being in the world, and you are Lord Alizar's representative here. Would you like me to continue?" Galeerial asked wryly. Aurum smiled gingerly.

"No, I think I get the picture."

"Good, because we're here." Galeerial inserted the key into the door and focused on the cavern sanctum of Sable. He focused on the Aer river, and the gray dragon. He turned the key and pulled the door open to reveal the flickering of twin torches illuminating only a narrow band of area surrounding the doorway. This was the place. Galeerial led the way, striding boldly into the chamber with Aurum, Grey and Rayner only a step behind him. As the last Cleric entered into the chamber the door swung shut and the torches went out. To their credit, nobody made a single sound at the abrupt shift into darkness. The soft glow of the Aer quickly faded into view as their eyes adjusted to the dark.

Blue eyes sprung to life, like fires in the gloom, as Galeerial became aware of Sable's presence. The blue light from his eyes seemed to seep out into the world as it slowly grew brighter and brighter until it settled into a comfortable glow. The Clerics stood assembled in a phalanx behind him as Galeerial formed the tip of a spear comprised of himself, Grey, Aurum, and Rayner.

"Are you here to kill me?" Sable asked. His hard, but even, voice echoed in the grand cavern. He was in his human form, and his serpentine tail flicked along the ground behind him.

477

"No. We're here, because I don't trust you, and I am not about to abandon Carin to go searching through another world for something that may not exist." Galeerial replied. "Consider them my advisors."

"And why, pray tell, would I tell them anything? Or you anything more than I already have? You insolent worm." A hard slice of wrath permeated his words. A shiver raced up Galeerial's spine as the fire in Sable's eyes flared into life. "I have given you knowledge, opportunity, and means. Armed with these three things, nothing is beyond your grasp. This is my domain. I can destroy even you, Ruin." Sable tilted his head, and Galeerial turned back to look at Aurum whose breath came in shallow ragged gasps.

"I can't...I can't touch the elixis." His brow furled in desperation. "I can't feel my legs." Grey leapt forward and grabbed Aurum as he collapsed towards the floor. A half dozen swords cleared steel as Aurum staggered into Grey's arms. The elixis had been holding his spine together in his mind. Now, it was gone. *This is bad. This is very bad. This is so very bad.*

"What did you do?" Galeerial asked evenly. Sable shook his head.

"You are so like a child, begging to play with the adults. Your knowledge is so limited. There is so much for you to learn; yet, you bind yourself to old decayed ways. You can never learn everything as long as your mind is surrounded by closed doors. Your friend can't touch the elixis because his body is protecting him from being overloaded by the presence of so much Aer. Aer is simply another manifestation of elixis." Sable turned to the Clerics. "And you? Galeerial came seeking validation. What are you here for false prophets?"

"The truth." The Clerics of Winter Crest echoed in unison. "We see the pathways of time and fate. You will reveal yourself to us, Sable."

"Fools, Galeerial. You surround yourself with fools." Sable berated him. Galeerial looked the dragon straight in the eyes.

"Who are you to be so unwavering in your confidence?" Cleric Rayner stepped in before Galeerial could answer. Sable turned to stare at the cleric. "You are not among paupers and servants. You are not among

478

children. We are Clerics of the Skyguard, and he is the Ruin of Lord Alizar. We are not lightly dismissed nor disregarded. Yet you do both. You have no fear. What are you?" Sable inclined his head.

"Well it seems that there is some wisdom among you after all. I'm of something higher, and this," he gestured outwards with both arms, "is my domain. Not all of us have as lofty of palaces as Merhelden, but we all serve our purpose. I don't meddle often in the mortal world, but in him," he gestured to Galeerial, "there is great potential. I believe in that potential." Sable finished. Galeerial watched his face. He had never been good at reading people.

"He's not lying." Grey said. "Though that doesn't necessarily mean that he is telling the truth." Grey approached Sable, leaving Aurum upon the ground. "What's your name?" He asked. The wizard inspected Sable's eyes and body as he spoke.

"I'm called Sable." He replied. "But you already knew that."

"What color are your eyes?" Grey continued.

"Blue." he replied again.

"Where are we?" Galeerial watched closely as Grey sauntered closer and closer.

"My domain."

"Why are you helping us?" Grey asked.

"I'm not." Sable replied. "I'm helping him." Sable gestured with a finger to Galeerial. *What is he doing?*

"Again, why?"

"Because the destruction of the Skyguard is not something that I want to see. And because Galeerial has the potential to be a valuable asset to the future."

"What future?" At this Sable's rigid gaze broke.

"Now, you are asking the right questions. A future in which I won't be bound to this domain. I know my place, but I dream of a greater life. A greater destiny. Is that wrong wizard?"

479

"No." Grey turned back to Galeerial. "He's not lying, or else he is lying about everything. Nothing has changed about his manner." Grey shrugged. "Take that for what you will."

"We see nothing about this being's future path." The clerics of Winter Crest replied. Galeerial looked from the clerics back to Sable.

"Satisfied, Galeerial?" Sable asked. "Or would you like to waste more time. You will find no friends in Cambria." At this Grey stiffened and turned slowly back to Sable.

"What do you know of Cambria?" Grey asked slowly. Sable looked at the wizard.

"I live at the source of the Aer: the same Aer that is in you, and Galeerial, and every living being in this entire world. I am connected to all of them through this place. Cambria, Carin, I know them all. Only icy death awaits you in Cambria. You and your wizard will need all the time you can muster if you are to return before angels rain from the skies." Silence stretched out between them as they stared each other down. "What are you waiting for?" Sable asked. Galeerial crossed the gap between them in three strides, and his right fist slammed into Sable's jaw. Sable didn't react to the blow at all.

"If you lay another hand on me, everyone here will die." Sable said calmly. Galeerial believed what Sable said to be true.

"If I find out that you are playing me, then I will tear you apart: piece by bloody piece. I will see the fear in your eyes before I kill you. Do you understand me?"

"Perfectly." Sable replied.

"Then we're done here." Galeerial turned on his heel and led the way back out of Sable's realm.

"We aren't done. Not even close." Sable's words echoed in the chamber long after Galeerial, and his companions had left.

Fear The Reaper
Thirty-Six

Rikard sat upon the floor in his room within the city of Terakeen. He and Dorian were clothed in full armor. Tomorrow morning the first ships set sail northwards. Rikard had already picked out his vessel, the *Emerald Twilight*. Its crew was strong, and they knew him from long ago. They would depart at first light, but Rikard had work that needed to be done first: work that began with the blade that sat in front of him. The eyes of Forlorn bore into him, but Rikard refused to back down. There was something about this sword. It was one of the blades of Midox, but it was more than just steel. It had called to him on the battlefield. It had called to him and no other. The blade had chosen him for a reason, and Rikard wanted to know what it was. That meant fighting on an entirely different battlefield.

He had found Galeerial earlier and spoken with him about the blade. He knew that he needed to fight this if he was going to be able to use this sword. He didn't understand the magic behind it all, but Galeerial had told him what he needed to do.

Don't be afraid.

Rikard's eyes focused on the sword.

"I have no fear." He replied calmly. He turned to Dorian who sat in silence beside him. "Are you ready?" Dorian nodded. Rikard wasn't sure what was going to happen, but since the moment he had picked up the blade, Forlorn had been pulling at him, as if the blade was trying to rip his mind away from his body. Rikard was going to surrender to that pull and find out just what exactly this blade was.

"I don't need to remind you that this course of action is unwise." Dorian counseled.

"We have been given the weapon of the enemy. It would be the height of foolishness to reject it." Rikard replied. "Besides, you ignored me when I counseled you about your wife; so indulge my own pursuit of stupidity." Dorian didn't reply, but a glimmer of a smile tugged at the corners of his lips.

"Well, Breva didn't turn out too bad; so maybe there is some hope in this after all." *Debatable on the first part.* Rikard said nothing. He was focused now. He stilled his mind and focused on simply letting go. This was a gamble. Rikard knew it, but he didn't have a choice. He needed to be better in every way. This was the start of it. Rikard reached out and grasped the claws of the wolf that adorned the hilt, and instantly, he felt the slow pull on his mind. It was like a gentle ocean tide beckoning and slowly weaning him out of his own mind and into some foreign darkness that he couldn't quite perceive. He relaxed his mind even farther, slowly but surely giving himself up to the pull.

Rikard tasted the blood from his tongue as the stream suddenly clawed at his mind ripping him forth. His every muscle screamed and cramped at once, and then he was gone.

Rikard couldn't feel anything tangible anymore. It was like the first time he had dreamed upon arriving to Carin. People didn't dream in

Cambria. He felt that same disconnected feeling lingered around him. It didn't last.

He screamed as his arms were ripped from their sockets, and he was hurled into invisible walls. The world went black, and he couldn't see anything. Still he wasn't afraid. His father had killed his fear, but he was in such pain; his mind burned to embers.

His back was twisted and cracked while he felt his mind slowly being shredded. His every memory was pulled out from him and shown before his eyes before being ripped away. Rikard bit through his tongue to avoid screaming again. He was Rikard Karandash, and Karandash was his creed. He was no-

"ARGH!" The bellow of pain hurled from his lips as his skin began to be pulled from his legs and torso one strip at a time. Barbed needles jabbed into his eyelids and ripped out chunks of flesh while he was flayed alive. Boiling blood began to pour down into his throat. He gagged, but it kept flooding his lungs. He couldn't breathe. He couldn't move.

Beg me for mercy human. The voice echoed in the chamber, and it ripped Rikard from his pain-filled mind. The daze of shock and pain had rendered his every thought black, but the voice gave him what he needed. It gave him a point, something to focus on as he struggled to breathe, but as he retched up his stomach, he forced it back down. He would not bow. He would not beg. He would win. Blood continued to pour down his throat, but he fought his lungs from hurling it up.

Hair was ripped from his eyelashes and chest. Hot coals jabbed into his eyes rendering him blind. His arms lay in front of him as he was forced to his knees by a blow that threatened to shatter his spine. The blood stopped flowing and instead a frozen arrowhead was jabbed down his throat and ripped back up.

Rikard couldn't focus on a single thought. Every time he came close a new torture would rip his ability to reason away. There was nothing to fight. He had no arms. He looked down dumbly at his ripped off limbs. Ants began to crawl all over his body, and they bit into his exposed flesh. Rikard howled in pain.

Rikard threw his mind away, but he had no memories with which to escape. All he had was that dark void in front of him. He hadn't blacked out, because he had nowhere to go. He had the void. He threw his mind into it: into the darkness. His body wasn't getting ripped to shreds by tiny wires ripping through his flesh, and his toes weren't being chewed through by locusts. Boils erupted on his skin, but he focused on the one image that he could never forget: the black. He focused on it, and the pain was something to be seen rather than felt.

He smiled. He had won.

Color exploded into a swirl of instantly changing flashes of white and yellow and pink that made him sick even as the smell of burning fat entered his nostrils. His stomach refused to obey his commands this time as he lost control of the black and collapsed back into the pain. The world swirled. Rikard squeezed his eyelids shut, but they were ripped off. The spinning explosion of colors sent his mind into free fall over and over again. A screeching sound tore into his ears: the sound of children screaming in pain. Bile filled his throat.

Every sense was torn into like a never-ending hurricane of disgust. Rikard desperately searched for some sense in the chaos, but he found nothing. He was drowning in a tempest of perception. There was nothing to focus any of his senses on; so he abandoned them. He instead grasped the pain, every burning and freezing, and tearing, and ripping, and screeching, every disgusting bit of it. The pain became his constant. It kept switching; yet the pain was always there in some form or another. He embraced it.

This was his victory.

The pain became like sunlight to a tree. It nourished him, and it gave him the constant he needed. He felt something change. Whatever, whoever was causing all this knew he was slipping out of the noose. The tortures became desperate as they tried to break his focus. His genitals were ripped off, and his ears flooded with the sound of screeching steel. The most noxious smells led him to vomit once again. His stomach clenched as the world spun. He sensed...something was coming. Then his mind buckled as the next assault hit.

484

The physical pain evaporated, and Rikard felt his body collapse to the floor. But he wasn't worried about that. He was focused on the next assault.

His shield of pain buckled and cracked as the strain of oppression, loneliness, despair, rage, shame, abandonment, paranoia, betrayal, insignificance, mockery and a hundred other emotions broke against him like a tsunami. It dragged him down, threatening to engulf him, until he found the one emotion that gave him strength: fear. He laughed at it. Those others bashed his wall of pain like drums, but this creature tried to use fear against him.

Rikard laughed. Fear was his conduit, and the creature reached to try and rip it away, but the damage had been done. Rikard used the fear to siphon away the rest of the attack and reinforce his shields once again.

Rikard tried to speak, to taunt his foe in some way, but his throat had been scoured, and he couldn't utter even the slightest of sounds. Instead he breathed. That first breath broke the rest of the spell, and Rikard felt a rush as the whole world went blank for a moment before he found himself on his knees in the darkness. He looked up and saw an azure beating heart enshrined in light before him.

Rikard staggered to his feet. With every step forward towards his goal, his wounds began to sew themselves back together. His eyelids grew back, and strips of flesh wove themselves back onto his legs and torso. Burns cooled and blackened skin regained its hue. His raw throat grew numb and then refreshed once again. Step after ragged step brought him closer and closer as tendons, bones, joints, muscles and veins grew back into his arms. Rikard winced, but kept his feet moving. Step after step, he moved closer and closer.

Closer and closer.

Closer and closer.

Until finally, he stood before the beating heart. This was what he had come for. This was his goal. His newly formed hand shot out and grabbed it in his hands.

You have proven yourself worthy. Rikard glared at the heart.

"This is now mine. If you want it back, then you will work for me. Is that understood?" Rikard asked.

"Perfectly, Sufferer." Rikard turned around to behold a flaming skull of a wolf with burning eyes. It hovered in mid-air at eye level and stared at him. It looked just like the hilt of Forlorn. Rikard tilted his head in the realization that he could think again. He looked down and saw his arms in front of him, and his body was back to what he knew it to look like. He didn't dwell on it. He turned to stare at his captor.

"Sufferer," a voice snarled from the depths of the skull.

"And you are what exactly?" Rikard replied.

"I could tell you, or I could show you." The skull moved forward until it was just a foot away, and Rikard found his eyes locked into the skull's own.

Rikard's mind exploded in a flicker of images. He saw a city so immense and majestic he could barely comprehend its scope. He saw the pillars that held it aloft rotting and crumbling one by one. He saw a large black infinite expanse that separated the city, and Carin begin to crack. He saw an army covered in darkness approaching the city, and a horned figure's hands curl around the neck of a shining warrior. A thousand images a second flickered through his brain before his eyes were released. Rikard flinched.

"You are a soul from the Dreaming." Rikard reasoned.

"I am. I and my brothers chose to be bound to these weapons by the being Frosh when the world was young." Rikard let no glimmer of recognition play out on his face.

"What did I just see?" Rikard asked.

"The Divide is breaking. The Shroud is on the move, and they lust for Merhelden and cursed Alizar's head on a pike. Veriel's Champion has awakened, and he searches for this blade. My soul was never meant to be forced into Materia. It was made for the Dreaming. The gaps grow wide indeed." The skull answered. Rikard grew silent for a moment.

"You fight for me now," said Rikard. The skull's jaw seemed to widen in a smile. "You kill whom I say, when I say it. Or I will snuff out your soul." The burning skull didn't even bother questioning the threat. "And my mind is my own. If you reach for it again, I will end you." The flame grew slightly diminished. "Now, set me free."

"Yessss. Free." The skull opened, and a gout of flame erupted from it billowing out. Rikard felt himself get thrown from the sword and back into his own mind. He looked up to see Dorian screaming at him. He looked down to see naught but empty air. Dorian held onto him desperately by a single hand.

"RIKARD!" He bellowed. Rikard glanced furtively around as the winter wind whipped past him. He was hanging from the balcony by his right arm which burned in pain. Rikard pulled himself up enough to grab the ledge with his left hand as Dorian hauled him up.

"By the Balance, Rikard. What just happened?" Dorian breathed as he collapsed to the ground. Rikard looked at his twin brother. The room was a wreck. The bed had been moved three feet, the dresser was in splinters upon the ground, and the cherry wood of the floor had been burned black.

"We need to talk to Aurum immediately." Rikard replied. He threw himself to his feet and grabbed Dorian's hand to help him up.

"That didn't answer my question." Rikard saw Forlorn still sitting on the floor, and he hooked it with his foot and tossed it up to his hand. As he grabbed the hilt he felt it hum in his mind, but the clawing was gone. He smiled in satisfaction as he sheathed it on his back.

"Just follow me." Rikard started to run as his mind sorted through what he had seen. If he was right then they needed to kill Veriel right now, for they were already out of time. Rikard sprinted through the hallway towards Aurum's room. Two pounds on the door brought Rikard face to face with his brother rubbing the sleep from his eyes.

"Rikard?" Aurum asked.

"Aurum." Rikard replied. He worked to formulate the words in his mind. "Whatever you had planned, it doesn't matter anymore."

"Rikard what are you talking about?" Aurum stepped back to let them in as he shook his head to finish clearing away the night's burden.

487

"Aurum, we need to hit Veriel right now. Me, you, Dorian, Galeerial, and The Bloom." Rikard's words trailed off as he saw The Bloom standing in the center of the room. Rikard turned and stared at Aurum before shrugging. What he did was his business. "Dorian and I need the edge the Heart of Fires can give us, and then we need to go after Veriel right now."

"Why? What happened, Rikard?"

"I…" Rikard struggled for the right word. "I entered the sword, and I saw things. They are all still a bit of a jumble in my head, but I do know that Veriel has more planned than we could possibly have realized. His army here in Carin is just a cover for his real army which is even now attacking that city you told us about, where you got your powers. I saw it, and it was under attack."

"Merhelden?" Aurum and The Bloom exchanged a glance as Rikard nodded.

"What do you mean you entered the sword?" The Bloom asked.

"When I held it, I could feel something tugging at my mind. I resisted, of course, but tonight I embraced it, and after a…struggle I conquered it."

"It was Paschen that showed you these things?" The Bloom asked.

"Paschen?" Rikard questioned.

"The burning soul of the wolf," The Bloom replied.

"Then yes." Rikard replied. "We use Galeerial's key to get to Illuvium. You will activate the Heart of Fires. Then, we blaze a trail of bodies north until we find Veriel." Rikard finished. Aurum nodded.

"That won't work." The Bloom cut in. Everyone turned to look at her.

"Which part?" Dorian asked.

"The part with the Heart of Fires." The Bloom replied. "The magic is too concentrated. That's why the Light Monks have to pass through Thanatos as part of their trials. It prepares the mind and body for the process. Everything fits together. Not to mention that you already have

488

Cambrian isterios. I don't know what would happen if you acquired a second."

"There is another option." Aurum said quietly as he strapped on his boots. "Lord Alizar. I can take you and Dorian to Acheron right now. He will find a way to activate the elixis within you. And then we could investigate that army. Time flows differently there. Months there are mere days in Materia." The Bloom nodded.

"It could work. I will leave tomorrow for Illuvium. Word has already been sent out recalling every Light Monk who has walked the Shaded Path to Illuvium. In three days time, an army of magic users will descend upon Veriel's army. With warriors such as you leading the rest of the world, no matter the force Veriel has assembled, there will be no standing against us." The Bloom replied.

"How long will it take to convince Alizar to help us?" Dorian asked.

"I was there for the better part of a year as time ran in the Dreaming training before I left and barely a week had passed in the real world. Time in a dream is vast." Aurum said with a shrug. "I also still need a new sword." Aurum said.

"I'm sure I could find Break out in the weapons gathered in the plaza." Rikard offered.

"I have a better idea." The Bloom smiled. "You take Rikard, Dorian and Joven to Acheron to feel the elixis, and I will take the Light Monks to Illuvium. After that, we will go to the redoubt. It is where Frosh spent his days working a forge on Parad. There are thousands of weapons there forged by his hand. We can arm the entire army with weapons of the finest caliber." The Bloom mentioned.

"Good." Aurum rose from his chair. "Gentlemen, are you ready to go?"

"I'm not going." Dorian's voice caused Rikard to turn back to his twin.

"Excuse me?" Rikard said.

489

"I can't leave our people. They cannot be left leaderless. Terel will step up to command, and then we will be back where we started. Tendra needs someone with her, and Joven may be our brother, but he's been keeping things from us. Soon we will need to have a reckoning with him. But now you two should go. The Five Pillars will move the armies northward for a rendezvous with the Light Monk army near Visir. We will be there, with all the strength of Carin behind us."

"We have a chance." Rikard was frustrated. "We have a chance right now to end Veriel for what he has done. We leave now, and we can end this in less than a week. You would trade that because you don't trust your people to be autonomous for a few days?"

"It's not a matter of trust Rikard; it is a matter of knowing the nature of the unu."

"That's right because you are one of them now. You are Dorian of the Thousand Hammers now." Rikard replied with a bitterness to his voice.

"How dare you?" Dorian shot back. Aurum and The Bloom had stepped back from them. "Why don't you say what is really bothering you Rikard?"

"You gave in!" Rikard veritably screamed it in Dorian's face. "You gave in. You know what the Orrery said, and still you gave in." Dorian set his jaw.

"I knew the risks when I took this job, and I have dedicated everything just as we all have to it. I killed my own surrogate father for it. Everything is on the altar for this. That was our agreement, and I have held to it."

"You damned me, and then abandoned me, Dorian." Rikard replied. "I guess it was too much to hope that you wouldn't do so again. Aurum, let's go." Rikard pushed past his brother's shoulder and into the hallway. He moved quickly and confidently to the balcony. Aurum was just a few paces behind.

"Do you want to tell me what that was all about?" Aurum asked.

"No. I want you to fly." Rikard stepped up onto the railing and into the night air before stepping off and plummeting downwards. The cold air

490

calmed him as he fell two stories before he felt Aurum's arms grab him under the armpits like two hooks and go streaking into the air.

"Rikard, I know…I know I have not been around for awhile, and even before we all came together at Sterin's Throne I maintained my distance from you all. But you have changed the most. I noticed it a little bit at the start of all this, but recently just watching you, you are different, callous, uncaring. What happened to you?" Aurum asked.

"Rayn got his head chopped off, and I'm sorry if I'm the only one of us who thinks that Veriel should get cut into little tiny pieces for that." Rikard replied.

"That's not everything, and we are all upset about Rayn. He was the best of us." Rikard nodded in agreement. "What happened with you and Dorian?" Aurum prodded. Rikard didn't say anything, but his thoughts ran back to Cambria, and to the Orrery of Words.

"What did the Orrery tell you Aurum?" Rikard asked. Aurum licked his lips. It was a very personal question. It was something that no one really talked about save for spouses and sometimes fathers to children.

"It told me that my heart's desire would be taken from me, and that I would be the ruin of the world." Silence was carried on the wind as they flew. "Among many other things, I never knew what the second piece of that meant, and it terrified me. I held the weight of the Orrery's words upon my shoulders for years and years. I was so scared that I would do something that would destroy the world. I was an architect; I designed things that thousands of people lived in, worked in, walked through. Every one of them I scrutinized to every detail so scared was I that one would fall apart killing everyone within. Not any more though. I don't know how, but the Orrery knew. It knew about all of this. Ruin is what and who I am now. I am Ruin. That is the name given to me by someone far greater than you or I."

"And you have just blindly given yourself over to this god's plan?" Rikard asked incredulously.

"Not at all, but…I saw Andusíl." Aurum said quietly, "and Hope." Rikard looked up curiously. "I know it sounds crazy, but I saw them and spoke with them, as I speak to you now. Rikard there is something past this

491

life, and I'll be damned if I go anywhere but to be with them. When you go to see Lord Alizar, perhaps you will get to see father." Rikard considered this for a moment. To see Rerem again, Rikard had never thought about what he would say to his father if he were to meet him in another life. Those kinds of things were not what he wasted time thinking about.

"This isn't a world I understand, Aurum." Rikard admitted. "What you can do, Veriel, the Radiance and The Bloom. This isn't my world. In Cambria, we understood everything. Here? When we arrived everything was simple and barbaric. Their myths were just that…myths. Now though? Gods granting magical power from cities that dwell in dreams. Swords with burning, torturous skulls inside them that can rip out your mind. I don't understand it anymore."

"Is that why you chose to try and receive magic?" Aurum asked. Rikard considered this for a moment.

"No. I chose that because I have to. Look at you, Aurum. I taught you everything about how to fight, and yet you were able to do more damage to Veriel than I because of your magic. If any random swordsman can kill me just because he has magic and I don't, then my death is meaningless."

"What about your life?" Aurum asked. Rikard said nothing, and the silence lingered between them. It was bitterly cold, but Aurum pushed his fire out to encompass them which more it more tolerable.

"We are close." Aurum said. Rikard shook his reverie away. The time for idle thought was over. He needed to get what he needed, and get out. Rikard watched as the deep black of Thanatos approached. He glared at it as they plunged downwards and burst through the outer limits. Rikard instantly felt his breath stifle as they flew forwards towards the black tower of Acheron. All color bled from his vision and the hairs on his arms stood on end. Nothing felt natural about this place. Rikard's muscles tensed involuntarily as his senses searched for something, anything to grasp onto in this cold, silence. Rikard didn't know what to expect, but as they circled the tower to the top, a window opened for them, and they descended lightly to the smooth black floor.

492

Rikard saw two staircases that led upwards made up of three steps each with one ending in a door of white and one a door of black. Beyond them was a pedestal upon which stood a book. Rikard imagined that the book was the being called Ohm, whom Aurum had told him about. All around him were images of the world around Carin, but Rikard didn't pay attention to them. He looked to Aurum who nodded to the black door.

"That door will take us to Merhelden."

"Where does the other one lead?" Rikard asked.

"If the black door leads to god, that means the white leads to the devil does it not?" Aurum replied.

"Hmmm." Rikard responded.

"Let us go." Aurum said, and Rikard moved gingerly towards the door. He took the first step, and then the second. He reached forward and touched the doorway. It reminded him of the Rift Gate that they had entered to cross from Cambria to Carin. As his finger touched it, Rikard watched as a ripple splashed across the surface. Rikard set his jaw and crossed over.

As he stepped onto the other side, he could feel the ethereal nature of the dreaming world enshroud him in a cornucopia of colors. He blinked several times and heard the sound of steel clearing sheaths. In an instant, Forlorn was in hand, and he was making long sweeping, tertiary blocking swings, but no blades came his way. As his vision cleared, he beheld four men. One was obviously the leader, for he stood apart and floated a dozen feet above the rest upon a throne of gold in a crimson sky. This was a man of power. Rikard could taste it.

The man was in a full long coat with heavy deep blue leather armor covering every inch of his body. A long dark steel staff was ended on one end by a polearm and on the other with a double bladed axe head. His hair was long and white and cascaded in light strings down his face and shoulders. His eyes carried a sharp glint to them, and his face was a deep brown. To his left was a gaunt being whose arms and legs seemed more like that of an insect than a man. His fingers ended in claws as did his long curled toes. He was shaved completely bald and wore a blue and black mail jerkin. To his right was a man whose entire body was covered in white lines

493

of fire etched into his burnt black skin. He wore simple cloth pants, and he held a triple bladed glaive that seemed to be made of black glass. Finally, there was a massive figure whose barrel chest was covered in plate mail. In his hand, he held a huge hand and a half sword that must have been five feet in length, and curved near the end. Symbols were etched up the length of it in some tongue that, even as Rikard read it sent a chill down his spine. Rikard focused on the center figure.

"Who are you to bear that blade," the figure who hovered above him looked down upon him, "Materian?" His voice was oppressive and throaty.

"I am Rikard." He replied. *Aurum wherever you are, some back up would be appreciated right now.*

"Do you know who I am?" He asked.

"No." Rikard replied still looking straight into the burning pools of his eyes.

"I am Talon; first among Lord Veriel's chosen." Rikard felt his blood go hot. This was what he had seen within Forlorn. "Now, kneel. Kneel before me or perish, human." Rikard closed his eyes for a moment before snapping them open with focus. He slowly raised Forlorn into a high guard.

"I kneel for no one." Rikard spat back. For a moment, no emotion played on either man's face, then oh so slowly a smile began to form on the elder being's face.

"Then you deserve your blade, Sufferer." Talon rose in his chair. "LET US REJOICE!" He bellowed. "For the fourth horseman has been found!" The crashing spears on shields turned Rikard's head behind him where he beheld an army of shrouded warriors. He turned back to Talon who looked down at Rikard with a silver glint in his eye. "Now, let us herald an apocalypse worthy of the Lord of Materia."

A Friend Forgotten
Epilogue One

Tendra knelt in the cathedral of Terakeen before the shiftstone statue praying for her cousin to be brought safely to her, and for Rowen. If asked she didn't know if she could honestly say that she believed that her prayers would be answered. They hadn't worked for her brother or for her father. Familiar words fell from her lips.

> All Father, who doth sit on high,
> thy greatness none can deny.
> Your arms welcome me this day,
> your glory is beyond me to say.
> Your forgiveness embraces all,
> your mercy saves those who fall.
> Protect me as I kneel before you,

495

save my soul from the evil I may do.
Thou greatness surpasses all earthly bounty,
may my actions bring you eternal glory.
And when I die and pass to you,
may I find peace in your arms too.
As my fathers before me and my sons beyond me,
I believe in Supremor with all I can be."

As she finished, she felt no different. There was still the cold emptiness within her heart. Jeric knew something was wrong with her, but he couldn't possibly understand. He couldn't understand what it was like being too late to stop her brother from being poisoned; her father from being cut down, and Rayn...if she had run when they had told her too, he would still be alive. His blood was on her hands. When she closed her eyes, she could still see his head perched precariously on Veriel's blade. His eyes an expression of shock and urging. Even as he died he begged her to run, to escape. He was dead because of her. There was no changing that.

Tendra thought about wandering down to the library, but instead found herself in the stables. She absentmindedly reached down and grasped a brush in one hand while running her fingers across the hairs on the mane of a beautiful silver mare with the other. She thought about her brush in the silver case her father had used on her hair. It was probably ashes at this point. She ran the brush down the length of the horse. She felt tired... so very tired. She wanted to sleep for an age and awaken to a better world that she hoped would someday exist. She sighed as she collapsed on one of the benches in the stables. She tried to get up, but she just wanted to sleep. She knew that the gallowglass would protect her should she actually fall asleep, but she knew that she would only be able to doze for a short while before she would drag herself back to her quarters.

The night was cold, and she wrapped her shawl close around shoulders. Jeric would be waiting for her back at their rooms, and that was part of the reason why she didn't return there immediately. If she kept him far away, he wouldn't die like everyone else. Tendra stood wearily. It was time to go to bed. She replaced the brush.

496

"This looks strangely familiar. Though it seems to me last time the positions were somewhat reversed." A silky smooth voice caused Tendra's weariness to drop from her like a weight. She hesitated to even turn around. It couldn't be. She slowly pivoted around to see Rowen standing just out of the shadows. He looked exactly how she remembered him with his mouth upturned in a sly smirk that called to her.

"I...I thought you were dead." She managed. She felt tears come to her eyes: tears of joy. Not everyone had died on her. Tendra's feet carried her towards him under their own volition.

"Yeah, death wasn't as pretty as you; plus she wasn't happy when I told her that I had already given my heart to another. So I got off the hook." Rowen's hand reached out and touched her hip where his dagger was hung. "Did you miss me?" Tendra couldn't say anything else; she simply threw her arms around him. She felt his arms embrace her. "I'm sorry I didn't come sooner, but I am here now, and I'm not going anywhere." He whispered in her ear. She believed him.

For the first time in a long time, she felt safe.

Homecoming
Epilogue Two

Galeerial and Grey stood within a cave inside the Rift Mountains to the west of Carin. In all Galeerial's days of ranging in his youth, he had never ventured to the Rift Mountains. Nor had he ever had any desire too. These mountains were shrouded in a perpetual fog, as if the unwavering abyss of the Rift had spilled some of its void out onto the area surrounding it. The stone was hard, craggy and brown. Nothing grew in these lands. Nothing grew in the shadow of the Rift. It was as if life was afraid to exist: afraid to defile the unnatural formation on the other side of these peaks. This was a dead land, and it brought a sinking feeling to Galeerial's stomach.

Grey had immediately taken charge upon their arrival guiding them directly to the cave passage, which had been guarded by a stone that didn't exist. Galeerial had watched aghast as Grey had seemingly vanished right through solid stone, but the wizard had reappeared a moment later to beckon him inwards. He had followed, and they had emerged in the chamber in which they now resided.

The chamber itself was simply a tunnel that had been bored out of the same stone that made up the entirety of the Rift Mountains that circled Carin. It was perfectly circular, which made walking downwards difficult due to the forced angling of their feet, but it was not the chamber itself that was important. It was what lay at the end of it.

Before them was a swirling rainbow of liquid crystal. Every color that he could imagine was wrapped in this silver meandering pathway that wound its way around the doorway to another world: a world that held the key to the salvation of his people. He would find the Spirit of Lights, whatever it was, and he would give his people the time they needed to live, to repent their mistakes, and to become what they were meant to be.

"Welcome to the end of the world, and, incidentally, the beginning of another." Grey gestured.

"Extraordinary." Galeerial replied breathlessly. He held a hand out towards it.

"Wait…wait…wait!" Grey hollered. Galeerial snatched his hand back. "I'm going first." Grey said. He winked at Galeerial who rolled his eyes. "You are going to want to hold on, because the journey is pretty rough." The wizard held out a small rope, and Galeerial bound it around his wrist.

The wizard approached slowly taking long deep breaths. He seemed to stretch as he disappeared into the sterling silver doorway. As he entered, Galeerial immediately felt himself being elongated forward. It was as if he was being pulled by the other side even as he gave himself to it. A cornucopia of colors erupted into his vision and swirled by him as he felt himself being twisted and turned in directions that he didn't even know existed. He couldn't see Grey any more, but the rope was still intertwined around his hand. His body was putty in the hands of the river that hurled him forward. He felt like he was being carried along a current which flowed in all directions at once. His body was alight with electricity as colors began to wash out. He was going faster, faster, faster.

He curved around the edge of infinity and began the faster than lightning trip back to whatever lay on the other side. His grip on the rope began to waver, but his muscles grew taut. He couldn't allow his brother to drift alone through these expanses. He fought with every erg of energy that he could muster yet still a thousand invisible hands sought to rip the rope away. An out of control gust of the current of ether grabbed Galeerial and sent him spinning dizzily around in endless circles.

Supremor help me.

Faster and faster, he twirled. Sound was meaningless in this whirlpool of silver as he descended downwards, downwards towards the end. It was like watching the heart of a hurricane. A small bastion of absolute calm existed there at the end. Galeerial strained against the current to cut straight there, but he was whipped around the side of the curve again, and again he tried and again he made no headway. But he was getting closer. The swirling ether was falling towards the calm. Galeerial relaxed his muscles and allowed himself to be swept swirling towards the exit.

Black lines began to grow in his eyes. His vision became a cracked mosaic, but still he held on. The door grew closer and closer.

He burst out of the opening in a tumble. He turned end over end into a cavern that looked much the same as the one he had just left. He finally came to rest almost on top of Grey. Grey groaned and struggled to right himself.

"I am so dead. We broke so many rules by leaving, as soon as the Torrentials find out I am back I will be dead like art."

"Why are you having regrets now? We are already here." Galeerial expressed coking an eyebrow at him.

"Yeah, but I never actually thought we would make it back through. You don't understand. This was such a bad idea, Galeerial." Galeerial tried to remember ever seeing the wizard afraid. He never had. Even as difficult as he had been, Grey had always been in control, even in Dynast the wizard had never seemed to be afraid, but he was now.

"What are you so afraid of?"

"You don't get it, Galeerial. We are no longer invincible. Rayn is dead. We spent years doing things that should have destroyed our group ten times over, but we survived. All of us survived. Not anymore though. We are no longer invincible. The Torrentials will find us. They can make us tell them where the Rift Portal is; they can make me tell them everything. Then, they will come, and they will kill everyone. This was such a…bad…idea." Grey's voice slowly grew quiet.

"What?" Galeerial asked. He turned at Grey's stare. A corpse lay near the edge of the chamber, and above it was a wall of ice covering the exit. The crossing chamber appeared to be the same as the one on their side only the opening was covered in a wall of ice. "I take it that wasn't here when you left?" Galeerial asked.

"No." Grey remarked. "In fact, I can't even remember the last time it snowed in Cambria. Grey pulled the Iron Men's ax from his belt, and moved forward to the wall. Galeerial ran his fingers along the wall of ice. Galeerial knelt beside the corpse. Heavy cloth covered the decayed bones. "Whoever he was, he died here after we came through. Let's look outside." Grey raised his ax and tapped it onto the ice wall shattering it. A cold biting wind made his bones instantly start to ache. The two of them walked together up the sloped chamber until they reached the surface. Outside they saw only white and black.

The ocean itself had frozen into a carpet of snow that stretched outwards in every direction. Thousands of leagues of winter raced outwards from them, but as Galeerial's eyes adjusted he saw an enormous mountain in the distance. A mountain, whose black shadow covered the land.

"By Supremor." Galeerial breathed.

"This…this wasn't…this isn't how it is supposed to be." Grey's words were almost lost in the sounds of the wind. "Galeerial, what happened to my home?"

The Drowned Flame
Epilogue Three

Finnerty filed into the one room within Illuvium that no one had ever been into. He would know; he had stood guard there for six months when he had been a Blinder, and no one had come or gone in that entire time. Since then, he had often enquired to see if anyone had but received endless negatives. Now, he knew why. Just this morning, each and every person here had been brought in to touch the half of the Heart of Fires that lay dormant at the bottom in preparation for the arrival of the three figures that stood at the bottom of the chamber. Every member of the Light Monks of the rank of Lustrous and above was within this chamber. Almost three hundred Light Monks. Something big was happening, at the bottom of the chamber, he could see the Radiance, the human Lord Aurum, the Hero of Terakeen, and one other figure that glowed a shimmering white. His bones told him that it was the Lady Bloom. Rumors of her return had been all over

Illuvium in the last few days. Now, she was really here. She was here to reignite the Drowned Flame and release the magic held within the Heart of Fires. Finnerty's pulse began to race. He was middle of the way down the massive three hundred foot cylinder. A single file footpath spiraled around the smooth gray stone and Light Monks stood shoulder to shoulder, each one carrying a torch that illuminated the entirety of the chamber with flickering light. He didn't know the two Light Monks to either side of him, but it didn't matter.

Finnerty came to a stop and peaked over the edge down towards where the Heart of Fires stood, or rather where half of it stood. The nine foot long tomb looked like a single massive slab of amber and within was the perfectly preserved corpse of Garen the Firstborn. However, at some point in history the single sarcophagus had been cut in two exactly in the middle of his face. Where the other half was, perhaps only the Radiance herself knew, but Finnerty did not. All he knew was that since The Bloom had become lost almost a thousand years ago, no magic had emerged from this particular half of the Heart of Fires.

Until now.

His pulse began to race as he heard the Radiance call out.

"Awaken the Drowned Flame." His hands were shaking. He had never been so excited, so terrified of the power that he was about to wield in his life. He craned his neck to watch as The Bloom stepped forward to the Heart of Fires. His heart beat like a drum as his breath caught in his throat. She reached out and touched it.

The world exploded.

Rapid pulsations of life reverberated through the chamber as the Heart of Fires roared back to life in a cacophony of light. Tongues of flame leapt as high as to come level with him, and Finnerty felt a single emotion: exaltation. Now, they would be able to enter this war as warriors and not peace keepers. Now, they would be able to make the true difference they had always wanted to make. The giants could no longer stand against them. He looked down at his hand and saw the olive fire crawl up his wrists and to his forearms. He felt power building around him as it began to seep into his every pore and drain into his soul.

Finnerty almost didn't notice it at first, so triumphant was his mind, but the sound of popping like seeds within a flame began to be heard from all around him. His head flashed to the left as he heard the sound.

Pop.

Finnerty was drenched with the blood and organs of the monk who had moments ago been standing next to him. He blinked heavily as he looked across the chasm as the popping came more rapidly.

Pop.

Pop!

POP!

Crimson droplets mingled with long strings of intestines and brain matter fell like raindrops past him as the popping continued.

The fire licked its way through his chest and onto his neck.

"No, No, No, No, NO!" he screamed as he felt the power breach his skull. He fell to his knees and called upon every ounce of discipline and willpower he possessed to stop this power from consuming him. He would not fall. He would not burst with this power. He would not-

POP!

www.ingramcontent.com/pod-product-compliance
Lightning Source LLC
Chambersburg PA
CBHW020626020726
47494CB00001B/65